ROYAL EL

RUTHLESS EMPIRE

RINA KENT

To the divine, raw chaos inside you.

AUTHOR NOTE

Hello reader friend,

Ruthless Empire marks the end of Royal Elite Series, and while there's still an epilogue novel for all the characters, Cole and Silver's book is the unofficial ending. Like you, this makes me so nostalgic and emotional. Like you, I'll never get over these explosive characters who will live inside me for eternity. I hope that you find the light despite the darkness in every book and with every couple.

Most of all, I hope you enjoy the unofficial conclusion and that Ruthless Empire bleeds in you as deep as it bled into me.

If you haven't read my books before, you might not know this, but I write darker stories that can be upsetting and disturbing. My books and main characters aren't for the faint of heart.

To remain true to the characters, the vocabulary, grammar, and spelling of *Ruthless Empire* is written in British English.

Ruthless Empire can be read on its own, but for better understanding of Royal Elite world, it's recommended to read the previous books in the series first.

Royal Elite Series:
#0 Cruel King
#1 Deviant King
#2 Steel Princess
#3 Twisted Kingdom
#4 Black Knight
#5 Vicious Prince
#6 Ruthless Empire
#7 Royal Elite Epilogue

Don't forget to Sign up to Rina Kent's Newsletter for news about future releases and an exclusive gift.

She's off limits. He has none.

There's a girl.

Beautiful. Popular. Fake.

And my obsession.

My fall.

Probably my damnation.

Did that stop me? Do I care? No and no.

There's a line between right and wrong. Moral and immoral.

And then there's her.

I cross every limit with blood-coated fingers.

She says she hates me.

I say I hate her too as I trap her, own her.

Make her all mine.

PLAYLIST

No One Knows Us—BANNERS & Carly Paige
The Black and White—The Band CAMINO
Medicine—Bring Me The Horizon
The Last Of The Real Ones—Fall Out Boy
The Sound of Silence—Disturbed
The Drug In Me Is You—Falling In Reverse
Why Are You Here—Machine Gun Kelly
Call You Mine—The Chainsmokers & Bebe Rexha
Castles—Freya Ridings
Old Wounds—PVRIS
Somebody Else—VÉRITÉ
Fall Down (Acoustic)—Zero 9:36
Maniac—Conan Gray
Empires on Fire—BANNERS
Move Me—Badflower
Time—NF
Colors—Kulick
Didn't I—One Republic
I Wish I Never Met You—Oh Wonder
Bad For You—AKA George
Tattoos Together—Lauv
You—James Arthur & Travis Barker
Monster (Under My Bed)—Call Me Karizma
Another's Arms—Coldplay
Natural Villain—The Man Who

You can find the complete playlist on Spotify.

ROYAL ELITE BOOK SIX

RUTHLESS EMPIRE

PART ONE

Cole

Age eight

There's freedom in chaos.

When my father used to say that, I didn't understand it much. Ironically, that piece of information remained in my head, floating around like a fact.

My father is a businessman. There shouldn't have been any room for chaos in his life, and yet, he thrived on it.

He knew that humans are chaotic by nature and that nature comes before nurture.

That's what the books say. I didn't understand them at first, but after the kidnapping, I returned a new person.

One day, I was coming home with my two friends, Aiden and Xander, and suddenly, everything turned black.

Masks were shoved over our heads, and then we were separated. I remember the darkness so well. It's not only about seeing the colour black. It's about breathing your own air and thinking you'll suffocate on it. It's about freezing until you can't feel your toes or your face.

The darkness isn't just a sensation. It's a phase of being.

That's what the therapist Mum took me to has been saying.

Were you afraid, son?

Did they hurt you in any way?

Touch you?

I answered no to all. It's the truth. The kidnappers didn't do any of that.

They didn't scare me, hurt me, or touch me. They just left me…alone.

It was a silent type of chaos. You can hear it in your head, but you can't see it with your eyes or feel it with your skin.

It's a deep suffocation that slowly but surely takes hold of you.

I didn't tell the therapist that. He wouldn't understand.

No one does.

Because no one knows what happened once the kidnappers released me on a deserted road. I didn't think about removing the bag that was strapped over my head—even though my hands were free.

I didn't think about my parents or home or my friends.

I didn't think about asking for help, even though that's the most normal thing anyone would do.

I did none of that.

Instead, I stood there, pulled my hands apart and drowned in the silent chaos all alone.

It was liberating, black, and so still. Nothing ruined it or interrupted it or ended it.

Constant silent chaos.

It was maybe hours or days—I don't remember.

Unlike Xander, I didn't fight to find my way home. He walked for hours and days until he finally returned.

In my case, some passersby stumbled upon me and called the police, who eventually sent me home.

I remember the tears in my mother's eyes, one of which had a purple bruise on the lid. I remember her embrace and how she held on to me sobbing, her voice echoing around me like a vice.

She was glad I'd returned and that I was safe.

I didn't hug her back.

I *couldn't* hug her back.

I just stood there, and while she cried, I thought about the chaos I'd left behind and if there was a way to bring it back.

Chaos is the only thing that makes me stop and stare. It's a pause button to my brain.

Not everyone likes chaos, though. I figured that out when my father took me to the therapist doctor because I didn't cry.

I couldn't cry.

All of a sudden, crying became something redundant. When I was younger, I cried while I curled in a ball in my bed.

I slammed my hands against my ears and pretended the shouting voices from outside weren't real. They were like the bogeyman.

What young me didn't know was that the bogeyman would never show up.

Our own house monster did, and he didn't stay still. He didn't keep his hands to himself.

Whenever Mum's screams echoed in the house, I made it my mission not to go out there. If I did, I'd only worsen the situation. She'd try to protect me and that would get us both hit and with bruises.

If I had bruises, Mum would hide me and not let me play with my friends until they were gone.

I don't know why I cried back then. It was useless anyway. None of our tears stopped him or made him pause.

We were just his things that he treated as he saw fit.

Being a successful businessman with an empire under his belt gave William Nash the name and the status. No one saw the monster behind his smiles. No one suspected his drinking habits or his firm hand that he didn't hesitate to use.

In public, he held me in his arms and doted on us. In private, he snapped the moment we said a word.

I learnt silence before I learnt talking. Silence gives you room to think, to plot. Talking only gets you in trouble.

After I met Chaos, I stopped crying, amongst other habits like wondering why Mum and I were stuck with him, or if I'd done something wrong by being born.

Chaos taught me many things, and the most important of all is: you have to start it yourself.

You can't wait for chaos to happen.

Dad is a master of chaos. He causes it every day. Every night.

It ends with Mum curled into a ball and placing ice to her face. She doesn't want me to look at her when she's like that. She does everything in her power to hide it—makeup, baking, smiles.

Lots of smiles.

She's inside now, hiding, crying.

I'm not.

I stand at the edge of the pool, staring down at all the red.

Chaos in its truest form.

For the first time since that day I returned home, I take a deep breath. A long breath.

I can breathe and it's not black. I can see and it's not the darkness. I can feel and it's not nothingness.

I don't know how long I stand there, watching and trying to remember what he said.

You're a monster.

He thought I was a monster.

Maybe I am.

I turn around like a robot, my body heavy and rigid, and leave. Not only the pool area, but the entire house.

Our mansion disappears from sight, but the scene in the pool keeps playing in the back of my head like a film.

The red.

The hand.

The gurgles.

And then…the silence.

You're a monster. He said something after it, but…I can't recall. I was too caught up in the chaos to remember.

It's late afternoon, so the dusk is orange and bright on the horizon.

Not knowing where I'm going, I stand in the middle of the street and watch the sun's slow disappearance behind the buildings.

Soon, it'll be dark. Soon, it'll be chaos.

My feet carry me to the nearby park. It's usually empty around this time because mummies take their kids home. It's a small park with tall trees and dark green benches similar to the one near the pool.

Maybe if I sit here and think about the park and the darkness, I won't think about the pool.

I should've brought a book with me.

I'm about to go back and get one when I notice a small figure huddled by the bench at the far end of the park underneath a large tree.

She's wearing a pink dress that has so much stuff at the bottom, making it twice her size. Her shiny, golden hair is tied in a long ponytail by a butterfly. The same butterfly is on the belt that surrounds her waist. She's hugging a doll that looks just like her and is even wearing the same dress.

That girl always does stupid things like that.

Silver often comes over when I'm playing with Aiden and Xander, but I don't like her.

She talks and argues a lot—like, a *lot*—and it ruins the silence in my head.

I should leave, but something stops me.

The tears in her eyes.

She constantly sprinkles her face in glitter as if believing she's the dolls she plays with. Now that she's crying, the glitter soaks in tears and fall in two rivulets down her cheeks.

Silver doesn't cry. At least, I've never seen her cry. I've wondered how she does that, and even though I don't like her, I've wanted to ask her and see if it's because she also thinks it's useless.

Now that I'm seeing her crying for the first time, I can't leave. I can't even move.

All I can do is watch the way moisture pools in her huge eyes. Their light blue colour darkens before those tears stream down her cheeks.

Her face is a mess, full with snot, glitter, and her endless tears. Her cheeks are red and her lips are rosier than usual.

Chaos.

It's come to me again.

I don't think about it as my legs lead me in her direction. She doesn't sense me, or rather, she can't. Aiden always says I move silently. It's because I learnt to tiptoe out of my father's reach.

But I never tell him or Xander that.

We're not supposed to say such things. We're proper people with proper manners and proper secrets.

Once I'm behind Silver, I pull on her ponytail. She gasps, then cries out.

That's what I usually do to kick her out of Aiden's house when she talks too much. She screams at us that boys suck and I should go to a bad place.

No idea why I did it just now. I don't really want her to disappear, but I also can't ignore the habit whenever she's in sight.

Silver lifts her head up, and when her eyes meet mine, they widen until they nearly swallow her face.

For a second, I stare at her, unable to do anything else.

I love that look.

I want to keep that look.

But how?

"What are you doing here, Cole?" She lets the doll—which

also has butterflies on its head—drop to her lap and hides her face in her tiny hands. "Go away."

I let go of her hair, annoyed she hid that look, and sit beside her. The big skirt of her dress could fit another person between us.

"Why are you crying?" My voice is quiet since I don't know how I should speak to her.

"What do you care?" She sniffles. "You hate me."

So she knows about that. "What makes you think that?"

I need her to tell me why she's crying, because if I know the reason, I can use it and maybe I'll be able to bring back the look from earlier.

Chaos.

"I just know you do." She manages to get out through her sniffles. "And I hate you, too."

"If you hate me, why are you hiding from me?"

"I'm not hiding! I don't want you to see me crying. No one sees me cry."

I fully face her, a smile on my lips. "So I'm the first?"

"Shut up and go away!"

"No."

"No?"

"This park is for everyone."

"Fine. I'll go." She removes her hands from her face. It's still full of tears and messed up glitter, but the look from earlier is gone. She's not surprised or taken off guard.

Why isn't she?

"If you stay, I'll tell you a secret," I say as she gathers her doll.

"What secret?" She doesn't attempt to move, her eyes widening again, but it's out of curiosity this time, not surprise like earlier.

The dusk's sun casts a golden hue on her hair and turns the blue of her eyes lighter and brighter.

"Are you sure you want to know? This secret will keep us together for life."

"F-for life?"

"Yes, Butterfly. For life."

She scowls. "Why are you calling me that?"

"What?"

"Butterfly."

"You have one on your hair." I motion at her dress's waist. "And on your clothes. Do you want to fly like one?"

"I do." Her expression brightens.

"Why?"

"Because, you know, they're so beautiful and everyone smiles when they see them. They bring happiness and light."

"They're cockroaches with wings."

"Shut up. Don't say that about them."

"There are some butterflies who die in a day."

A crease forms in her forehead as she folds her arms. "You're a meanie."

"And you're unrealistic."

"I'm leaving."

"I thought you wanted to know the secret? Or are you a coward?"

"I'm not a coward."

"So you want to know?"

She nods discreetly. Silver might talk a lot, but she doesn't like to ask for things. She also doesn't like to put herself out there.

I noticed it in games. Whenever we play, she asks to go last so she can observe the others. Of course, she doesn't, because I steal the last position from her every time. Aiden and I usually win against all of them.

Xander and Kim don't care; they only like the act of playing games, but Silver always stomps out angrily, then returns the next day demanding a rematch.

"I'll tell you if you tell me yours," I say.

Her brow furrows. "Mine?"

"Why are you crying?"

She crosses her arms again while still holding her doll. "I'm not telling you."

"I'm not telling you either, Butterfly."

She glares at me, jutting her lip forward. It's adorable.

It's weird to think of someone as adorable on a day like this…I *suppose*. But since I met Chaos, I've realised normal was never for me in the first place.

Finally, Silver sighs. She stares down at her dress's skirt and plays with the butterfly at the waist. "I overheard Mum and Dad fighting and saying they're getting a divorce."

Disappointment grips me like when those passersby found me. Why is it so boring? "That's it?"

"What do you mean, *that's it?*" Fresh tears pool in her eyes. "They always fight and scream and say mean things to each other. Now they're going to get a divorce. I'll be like Sally from class. My life will be divided between two parents and two homes. We won't live together, have holidays together, or travel together and…and…I don't want that!"

"Okay."

Her head snaps in my direction. "Okay? I tell you everything and all you have to say is *okay?*"

"Yeah, good luck." I start to stand, but she clutches me by the sleeve of my T-shirt, keeping me in place.

"You don't get to leave, Cole." She pulls me down with a force I didn't know she had in her. I lose my balance and fall on my back on the bench.

The sting creeps all the way up my spine.

Silver straddles my waist, her big skirt covering us both as she places her palms on my shoulders.

If I wanted to push her away, I could, but I don't want to. This close, I notice the tiny freckles lining her nose that I haven't seen before. Tears glisten in her eyes, and the view from the bottom allows me to look at the clear contours of her shadowed face.

It's...beautiful.

"You can't leave. You're the first one I ever told that. You have to take responsibility for it. Papa says everyone is responsible for how they react after they see things. If you ignore something bad, you're a bad person." A tear falls from her eyelid, straight on to my cheek, and drips to my mouth, making me taste salt.

"Who do you hate the most between them?" I ask quietly.

"I don't hate my parents."

"You must. If they're fighting, one of them is causing it, right?" I pause. "In my case, my father does, and I hate him."

I don't know why I tell her that. Could be because I want to conjure that look from earlier, or simply because I want to say it out loud for once in my life.

"Why do you hate your father?" she asks.

"This is about you. Who do you hate the most?"

"I don't hate her, but I don't like M-Mum sometimes." She stares away as if she doesn't want to admit it.

"Why?"

"Because she dislikes everything and keeps telling me I need to act like a lady. I can't play outside or invite my friends over. I can't run to hug Papa when he comes home. I can't cry or scream. So I do it here, you know." She motions at the park. "I cry and scream here when no one is around."

"She'll want to take you when they divorce."

She sniffles, her eyes doubling in size as she stares at me again, then she violently shakes her head. "No. I don't want that."

"When other adults ask you, tell them you want to stay with your father."

"And...and they'll let me?"

I nod. "That's what Sally did. She chose her mum and they let her live with her."

"Does that mean I'll never see Mum? I don't want that."

"You will, but you'll stay at home with your father most of the time."

She draws a crackled breath, offering me a small smile. "Thank you. I'm glad you're the first one I told this."

"Me, too." I get to see her like this when no one on this earth ever will.

Suddenly, a thought takes over me and becomes a need.

Just like the need I had when I wanted more chaos.

"Now tell me your secret," she demands, still fighting with the remnants of her crying.

I grin. "I want to be your first."

"My first in what?"

My thumb wipes the moisture under her eyes. "In everything, Butterfly."

"Then I want your firsts, too." She juts her chin. "Promise me."

"Promise."

TWO

Doll Master

Hello.

You don't know who I am, but I know who you are.

I'm the monster under your bed and the bogeyman in your closet.

I'm the unknown.

You don't see me unless you look for me, and even when you do, are you sure you've looked hard enough? Searched thoroughly enough?

Here's something you need to know about me: I like dolls.

Or rather, one particular doll.

My father didn't let me play with dolls. He said he didn't like them and they weren't for me.

So I hid my doll and proved him wrong.

Now, I'm proving everyone wrong.

Including you.

This is the story of my new favourite doll after I lost my most precious one.

I didn't believe in love at first sight until I saw her.

And I mean, *all* of her.

The porcelain skin, the baby blue eyes, the golden hair, and the pink dress with ribbons and tulle.

It's like she was made for me.

She was.

My own doll. My special doll.

I was broken the first time I saw her. I was about to make a decision I'd regret for the rest of my life, but she showed up. She was there, beautiful and crying, and I knew I had to keep her.

I already had a doll before, so I hadn't paid her any attention.

Now that my doll is gone, I finally see her.

Crying, speaking.

My previous doll didn't do that. Not really.

Her golden hair camouflages her face and hides her from the world, but eventually, she'll be completely visible to me.

There's an art in being a doll master. You get to see and notice things no one else sees or notices. Not even the dolls themselves.

Masterpieces in the making.

I can recognise a masterpiece even before it's fully formed. That's why I'm the best doll master you can ever find.

That is, *if* you can find me.

You can't.

And neither can she.

I've mastered the art of deception, of hiding, of being invisible.

Sometimes, even *I* don't see myself.

Even *I* find trouble in recognising what I've done. What I can do.

My limit has been myself, but today, I've let go of the last shackle.

Now, I have a new doll. My prized possession.

Silver. My beautiful little doll.

Welcome to my world.

You'll find it fun.

Eventually.

Oh, and don't search for me. You won't find me until I let you. And when I finally show up in front of you, all you'll be able to do is shatter into bloody pieces.

I smile at the thought.

Time to start my homework.

Run, doll.

Hide.

And don't ever, ever look under your bed.

THREE

Silver

Age eleven

I have to stay with Mum this weekend. I don't like it.

She takes me to parties and brunches and makes me wear dresses and sit with her friends' children.

I want to stay with Papa and listen to his friends. They're cool people—Papa's friends, I mean.

They own the whole country.

Papa says no, that the Conservative Party doesn't own the UK; they just govern it. And the only reason they do that is because they gained the people's vote.

I don't care. They're cool and they own the country in my mind. They know a lot of stuff about stuff, and they make me feel so important when I help our housekeeper bring them tea. Papa always asks about my opinion and lets me read his favourite books.

When I grow up, I'm going to be him. I'm going to stand in front of many people in the parliament and defend my beliefs.

Mum is also in the Conservative Party, but she's from the loser faction—or that's what Frederic, Papa's right-hand man, says. He tells me Mum is from the faction who nominate a leader who never wins the internal elections.

Being members of the same party should've given my parents a reason to stay together, but they somehow managed to find a way to disagree, even while having the same general beliefs.

Anyway, Mum's friends aren't cool. They're snobs and frequently make me feel like I need to walk the line around them.

Papa's friends are way better.

But this weekend, I have to go to Mum's. I asked Papa if I could stay with him, but he says she's my parent too.

If I don't go, Mum will come and pick a fight with Papa all over again. Mum doesn't shut up—at all. She made the divorce and the custody process so messy, I still have nightmares about it.

But she's my mum, and I don't like seeing her alone. For three years, I tried bringing her and Papa together again by suggesting we have holidays together, but they always, without fail, ended them with a fight. It's like they look for opportunities to argue.

I guess I can survive the weekend.

But first, I need to get ready. That's why I'm sitting in the park alone. I wore my navy blue dress with matching flats and I have my hair loose, falling down my back.

One hour until I have to meet Mum's friends for lunch.

I can do this.

I sit cross-legged on the bench and place my hands on my knees. I'm meditating. It's a trick Helen taught me to use when my thoughts are all over the place.

Helen is way better than my mum in being quiet. She listens to me and does my hair and gives me gifts. She taught me tricks to make better tea and she lets me be with her when she's baking.

If her son, Cole, wasn't a pain in the arse, maybe I would've spent this hour with her instead of being alone.

I don't like boys in general. They act like pigs, are annoying, and don't let others be at peace.

All they care about is pulling pranks. Especially Aiden and Cole. I still want to punch the tosser Aiden for tripping me the other day.

But who I hate the most is Cole. He offered me his hand to help me up and then he pulled on my ponytail and said, "Go cry in the park."

I hate that he knows how important this place is to me. He's been using it to taunt me every chance he gets. Sometimes, he follows me here just to make fun of me. He doesn't do it in front of the others because everyone believes Cole is a good boy.

They think Aiden is slightly mischievous and Xander is the bad boy, but they don't know that Cole is a first-class wanker.

I tried finding another special place other than this park, but I couldn't. This is where I had my first picnic with my parents. Or maybe it wasn't the first, but it's my first happy memory, so it became my sanctuary. My escape from the world.

The wanker Cole won't take that away from me.

Happy thoughts. Don't think about Cole. Happy thoughts.

As soon as I return from Mum's, Papa will hear me play the piano piece I'm practicing for an upcoming competition. Helen will teach me how to make cakes. For some reason, I never get it right. I'm better with preparing tea.

Someone pulls on a strand of my hair and I groan, my eyes snapping open.

Cole sits beside me, smiling. He does that a lot—staying silent and having that infuriating smile all over his face.

He's not saying anything, but his expression feels like a taunt all on its own.

"What do you want?" I snap.

"This park is for everyone, Butterfly."

Ugh. I hate it when he calls me that. It's a reminder of that day I showed him my weakness when I shouldn't have.

Though his advice worked. When I told the judge that I

wanted to stay with Papa, he didn't hesitate to give my father custody. Mum didn't talk to me or Papa for a week and I had to go apologise to her about it before she would forgive me.

I'll never tell Cole I'm thankful. That means showing weakness in front of him again and he'll use that against me for years to come.

That day was black in both our lives. When I went home, my parents sat me down and announced they were getting a divorce. I cried myself to sleep that night.

The following morning, I found out that Uncle William, Cole's father, tripped in his pool and hit his head against the edge. He died around the time Cole was talking to me in the park.

Cole's life has never been the same since then. He doesn't say it, but I kind of feel it.

Mum and her friends keep saying Helen became a rich widow who has so much money, she won't be able to spend it in her lifetime.

Cole didn't cry at his father's funeral. He doesn't cry in general, but I thought he would that day.

However, he didn't even shed one tear.

He spent the entire ceremony clutching his mother's hand as she sobbed. It was like she was crying both Cole's and her share.

That day, I gave Cole my Snickers bar. I only get one every three days—Mum's rules because I have to watch my diet—and I figured since he was sad, the chocolate would make him feel better.

He glared at it, then at me, before he told me to eat it in front of him. I did, secretly happy I could get my chocolate. While I was still eating, he told me I was selfish. I threw the rest of the chocolate bar on his chest and left.

He's been a wanker ever since. He makes me think he wants to spend time with me, just to say mean things while smiling.

I hate it when he does that.

I hate his smiles and his chestnut hair that he keeps long enough to be ruffled by the wind. I also hate that his eyes are a green so rare, it's mesmerising. It's not foresty like Kim's, no. It's also not like the grass everyone can stomp on. It's like the tip of the tall trees where it appears light but it's in fact dark and deep. High and mighty and far.

So, so far, it's almost impossible to climb up to it.

"Are you still mad because you lost in chess earlier?" He smiles. "You're a newbie."

"I'll win next time. Whatever."

"You can't win against me, Butterfly."

"Of course I can. I won in the piano competition. Hmph."

"That's because I let you."

"That's what losers say."

"You don't want to challenge me, or I'll make you cry again."

"Go to hell."

His grin widens. "Whoa. Big words, Miss Prim and Proper."

I narrow my eyes on him. "What would it take for you to leave me alone?"

He pauses for a second, seeming to seriously consider my offer. Then he taps his cheek. "Kiss me here."

"I won't!"

"Fine." He lets his arm drop to his side before he sneakily pulls on my hair.

"Ow!"

"What?"

"I told you not to do that anymore."

"You didn't give me what I wanted. Why should I give you what you want?"

"You're such a…a…"

"You can't find the word?"

"A tosser!"

"I'm fine with that. Are you going to kiss me or should I bother you until Cynthia comes to pick you up?"

"Why do you want me to kiss your cheek?"

He lifts a shoulder. "Because."

"Tell me why or I won't do it."

He pauses, his smile disappearing. Cole doesn't like it when he's cornered. Finally, he speaks quietly. "You haven't done it to any other boys."

It's my turn to smile. "Because you want my firsts?"

He nods. "Now do it or I'll pull your hair again."

"Say please."

"I'm not saying please," he mocks. "Do it or I'll pull on your hair."

"Then I'll just kiss Aiden's cheek and you'll lose that first forever."

Cole's nostrils flare and I fold my arms, feeling smug.

"You'll regret this," he says.

"Don't care."

He takes a deep breath. "Please."

"Please what?"

"Silver," he warns. He only uses my given name when he's mad or wants me to do something.

"You have to say the whole sentence."

He grits his teeth but speaks in a calm voice. "Please kiss me on the cheek."

I do.

Placing a hand on the bench, I lean over and brush my lips against his right cheek. The contact is brief, but for some reason, my face heats and I quickly pull back.

He's smirking.

Why is he smirking?

Cole taps his left cheek. "Now, the other one."

"We only agreed on one cheek."

"We only agreed on *a* cheek, we didn't specify which one. I wanted the left one."

"Fine." I want to feel his skin again anyway.

He leans in slightly so his left cheek is in front of me. But the moment my lips are about to make contact with his skin, he abruptly turns his head and his mouth seals to mine.

For a second, I'm too stunned to react. His lips are soft and feel fuller than they look.

And now, they're on mine.

I reel back in shock, covering my mouth with the back of my hand. My cheeks are so hot, I feel like they'll explode.

"W-w-why d-did you d-do t-that?!" I point a shaky finger at him. It's like I can't speak anymore.

Another smirk lifts his lips. The lips I just kissed. "Because."

"Cole, you…you…"

"Tosser?" he completes for me, tilting his head.

"I wish you'd die —" I pause, realising what I said. Those words should never be said, not after what happened with Mum recently. "I didn't mean that."

"I'm fine if you do. Besides, you're the only one to blame for this."

"*Me?*"

"I told you you'd regret it. Don't threaten me again, Butterfly. You'll never win against me."

I hit his shoulder with a closed fist. "Go away!"

"Or what? You'll stop acting like a lady? You already have. Ladies don't punch."

"Shut up and go."

"All right, all right. A deal is a deal. I'm going." He staggers to his feet, still smiling in that infuriating way, taunting me, making me want to punch him in the throat.

"I hate you." I glare up at him. His shadow is camouflaging the sun and his presence is blocking everything else.

He ruffles my hair, making the golden strands fly everywhere, before he places a palm on the top of my head and leans down so his face is level with mine.

There's no smile on his lips as he speaks with an edge to the tone of his voice. "Hate me all you want, but keep our promise. All your firsts are mine."

FOUR

Silver

Age fourteen

My mum said I could do better.

I could be more sophisticated, more elegant, and just…more.

I pushed Kimberly away because if I hadn't, Mum would've hurt her in some way. Mum's too direct and doesn't think twice before saying truths—no matter how ugly they are. She doesn't care about who she crushes on her way to success. She doesn't stop to think about the consequences for other people. She simply doesn't feel like the rest of us do.

Or if she ever did, that part of her died after the divorce. Or, rather, three years ago. It's like she killed a part of herself in that tub.

Since then, I don't want to test her in any way. If she says I'm to change friends, I change friends. If she says I shouldn't wear a certain thing, I don't. If she says I shouldn't listen to rock music, I don't. At least, not in public. Everyone knows me as a piano girl, and I'll remain that way.

It's not that I don't like playing the piano, because I do. However, I prefer listening to other types of music with thought-provoking lyrics.

Mum calls it the devil's music.

Before I know it, my life has become an image. I act a certain way, speak a certain way, and even walk a certain way. I have to sway my hips gently, but I can't walk too slow like a slut or too fast like a nerd.

I'm a lady. Just like Mum.

Papa sat me down and told me I didn't have to follow her instructions or be threatened by her. But Papa didn't see what I saw. Papa wasn't there.

I love him more than the world itself, but he's not me. He wasn't split up between two alpha parents with god-like personalities. He wasn't forced to see one of them hit rock bottom.

As soon as I told him I wanted this, he didn't bring up the subject again. Papa might be a feared politician with strict rules and steel-like opinions, but he respects my wishes above anything else. And for that alone, I'm grateful to him.

I haven't been able to say it as much lately. Part of being a lady is not showing your emotions. If you do have to show them, they shouldn't be your real ones. Those need to be always hidden where no one could find them.

I know people at school call me a bitch, the queen B, but I don't mind.

Being a bitch means I'm doing a perfect job of hiding my emotions and I don't have to live that nightmare again.

It means I get to keep all my pieces together.

So I've played the bitch role so well until no one can see through it. I've picked fights just to come out as the winner. I've played games merely to prove that I can.

Even Kim, who used to be my closest friend, believes the transformation and now calls me a bitch herself. Sometimes, I want to send her a text and tell her I'm sorry, but at the last minute, I change my mind. There's something a lot bigger than friendship at stake and I would never gamble that.

Mum says it's lonely at the top and I'm starting to understand what that means.

Her friends have started to drift away the more she climbs the party's ladder, establishing herself as the most beautiful female politician who can actually rival men. A while ago, a reporter asked her if she used her beauty to get what she wants, and she said the famous line, "I came here to talk about a very serious, very urgent problem, and that is public housing. Can I share my thoughts, or do I have to sit and dodge comments about my face before I'm able to do so?"

That gained her a lot of popularity on social media and with women's associations.

"Thank you, Derek." I peek at Papa's driver through the window after he drops me off from school at Helen's house. "Don't forget to drink the tea I gave you earlier. I made it myself."

"I wouldn't miss it." He grins, showing straight, white teeth. He's in his late twenties and helps Papa a lot with his work. "Have fun, Miss Queens."

"It's Silver." I wave at him as the car disappears around the corner. Papa said he'd pick me up later, even when I told him I could walk home.

The housekeeper, Isabel, lets me in with a huge smile on her face. She's the only help Helen allows and she only comes twice a week. Isabel motions that Helen is in the kitchen.

I place a finger to my lips and tiptoe there, abandoning my backpack on the sofa.

Spending time with Helen is one of the highlights of my week. Papa has become busier with the party since he became a secretary of state. I participate in his meetings, but he barely has time for me—or for himself. It kills me to see him so alone and getting older by the day.

However, I've been spending most of my time with Mum and it's hardly fun.

When I'm with Helen, we talk and bake—or more like, she bakes. I continue to suck at it. Yet Helen has never given up on me and keeps teaching me.

We meditate together and she still does my hair and tells me I'm the perfect daughter she never had. Maybe hearing those words my own mother rarely says to me is what keeps me coming back here.

It's certainly not because of her arsehole son.

I hate Cole Nash.

I despise him from the bottom of my heart.

He's levelled up from pulling my hair and taunting me to playing games. He loves those a lot—games, I mean. The belief that he has control over someone.

And he's becoming popular, too—he and that other wanker, Aiden. I don't know what girls see in them. They're both *yuck*.

Xander and Ronan make sense. At least they're charming.

Oh, wait. Everyone thinks Cole is charming as well. He smiles at them and offers to help with their homework, like he's the prince from their favourite fairy tales.

Idiots.

They don't know that everything is a game to Cole. If he compliments someone or acts nice to them, it's usually because of a dare he has with Aiden on who gets whose favour.

While Aiden does it the brooding way, Cole charms himself into it. It's about who wins, but it's also about the process.

Cole thrives on games and he's been playing them for years. He likes to think everyone is a piece on his chessboard and that he can control their fate.

Aiden likes playing the king who comes out a winner, but Cole strives to be the player who controls not only the king but also every piece on the board.

We mostly avoid each other. The more I see his true self, the more he sees mine. I hate that.

We can go days not speaking to each other, not even when Helen or Papa is around. Then he'll come out of nowhere and provoke me—or challenge me. It can be as simple as a biology test, or a piano competition, or even who holds their breath underwater the longest.

I rise up to every one of them.

I'm Sebastian Queens and Cynthia Davis's daughter and I'm as tenacious as my parents. No one gets past me.

No one.

He usually wins and laughs at me, though. I swear he only keeps being the first in class just to piss me off and call me Miss Number Two. Sometimes, even Aiden will push me off the second place simply to prove he can.

Both of them are major wankers.

They have football practice right now, which means I can spend time with his mother in peace.

Couldn't she have a different son? Ronan or Xander would do. Hell, even Levi, Aiden's cousin, would be fine.

It had to be the one I hate the most.

The one who makes me feel fake whenever he looks in my direction at school.

Helen stands in front of the refrigerator with her back facing me. She's wearing chic trousers and a pressed shirt. Her light chestnut hair is tied in a neat bun that shows off her soft cheekbones and enhances the size of her hazel eyes.

Helen is a bestselling crime thriller novelist, so she doesn't usually dress up at home. She only does that when she has to meet her agent or something.

I sneak up behind her and hide her vision with my hands. "Guess who?"

She hums. "A beautiful girl with baby blue eyes and the shiniest blonde hair who's wearing pink?"

I laugh, removing my hand. "Uniform, Helen. Colours aren't allowed, but hey, my watch is pink."

She turns around and hugs me. She smells of strawberries and spring. If I had to pick a part that I love about Helen the most, it would be, without a doubt, the way she hugs. It's like she engulfs you and saturates you with her warmth.

Papa rarely hugs me ever since Mum told him he's the reason I'll stay a little girl. Mum seldom does it, so Helen is basically my only source.

She pulls away. "Are you ready for baking?"

"Weren't you on a deadline?"

"I finished early. So we get to bake all the cakes."

"All?"

She nods.

"Can we make a Snickers cake?"

"You and that chocolate." She smothers a soft laugh. "Yes, we can make that."

"Yes! You're the best." I kiss her cheek and she laughs again.

Helen and I get to work, and as always, I'm her sous-chef. She has a way of mixing ingredients that makes her fit to be a chef if she ever considers changing careers.

"You look beautiful, Helen," I tell her as we mix up eggs with butter.

Her warm smile makes an appearance. "I do?"

"Of course you do. If you go out there, you'll come back with ten men."

"Silver! Where have you heard things like that, honey?"

"The girls at school."

"Wow. Kids these days are unpredictable."

"I mean it, Helen. You're still young and beautiful. Oh, and rich. Mum says that's what matters the most."

Helen's eyes cast downwards. "Not in all cases, honey."

Ever since her husband's death six years ago, Helen has dedicated her life to her wanker son and her work. She became a bestselling novelist and built a name for herself, but I can sense how lonely she is.

Like Papa.

Oh. *Like Papa.*

A wicked idea comes to mind. I can tell Papa to come pick me up early and then pretend to be asleep so he can spend some time with Helen.

I gave up trying to patch things between him and Mum some time ago. All they do is fight, so maybe it's better for both their sakes to see other people.

I get into action before I can even think about it. I text Papa, and when he doesn't reply, I text Derek so that he passes on the message.

By the time Helen and I are finished with baking, I pretend I'm sleepy. Helen tells me to use any room down the hall to take a nap until my Snickers cake is ready.

I'm definitely taking that home with me. I don't have to tell Mum about it.

The moment I lie on the bed and place my head on the soft pillow, I somehow fall asleep.

I dream of Helen and Papa's wedding. I'm smiling, happy even, and I'm wearing a princess dress like the one from that Cinderella remake, but pink.

Then I see who's standing beside me at their wedding.

Cole.

Cole becomes my brother.

He's laughing so loud that I wake up with a start.

Damn it. Why didn't I think of that before I came up with the plan?

I was too focused on Papa's and Helen's loneliness that I forgot the small but horrible detail of Cole becoming my brother.

No. Nope.

I'll have to find other people for Helen and Papa. I'll never live under the same roof as that crude, stupid —

"Bad dream?"

I gasp and almost jump off the mattress. Cole is sitting beside me, leaning against the headboard and reading from a book called *Norwegian Wood* by Haruki Murakami. His hair is damp and falls on his forehead. He's wearing cotton trousers and a simple white T-shirt, which means he just got out of the shower.

I can't help inhaling the scent of his shower gel. It's like cinnamon and spice and I've become so used to it in a weird way lately.

I wipe my mouth in case there's drool or something. "W-what are you doing here?"

"This is my room," he says without looking up from his book.

He does that a lot, reading. Like a nerd, making all the girls watch him and say he's so swoony. So attractive. So hot. He's not.

"It's not your room." I do a swift glance to make sure. Of course it isn't. Considering I make it my mission to avoid his room, I would've known if it were.

"I made you look."

"You're such a wanker." I fold my arms over my chest, glaring at him.

We remain like that for a second too long. He's reading while I continue to glare, trying to figure out what the hell girls find attractive about him.

Yes, he has beautiful eyes that seem mysterious like the top of trees no one can reach. His hair is soft and a bit long, so that's cool, too, I guess. His face is generally pleasing to look at, yes.

But his personality is rotten.

Why does he keep attracting everyone so much?

"You went to a charity event with Aiden?" he asks quietly, still staring at his book.

"I did. We were with Papa and Uncle Jonathan."

"And what did you do?"

"We had fun."

"Define fun, Butterfly."

"We talked to some of Papa and Uncle Jonathan's friends, and they said we're smart kids who'll be perfect heirs to our fathers." I grin at that memory, I love when people compare me to Papa. "Then we ate and we played chess and we danced and —"

"You danced?" he cuts me off, finally lifting his head from his book to glimpse at me.

I nod.

"How?"

"What do you mean, *how*? We danced a bit of a waltz."

"Waltz," he repeats, glaring at me as if he wants to punch me. If I didn't know Cole doesn't punch or hit anyone—not even jokingly—I would've run from the room.

The silence stretches until it becomes uncomfortable. I hate long periods of silence, it makes me squirmy. Mum's voice echoes in my head over and over again.

A lady never feels awkward.

"Then Aiden and I went outside," I continue. "We snuck and ate more dessert behind the staff's back and —"

"Shut up."

"You're the one who asked what fun we had."

"And now I'm telling you to shut up." He slams his book closed and although the sound isn't loud, I flinch in place.

I should probably go. Not only to escape this atmosphere, but also to find Papa before my plan comes into play.

"Show me your titties," Cole says out of freaking nowhere.

My eyes widen so hard and I swallow as if that will somehow erase what I've heard.

His face remains neutral, even though his lips twitch as if to smile—or smirk.

"N-no!" I cross my hands over my chest.

"I could've seen them when you were asleep."

If my jaw could hit the floor, it would about now. I pull the sheet to my chest, my voice small and wrong. "D-did you? See them, I mean."

"No. It's more fun if you do it."

"Well, I'm not doing it." I narrow my eyes into slits.

"You will eventually, so you might as well start now."

"Nice try. No."

He shrugs as if it's the most normal occurrence in the world. Ever since I started growing breasts, Ronan and Xander won't stop asking things about them, like can they touch them? No. Do I stare at them all day? No. Can they get a picture to compare to the other pictures they have? No—and I didn't even ask what other pictures they have.

Cole has never once paid attention to them. It's the first time he's mentioned them. But Cole has a way of watching things that never alludes to what he's actually thinking or feeling.

"Do you want a dare?" he asks.

I jut my chin. "What are the stakes?"

I've learnt to always ask about the stakes before we start, because Cole plays unfair. I'm really beginning to think he loses just because he forfeits.

And that's a low blow to my pride.

"If you win, I do something for you. No questions asked. And vice versa."

"I'm not showing you my breasts, Cole."

"You mean tits?"

My face heats. Why does he have to be so crude? "Well, I'm not showing them."

"Okay."

"Really?"

"Yeah. Promise."

"What's the dare?"

He throws the book in my lap. "Pick a page, then tell me to read any line."

"That's ridiculous. You can't have possibly memorised the whole book."

"Then you'll win."

I nibble on my bottom lip, contemplating this. Cole has an excellent memory but it doesn't go as far as memorising a book. Besides, he's just started reading this one. I know, because he was reading something called *Nausea* yesterday.

Only Cole would read weird books like that when all the other boys are hiding porn. Ronan and Xander sure are.

If he's stupid enough to make this bet, so be it. I open the book, hiding it away from him. "You're going to be my slave for a week, Cole."

"Is that what you wish?"

"I'm going to make you regret everything you've done to me." I pause at a page and the line at the top catches my attention. "Page one eighty-eight, paragraph two."

A smug smile lifts my lips, my mind already full with different ways I'll torment Cole.

"'Never mind,' I said. 'Both of us have a lot of feelings we need to get out in the open. So if you want to take those feelings and smash somebody with them, smash me. Then we can understand each other better.'" He doesn't even miss a beat.

My eyes must double in size as I stare between him and the book. It's the same line, word for word.

No. No.

I point a finger at him. "You cheated!"

"You were hiding the book like your life depended on it, Butterfly. You think I could cheat?"

"Then you knew I was going to pick it."

"How would I know which page you'd choose, let alone which line?"

"I...I demand a redo."

"No. You lost and now you pay up. Unless you're a quitter."

"I'm not," I groan, throwing the stupid book

away—though I'll probably read it later. I like that line. "What do you want?"

"I'm going to kiss you and you're going to let me."

Before I can form a thought, he palms my cheeks and brushes his lips against mine.

They part open of their own accord and Cole takes control of my lips. He kisses me slowly at first, tasting me and making my entire body shiver. I don't know what to do, so I remain still.

I've thought about kissing before—more specifically since that day he tricked me into kissing his cheek but turned his head at the last second.

His lips are firmer than back then, and when he slips his tongue against mine, he tastes of his favourite lime gum. My toes curl and my limbs shake with whatever force he's injecting into me.

Why does kissing him feel so good?

It's not supposed to, right? I hate him.

And yet, the more he glides his tongue against mine, the more I want it to last, the harder I need it to.

When he pulls away, I briefly close my eyes to steady my breathing. Wow. Is it supposed to feel as if I'm floating out of my body right now?

"You're not bad compared to the others," he says.

The others.

Plural?

My eyes snap open and I shove him away with a force I didn't know I possessed. "Don't you ever touch me again."

I storm out of the room with tears in my eyes.

I hate Cole Nash.

I despise him.

FIVE

Cole

Age fifteen

Existence, or the lack thereof, is intriguing.

I remember the first time I picked up *Nausea* by Jean-Paul Sartre from one of Mum's shelves. It was covered with dust, not having been touched in years.

I remember reading it in one day. I was twelve. I didn't understand much of it back then, but every time I reread it, I get these bursts of nothingness.

Other people would steer clear from that, but I keep coming back for more. I read about the existentialism theory and followed all of Sartre's counterparts, and while I'm not a believer in the theory—or in anything in general—I still find myself engrossed in Sartre's main character in *Nausea,* Antoine Roquentin.

A lonely man suffering to come to terms with his existence while being horrified by it.

When Mum saw me reading the book, she said she pitied him because he didn't have anyone to understand him. Antoine is, in her mind, the worst-case scenario for writers who delve too deep.

Mum might be a novelist herself, but she's into what I call

thought-provoking fiction. She writes books about the darkest parts of human nature, psychopaths, serial killers and cults. She writes books where villains are the main characters and she doesn't try to romanticise them. That's what makes her plots heart-pounding.

No matter how much I love Mum's talent and her literary genius, I think she missed the point in *Nausea*. It's not that Antoine didn't understand himself; it's that maybe he understood too much, which became a burden.

I didn't tell her that, or she would've given me that look. The one where her brow creases and she watches me closely as if looking for signs from her serial killers' articles cheat sheet.

Then she would've booked me an appointment with the therapist so I could talk it out.

It's been the same endless cycle since my father died. Over the years, I've learnt to keep my most unconventional opinions to myself. Whenever Mum says I sound a lot older than I am, it's usually my prompt to cut back and mimic those surrounding me.

Especially Xander and Ronan; they're the most normal amongst the four of us—or as normal as they can get.

I've been having my suspicions about Ronan. His overall joyful personality sometimes seems to be the camouflage of something.

He's now grinning like an idiot as we gather in the Meet Up—the cottage Aiden's late mother left him. We usually come here after games with other team members. Today, however, it's only the four of us because Ronan said it's a special occasion.

"Lady and gents—and by the way, the lady is you, King." He hops on the table, feigning to hold a microphone in hand. "We're gathered here today to celebrate the holy deflowering of Aiden King. He finally lost his virginity. Let's hear it for him!"

Xander howls as he jumps on the table and grabs Ronan by the shoulder. He's one to talk, the hypocrite.

"Shut the fuck up, Astor, and get down," Aiden says from beside me. He appears bored as usual. His grey eyes are bland and about ready to commit murder to interrupt the vicious, dull cycle.

I know that feeling.

Unless there's chaos, it's as if the world is permanently grey and there's no way to inject colour into it.

For me, it started after the kidnapping. Maybe I had some issues before, but that darkness—that first taste of chaos—sealed the deal for me.

Aiden is the same, although his case is deeper. Xander and I were taken for two days and weren't harmed. Aiden spent an entire week in chaos and came back with scars.

Is he special? Is that why Chaos kept him for longer?

Since then, he's been making it his mission to instigate battles and wars. Or rather, it's become *our* mission. Me, because I'll take any chance to meet Chaos again, even if it's brief. Him, because he loves the challenge. He isn't labelled Conquest for no reason.

They came up with these names for us at school because of football. Xander is War, which is understandable, considering he's like a bull striker. Ronan is Death because he kills any attempt at attack from the midfield. I'm Famine. According to them, silent but deadly.

I'd say I'm always hungry for more. More information, more books, more *chaos*.

"Admit it, Aiden." Ronan directs his imaginary mic at him. "It's because of my recommendations."

"Fuck off." Aiden doesn't miss a beat.

"You don't have to say it out loud. I get it in the small space in my heart." Ronan grins, running his fingers through his messy brown hair in a smug way. "I was the first to lose my virginity. You're the last. Guess who wins?"

A slight smirk crosses Aiden's lips. "How about Knight and Nash?"

"Knight was right after me." Ronan squeezes Knight's shoulder. "Was that night with that twin fun or what?"

"Are you sure, though?" Aiden glances at Xander, who flips him off with a dimpled smile.

"*Mais bien sûr,*" Ronan dismisses Aiden. "Cole was… Hey, wait a second. When was it?"

"Miss Goldman," I say and focus back on my book.

They don't need to know the details. Besides, if they find out, Ronan will make a fucking show out of it. He makes it his job not only to start a rumour, but also to spread it until it reaches other schools.

He's shit with secrets.

"Ooh, right." Ronan grins, then pouts. "You're the winner in quality, but I'm the winner in quantity. Aiden is last."

The latter flips him off and he returns it as the door clicks open.

Only six people have access to the Meet Up. Four of them are here and the fifth is Levi, Aiden's one-year-older cousin, but he disappeared with a girl, which leaves just one option.

My head lifts from the book as she comes inside, holding a grocery bag and juggling her backpack on one shoulder.

Chaos.

My entire body sharpens whenever she's in my vicinity. It's been getting more noticeable over the years. Every time she's there, I have this urge to get up, grab her, and take her… somewhere.

Anywhere.

It doesn't help that every day, she's been growing from that kid Barbie doll to this girl with long, toned legs and an hourglass figure that keeps sharpening with time. Her tits are perky, high, and big, straining against her jacket whenever it's closed—like now.

Her face has this symmetrical quality to it. Her eyes are huge and a clear blue, and when you're close enough, you can see the grey flecks in them. Like a symphony of colours. The small freckles on her nose have been slowly disappearing over the years and she's been hiding the traces with makeup. Her lips are full and have a perfect teardrop at the top that I haven't been able to stop staring at since the day I sucked on it about a year ago.

No. It's not only her lips that I haven't been able to stop staring at.

It's *her*.

All of her.

And it's not only because of that kiss or the almost-kiss before that.

It all started that night. It started with chaos and refused to end.

I still don't like Silver Queens. And not because she acts like a bitch to everyone at school, but because she's not actually a bitch. She'll go out of her way to snitch to the principal on anyone who bullies Kimberly, but she won't talk to her. She'll even hurt her if she feels her ex-best friend, Kim, might get close to her.

She shuts Summer and Veronica up when they make the other students do shit for them while she sits at parties like she's a queen, accepting the peasants' offers at her feet.

The sorry fucks line up to ask her to dance, only for her to tell them she's not feeling like dancing, but they can sit with her.

She's plastic. She's becoming more and more a replica of her mother, and the worst thing is, I don't think she even realises it.

When her eyes meet mine, she pauses for a fraction of a second before she harrumphs and directs her attention at the others.

Since that day in our guest room, Silver has made it her mission to avoid me and never stay alone with me. Whenever we meet at my house by accident—because I make her think I won't come back at that time and then show up anyway—she pretends I don't exist.

Like now.

It's a game we play. Pretending the other doesn't exist.

I still pull on her hair every chance I get. She's lost that awed, surprised look over time, but it's one of the rarest moments where she'll stare up at me with wide eyes. They usually morph into glares way too soon, but that brief second is worth it.

Silver still tries to compete with me every chance she gets. She loses most of the time. In the beginning, I used to forfeit to see her eyes widening in a different type of way—with happiness—but lately, she's been pissing me off with all the fuckboys she sits with at parties, so I make sure to see her lose.

I make sure she falls at my feet.

She stands up every time, though, and swings back even more determined. It's one of her most admirable qualities. It's like she can climb a mountain, then destroy it if she puts her mind to it.

I'm that mountain in her life right now. The one she'll never be able to reach the top of. I won't let her. I'll keep her hanging on to me because I need the chaos she brings to the solid exterior. The way she digs her nails in and disrupts the boring cycle.

If I give in to her, if I allow her to have her way, everything will snap back to normal, and I don't like normal.

"I brought snacks Helen and I made." She carries the bags to the kitchen area.

"Are there any crisps?" Ronan helps her and she nods.

Xander follows, rubbing his hands. "I get half the crisps."

"No!" Ronan brings out an imaginary sword. "Fight me for it, peasant."

Xander brings out his own imaginary sword and they start jumping like monkeys around Silver.

"You mean, Mum made them and you just watched," I say, feigning to read from my book. I can't concentrate on words when she's around. I always have this overflow of energy that starts in my chest and ends in my dick.

"Funny because you weren't there," she shoots back.

"I don't have to be there to know you suck at cooking, Silver." I don't use her nickname when anyone else is around. If I do, they'll pick up on my abnormal attachment to her.

That means weakness.

And I already made a promise to myself that there would never be another moment where I'm weak.

I did it once. Never again.

I don't lift my head, but I feel her glaring at me from across the room. I like to think her hatred is black hands, and they're punching me metaphorically when she's not within physical reach.

She still hits me whenever possible. Sometimes, it's stomping on my foot or elbowing me in the side when no one is looking. Other times, it's a straight out punch to the chest, but that's only when we're alone. She thinks they hurt, but they're like a toddler's caress.

Silver has an outside image and an inside one. They never overlap and she's becoming an expert at juggling her two lives. One is Daddy's little girl, her mother's perfect daughter, and the top student, piano player, and classical music lover. The other is everything else. Like listening to rock music and eating Snickers bars in secret. The punches, too. That's why I did everything to bring them out.

I'm the only one who brings them out.

"You've been on the same page for ten minutes," Aiden says from beside me, his voice low enough so that only I can hear him.

Silver is trying to pacify Ronan and Xander's fake fight. A pacifier—that's what she is deep down. However, she's been slowly but surely trying to get rid of that part.

I flip the page. "I'm engraving the words to memory."

"Lie. You have a photographic memory, so you engrave pages after a minute, or is it seconds?" He pauses. "Maybe you're distracted."

I lift my head from the book. Aiden is watching me with a sadistic smirk on his lips. Was I not careful enough? Did I somehow raise his suspicions?

"What are you talking about?" I play the nonchalance card I'm so good at.

"Silver Queens, huh? I should've seen it coming with the amount of time she spends with Helen."

"She only comes over for Mum."

"Sure, did I say anything?" He pretends to push his black hair from his forehead. "In that case, is it okay if I fuck her?"

My hold tightens around the book, but I try to keep my expression the same. It's a tool I've found works in most situations. If you stay calm, it'll eventually go away.

If I tell Aiden no, he'll figure out my fixation and use it against me every chance he gets.

But I know something... Silver can't stand Aiden. She thinks we're both wankers and doesn't miss a single chance to tell us that. She wouldn't touch him with a stick.

Besides, I have a way to make her hate him even more.

"Sure, if you're into bimbos." I smile.

"You and I both know she's a not a bimbo."

"Uh-huh."

"You think I won't be able to do it." His smirk widens. "I love it when you underestimate me, Nash. I really, *really* do."

"Be my guest." I focus on the other two. "Hey, Ronan. Why don't you tell Silver what we're celebrating?"

"Oh, right." Ronan pauses his fight with Xander and clears his throat. "Aiden lost his virginity to his father's secretary yesterday. He's finally a man."

"I didn't need to know that." She makes a disgusted face as she opens the container on the counter.

Bingo. I just made Aiden lose before he started to play. That's how it's done.

"You fucked up, Nash," Aiden murmurs to me. "Now, I'm taking this to the next level."

I can't resist the smug look that pulls at my lips. "Best of luck."

"Hey, Ronan," Aiden speaks in a neutral tone. "Why don't you tell her the order of how we all lost our virginities?"

"*Mais bien sûr.*" Ronan points at himself. "I'm number one, of course—no need for applause—then Xan, and then Cole with the bombshell Miss Goldman, and the loser Aiden is last."

Silver pauses opening a container, her fingers freezing on the handle.

Fuck.

The change in her demeanour is short, but it's there. Her eyes are cast downwards, so I can't see the look in them. However, she purses her lips for the briefest second before she goes back to normal, and by normal, I mean the mask she wears every time she gets up in the morning.

Silver Queens is the most popular girl at school.

A piano prodigy.

The school's queen B.

And fake.

She's so fake, I can taste the bitterness of it on my tongue.

"You guys are pigs," she says with her haughty attitude, but there's a slight tremble in her voice at the end.

"You insult me." Ronan grabs her by the shoulder, speaking in a dramatic voice. "Pigs don't have my package, love."

"Thank God for that." She slips from underneath his hold. "I'm going home. Papa's waiting."

"And we can have all the crisps?" Xander asks.

She waves a dismissive hand at him as she strolls into our area to pick up her backpack.

Aiden stands, giving me a sideways smirk. "Can your driver drop me off?"

No, thanks. She'll say, *no, thanks.* That's what she tells Aiden every fucking time.

"Sure." She grabs her backpack with stiff fingers.

"Drop me off, too." I stand.

For some reason, I feel that if she walks out with him through that door, everything will be screwed up, and it won't be the chaos I love so much.

It'll be chaos I can't control, like when I was a kid, standing at the edge of the pool.

She snaps her head, finally looking at me. I wish she hadn't. I've never seen that look in her eyes—malice mixed with hurt and disappointment and something else I can't put my finger on.

Something so deep and raw, it's almost like the time she pinned me to the bench and soaked my cheeks with her glitter tears because she couldn't hold them in.

She's not crying now, though, and that's way fucking worse.

"You can go to hell," she tells me as Aiden steps to her side.

She leans in to whisper, "You don't know what I'm feeling right now, but I'm going to make you regret it."

I reach out a hand for her, but all it finds is air.

The moment the door closes behind her and Aiden, something inside me slams shut too.

SIX

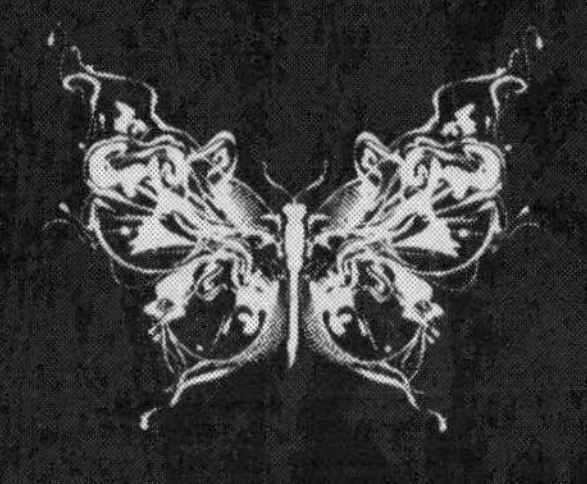

Silver

Aiden and I are at the back of Papa's car, sitting side by side.

The moment Derek drives away from the Meet Up, my breathing turns faster and harsher, as if I've been running.

As if I'm climbing a mountain and have no way to get down. Then I'm falling and there's no landing in sight. It's a fatal fall, the type that crushes your skull and destroys your body.

I stare out the window and focus on the empty road to not think about what I've just learnt.

The distraction doesn't help. The inhaling and exhaling don't help either.

There's a weight on my chest that won't go the hell away. It's suffocating me the more I gulp air into my lungs.

All I want to do is scream until my voice turns hoarse and I can't scream anymore.

I retrieve my phone and pretend I'm scrolling through my vain chat room with Veronica and Summer. It's all about gossip and the latest makeup and fashion trends. The stupidity itself should somehow cool my head.

It doesn't.

The only image going on in my mind on a freaking loop is

Cole having sex with our head nurse. He was *having sex* with her.

As in they were naked and he kissed her.

Tears fight to spill free, but I turn away from Aiden and widen my eyes so they stay there. I won't cry. I'm not going to cry because of that arsehole.

So what if he has sex? I don't care. Why should I care?

Cole can go to hell for all I care.

I hate him. The one good thing about him is that he's Helen's son. That's it.

That's *all*.

Since that day he kissed me, I knew Cole wasn't for me. I just knew it. The moment he compared me to others, blatantly declaring I was only one of his conquests, I decided I would be the conquest he'd never win.

He might make me lose at studies and piano and sports, but he'll never make me lose at this game.

And I meant what I said. I'll make him regret it.

My firsts?

Screw him. He lost the right to those the moment he didn't save his firsts for me.

Cole might act like I'm a fly in his vicinity, but he gets unnecessarily aggressive when he knows Aiden and I have spent time together behind his back. We only do it because Papa and Uncle Jonathan are close friends and we're often invited as a set.

And by unnecessarily aggressive, I mean he'll accept Aiden's challenges, even when he usually doesn't. He makes sure to win every time too.

Cole doesn't just win. He crushes. Then he walks all over you as if you never existed.

I lay the phone on my lap. "Out with it."

Aiden throws me a glance. He has a permanent 'piss off' look etched on his features. And while he's relatively handsome with his styled black hair and sharp features, I don't know why the girls find him attractive and nearly blend in with the walls whenever he passes them by.

He's annoying and entitled and has sociopathic tendencies. If they tried looking behind his exterior for a second, maybe they'd figure that out, but girls like Summer and Veronica say stuff like, 'but he's so hot' as if that will save them when he ends up choking the life out of them.

"Out with what?" he asks.

"Derek and I know you don't enjoy our company, so why did you want to catch a ride?"

"For your beautiful eyes, Queens."

"Eww. Don't ever try that again with me. I literally want to throw up."

He smirks. "You wouldn't want to throw up if it were Nash, eh?"

"Fuck him and you."

"Someone is triggered."

"What do you want, Aiden?" I grit out through my teeth. "If this is some sort of game between you two, I'm not playing. I'm not a pawn on either of your chessboards. I'm a queen on mine."

"Interesting." He fully faces me. "But here's the thing, this can be your game too."

"My game?"

"Revenge. You said you'll make him regret it. Do you know the best way to do that?" He lowers his voice so Derek doesn't hear. "Losing your virginity to me."

"You must be out of your mind if you think I'd let you touch me." I flip my hair back. "If we were the last two people left on this planet and our children were the only hope for humanity, I'd vote for extinction."

Derek's lips twitch in a smile in the rear-view mirror and I smile back at him. He understands me.

"Unfortunately, that's mutual," Aiden says. "The only good thing about you is your ability to rile Nash up."

I fold my arms over my chest. "Why unfortunately?"

"Because I won't be able to fuck you and win against him."

"Who says it has to actually happen?" I smirk. "We just have to make him believe it did."

Aiden mirrors my smirk; his, however, appears more wolfish. "I like the way you think, Queens."

"I'll take that as a compliment."

"What do you say we become allies and crush him?"

"Crush him how?"

"In a way he'll fall at your feet like a puppy."

I don't want that. I only want him to feel the pain he inflicts on me. I want to hurt him as much as he hurts me.

I want him to look in the mirror and hold back screams because he's been making me feel invisible.

Since that night, I've never been invisible to him. But lately, he'll pass me by and greet Veronica and Summer, but not me. He'll smile at them, but never me.

It's like he's punishing me for something I've never done. Okay, so maybe I did the same, but he started it.

Or did I?

I don't remember. Either way, he's at fault. I refuse to lose to him or anyone else.

I focus back on Aiden. "How do you intend to do that?"

"Give me your phone."

"What are you going to do with it?" I ask suspiciously.

"Just give it."

I unlock the device and pass it to him.

He types something, then shows me. He texted Cole from my phone.

Silver: We sent Papa's driver away and guess what we did?

Cole sees the message but doesn't reply.

Aiden's lips pull in a smirk as he types again. He's so keen about details, he even included how I address my father.

He sends another text and shows it to me.

Silver: Aiden fucked me so hard, I'm so sore and can't move.

I gasp, bile rising to my throat at the image he's painted in Cole's head about me. "Why did you do that?"

"Isn't that what you want him to think?"

"Yeah, but not that way."

"Believe me, he needs to get the crude details to react…" he trails off and brings out his phone. Cole's name flashes on his screen. "Speak of the devil."

"Are you going to answer?" I murmur.

"No. It's better to keep him in suspense, don't you think?"

"Why, of course." This is my revenge. I didn't throw myself away and have sex just to spite him, but Cole thinks that.

That's the only part that matters.

My phone buzzes with a text from an unknown number. Aiden starts to look at it, but I snatch it away.

I don't want him, of all people, to know about that part of my life. We might be allies, but I don't trust Aiden, not even a little. If he thinks disclosing this would benefit him in any way, he'd do it in a heartbeat.

One peek at the text causes my skin to prickle.

Unknown Number: I love the new watch.

I've been receiving these types of texts for the past few weeks. At first, I liked how someone praised my piano playing and said I have the best dresses.

It's when they started to describe my daily routines and the clothes I wore outside that I recognised I might have a stalker.

The only reason I've ignored it is because they've just been harmless texts. Besides, Papa is preparing for an important internal campaign. I won't, under any circumstances, divide his attention.

Mum is also in that campaign, and if she knows about this, she'll raise hell and take it to social media. That's the last thing I want.

So for now, I've decided to keep it to myself. If it gets more persistent or creepy, I'll tell Papa or maybe Frederic. He's PR-savvy so he'll know how to deal with it.

We arrive at my house first. "Derek, please drive Aiden home."

"I'll keep Nash on the edge." Aiden winks. "This is going to be so fun."

No. It's not fun. I might want to get back at Cole and I won't allow him to throw me the short end of the stick, but I don't enjoy this.

It's just a necessity.

Aiden, however, is finding the most joy in it.

I'm about to step out when Papa peeks in from the passenger window. "Aiden, perfect. Come join us."

An automatic smile lifts my face the moment I see him. I barge out of the car and squeeze him in a hug. "Papa! What are you doing home this early?"

He strokes my hair back—it's a habit he started from when I had a fever ever since I was young, and it usually puts me back to sleep. Even now that I've grown up, he still does it.

I've always loved it when I'm sick. It's the only time my parents nurse me all night without fighting.

Papa is a tall man with a darker shade of blond hair than mine. His eyes are a light brown that turn to mesmerising hazel under the sun.

He's wearing his three-piece Italian cut suit and he still has his leather shoes on, which means he recently got home. He usually changes into a cardigan sweater as soon as he leaves the office. Unless he has company.

His next words confirm my suspicions. "Jonathan and I have something important to discuss with you and Aiden."

"Is this about a fundraiser?" I ask.

"Let's talk in the house." Papa nods at his driver. "Thank you, Derek. That will be all."

Aiden follows us inside as I keep hanging on to Papa by

the waist. I feel like I haven't seen him in an eternity. Not only has he been busy lately, but Mum has been dropping in unannounced, demanding I spend time with her and complaining that I never do anymore.

The guilt trip frequently works and I end up in her flat before I know it.

We go into Papa's office. It's as big as a conference hall with photos in black frames of previous leaders of the Conservative Party who Papa looks up to.

The wood and the chandeliers give a hint about Papa's ancient roots and how much he believes in classical with a modern twist. Everything in his office has a time and place. You never find papers stacked on top of each other or in disorder.

He's all about law and order to the point he uses it as the slogan of his campaign.

There's a conference table in the middle with a presentation board and everything.

We head to the adjacent lounge area that has brown leather sofas and chairs. Uncle Jonathan is already sitting there, sipping from a glass of scotch and scrolling through his tablet on what looks like the FTSE 100 Index.

Aiden is a replica of his father appearance-wise. They share the same black hair and dark grey eyes. Uncle Jonathan, however, has a sharper edge and he's frightening with his enemies. He's crushed countless companies and rivals until they either disappeared off the face of the earth or agreed to his conditions. All he cares about is profit and going forward.

I'm glad Papa is his friend, not his enemy. Upon seeing us, he places his glass and tablet on the table. "Wonderful, both of you are here. Saves us time speaking to you separately."

"Sit down." Papa motions at the sofa as he settles in beside Uncle Jonathan.

"What's going on?" I ask after Aiden and I sit next to each other.

"Jonathan and I were talking," Papa starts. "And we think it would be a marvellous idea to join our families through marriage. That is, only if both of you agree."

If I were drinking something, I would've spat it all out right about now. It shouldn't be a surprise that Papa and Uncle Jonathan would want to join forces, but I never thought it would be this soon or in this way.

"Aiden has no reason to disagree." Jonathan raises his brows at his son. "Isn't that right?"

"I'm fine with it," Aiden says.

My eyes snap in his direction, asking him without words, what the hell he's doing.

"Remember what I told you about becoming allies?" he whispers.

"But we're only fifteen," I tell Papa.

"There will be no marriage until at least after university, Princess. This is just putting the rocks in place."

"Or rather, the chess pieces." Jonathan sips from his drink.

I know the whole meaning behind this. Papa is a secretary of state who can help Uncle Jonathan, and in return, he'll push him in the next elections towards Papa's most coveted dream—becoming the prime minister.

He's already gathering votes to become the leader of the Conservative Party, and by the next general elections, Papa will be the strongest leader of the country.

I want to help him with everything in me. I really do. But… something in my chest aches at the thought of being engaged to Aiden when —

No.

I won't let my brain finish that thought.

My phone dings, and I apologise, pulling it out to shut it off. The name on the text notification stops me in my tracks.

Cole.

It's almost like a sign. He messages me now to stop me before it's too late.

My heart thumps so loud as I open the text.

Cole: You and Aiden deserve each other. You're a bitch and he's a psycho. One day, you'll fall, Butterfly, and I'll stand there and watch as you burn.

Something breaks inside my chest.

I hear it, feel it, I just can't see it.

My eyes burn with tears, but I inhale deeply, disallowing them from spilling.

I'm a lady.

Ladies don't cry in public.

"You don't have to do it if you don't want to, Princess." Papa smiles at me with so much warmth, I want to hug him all over again. "You know I'll never force you to do anything."

"I want to do it." I manage a smile. "I'll be engaged to Aiden."

I'll help Papa.

And most importantly, I'll get over the cancer that's been eating at me for years.

The cancer without a cure. Cole.

SEVEN

Doll Master

I've watched for long enough.

Waited for long enough.

The time has come to take the next step.

My beautiful doll has been growing up into a woman every day in front of my very eyes. She's been becoming this next upgrade I cannot wait to touch, to run my fingers over.

To taste.

The problem with my pretty little doll is that she spends a lot of time with non-important people like her bitch mother whose only good quality is that she gave birth to her.

Or those friends who make her look stupid when she's anything but.

My doll will keep growing up, and the more I see her, the surer I become about how she deserves to be number one in my collection.

The others aren't like her. They never will be.

I used to be fine watching from the sidelines, being proud of my creation and of how she was turning out.

I liked the fact I knew about her and she didn't know about me.

Isn't invisibility a wonderful thing?

I'd played it before when I hid from my father. All I had to do was look at my doll and pretend he wasn't there.

Other days, I'd go to the closet.

Hiding in the dark isn't hard. At first, you see nothing. Then you might get scared. Then you feel things pulling you by the limbs, and soon enough, you become friends with those things.

The monster under the bed understood me when no one else did. He listened to me when no one else would, and for that reason, he's my friend. All my demons are my friends. They sit with me when I plan and they're there when I watch my pretty little doll.

But my demons and I don't like being ignored. We've been on the sidelines for years now, watching quietly without making a sound.

A few weeks ago, I decided my pretty little doll should start getting acquainted with her master.

I chose an untraceable method, of course. So even if she freaked out and told her daddy about me, they wouldn't be able to find me.

She didn't.

My little doll can be an attention whore, which is understandable with the bitchy mother she has. My first text to her was, 'You played the piano perfectly today.'

She read it with a furrowed brow and then she smiled. She lost that day and no one tells those who come second that they played perfectly. All they say is better luck next time.

However, Silver didn't need luck. She needed encouragement and I gave her that.

Ever since then, I send her texts to compliment her, but also to tell her without being specific that I'm close. Maybe not enough to smell her—her scent is of cherry and Chanel most days—but I'm there.

I watch her.

I listen to her.

And one day, I'll own her.

EIGHT

Cole

That night, I don't sleep.

I can't.

Not that I usually have a good sleeping cycle. I'm the type who stays up all night, then sleeps one or two hours before I have to wake up.

I've always thought sleep is a waste of time. Why sleep when you can read?

But the reason I can't sleep isn't because of reading. In fact, I haven't been able to touch a book since I got home.

I barely had dinner with Mum, and since then, I've been staring at my phone—the text Aiden sent right after Silver messaged me.

Aiden: Hey, how do I remove virginal blood from my dick? Should I just wash it?

I called him immediately, but he didn't pick up.

It's only a trick. A fucking game of Aiden's.

Silver wouldn't let him fuck her, she sure as hell wouldn't give him her virginity. Silver might act high and mighty, but she believes in all that lady bollocks. She wouldn't lose her virginity in the back of a car and with someone she's not even dating.

She wouldn't.

Unless if she wanted revenge.

I'll make you regret it.

Her words echo in my mind like a twisted song, the type where I want to smash the CD against the wall.

I keep filling my head with thoughts like, *Silver wouldn't pull herself down or do something out of spite.* She's a snob in a way, and thinks ruining oneself is stupid.

But then again, she started hanging out with those fuckboys after I kissed her and told her she's not bad compared to the others.

She's vindictive and refuses to lose, even when she's down.

Fuck.

I jump out of bed and then storm outside. I stop by the pool and stare at the luminous blue surface. I constantly think it'll somehow turn red.

The reason I stop and stare at it every time isn't out of fear, it's out of my need for chaos.

The only time I go near that pool is when Silver is swimming with Mum in her one-piece suit. Her nipples show through the material and I always come close to have a better view of them. Then, after I get my fill, I tell her about it just to see her eyes widening and her cheeks turning red.

I hop on my bike and head towards Aiden's house. I'm not one minute in before the sky starts pouring. I'm soaked within seconds but I don't stop pedalling, not even when the water blurs my vision. It takes me fifteen minutes on full speed. I'm breathing harshly and there's no one in the streets. It's almost a scene from a crime thriller novel.

And maybe I should end it with a crime.

As soon as I arrive, I throw the bike down and hit the bell. Their butler lets me in and offers me a towel, pointing out that it's past midnight. I couldn't give a damn about that, so fuck him and his towel.

I storm up the stairs to Aiden's room. It's dark when I barge inside. It's only when lightning strikes in the distance that I see his silhouette. He's sitting on the bed, staring at something in front of him. I hit the light switch and he squints as I interrupt his session with his chessboard. He's been playing against himself again. In the dark.

"Hey, Nash. You couldn't sleep either?"

My breathing is choked, chest rising and falling so hard I couldn't speak even if I wanted to. Droplets of rain fall from me, soaking the carpet.

He tilts his head. "You look like a rat out of the sewer."

"Silver wouldn't fuck you in the back of her father's car." I pant. "She's conservative and we both know it."

"And yet, she did. I already washed the blood off my dick. I wouldn't have if I'd known you have a virginal blood kink."

I'm panting like a dying dog. "You're lying."

Though I can't tell for sure, considering his unchanged features. Usually, I'm good at reading people's expressions and knowing if they're lying or bluffing. I've been slowly trying to seem completely unaffected while I lie myself.

It's not hard. You need guilt to show those signs in your body language. I lost that ability a long time ago.

Problem is, Aiden lost it too, so you never know when he's lying or telling the truth.

"What's in it for you, Nash?" He stands up and stalks towards me. "You don't want me with her?"

"Why wouldn't I want you with her?"

"I don't know. Let me take a wild guess. Hmm." He feigns a thinking position. "Feel threatened, maybe?"

"You wish."

"Don't tell me you rode your bike all the way here in the middle of the pouring rain at midnight just to tell me you don't care."

"That's exactly it. I don't care. I stopped caring about anything a long time ago." I pause, continuing to catch my breath. "Still, Silver wouldn't have done what you're trying to convince yourself and me of. She believes in things."

"Like stability, law, and order?"

"Yes."

"That means she would have done it with her fiancé, don't you think?"

I stop breathing for long seconds until my lungs burn. "What the fuck are you talking about?"

"From today onwards, Silver and I are engaged. We accept congratulations starting this Sunday. You can drop the gifts at the post office."

"You're *what?*"

"Engaged? She's my fiancée? We'll get married and have kids? That includes fucking on a daily basis, by the way."

I lift my fist to punch him, but the smirk on his face stops me in my tracks.

He's playing with me. He knows I never resort to violence and he's now using this masquerade against me.

"Come on." He motions at my hand. "Finish what your head is telling you to do."

"Was this Jonathan and Sebastian's doing?" I ask.

"And us. Nothing would've happened if she and I hadn't agreed."

"She agreed." My hand drops to my side, the fight inside me withering to nothing.

Silver agreed to become Aiden's fiancée.

What the hell is this thing breaking inside me?

"Of course she did. It's me. Besides, you pushed her my way, Nash, and do you know what I'll do now? I'll play all the games you never wanted to play before."

"And you'll lose every fucking time." I turn around to leave.

"Can't wait," he calls after me. "She has a tight cunt that I'm looking forward to tasting again tomorrow."

I swing back and this time, I smash my fist in his face. He winces, clutching it, but he laughs out loud, the sound echoing in the room.

"What was that for, Nash? Do I smell jealousy in the air?"

"That's a declaration of war. It might not be tomorrow or next year or even the next decade, but I'll find a way and crush you."

"Good luck with that. In the meantime, please enjoy my and Silver's engagement."

I storm out of the house before I throw the fucker out of the window. I jump on my bike and ride it in the rain.

For hours, I just roam the empty streets, my chest rising and falling heavily as the downpour drenches me. My T-shirt sticks to my back and my wet hair glues to my temples.

My head crowds with chaos so strong, I can't begin to solve it. I usually need the beginning of the riddle, and no matter how much the thing is tangled, I'd figure it out. I'll find a way and solve it.

Not this time.

This time, it's almost like the chaos isn't in my head—it's in my chest. It's aching and beating in and out of synch. Something tells me it's not because of the rain or the cold.

She ruined it.

She ruined everything.

She killed the small living part in my chest, and now, I'll kill her in return.

It might not be today or tomorrow, but Silver Queens will pay for this pain. I'll make it slow and torturous, just like the thing dying in my chest.

I only return home around five thirty in the morning because it's close to Mum's waking time and I don't want to worry her.

She worried enough for a lifetime when William Nash was alive.

I shrug my wet clothes off and stand under the shower for half an hour before I step out and put on my uniform, then join Mum downstairs.

The sound of humming stops me at the entrance to the kitchen.

Mum.

She's singing.

It took her seven years, but Mum is singing again, and not only that, but she's also doing it with a smile on her face as she checks the oven.

When I was a child, Mum used to sing me to sleep or when she made breakfast like this. She has a soft voice made for lullabies and sweet dreams. Over the years, William killed that voice. She stopped singing and even stopped writing. She went into a slump for the last three years of his life.

She picked up writing again soon after his death, even though she battled with depression. It was her outlet, something she found refuge in. However, she never sang again and I thought William had taken her voice with him.

Now, she's found it. She dug it from the grave and got it out.

I drop my messenger bag on the chair and hug her from behind. "How is the best mother in the world?"

"Oh, darling." She places a hand on my cheek and tiptoes to kiss me on the forehead. She hasn't stopped doing that since I was a kid. "Have you stayed out?"

"How do you know that?" She shouldn't. Her pills make her go out from ten to six. "Have you not been taking your pills, Mum?"

"No, I don't need them to sleep anymore." She smiles. "At least, not every day. Now, young man, where did you go?"

"Aiden's. We were playing and lost track of time."

"You better not have ridden your bike in the rain."

"Is that my favourite citrus cake?" I kiss her on the cheek and take the plate before settling at the counter.

She shakes her head and starts dragging things in front of me as I eat my slice of cake. There's coffee, juice, jam, eggs, bacon, toast, butter, and what's fit to feed an army. Mum has always cooked things that feed a large family.

"You've been radiant lately, Mum."

"I have?" She touches her chestnut hair that she's started to let loose. Her eyes sparkle, and it's the most beautiful view. She has lived as a shell of herself for years. Even after William's death. Once, I heard her tell Ronan's mother that, sometimes, she thinks maybe William will come back.

That's when her mental health takes a sharp dive and she doesn't get out of bed for days. She doesn't write or take jogs, she just hides in her room.

Lately, it's as if life has been blown into her, and I know why. She's been going out a lot lately for tea with Ronan's mother or for dinners with the company people—*people* because Mum doesn't like anything about William's business. She's only keeping the fort until I'm of age to take over.

However, Mum hasn't really been going for tea or to those dinners. For one, Ronan's mother is often out of the country with her husband. For two, Mum has been dressing more elegantly than usual.

I figure it's a man, but I want to hear it from her. If he's making my mum happy, I'll give him a chance. But if he as much as gives off any 'William Syndrome' signs of violence, he'll end up in that blood pool.

"Listen, honey." She stands across from me. "Ever since your father's death, you've been my world and the reason I've held on to life. You're everything to me, Cole. I need you to know that."

"I do." She's tried. In her own way. But Mum and I are already broken beyond repair.

Or I am, anyway.

No breakfast she prepares can fix the close relationship we could've had.

William took that with him.

Seems as though Mum has found the glue that's put her back together.

"I'm happy, you know that?" She touches her hair again. "I met someone and we've been going out for nearly a year now. I didn't want to tell you about him until I made sure we were serious. We are, darling. He makes me feel like I deserve a second chance and it'd mean so much to me if you accept him."

"As long as he's not my age," I joke.

"No, of course not." She smiles awkwardly. "But he's someone you know."

"Someone I know?"

She swallows. "Sebastian."

I nearly drop the unfinished slice of cake to the plate. Not much surprises me, but this definitely does. "Sebastian Queens?"

She nods.

"Silver's father?" I know I'm starting to sound redundant and like a fucking idiot, but it's like my brain is unable to process the information.

"I know you two don't get along so much, but Seb and I are hoping you'll be closer with time."

Seb. She's calling him Seb. They're already close.

And now I'm getting unwelcome images about Silver's dad and my mum.

"Honey?" Mum's face contorts. She keeps touching her hair and her apron and her hand, which means she's getting out of sorts.

The idea that I won't accept Sebastian is throwing her in an endless loop. If I tell her no, she'll choose me—I have no doubt about that—but she'll relapse back to acute depression. She'll need her meds again. She won't put on makeup or let her hair loose. She'll stop singing and jogging and getting out of bed.

I'll never hurt my mother that way.

When I was six and William threw a pan at me, she hugged me and took the entire hit on her back. Then he kicked her in the ribs for getting in his way. She had those bruises for weeks. She cried in the shower every night.

But she still protected me every time William came after me, taking all the beatings on my behalf.

She still loved me, even when she was at her lowest.

"I'd love to meet Sebastian as your prospect other half, Mum."

Her features light up. "R-really?"

"Really." I stand, round the counter, and engulf her in a hug. "I'm happy for you."

"Oh, darling." She cries into my neck. "You don't know how much this means to me."

I pat her back. "And you don't know how much this means to me."

Silver hates me, but soon enough, she'll be forced into having every dinner with me.

And she'll pay.

I might not like Silver Queens, but I've always considered her something sacred.

And mine.

She ruined that.

She ruined everything.

NINE

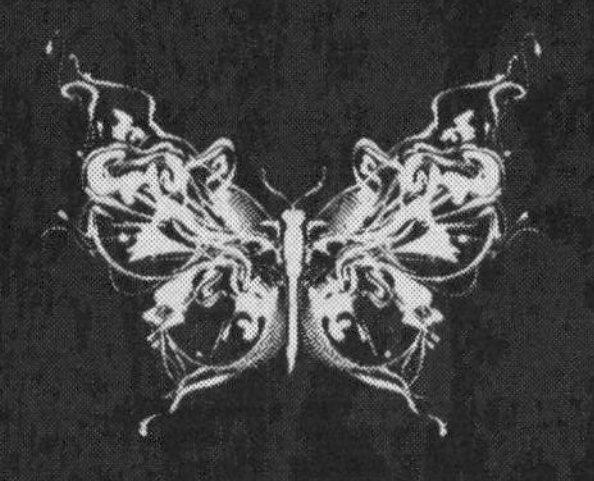

Silver

The following day, I don't go to school.

As soon as Derek stops in front of Mum's building, I rush out, my heartbeat nearly eradicating me altogether.

Mum lives down the centre of London, where it's noisy and the traffic is suffocating. It's her way to stay amongst people—even if they're the most annoying type.

The concierge, an old man with a beard, greets me and I gulp so I can speak over the tightness in my throat. "I-is Mum upstairs? Did you check on her?"

"Mrs. Davis asked us not to disturb her."

My knees weaken. I nearly fall right there and then.

No.

No, Mum. You promised.

He's saying something else, but I don't listen to him over the buzz in my ears. It's like I'm pushed a few years back. It's the same scene, the same foreboding, and the same deadly fear.

It's all there.

I hit the lift's button, but it doesn't come down.

I storm towards the stairs and take two at a time. My knees still shake, but I manage to go all the way to the tenth storey. I'm panting, my uniform's shirt sticks to my skin, but that's the least of my worries.

The moment I'm in front of Mum's flat, I just stand there. My limbs freeze and it's like someone has cast a spell on me. I can't move.

Oh, God.

Maybe I should've told Papa before he went out to work this morning. Maybe I should've had Derek come up with me.

I don't want to go in there alone.

I…I'm scared.

My heart thrums loud in my chest and a shiver shoots up my spine, engulfing me whole.

Go, Silver.

You have to go.

My fingers are stiff and cold as I hit the password to her flat. The sound of the lock clicking open echoes in the silence of the hall like doom. I flinch, even when I try to keep my composure.

My hand strangles the strap of my bag as I tiptoe inside.

The first thing I see is black.

It's so dark, I can't make out my own hands.

Then the smell of something rotten follows. Something like meat and alcohol.

A sob tears from my throat as I run inside. "Mum! Mum!"

I trip over a table and my foot stings. I throw my bag down and continue hobbling towards her bedroom. I've learnt the way by heart and can reach it even in the dark.

My fingers tremble, hovering over the light switch. What if I find her on the ground like the other time? What if I'm too late? What if —

I hit the button and freeze in place.

Mum sits in front of her console, her blonde hair falling on either side of her face and stopping a little under her neck, dishevelled and all over the place.

Her cobalt blue eyes are bloodshot and lost in the mirror. Streaks of mascara mark her cheeks, and she holds a red lipstick in her hand that matches the colour on her lips.

Her other hand clutches a half-full glass of red wine. Her satin nightgown is creased and the robe is tied wrong around her waist, but it doesn't hide her model body or her exotic beauty that everyone in the media talks about.

The model politician. Beauty can be smart.

That's Mum in their eyes. A successful, beautiful woman who can debate in the parliament for days. But they don't see the woman I see. They don't witness her like this, lost somewhere no one can find her.

"Mum..." I approach her slowly, a tear sliding down my cheek.

Her head turns in my direction like a robot. For seconds, she stares at me as if I'm a stranger, as if she's seeing me for the first time in her life. Then slowly, too slowly, her lips pull up in a warm smile.

"Babydoll, what are you doing here? Shouldn't you be at school?"

"You haven't answered my calls since last night." My voice breaks at the end as I wrap my arms around her neck in a tight embrace. "Why didn't you answer?"

"My battery died. I forgot to charge it." She pats my back.

"I was so worried, Mum." I sniffle into her neck, stopping myself from telling her I didn't sleep a wink last night. If I hadn't known Papa had an important meeting this morning, I would've made him drive me to her in the middle of the night.

"I'm okay." She pulls away from me and scowls. "Why are you crying, Silver? Ladies don't cry in front of other people."

"Mum...let me tell Papa so he can help you —"

"We spoke of this before," she cuts me off, her tone turning firm like she's in a debate. "Sebastian has no involvement in my life anymore. If you tell him anything about me, I'll consider it a betrayal."

"But, Mum..."

"He already thinks that I'm on the wrong side of the party

and he's on the right one. Not only has he decided I'm no longer good enough for him, but he also took you away from me, my beautiful baby girl."

"I'm here, Mum. Do you…do you want me to move in with you?"

"Absolutely not. That will seem as if I'm asking for pity after I announced I want to focus on my career."

I wish Mum would stop thinking about the media, the press, and her friends when she makes her decisions. I wish she'd look in the mirror—*really* look in the mirror—and base those decisions on not only her reflection, but also the woman on the inside.

I wish she'd stop trying to prove herself to her dead father who pushed her to be a perfectionist, or to my dead grandparents from Papa's side who criticised her for everything. They wanted their prodigal son to marry an aristocrat's daughter, so when he married Mum, they kind of made her life hell as revenge. Nothing was good enough in their eyes. So she took it out on Papa. It was a vicious cycle.

But I learnt to stop wishing for things when it comes to my mum. She'll only do what she thinks is good for her image and her career.

That's why she's been making me slowly but surely change to fit that image.

"Okay, happy thoughts." She shows me her red lipstick. "This one is amazing. Let me try it on you."

"Mum —"

"Stay still." She places her glass of wine on the counter and paints my lips, then looks at me with awe. "Look at you growing into a wonderful young lady. You're my pride, Silver. It's because of you that I survive this rotten, man-infested world."

"Then please answer my calls next time." I'm still high off the adrenaline, slightly trembling from thinking I'd lost her.

"I will. Now, happy thoughts." She smiles, and it's radiant.

It's the reason her snobbish friends are jealous of her—because she's the most beautiful amongst them all. She's the one who attracts attention and gets invited to radio and talk shows.

"I got a perfect score in maths."

"I'm so proud of you." She strokes my cheek and I lean into her touch, fighting the tears that are about to break free.

I would do anything to keep that expression on her face, so I say, "I…I got engaged to Aiden King."

"Really? Jonathan's son?"

I nod, and for the first time since yesterday, it doesn't feel like the most horrible decision I've ever made.

"Look at you, Babydoll, scoring so high when you're so young." She sighs dreamily. "You're the best thing that I got out of that bastard Sebastian."

I wince. Sometimes, I think Mum forgets he's my father and that she shouldn't project her hatred for him on me.

Both of them do it, actually, but Papa is more passive-aggressive about it. Mum is too direct.

Since their divorce, I feel like I age three years for every year. The only things I care about are making Mum happy enough so her mind won't lead her in the other direction and spending time with Papa in an attempt to reduce his loneliness.

When it gets too much, like *too* much, I go to the park and cry. In those dark moments, I wish they would never have given birth to me, or I imagine how my life would've been if I had whole parents like Ronan's or Kimberly's.

Every one of those times, Cole has found me in that park. It's like he hunts me down just so he can catch me crying.

He sits beside me in silence, mostly reading from a book, and that's enough to make me stop crying.

It's enough for my tears to turn to hiccoughs before they eventually disappear.

I hate that he has the ability to calm me down by his presence alone, but I keep my mouth shut about it. I've accepted it because we share secrets. He knows something about me no one else does and vice versa.

So his betrayal yesterday stung more than I like to admit. It cut me open and is still refusing to be sewn back together.

I might have hurt him back in the only way I knew how, but unlike what I thought, it doesn't make me happy.

Not in the least.

If anything, it smashes a heavier weight on my chest.

"Come on, Mum. Go shower. You have to be in that radio studio today, remember?" And yes, I have both my parents' calendars on my phone. I'm that desperate to be the breeze that makes their lives easier, not harder.

She stands up on wobbly feet and takes my hand in hers. "Remember, Babydoll. Men are only to be used. Feelings and all that stupidity was invented by unsuccessful people. Your worth is what you offer to the world—your beauty, your intelligence, and your competitiveness. No man should steal those from you." She lays a hand on my heart. "Seal this." Mum taps my temple. "And you'll win using this."

Then she goes to shower. I wait until she gets in her car before I leave. I'm going to listen to her radio show to make sure she's doing well.

Though I have no doubt she'll nail it. Mum is a goddess outside the walls of her flat. She allows no one to see her weaknesses. She never gets flustered, not even during the divorce when the reporters didn't leave us in peace. Papa appeared exhausted and a bit sad at that time, but she put on her best designer clothes and makeup, took all the questions, and told them their decision was amicably made right after she finished a yelling session with Papa.

"Where to, Miss Queens?" Derek asks from the driver seat. I feel sorry for him. Not only does he have to stick to Papa's hopping schedule, but he also drives me around whenever I wish.

I consider skipping today. My head is mush and I could use ten hours of sleep.

But that would mean running away, and I don't do that.

I'm the type who runs straight into the middle of the danger instead of shying away from it. If I'm to be killed sooner or later, I will find a solution or die trying.

It'd be worth it.

"To school," I tell Derek as I scroll through my phone.

My Instagram feed is full of Papa's campaign friends. There's a picture of him and Uncle Jonathan participating in the opening of a childcare centre yesterday. That must have been where they came from.

There's a picture of Mum in LBC's official Instagram page as a guest for today's political talk. She looks so radiant in that shot, her smile to die for.

I upload the selfie I took with her before she went out, where we're smiling at the camera, and caption it: *Proud of you, my heroine. #VoteforWomen #WomenforWomen #SuperWoman #CynthiaDavisPoliticalTalk*

I schedule another post for later. It's a picture I took while I was helping Papa put on his tie yesterday.

In the caption, I write: *Voted as the best father in the world by yours truly. #ProudDaughter #SebastianQueensForTheWin #GoTories*

Whenever I post a pic with one of them, I feel guilty if I don't follow up with a pic of the other one.

People say you get used to it with time—the double holidays, the double dinners, the double birthday celebrations—but you don't. Not really.

Especially when one parent is lonely and the other is depressed.

I scroll further and find a picture from Aiden uploaded around one in the morning. It's a black and white shot of his chessboard.

The caption says: *The war has started. Nash?*

Cole doesn't use Instagram or any social media. All pictures of him can only be found on Aiden's, Xander's, and especially Ronan's Instagram accounts.

Does Aiden's post mean Cole paid him a visit last night? I squash that thought away before I can allow my heart to soak in it.

He wouldn't have. That would mean he cares, and he doesn't.

Or, rather, he does, but only if it's part of his sick games.

I reread his text from yesterday, and the chest tightness I felt when I first saw it swallows me again.

I hate him.

We arrive at school and I thank Derek, then give him a spare bottle of juice on my way out. "Have a wonderful day."

As soon as I'm out of the car, I lift my chin up, square my shoulders, and walk with my nose practically in the sky. I ignore the ones who tell me good morning and I pretend the world doesn't exist.

If I talk to them, they'll start thinking they can be my friends. No one can. That would mean they'll get close enough to read through me, and I won't allow that.

My phone vibrates with a text. I retrieve it as I go into the piano room. I have a competition coming up in a few days and I need to perfect my "Moonlight Sonata". I already took a leave from my morning classes so I could focus on this.

Both my parents are going to be there and I need to do this well. No. I need to win.

The moment my eyes fall on the text, I stop in my tracks.

Unknown Number: Your lips looked beautiful painted in red. Why did you remove it?

I swallow, slowly doing a sweep of the school's entrance, trying to see if anyone is watching or following me.

After I took the picture with Mum and she left, I removed

the lipstick in her building's lounge area. It means someone saw the post on Instagram and is now seeing me at school.

My shoulder blades snap together and a sense of foreboding slams into me.

Quickening my pace, I head towards the piano room on shaky legs. I place my bag on the chair, settle in front of the piano, take a deep breath, and let my fingers move over the keys.

The trembling fades with each note.

It's almost like being thrust into a different world, but not really. As the notes escape the piano and get lost in the air, I'm in a peaceful world where the sun shines every day, not like a unicorn, once in a lifetime. In this world, my parents are together, Mum doesn't have dark thoughts, Papa isn't so busy, Helen isn't so sad and...

Dark green eyes barge into my image and I want to chase it away, but it won't go.

Something dainty wraps around my neck. My fingers miss a note and the sonata is interrupted by a noisy sound.

My head lifts to be greeted by those green eyes from my image. Have I somehow managed to conjure him into life?

Don't be an idiot.

Then I notice the necklace he's clicked around my throat. It's dainty sterling and has a small butterfly pendant, its wings wrapped in an infinity symbol.

Whoa. It's so beautiful.

It's nothing like the expensive necklaces Mum gets for me that I only wear when I'm out with her.

I stare back at Cole to find him leaning on the piano, legs crossed at the ankles and his fingers running over the black keys without pressing them.

But his entire attention is on me. I take a moment to see him, the boy, the damnation, Helen's son who doesn't deserve to be.

His hair is tousled. Sometimes, I wonder if he bothers to

comb it after showers. His physique has started to fill Royal Elite Junior's uniform. Even the hollow of his neck has become muscled. His shoulders have broadened, his legs have lengthened, and in no time, he's become way taller than me.

He's so different from the boy who sat beside me that day at the park. The boy who saw me cry and was about to leave until I made him stay.

One thing hasn't changed, though. His eyes.

They're still as hard as back then. Others might find them mesmerising, but I've often found them a little bit haunted, a little bit mysterious, and a little bit frightening.

Cole might be the best at hiding his expressions and feelings, but he can't hide what I see in those dark greens. They have a language all of their own, yet right now, I can't figure out what they are saying.

My fingers shake, only a little, before I drop them from the necklace and speak in a smaller voice than I would like, "What is this for?"

"Our new beginning."

"Our new beginning?"

"Yes. Sebastian didn't say anything?"

Papa did mention he'd tell me something at dinner tonight, but I thought it was about his upcoming travel plans.

"What is he supposed to say?" And why does Cole know about it and I don't?

He remains silent, almost as if he's testing my nerves. Scratch that. He's absolutely doing so.

Then he smiles. It's blinding, his smile. He doesn't do it often, but when he does, all I can do is stop and stare. "Congrats on the engagement with Aiden."

My heart drops and it takes everything in me not to cry. He's congratulating me? Not that I expected him to tell me not to go through with it after that text, but I thought he'd at least be upset about it.

He's congratulating me. Seriously?

"Deflowering and an engagement all in one day," he continues in that calm, infuriating tone. "You work fast, just like your mum."

"Don't you dare bring up my mum." My voice raises. "You have no right to talk about her."

"Why, Butterfly? Afraid you'll turn out just like her?" He leans over so only a small breath separates us. "Here's a reality check: with someone like Aiden, you'll end up worse than your mother; you'll end up like *his* mother. You'll be found dead after long hours of suffering in the middle of nowhere."

I raise my fist and punch him in the chest, my eyes stinging. "Screw you, Cole."

I'm about to remove the necklace and give it back, but he says, "If you remove that, I'll take it as you're forfeiting."

Pursing my lips, I drop my arm. Why does he know the right buttons to push? There's nothing I hate more than losing before even starting.

"Go away," I dismiss him. "I don't want to see your face again."

"That would be hard, considering the family ties and all."

"What?"

"Mum and Sebastian are dating."

Oh, God.

If my jaw could hit the floor, it would right about now.

My plan from a year ago worked. A part of me is thrilled that Helen and Papa have their second chance, but the other part, the one who's staring at those soulless green eyes, makes me pause.

Cole is Helen's son.

If this goes any further he'll be...

No. Nope. I won't allow my brain to voice that thought.

"Do you know what that means, Butterfly?"

I shake my head frantically, not wanting to think about it.

He places both his palms on my cheeks until his lips hover an inch away from mine and then, just like that, he brushes them against my mouth once before he claims it in a kiss.

It's nothing like the one from one year ago. It's not mere massaging of tongues and innocent strokes. This time, he devours me, our teeth clinking together while he aggressively kisses me.

His fingers dig into my skin as he angles my head up and plunges his tongue inside, swirling it against mine. It's like he can't get enough.

I can't get enough.

There's a voice in my head telling me I should stop this, but I'm too drunk on his taste, on the way he grabs me and eats me alive, to listen to that voice.

As he pulls away, he bites my lower lip, making me wince. Then he whispers near my jaw, "I'll take good care of you, baby sister."

His words bring me out of my stupor, but I'm still too numb. I can't even move my hands up to punch him.

"Don't waste your time practising." He makes a loud note by hitting several keys at the same time. "I'll win the competition."

Then he turns and leaves.

"I hate you!" I scream at his back and he just waves two fingers without turning around.

My breathing comes in and out in a frenzy long after he's gone. I can't calm down. I keep licking my swollen lips without even realising it.

I'm going to hurt him as much as he hurt me.

I'm going to ruin him.

I bring out my phone and dial Papa. He picks up after two rings. He might be busy, but never too busy for me. Besides, he knows I won't call him unless it's urgent.

"Is everything okay, Princess?"

"No, Papa." I adapt my slightly spooked, slightly appalled voice that I learnt from Mum. "I just saw something and I'm not sure if I should tell."

"This is me, Princess." His caring but firm tone makes an appearance. "You can tell me anything."

"But it might get someone in trouble."

"If they put themselves into trouble, they deserve it. Law doesn't protect the stupid."

"It's our nurse, Miss Goldman."

"What about her?"

"I was passing by this morning and I heard her making strange noises. I thought she was hurt, but when I peeked in, I saw her…" I take a dramatic pause.

"You saw what?"

"I'm so embarrassed to tell, Papa."

"You should never be embarrassed to tell the truth."

"She had her mouth around a boy's penis," I blurt.

"Oh, Princess. Don't worry. I'll take care of this."

"Should I tell the principal? I didn't see the boy's face."

"No. I'll be the one to talk to him. When you go to school tomorrow, that nurse will be history."

"Thank you, Papa. I love you."

"I love you, too, Princess. See you later. I have news for you."

"Can't wait." I manage a forced smile as I hang up.

One out of the way.

She shouldn't have touched an underage kid in the first place. That scum is a paedophile and I'm doing society a favour by using Papa's power.

Cole thinks he can win in everything, but he doesn't know the small ways I'll always win against him.

My fingers run over the necklace.

If he wants a war, then war is what he'll get.

TEN

Cole

Age sixteen

Is there a place in literature or psychology books that states when you should realise you're not…normal?

I've had my suspicions since that night when I stopped crying once and for all, but lately, I've been noticing the abnormality more than usual. I've been reading books about deviant behaviour and thoughts. The thing is, those theories don't really apply to me.

I've never looked at a kitten or a puppy and decided I wanted to hurt it or felt the urge to. If anything, I think people who have such thoughts are cowards. They want to do greater damage, but they latch onto creatures way weaker than themselves who can't do anything to stop them. Those people are pathetic, and I'll never belong in the same bracket as them.

That leaves me with little to no choices as to where I should be put. Do I have anti-social behaviour? Do I want to hurt people?

The answer to the latter is no. I don't care about people enough to want to hurt them.

Besides, I love my mum. In my own way. She's the reason I still believe there could be something else for me.

Chaos is still one of my secret tendencies, though.

Whenever I find the opportunity to bring it back to the world, I do. Since we play football, I usually get that chance by instigating a small fight here, a rivalry there. It brings flavour to the other players' boring lives, so they should thank me for it.

If chaos is the only thing that makes sense, what does that make me?

Chaotic?

I don't think so. I enjoy watching chaos from afar, but I dislike being in the middle of it.

There is unwanted chaos in my life—the type I can't seem to control no matter how much I try.

Like the fucking scene in front of me.

We're at the Meet Up, watching a football game between Arsenal and Tottenham. Everyone here cheers for the former. I do, too, but only so everyone thinks I actually give a fuck. I don't.

Ronan and Xander are making a ruckus, kicking and screaming as if they're the ones playing. Captain, Levi King, shushes them so he can hear the commentator.

Unlike his cousin, the current captain of Elites—Royal Elite School's football team—is more open, but still a control freak like everyone in the King household. They could use personal psychoanalysing from Freud himself—if he were still alive, that is.

Aiden is sitting across from me with Silver by his side as he places a hand around her shoulder. They keep whispering things to each other before she laughs discreetly and he smirks with mischief like the bastard he is.

She doesn't give a fuck about football. At all. And yet, she makes it her mission to watch it and put on a show with Aiden.

And I know it's a show, because on normal days, they can't stand each other. They only pull this shit in front of me. I know it's a game.

Her way of revenge.

His way of being a dick.

Despite knowing all that, I can't purge it out of my head. I don't watch them, not when they can sense me, but I see them all the time. I fucking hear them, even if the TV's sound is loud.

This is the unwanted chaos I don't understand. If I know it's fake, why the fuck am I so hung up on it?

Why do I want to stand, punch Aiden in the face, and devour her lips in front of him so he knows who the fuck she belongs to?

Perhaps this is what it feels to be the victim of chaos. That chaos is Silver.

Not Aiden. It's all on *her.*

Since our parents started officially going out together and she decided Aiden, the fucker, deserved her virginity and the title of her fiancé, I've turned her life into hell.

There isn't a field I haven't made her lose in. I used to at least leave piano alone, because she'd have this proud expression when she won, and she'd take a picture with both her parents and post it on social media with the happiest caption.

But she killed that part of me, so now, I win everything. And I mean every-fucking-thing. Down to the simple credit homework.

I don't only win, I crush her. I don't only push her to be Miss Number Two, but I also win with a large gap that makes her doubt everything.

Soon after, she gives me that glare, tells me she hates me, and then goes to the park to eat a small Snickers bar and cry on her own.

While she does so, she usually curses me aloud like a madwoman speaking to herself. I watch every moment until she goes back home, smiling and hugging Sebastian as if nothing happened.

That's the thing about Silver. Her happiness is visible to

the entire world through her social media and her hashtags, but her misery is only for herself.

And me.

There's always me.

It's not Aiden whom she comes back to for more. It's not Aiden that she'd demand a redo with. It's me.

Always *me*.

Silver never gives up. Never.

You can bury her under ten metres of dirt and she'll dig her way out and demand a rematch.

Her phone dings and she pulls it out to stare at the text. I lean on my hand, pretending to watch the TV or Ronan and Xander's show. In reality, I'm only watching her. The slight parting of her lips, the way her shoulders tighten a little before she throws the phone back in her pocket and feigns interest in whatever Aiden is telling her.

She's agitated. No. Not just agitated. She's scared.

Usually, it's something to do with her mother's well-being, but lately, she's been disappearing without a word and spending less time with Mum.

In the beginning, Silver did her best to resist her dad's relationship with Mum, but it only took her a talk with them during the first introductory dinner to change her mind.

I went to the restroom and when I came back, I overheard her tell them she's happy they get their second chance and that she'd secretly planned for this and she'll do her best to help out in anything.

Secretly planned for it. Which means she wanted it.

After that, she did as promised. Silver became their perfect daughter. Her only problem is me. She can't feign getting along with me when she constantly, without fail, tells me she hates me every day. It's her mantra.

Mum told me not to be mean to her, but that's the thing, I'm not. At least, not in front of them. So they always think the problem is with Silver, and the reason she won't get along with me is her secretive way to resist their relationship. Her frustration and inability to tell people I'm actually mean and have them believe it gets her more riled up against me.

Did I mention that I like creeping under her skin? It's the only time when she's not putting on a façade and letting out her genuine emotions. It's just anger, but it still counts.

The change in her patterns lately hasn't escaped me. She lets her father's driver pick her up early. She doesn't go out late and she's been having that expression when reading her messages sometimes.

It's hardly noticeable since she's mastered hiding her reactions.

Aiden sure as hell doesn't pick up on it—or care enough to.

He fucks girls he literally doesn't remember the names of. She's aware of this. She caught them once, but she just threw his jacket at him and told him they had a fundraiser to attend.

Aiden is nowhere near her ideal. I know because she writes about that in her journal.

And yes, I read her journal whenever Sebastian invites us to dinners at his place.

Surprisingly, she doesn't write much about me except. *I hate him. I wish he wasn't Helen's son.*

That makes two of us.

She calls Aiden a pig and says how much she can't stand him on almost every page, but she's still with him anyway.

The other time, I told him I'll accept all his challenges if he breaks off the engagement with Silver.

"It's not a child's play, Nash," he said. "Jonathan won't let me."

"You want me to believe you're afraid of your dad?"

"No, but I know how to pick my battles with him." He grinned. "Why, Nash? Are you finally admitting your black heart actually has a spot for another human being?"

When I said nothing, he continued, "Or are you being a doting older brother who'll come at me with an axe if I hurt his sister?"

She's *not* my sister.

But I didn't say that so he wouldn't latch onto it and perhaps even tell her. I've been using that taunt to make her go crazy.

Mum and Sebastian are still dating, and considering the latter's commitments and Mum's writing schedule, I say they'll break it off soon.

They care about their respective careers more than emotional balance—especially Sebastian.

Since he'll undergo important general elections soon, I have no doubt that both of them will call it quits. Mum doesn't like the flashing of cameras and attention, and she won't let them label her a politician's wife. Now that they've had their adventure, each will go back to their respective world.

And that's when Silver will be mine.

This time, I'll swallow her so much into my chaos, she'll never find a way out.

Aiden says something and she laughs. Fuck them.

I stand up and tell Levi, "I'll be right back."

He nods and I go through the back entrance and stand on the porch that overlooks the tall trees in the forest visible from here.

I retrieve a cigarette, light it, and take a drag. It tastes like shit, but the nicotine allows my brain to loosen up a little and stop being stuck in its messy chaos.

It's the only addiction I allow myself, although I just smoke once or twice a week or when the chaos gets too tangled.

Ronan says I'm addicted to books and I should seek therapy, but fuck him. He's only literate because his father is an earl. No kidding, he's the type who'd say, 'How do you read this shit? There are no pictures in it.'

Reading is one of my defence mechanisms to not get caught up in the world. The world makes me think of worldly things, like that night, and I hate that night.

So I redirect my thoughts to the one thing I didn't hate about that night. The girl with a butterfly pin and a doll.

Silver wrote in her journal about it.

Cole saw me cry today. He didn't hug me as Xander does to Kimberly whenever she cries. He wanted to leave, the tosser.

But he told me divorces happen and that Papa and Mummy will probably be happier apart.

I hate that.

Cole also told me his secret. He wants to be my first. I told him, I'll only do that if I'm his first too. Otherwise it's not fair.

Papa says to always negotiate so it's fair.

And now, Papa and Mummy won't be together anymore. I can't stop crying.

Why did they get married if they don't want to be together?

Why did they give birth to me?

And yes, I recall every entry I read. I usually memorise anything by reading it once. I took special care of her journal. Now all her words, her vents, and her confusions and fake personality are integrated into my head.

When I grow old and my memory starts demanding to delete files to be able to remember others, I'd choose her stupid journal over books by philosophers and psychologists any day.

Chaos.

She's fucking chaos.

I step out into the night and through the trees. Twigs crush under my boots and I ignore them as I continue on my way.

The moon is bright in the sky tonight despite the freezing weather. I left my jacket inside, so I'm only in my uniform's trousers and shirt.

I arrive at the small lake beyond the trees and stand at the edge of the deck, staring at the moon's reflection in the calm water. I don't know how long I remain there. Something about it is bugging the fuck out of me.

It's not red.

How come it's not red?

It should be red.

"Cole?" A soft voice calls from behind me. "What are you doing?"

I turn around and face her, but I don't move from the edge. Under the moon's light, she appears like a blue shadow. Her hair falls to her back and the butterfly necklace glints. She's never removed it in public. Not even once.

But it's not because she cares, no. It's because it means she admits defeat if she doesn't wear it.

And that's exactly why I said those words—so she'd keep me with her at all times.

"Are you stalking me?" I ask.

"You wish."

"Then why did you follow me all the way over here?"

"Papa called and said he made reservations for dinner. Derek will pick us up."

"Message received. Go back to Aiden."

She scowls, but she doesn't make a move to leave. "Are you still smoking that death stick?"

I blow the smoke in her face, making it scrunch. "Obviously."

"You're a bastard."

"If you keep complimenting me this often, I'll think you have a fixation on me."

"In your dreams."

"You don't want to know what's in my dreams."

"We agree on that." She stretches her hand. "Give me your phone, I need to make a call to Derek. My battery died."

"What do I get in return?"

"My begrudged thank you."

I smirk as I retrieve my phone and unlock it. Silver makes her call, glaring at me the entire time. Once she finishes, she's about to return it, but then she focuses back on the screen.

She must've touched a button. Her cheeks heat as her eyes widen and that look returns. The look from eight years ago.

It's the fucking same.

I've seen hints of it, but never this identical awe.

"W-what the *hell* is this?" She thrusts the phone into my face.

It's an image of Hope bound to a chair, half-naked, and giving me a seductive look. "Hope. She's a senior."

"I know it's Hope, b-but w-why is she tied like that?"

"Because she likes it." My voice lowers as I blow another cloud of smoke in her direction. "And I like it too."

Silver's face doesn't even scrunch at the smoke. It's caught in that eternal awe-filled look. Or maybe it's fear?

Her blue eyes darken and her throat works up and down with a gulp.

"You're…sick," she breathes out, even as her cheeks redden under the moon.

Silver throws the phone in my hand, turns around, and marches out as if her heels are on fire.

Sick.

Maybe. Probably.

And part of my sickness is her. My Butterfly.

My chaos.

ELEVEN

Silver

Age Seventeen

Timing is important.

Papa says that timing is the most important thing in the world.

You can't start something a little too early or a little too late. A fraction of a second can make a difference not only in deciding crucial events but also in defining a person's life.

I learnt the importance of timing from both Papa and Mum. Considering their political careers, time plays a huge tribute in their lives. They never go over the time given to them to speak in parliament. They just say precise information that doesn't only relay their point, but also makes their opponents pause and think about a possible retort.

And yet, lately, I've been having this nagging feeling that I missed the timing for something.

What, I don't know.

It couldn't be piano practice or my weekends with Mum or even Papa's house briefings.

Lately, it's like we have the parliament at home. Everyone is there, led by Frederic, and it's almost like early elections. While I love talking to Papa's friends and getting caught in debates, I don't like the feeling of emptiness the further he gets away from me.

Mum has been doing well, even after Papa started dating Helen. Actually, it's too well that it's beginning to raise red flags. She now goes out on dates to seek out a potential man to step on—her words, not mine.

Is it Mum? Is that why I feel the timing is wrong?

I send her a text to tell her I love her and miss her.

If we weren't in the middle of dinner, I would've called, but Papa doesn't like it when I talk to or about Mum in front of Helen. Not that she minds, she told me so herself. She said Mum is a part of who I am and no one can take her away from me.

I hugged Helen to death for saying those words.

Papa is wonderful, but he doesn't understand my constant concern about Mum. He says she's the adult and should worry about me, not the other way around.

But Papa doesn't know about Mum's mental state. All they do is fight. Even after nine years of divorce.

The four of us sit around the smaller table in the kitchen. Helen doesn't like the bigger dining room when it's only us. She said it feels impersonal and lonely while this one is cosier and gives a familial vibe.

I consider everyone here family—except for the one sitting opposite me.

Cole eats the steak and compliments his mother's cooking and Papa for picking the Korean beef. Then they strike up a conversation about the economical exchanges with South Korea and the benefits of it.

That's Cole to a T. One, he knows everything about everything. He even throws out numbers and statistics. Papa's friends love him because he agrees with them. Not in a way that seems like a follower's, but more like someone who did his homework, refused all the others, and settled on them. He makes it seem as if he likes them, not because he has to, but because he wants to.

Liar.

He's the biggest liar alive. There's nothing coming out of his mouth that I believe as the truth anymore.

Cole has mastered the art of lies so well, he can even manage to convince you that the truth might also be a lie.

He's too much into mind games and seeing people trip over themselves. Watching someone flustered because they didn't see a question or a situation coming their way is his favourite pastime.

He turned eighteen over the summer, but it's almost like he's twenty-five. Granted, all of us learnt to become mature since a young age; we couldn't smile wrong in front of people or speak wrong or even breathe wrong, but he takes it to a whole different level.

Cole is perfect on the outside but rotten on the inside.

Ever since I saw that picture of the bound girl, I've realised how deep he actually runs, how far and how fast he can go. That he can be way worse than what I know.

And I hate that my first reaction to that image was intrigue.

Why the hell would I be intrigued about that depravity? Cole and his sick ways can go to hell. I'm Sebastian Queens and Cynthia Davis's daughter. I'm the most proper teenager you'll ever find, and my view on Cole is a definite no.

Now, if I stop glaring at him, it'd be good.

He catches me staring across the table and smiles like a damn gentleman. "Silver also believes in relationships with Asian countries, don't you?"

"I do, but I also disapprove of the government's policies of dealing with dictators' regimes just because we can sell them weapons and fill our safe."

Cole raises a brow. "Are you suggesting we should use our arsenal and hit them, you know, to be superheroes?"

"No. I'm merely saying we should pressure them, not leave them to do as they please to their people."

"It's their people. Why should we care?"

God. He's infuriating.

If it were someone else, I would've kept my cool and gone on with the debate, but the way he's egging me on with that deceptively calm tone gets on my nerves. Or rather, *he* gets on my nerves.

Everything about him does, from his hair that's become longer to his eyes that have turned more piercing to his damn jaw that sharpened overnight.

"You know," I speak in my calmest tone. "That philosophy of 'It's not my problem. I don't care' is what's ruining the world."

"And yet, some do it so well." He chews on the beef leisurely. "They can even pretend they don't care about themselves or their old friends."

The jab is at me for the way I watch Kim from afar but still throw bitchy remarks her way.

I always, without fail, find Cole's gaze on me after I tell Kim to piss off. It's more than disappointment in his eyes, though. It's pure hatred.

He hates me at school. He can't stand to be near me and he makes it known by secretly pulling on my hair every chance he gets.

"That's better than pretending you care about everyone when you don't." I pause, feigning nonchalance. "General you."

"You kids are always at each other's throats." Helen laughs, serving me more juice.

I'm weird. I drink juice with my dinner and Helen respects that. Isn't she the best?

It's Cole who snickers at me from across the table and I scowl at him as I take a sip of the apple juice.

"Their debates are fun." Papa smiles at us. "Our dinner table is going to be so lively in the future once Helen and I get married."

I choke on the juice and cough as Helen helps me by patting my back.

"Sebastian!" she scolds. "We agreed to talk about it after dinner. Look what you've done to Silver."

"I'm sorry, Princess." He offers me a napkin. "I'm probably too excited for the news. Helen and Cole will move in with us. Isn't that wonderful?"

No.

No, it's not.

Lately, Helen has been complaining about coming out of her work zone and Papa has been saying he can't find time to meet with her anymore, so I figured they'd break up sooner rather than later. I thought it was a fling, but a fling can't go on for three years, right?

How stupid can I be?

Drinking from the cup of water Helen offered me, I stare at Cole across the table. He's paused mid-cut through his steak, but aside from that, there's no reaction.

"Are you okay, darling?" Helen asks me. "Is something wrong?"

Yes. Something is wrong.

That premonition about timing hits me again. Something is definitely wrong. I can't let them do this.

I don't want this. I'm not even sure why. I love Helen and the way she chased away Papa's loneliness, but I don't love this.

I have to do something. *Now.*

"Papa, I —"

"Congratulations, Mum." Cole stands up and hugs her, and her face breaks into a radiant smile. He then shakes Papa's hand. "Congratulations, Sebastian."

"Thank you, son."

Congratulations?

Congratu-fucking-lations?

Why the hell did he do that? Why is he giving them his blessings?

No.

This can't be happening.

"Princess?" Papa stares down at me with a creased brow. He's disappointed in me for not being like Cole.

He hates that I'm making Helen even slightly uncomfortable.

What the hell is wrong with me?

I stand up on wobbly feet and flash the showtime smile I've perfected so well. "Congratulations, Papa, Helen. I'm so happy for you both."

I'm not.

If there's a place lower than hell, I deserve to be there. Why am I not happy for them?

It's because of Mum, right? I'm the number one believer in her romance with Papa, despite all the fights, and I've hoped that someday down the line, they'd eventually get back together.

Especially since, until Helen, they hadn't actually seen other people after their divorce.

However, that's not the thing that's gripping my heart in its black, merciless claws.

I force myself to listen as they talk about the wedding preparations and that they need to do it soon, before the elections.

They agree on my birthday, a 'double celebration', Papa says.

I open my mouth to scream, NO, but instead, I say, "I promised to call Mum. Can I go?"

"Why, of course." Helen strokes my arm, her features creasing. "Are you okay?"

"Yes, perfect. I can't wait to tell Mum the news."

"I'm afraid she won't be as acceptant of them." Papa cuts through his meat with a neutral expression.

"What are you talking about? Mum will always be happy for you." My voice is on the verge of a breakdown. I need out of here. Now.

And I need to stop trying to look at the arsehole across the table. He wouldn't help. He ruined it.

"Cynthia? Happy for me?" Papa lifts his head. "Are we

talking about the same Cynthia Davis who's currently gathering people to vote down my bill?"

"She means no harm. I'll be right back."

I fly out of the scene as fast as I can. I don't know how I ascend the stairs, but the moment I'm in my room, I fall to a slumped position on the bed, my heart nearly beating out of my chest.

The need to cry hits me out of nowhere and I can't control it.

What is happening to me? Why do I feel like I missed the greatest timing of all? Like I screwed everything up?

My door clicks open. I feel him before I see him.

There's something about his presence that has become familiar over the years. Even in the park, I feel him before he shows up.

In school, I know when he's there before I step into class.

It's a curse.

One I haven't been able to get rid of since he first called me Butterfly and wiped my tears, getting glitter all over him.

Cole stands at the door, placing a hand in his jeans' pocket. He has bloomed over the years to become tall and with a muscular athletic body that all the girls swoon over.

It's not only because he's part of the football team and one of Elites' four horsemen.

He's nicknamed Famine because, while he's mostly silent, he's deadly in attacks. He sneaks up on you out of nowhere and kills you a slow, torturous death.

The girls think he's the whole package—smart, hot, rich, and an athlete. I can almost hear Summer and Veronica say I'm so lucky to be his stepsister.

I'm not.

I don't want to be his anything.

"Are you hiding to cry alone again?" He appears calm, bored even.

"I'm not crying."

He motions at my eyes as if proving a point. I wipe them harshly with the back of my hand. "Those aren't tears."

"Sure, if you say so."

"What are you doing here, Cole?"

"I need to call Mum. Oh, wait, mine is downstairs."

"Get out."

"I should start picking a room. I think I'll go with the one next to yours."

"Are you rubbing it in?"

"Rubbing what in?" He approaches me with steady steps. All his nonchalant mood evaporates and his voice turns more lethal by the second. "You set them up. You gave them your blessing. You said, 'I'm glad both of you are getting a second chance.' Remember that, Silver?"

I rise to my feet, pointing a finger at him. "You didn't say no either. You let them. You freaking congratulated them just now!"

"You started this whole mess." His voice is calm, but his shoulders are rigid as he towers over me. "You let Aiden fuck you in the back of a car and then got engaged to him."

"That's because you didn't keep your promise. If you didn't save me your firsts, why should I save you mine?" That need to cry hits me again and I lower my head. "It doesn't matter anyway. It's too late now. It's —"

He lifts my chin with two fingers and slams his lips to my parted ones. I gasp against him, my head swirling with dooming thoughts and my body bleeding, trembling, craving more.

So much more.

For a second, I let him kiss me, my heart and my chest tingling with a thousand emotions but none of them intelligible.

No.

This is wrong.

I place two hands on his shoulders and push him away. "W-we can't do this."

"Why?" He doesn't leave my vicinity, his chest nearly colliding with mine.

"Because we're going to be siblings."

"Here's the thing, Silver. You're not my fucking sibling. Never were. Never will be."

My protests fade into nothing as his lips find mine again. They're less urgent but more desperate, possessive. Almost like he's claiming not only my lips but also something deeper and stronger inside me.

This time, I moan against his mouth. This time, I don't fight him. Instead, I let myself fall into the sensation.

It's as if I've been lost and now I've found refuge. Every time I've seen him with a girl, I've wondered if he was kissing her the same way he used to kiss me. I've wondered if he was erasing me with the others. And all I wanted to do was punch them so they'd never get in his vicinity again.

"Do you let Aiden kiss you?" he speaks low, almost threateningly.

I'm too stunned by the force of his touch to answer. His hand moves to my arse cheek and he pinches the flesh.

My eyes widen as my legs shake with a foreign sensation.

"Do you?" he repeats.

If I tell him no, he'll know it's just a game, and I can't do that. Aiden is my only effective weapon against Cole. I can't lose him.

"So that means he does." The deceptive calm in his voice makes my spine turn rigid. He doesn't like it. At all.

"And you let him." He releases my arse, reaches under my skirt, then cups me through my underwear.

I try to clench my thighs, but I can't. I don't want to. If anything, they fall open slightly, giving him more access.

A violent shudder tingles at the bottom of my spine and ends in my core as he runs his fingertip up and down my folds. He pushes the cloth aside and thrusts a finger inside me.

I nearly topple over at the intrusion. Holy hell.

This isn't the first time there's been a finger inside me. I do it myself some nights, but it's never felt this overwhelming.

What is this feeling of utter abandon?

"Do you get this wet for him, too?" he whispers the dark words against my lips. "Do you soak his hand like you soak mine?"

He adds a second finger, eliciting another deep moan from me. My heart nearly falls to the ground as his rhythm takes complete control of my being.

I know it's wrong. I know I shouldn't let him touch and unravel me this way.

But I can't stop it either.

It's like I've waited for this, and I'll be damned to put a halt to it now that it's here.

A sudden rush of adrenaline zips through me, and I grip Cole's shoulder as he thrusts into me harder and faster.

My moans rise in volume, mixing with the sound of his, in and out, and permeating the air.

"Answer me," he speaks slowly, his voice hoarse with arousal.

I shake my head violently.

"Fucking answer me, Silver."

"No…I-I won't…answer…ohhh…" My words end on a needy whimper as I fall apart around his fingers.

He grunts as his lips claim mine in a long, devouring kiss filled with bites and harsh licks. It's like he's eating me alive and saving the remains for later.

"Cole, are you there, darling?" Helen's voice comes through the door. "We need to go."

I pull away from him with a start, but I can't get far since his digits are still inside me.

The realisation of what I've done smashes straight into my face.

Oh, no.

No, no, no.

"Let me go," I hiss, shoving at his chest.

"Why?" He smirks, wrapping an arm around my waist. "Afraid Mum will come and see my fingers deep inside your soaked cunt?"

"C-Cole!" My cheeks heat as I stare between him and the door. I didn't lock it, and I doubt Cole did. If she comes in, that's exactly what she'll see.

"Afraid to lose the good girl award, Butterfly?"

"Cole, let me go this second or I swear…"

"Or what? Go on. Although, a word of advice, it's not wise to threaten me when I have my fingers inside you."

He scissors them and I nearly fall onto his shoulder, the wave from earlier restarting as if it never ended.

"Silver?" Helen calls.

"Cole!" I whisper-yell.

"I'll let you go on one condition."

"Fine, just let me go." I'd do anything so he'd get away from me right now.

He slips from me. A mixed sense of relief and emptiness hits me at the same time.

What the hell?

As soon as I release a breath, Cole lifts the two fingers that were inside me to his lips and sucks them into his mouth in one go, not breaking eye contact with me.

I couldn't look away even if I wanted to. My pussy clenches at the image. My lips part.

Shit.

He then places them in front of my mouth.

"Are you insane?" I speak low. "No."

"Remember. You said anything, Butterfly."

"Anything but this."

"You should've specified it then. You made a mistake and now I want you to suck yourself off my fingers."

"Cole…" I clench my thighs at the image.

"Do it before Mum comes in."

Damn him.

With one last glance at the door, I take his digits into my mouth. He watches me with a rare gleam in his eyes. It's like the sun is shining on the green in them.

For a second, I'm too lost in his eyes, in the feel of his fingers as he glides them against my tongue, making me taste the remnants of me and lime from when he put them in his mouth.

Now I want to keep tasting lime until I can't.

Until lime becomes the most forbidden taste on earth.

It's wrong, isn't it?

Absolutely wrong.

I slide my mouth away with a pop and his brows scrunch.

"Helen is waiting for you," I murmur.

"This is the last time I'll have to leave after dinner, Butterfly." He leans in and brushes his lips against my nose.

"I hate you."

Cole pulls on my hair, hard, then turns around and leaves.

My legs fail to carry me anymore and I fall on the bed with tears glistening in my eyes.

You can't do things a little too early or a little too late.

Timing is important.

And I just messed it all up.

TWELVE

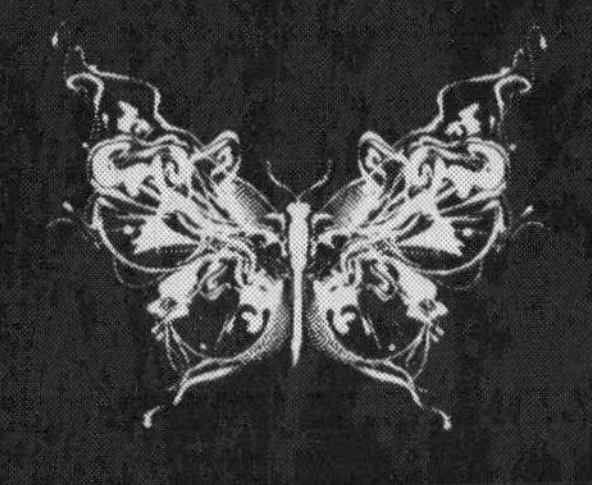

Silver

Papa and Helen get married on my eighteenth birthday as they planned.

Happy birthday to me.

I did everything I could in the background. I tried to secretly tell Helen that Papa is very busy and never actually puts time aside for home and that's why Mum divorced him.

I told Papa that Helen's career is at its top level and she'll continue writing her bestsellers instead of being a housewife.

I even stooped so low that I got Mum involved. She came over to tell Papa that he's disgusting for bringing another person to his daughter's life when the elections are so close.

He brushed her off.

I hated myself for being the type of bitch who's out to sabotage her father's marriage. That's not me.

There's nothing I want more than to see Papa and Helen happy.

If only she didn't have a son. Or had a different son.

After I realised there was nothing I could or should do to stop the wedding, I helped Helen with the preparations, and a minute ago, I watched them seal it.

Yesterday, I cried in the park.

Last night, I cried in the pillow.

Today, I cried when they were pronounced husband and wife. However, cried is an exaggeration—it was a couple of tears and I quickly wiped them away, pretending they were happy tears.

More like mourning tears.

The moment I stood there witnessing the union of Papa and Helen, something inside me died and I knew I'd never be able to get it back.

I missed the timing and now I'm paying the price. I shouldn't care, but it's the only thing I keep thinking about: missed timing.

There's no time machine to take me back to last month or to last year or to that damn night I set Papa and Helen up together while Cole kissed me upstairs.

We have a small reception in our house only for friends and family, and by that, I mean Papa's party members. They fill the garden and chat amongst themselves about the elections.

It's a rare sunny afternoon and it gives the gathering a glowing aura. Papa looks dashing in his black tuxedo and the bowtie I personally put on him. Helen wears a simple beige dress that complements her skin tone. Her hair is pulled up in an elegant way and she appears so happy as she puts her hand in Papa's arm.

He, too, has been caressing her hand every chance he gets. I've never seen Papa smile this much for no official necessity. It's almost as if it's permanent.

I'm happy for him, I am, but I still can't chase away the lump in my throat, no matter how much I swallow.

God. Why am I such a horrible daughter?

Papa needs this. Helen needs this.

I just have to suck it up and move on. I'm good at moving on. At pretending. At being someone everyone envies and wants to be.

My fingers reach for the necklace around my neck, but I quickly drop my hand before I touch it.

I need to keep it together.

I help the catering guys, directing them to the kitchen. Since Mum left, I've always taken care of these things; I became an adult at a young age. I guess Helen will take that burden away from me now.

Not that I ever considered it one.

Ronan and Xander join me to steal food.

Xander has a blond exotic look with piercing blue eyes and charming dimples. The worst thing about his whole package is that he's very well aware of it and uses it every chance he gets.

Ronan, too. He's developed a charismatic personality that he takes advantage by shagging everyone who wears a skirt.

They both showed up with their parents. Ronan's father, Earl Edgar Astor, is one of Papa's friends and a crucial sponsor like Uncle Jonathan.

Xander's father, Lewis Knight, is a powerful member in Papa's party and basically his right hand—besides Frederic.

I've been thrust with these guys since a young age whether I liked it or not. Not that I dislike them—they're actually fun—but I'll never tell them that so it doesn't get into their already big heads.

I swat Ronan's hand away from the container. "Stop it."

"Hey!" He stuffs a scone in his mouth. "Food is free. Don't be a snob, *chéri.*"

"There's an open buffet outside."

"Nah, my father glares at me when I eat this much in public." He steals another one. "I have to do it in secret like a proper gentleman."

"Amongst other things you do in secret." Xander winks at him.

"*Mais bien sûr.*" Ronan grins. "Remember those tits?"

"Ronan!" I scold.

"What? You didn't show us yours, so we had to outsource it." Ronan stares at my cleavage. "Unless you changed your mind."

"I might." I open more containers on the counter.

"Really?" both Ronan and Xander nearly shout.

"Really. I have one condition, though."

"I'm in." Xander smirks.

"*Moi aussi.*" Ronan swallows the food in his mouth. "Threesome anyone?"

"What's the condition?" Xander insists.

"Wank a cactus." I give them a smug look.

Both their expressions fall when they realise I never planned to go through with it anyway in the first place. They can be so dramatic sometimes.

"Pass." Xander sighs.

"Silver, *mon amour,* your tits are beautiful but not beautiful enough to have me cause damage to Ron Astor the Second."

"Ron Astor the Second?" I ask.

"That's his dick." Xander rolls his eyes.

"Ew, I can't believe you named your dick."

"All healthy males do. Not my problem you only get close to psychos." Ronan grins and snatches another dessert from between my fingers to devour it as if he's been starving.

"So, new family, huh?" Xander waggles his brows, flashing me his dimples.

"It's just Helen." I continue with my task.

"And Cole." Ronan follows me like a puppy to steal from every container I open.

I swat his hands away.

"What? I'm tasting them for you, *chéri*. You should thank me. Anyway, where was I? Right, Cole. How could you forget him?"

It doesn't hurt to try.

Today, I haven't held eye contact with him. I've passed him by every time I can. I haven't looked at his pressed suit Helen is so proud of. I haven't spoken when people are congratulating us for becoming siblings.

I've simply kept my mouth shut and played "Moonlight Sonata" in my head. I've pretended I'm somewhere out of here.

Somewhere where *he* isn't outside accepting congratulations and acting as if this is the happiest day of his life.

Why can't I do that?

Just why?

"Where's Aiden?" I ask instead.

He showed up with Uncle Jonathan, but then he disappeared somewhere out of sight.

"Why?" Ronan grins. "You miss him?"

Not in a million years. "We need to take pictures."

"He's probably playing chess against himself." Xander sips from a glass of champagne and grimaces. "This shit is awful. Do you have any Vodka somewhere?"

"We have no relationship with the mafia, thank you very much."

"You don't have to be a bitch about it." He messes up my plates for good measure before running away.

I nearly hit him with a pan. Ronan steals one more scone and jogs away, too, before I can catch him. He almost runs into Mum on his way out.

"I'm sorry, Ms. Davis." He takes her hand in his and kisses the back of it. "Is it only me or have you become even more beautiful over the years?"

She laughs, the sound throaty. "You're such a darling, Ronan."

He bows to her like the proper gentleman he'll never be and leaves.

Mum joins me at the counter, walking in that confident, lady-like way. She's wearing a red dress. No kidding. Her golden locks are styled like an actress's and she has perfect makeup made for models.

When I told her she's not supposed to look better than the bride, she said, "Nonsense. Do you want the media to say Cynthia Davis is heartbroken over her husband's remarriage? I need to look my absolute best."

That was after she cried in the bathroom and I hugged her, crying too, but for different reasons.

Yes, I now realise my parents will never be together, but I lost something else too.

"How many times have I told you that you don't have to do this, Babydoll?" She glances down at the containers with distaste. "Your father pays people for that."

"I just want to help."

"Go outside and take pictures. That'll be your greatest help. But don't you dare play the piano and appear too happy for him."

"I'll go out in a bit." We have that dreadful new family picture we need to take.

"Helen looks awful in that dress. She should've put in more effort."

"Mum..."

"What? I'm just saying. I'd hoped for some competition, but she doesn't even stand a chance. Ever since school, she's always been a nerd."

"Can we stop talking about Helen?"

"Fine. I can't believe your scoundrel father invited the entire party," she hisses under her breath. "It's like he's out to embarrass me and make me look pitiful in front of them."

Or he just wanted them to share his happiness. But I don't say that, or Mum would go bonkers. She constantly thinks I'm siding with him anyway.

"You can leave, Mum. You don't have to stay."

"Cynthia Davis running from her ex-husband's wedding. Do you want to see that in tomorrow's headlines? I thought you were on my side, Silver."

I'm on both your sides. I want to yell, but I don't, because that will freak her out more than the words themselves.

"Well, are you?" she insists, her brow furrowing.

"Of course I am."

"That's my Babydoll. Now, come here. Let me look at you." She takes me by the hand and spins me around so she can get a full view of my soft pink dress with tulle as a skirt. It stops a little above my knees and is tight at my breasts and waist. My hair is straight and falls to the small of my back in thick blonde strands. I have worn light pink lipstick to match.

"I'm so proud of how you've grown up into a fine lady, Babydoll. Happy birthday." She kisses my cheek and I nearly break then and there.

Papa and Helen did wish me a happy birthday this morning, but they seem to have forgotten all about me now. Not that I blame them, but still.

It's the first time Mum is one step ahead of everyone.

"Your father is a selfish bastard for scheduling his wedding on your birthday." Disgust is written all over her face. "He was out to ruin your special day."

"Mum..." I trail off.

"What? I'm only stating facts." She pulls out her phone and brings me to her side. "Let's take a picture."

My lips curve in an automatic smile as I stare at the camera. It comes too naturally to me now, I don't even have to stop before I fake it.

Mum posts the shot on Twitter with the caption: *Having the greatest fun on my only daughter's eighteenth birthday. This girl right here is the future. #MotherandDaughter #ReplicaofMe*

Almost immediately, the comments filter in about how she looks like my eldest sister, not my mother, or how I turned out stunning like her.

It's the type of comments that Mum thrives on. The type she screenshots and sends me in our chat. She saves each and every one that says I'm taking after her, not Papa, then forwards it to the both of us.

I can't help stealing a look at her wrist. It's covered with a thick watch, but I can never forget what that watch is hiding.

For the rest of my life, I'll constantly worry that Mum's black thoughts will one day take over and I'll lose her.

Cole has always said I'm Mum's puppet and that I'm turning like her, but that bastard didn't see what I did. He didn't walk in on a pool of blood and nearly faint.

If being her puppet will allow me to keep her, I don't mind. That's why I never, *ever* antagonise her. Since the divorce, I've learnt to bottle all my thoughts and feelings inside, put on a mask, and move along.

It's been the safest choice for everyone.

Just not for me.

The same wave from earlier is about to hit me again, and I have no confidence that I'll be able to hold it in when Mum is around.

As much as I want to protect her, sometimes I hate it. I hate that I can't sleep at night, thinking about what she could be doing, or that I have to call her first thing in the morning and five times a day like a clingy boyfriend.

I'm not supposed to have had these bursts of anxiety on a daily basis since I was freaking eleven.

"I'm going to get the camera from Papa's office," I tell her.

She says we don't need that since my pretentious father has paid a ton of photographers, but I deflect and leave the scene anyway.

I ignore all the chaos in the house and smile at Papa's friends, accepting their congratulations. I slip out of their usual questions about who would I vote for if I was given the choice between Papa and Mum.

As soon as I'm inside Papa's office, I close the door and lean my forehead on the cool surface.

My shoulders shake and my head is about to explode from the pent-up thoughts crowding inside it.

"Why can't this day end already?" I mutter under my breath.

Then the voice that comes from behind me shuffles all my cards, "Bored already, Butterfly?"

THIRTEEN

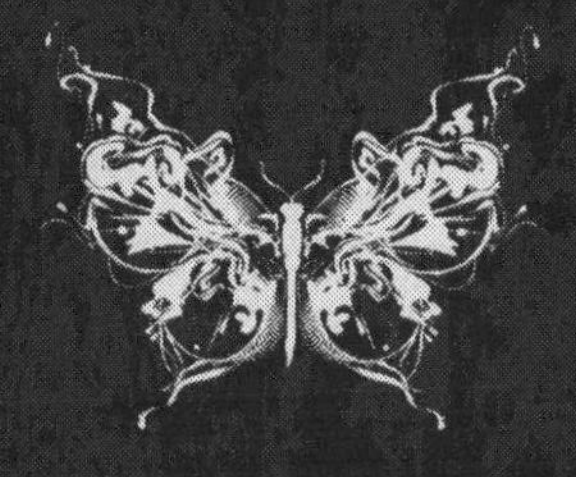

Silver

You can run, but you can't hide.

I didn't believe in that saying until this moment.

Over the past weeks, I've done everything to run away from Cole, avoid him, not look at him. I even went as far as feigning exhaustion to not stay in the same room as him.

But here I am, trapped with him in Papa's office.

Sure, I can go outside. I can open the door and run again, but that will look cowardly and I'll never do that.

Taking a deep breath, I slowly turn around and see Cole for the first time today, like *really* see him, instead of pretending to while I avert his gaze.

Cole sits on the edge of Papa's conference table, reading from a book titled *The Rule of Law* by Tom Bingham.

The dark blue suit pants mould to his muscles and tighten at his strong thighs with his sitting position. He's only in a white shirt and a black bowtie, the jacket lying neatly on the chair beside him.

His chestnut hair that has darkened over the years is styled back, showcasing his forehead and the sharp lines of his face. His green eyes fall on me as his lean fingers hold the book—fingers that were inside me a few weeks ago. Fingers that brought me to a height I've never experienced. Fingers that —

No.

That was a mistake. We're siblings now. A family. That nonsense will never happen again. It'll destroy my parents' careers and even Helen's.

Cole and I are over.

Completely, utterly over.

And we didn't even start yet.

"There you are." He smiles, and it's flat, bland, almost menacing. "Were you avoiding me or was I imagining it?"

"Imagining it." I fold my arms, adopting my firmest, most unaffected tone. "Why would I avoid you?"

"I don't know. It might have something to do with how you ran away from me the last couple of weeks." He flips a page, even though he's not reading. It's like he's absentmindedly keeping up with his usual pace. "You do realise you can't avoid me forever."

"As I said, I wasn't."

"You're such a liar, Butterfly." He strokes his fingers over the edge of the book. I want to look away, but I can't. It's like he's cast a spell on me and now all I can think about are his fingers and my thighs and —

Focus, Silver.

"Why would I even need to lie to you?" I raise my nose. "You give yourself so much credit, Cole."

"Then what are you doing here?"

"I came to search for Aiden. We have pictures to take."

He remains silent for a beat too long, watching me in that unnerving, quiet way that makes me want to snap out of my skin or hide underneath the carpet.

Cole has always had that effect on me. I've denied it, I've run away from it, but it doesn't disappear.

Just because you don't look under the bed, doesn't mean the monster isn't there.

He is. Waiting. Biding his time for the right moment so he can come out and play.

The only way to escape is to never, *ever* look. I was so close to breaking my own rule that day in my room, but it won't happen again.

"He's obviously not here." I turn to leave.

"You're running away again." His calm voice stops me in my tracks.

"No, I'm not."

"Yes, you are. Word of advice, never give me your back." In a second, he's behind me, his hot breaths tickling my skin. "I'll take it as an opening to attack."

His index finger traces down the bare skin of my shoulder all the way to where the top of the zipper rests. Goosebumps cover my flesh. My breathing turns choppy. His touch is so sensual, but I know, I just know it's only an appetiser to what he's truly capable of.

"You're wearing a dress like the one from that day ten years ago." He grabs the zipper and slowly glides it down my back. "It's on purpose isn't it, Butterfly?"

"N-no, don't flatter yourself." My voice is weak and sounds wanton, even to my own ears.

He slides his fingers down my exposed back. I close my eyes, my forehead falling against the door. A whimper fights its way out, but I bite my lip against it.

Why does this feel so good? Why are my legs opening of their own volition?

His breaths against the shell of my ear and his presence behind me send bursts of pleasure down my spine and right between my legs.

"C-Cole..." It's supposed to be a protest, but it comes out as a messy, lustful moan.

"Say it again." He skims his lean hand over my naked back before he stops at the middle, easily pinning me against the surface. "My name with a moan."

"N-no."

"No?" His other hand wraps around my throat. It's not hard enough to cut off my air supply, but it's firm, with the intention of keeping me in place.

I gulp, my body sharpening to attention as if I've been suddenly driven to the midst of an adrenaline high.

His teeth find the shell of my ear, nibbling slightly. His voice is that deceitful type of calm that gains an edge with every word. "Are you telling me you haven't been thinking about my fingers inside that tight cunt, Silver? That you haven't touched yourself to the memory or thought about them every time you saw me and fucking avoided me?"

My lips tremble at the onslaught of everything. His words. His mouth. His fingers around my throat.

Everything is too much.

"Because I have." He pushes his hips into me and an unmistakable bulge settles against my arse cheeks.

He's hard.

Cole is hard for me.

"Ever since you fell apart around my fingers, I've been fantasising about taking you in every fucking position."

I can feel myself falling. My walls crumbling and my beliefs scattering around me in shreds. All I'm itching for is a taste, a moment, a second of what happened back in my room.

No.

I *can't.*

I elbow him hard enough that he backs up a little. I use the chance to get away from his hold, clutching the front of my chest so the dress doesn't fall off. It has a built-in bra, so I'm only wearing knickers underneath it.

My breathing is high-pitched and loud like an animal's as I stand by Papa's conference table. Papa's office. This is Papa's office. What is wrong with me?

Reaching behind me, I zip up my dress and try to regulate my breathing.

Cole is still by the door, staring at me like a predator who can't decide what to do with his prey. Although he already has.

He's not the type of person who would start anything before figuring out the entire situation. He's one of those who knows the ending before hitting Play.

It takes him one second, two...

He stalks towards me, slowly but surely.

"Stop right there, Cole." I'm so glad my voice doesn't shake.

"Why? Because you don't want people to know you have the hots for your stepbrother?"

"I do not." My words fracture at the end and I hate him.

I *hate* him so much.

"I have Aiden," I challenge and then immediately regret it when the green of his eyes darkens to a frightening bottomless colour.

"Fuck him."

"I-I hate you."

"Doesn't mean I can't fuck you."

"You hate *me*."

"I still don't find the reason why that should get in the way."

"Our parents are married."

"So what?"

"We're siblings to everyone!" I cry out, no idea if it's at myself or him, because the closer he gets, the more I'm frozen in place.

One, I don't want to run away like a coward, but also, I don't want to move.

Ever.

He stops a small distance away and stares down at me. "So fucking what?"

My vision blurs as I peek up at him with the last pleading look I can manage. "W-we can't do this."

"And yet, you want to."

"W-what?"

His voice drops. "I can smell your arousal, Butterfly."

Before I can protest, he flips me over so my cheek and front are glued to the smooth surface of the table. His hand wraps around my nape, caging me in place.

"Cole, we can't."

"And yet, we will." The finality of his words hit me.

We will.

The fact he's taking it from me gives me some sort of peace.

I didn't choose this.

I'm not ruining my principles.

He is.

He's the one doing destroying every belief I had. It's all his fault, not mine.

My heart skyrockets as he yanks up the tulle of my dress and bunches it around my waist. Cold air bathes my skin as he pulls down my underwear, letting it pool at my feet.

"Look at your cunt all soaked and ready for me," he rasps as I hear the sound of his belt.

"It's not." I breathe against the wood, forming condensation on it.

"Do you think if you deny it, you'll get away with wanting it? Is that it, Butterfly?"

Yes. But I won't say that.

I won't.

He slaps my arse cheek. Hard. The slap reverberates in the silence of the office and I gasp as the sting registers. But it's not because of the pain. It's because of the clenching of my thighs that came with the pain.

What in the actual hell? There's definitely something wrong with me.

"Your habit of not answering my questions will have to change." His cock meets my entrance and my hands grip the table.

This is happening.

This is happening.

I close my eyes, trying to think of important things like birth control. Okay, I'm on the pill. Phew.

No. I shouldn't be happy that I'm on the pill. I should think of why this can't happen and that I need to stop it.

Nothing comes to mind. Absolute desert.

"Anyone could walk in on us. Did you know that?" he murmurs in a sadistic tone.

My gaze snaps to the door. It's not locked. Papa or Frederic or one of their friends could come in here to use the phone any second. They'll see us like this.

Why doesn't that terrify me as much as it should?

Cole tightens his hand around my nape. "Maybe that will ruin the wedding."

"No, I don't want that."

"Oh, but you do. You've been wishing for it for weeks, Butterfly. You're not as good a girl as you make everyone believe you are."

"Shut up."

"You're fake, but not with me. Never with me."

"Shut the fuck up, Cole."

"Uh-oh, Miss Prim and Proper is cursing."

"I hate you. I hate you so much."

"You know, I was going to wait until they broke up to make you mine, but they made this decision." He leans over so that he covers my back, then wraps his hand around my hair and fists it tightly. "And I made mine."

He thrusts into me in one ruthless go.

I cry out, my eyes screwing shut as the pain stabs me.

Oh, God.

It doesn't matter how wet I am. He's big and I'm too tight. It hurts.

"Fuck." He stops before I feel his warm breaths on my skin. "This is your first time?"

"Obviously, dickhead," I strain, my voice trembling.

"Open your eyes."

"No."

"Silver, open your fucking eyes."

"Just get it over with."

"Silver," he warns.

I know he doesn't use that tone a lot, if ever, so I slowly peel my lids open. My breathing cracks when I find him staring down at me.

If I expected pity, there's none. Instead, there's a hint of concern, but most of all, his eyes shine with a possessiveness so tangible, I can taste it on my tongue.

"I'm your first," he says with what seems like awe.

I nod, even though he didn't ask a question.

"Why am I your first?"

"It doesn't matter."

"Liar." He starts moving inside me and I grip the edge of the table tighter as he rocks his hips gently.

He's letting me get used to his size and to his rhythm. Oh, wow. I never thought there would be this side to Cole.

Soon enough, the initial sensation goes away and it's almost… pleasurable.

A whimper falls from my lips when Cole releases my hair, then massages my clit. The pain vanishes, and a wave pulls me under.

His pace picks up with every stroke of his fingers. A loud sob tears through the air, and I realise it's mine as I fall apart.

I didn't even last a minute.

My orgasm engulfs me until all I can recognise is him at my back, in me, all around me.

Cole holds my nape to the table and fucks me hard and wild. He fucks me like he's taking all the previous years out on me with each of his ruthless thrusts.

I fall again, or maybe it's the first fall bleeding into the second one. I can't see straight, let alone think right now.

All I can do is feel him—his power, his presence, his need for more that mirrors mine.

He doesn't stop.

Not when I'm moaning or whimpering or sobbing my orgasm. It's not until I can't stand and am nearly ready to collapse that he pulls out of me. A hot liquid drips between my legs, and I close my eyes, soaking in the sensation.

Still holding me by the neck, Cole gathers the cum that's dripped from me and fucks it inside me with two surprisingly gentle fingers until I'm nearly begging for another orgasm.

I'm sore and feel used, but at the same time, I still want more.

So much more.

The realisation of what I've done hits me right there with my head against Papa's conference table.

I betrayed my own principles. My beliefs. My parents.

And it's all because of him.

Cole.

He used me and ruined me beyond repair.

And I know, I just know, that from now on, nothing will ever be the same.

"Happy birthday, Butterfly," he whispers against my ear. "You're now mine."

FOURTEEN

Doll Master

My little doll has turned into a woman.

The way her body contracted and her blood trickled down her thighs mixed with cum is a sight I'll never forget.

It's art at its truest form.

It's a masterpiece.

And I'll have it unfold over and over again.

Blood looks exquisite on her porcelain skin. Almost like it's made to smother her flesh, bathe it, creep over it instead of underneath it.

My Barbie doll doesn't realise how beautiful she is. How exquisite. She has a smile to die for, lips to devour, and eyes to stare at for eternity.

People at school call her a bitch, but they're just jealous of her beauty, her grace, and her mind. Her intelligent, bright mind. It's the reason why her beauty is enhanced. She's not one of those bimbo dolls I get tired of after one glance.

She's not shallow like them, stupid like them, hollow like them.

She's the whole package.

She's what I've been searching for my entire life while I kept myself busy with their forgettable bodies.

I spent years being patient, slowly creeping under her skin, but not too obviously.

You can't be obvious with dolls. People say they don't see, but they have eyes. They say they don't feel, but they have skin. They can bleed too if you run a knife over their bodies.

Dolls need to be treated carefully, dressed carefully, washed carefully.

Watched carefully.

You can't let them suspect you. Instead, you have to be the most important part of their lives. Their doll master.

The one who dresses them, washes them, does their hair.

I stare at a picture of her asleep on her side in only her T-shirt and no underwear. I groan as my release comes in waves.

I retrieve my spare phone, coat her pictures with my release, then type with the same fingers.

Unknown Number: You look beautiful today, like a rose finally deflowered. Happy eighteenth birthday. You're a woman now.

My doll.

My masterpiece.

Now, she'll never get away from me.

PART TWO

FIFTEEN

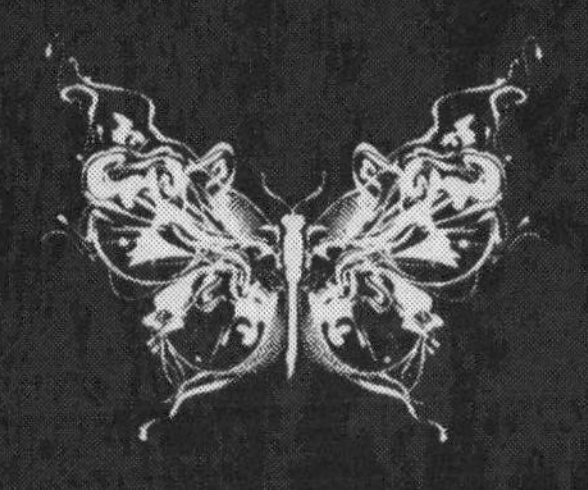

Silver

When I go to school the following day, I'm not focused. Everything seems to be out of control. *Everything.*

One, Mum got drunk at the end of the reception and she kept asking what Papa sees in Helen anyway. Is she prettier than her? Better accomplished? She said even her books seem like they're written by a psychopath.

I told her that all crime thriller books need to be frightening in some way. Helen's books always give me a chill and that's why they're so successful.

I had to ask Derek to help me drive her home. We'd barely gotten her in the car and she had a fight with Papa—again. Thankfully, it was away from the reporters or their other party members.

They screamed at each other and it was like a flashback from the divorce time.

After I tucked Mum safely in her bed, she hugged me, kissed me, and told me she was sad and that she didn't want to be sad. So I stayed with her until she drifted off to sleep.

By the time I returned home, the reception was over. Papa and Helen had already retreated to their room. They decided against a honeymoon because of how busy they both are.

I was all alone with the catering staff, and Ronan and Xander, who didn't leave my side. I was thankful to them in a way words can't express, so I let them have all the food and alcohol they liked.

Cole just sat there, reading from his book as if nothing had happened. As if he hadn't broken my world to pieces and made me walk unevenly all night. I had to feign spraining my ankle—to which he smirked at, the bastard.

This morning, Papa's party friends and political life has returned at full force. Helen prepared them tea and told me to go ahead to school and not worry about anything.

Then there's the damn text I received yesterday from the unknown number.

A rose deflowered.

He watched me. He saw me do it with Cole.

What if he tells Papa, or worse, the media? That would screw up everything.

Everything.

Since I received the text, I've been watching my surroundings as if he'll come up from the shadows and attack me.

When I was younger, his texts were non-harmful ones, just compliments, like any comment on my social media posts, but a year or so ago, I finally started to see them as disturbing.

No one should know so much about me. My morning routines, from my favourite Chanel perfume down to the type of shampoo I use.

But the last text pushed every boundary I could've had. The fact that he was there, in Papa's wedding, and possibly saw me coming out of his office is more than disturbing.

The reason why I feel like I'm suffocating is because I can't show this to Papa anymore, or even to Mum. She'll kill me if she knows I slept with my stepbrother.

And Papa will give me that disappointed look he saves for his party members who act like brats and cause a media ruckus.

Even Frederic is out. He'll immediately tell Papa about it.

It's all because of him. Cole. The bastard.

Why did he have to do that? Why did he have to make us fall into a hole of no return?

If I tell him about it, maybe he'll —

No.

This stalker—or whatever—won't get to me. Papa once taught me a trick that should exist up every politician's sleeve—doubt.

If someone makes you doubt yourself and your core principles, they can easily destroy you. They're using you to ruin you. It's like when the body self-destructs.

That's what the stalker is doing. He's trying to make me panic, and as a result, I'll make a mistake that he'll use to his advantage.

You've got the wrong person for that, arsehole.

I'm the daughter of Sebastian Queens and Cynthia Davis. It takes more than stupid texts to scare me.

Lifting my head, I walk through Royal Elite School's hallway. RES goes way back to medieval times. Its ten towers show the majestic power of this place, and to what levels it can take you.

Papa, Mum, and even Helen walked the halls of this school. It's where they met the first time. After that, Papa and Mum studied at the same university and got engaged. Unlike what the media said about them, it wasn't an arranged marriage between two powerful families. For one, apparently Mum's family, which has a long chain of secretaries of state, wasn't good enough for Papa's parents.

They already had power, so they wanted nobility. Papa chose her over some noble family's daughter, and although Mum smiles when she retells that part of their story, she follows it with a scowl and says they chose that misery willingly.

That's what she calls their marriage, by the way. Misery.

Now, it's my turn to make the right decisions and take the most advantage of the school. It's the beginning of our last year and I know exactly where I'll be at the end of it.

In Oxford, studying politics and international relations. For that, I'll be at the top of the class. Screw Cole if he thinks he can take that away from me.

Near the seventh tower, I spot Aiden cornering Elsa, better known as Frozen. I glare at them.

Since the start of the year, Aiden has been obsessed with her. Okay, maybe his obsession started two years ago when she first came into RES. However, he never acted on it. He just watched from afar like a psycho.

But something happened this year, and he's been gravitating towards her like a magnet to steel.

I can't let that happen.

Aiden is one of my cards against Cole. Scratch that. He's my *only* card against Cole.

I need the engagement to push my bastard of a stepbrother away, and that girl is ruining my plan.

She's always shoving Aiden away anyhow, so I've been doing her a favour by keeping his psychotic claws off her.

She'll thank me for it later.

Okay, maybe she won't, but hey, the sentiment is there.

I'm about to go and break them off when a sinister presence appears by my side. Cole smirks down at me as he clutches his books. He's been in an awfully good mood since yesterday.

"I could've driven you to school, Butterfly. You know, with how you sprained your ankle and all."

"Screw. You," I hiss under my breath.

He laughs, the sound echoing around us like a halo.

I can only stop and stare when he laughs. He doesn't do it so often, and when he does, I want to catch it and tuck it away for safekeeping.

Snap out of it, Silver.

"Your compliments are music to my ears, even better than your piano playing." His lips brush against the shell of my ear. "And I love your piano playing."

My heart beats so loud, it's about to burst free of its confinements. It's the first time he's said that.

"Then why do you always make me lose in competitions?" I whisper.

"Because you act like a bitch."

I wish I could punch him right now, but since countless students are buzzing around us, I can't.

Cole must realise that, too, because his lips lift in an infuriating smirk. No, he didn't only realise it, but he planned it all along. He loves taunting me in public, knowing that I can't react to it. I swear he lives to torment my existence.

I can't believe he was inside me yesterday. He pushed me to the table and touched me and fucked me and –

No.

I swallow the desire that bursts to the surface every time I recall what happened. *Stop thinking about it. Just stop.*

Huffing, I stride in Aiden and Elsa's direction to continue my mission, but he places a hand on my arm, stopping me in my tracks.

"This is one of the bitch moments that make me retaliate, Silver." His voice is still calm, but the fact he's calling me by my name means he's either pissed off or annoyed. Or both.

"Well, I don't care what ticks you off, Cole." I wiggle away from him because his touch makes me feel things I shouldn't— even through my jacket and shirt. I clutch my hip and glare him down. "Besides, Aiden is my fiancé."

He narrows his eyes but soon schools his expression. "So what? It's not like you'll marry him."

"What makes you think I won't?"

"Are you blind?" He steps slightly behind me so both of us are watching the scene ahead. His voice drops in volume as his breaths warm my ear. "Can't you see the way he looks at her? He'll never give you that, Silver. No one will."

I tighten my grip on my hip, but it's not because of Aiden and Elsa—I couldn't give too shits about them.

It's the last part of what he said.

No one will.

Why? Am I going to end up alone and sad like Mum? Will I have a daughter and make her worry about me twenty-four seven?

"Break it off." Cole's voice brings me out of my stupor.

"What?" I stare back at him.

"The fake engagement. End it."

"It's not fake."

"Sometimes, I think you know me the best, and other times, it's like you don't know me at all." He's not touching me, but his close proximity is enough to make me aware of every word leaving his mouth, of his scent oozing with cinnamon and lime. Of his body warmth that mixes with mine.

For someone so cold, he's so warm. I felt it. Hell, I still feel it with every step I take.

No baths or self-care home remedies will be able to remove the feel of him inside me.

"Did you really think I didn't figure out you and Aiden were doing this whole thing to spite me?"

"W-what?" He knew all along?

"If I'd had the slightest doubt, it was eliminated when I knew you'd saved your virginity for me."

"I…didn't."

"Why are you such a liar, Silver?"

"Why are *you?*" I elbow him discretely so no one else sees it.

He barely winces before his grin returns to the surface. "If you don't end it amicably, I'll step up. Believe me, you don't want me to step up, Butterfly."

"You don't scare me, Cole."

"But I can do other things to you."

"In your dreams," I hiss low enough so no one hears.

"We'll see about that." He motions at Aiden. "I was thinking about telling Aiden about our first time—*your* first time."

"He wouldn't mind. We're open like that."

"With Elsa in the picture, I wouldn't be so sure." He tugs on my hair. "End. It."

And then he disappears from my back, leaving me empty.

No. Screw him. I'm not empty.

I focus back on Aiden and Elsa. She's telling him something, or rather, yelling something at him, but he only smirks like the bastard he is.

Cole is right. It won't be long before Aiden dumps me for her.

I hate it when Cole is right.

A new plan forms in my head. Elsa is jealous of me and she doesn't even know about the engagement. Aiden wants her to be jealous because that would mean she cares about him, and his ego needs that confirmation more than anything.

I'll make a deal with him; we stay engaged and I won't mention a word about it to his precious ice princess.

In return, Cole will stay away.

Perfect.

"Hey, Sil." Veronica and Summer join me as we go to class.

They're both blondes—not naturally so—and their lives are all about the latest fashion and makeup trends and the best way to spend their daddies' money.

Shallow doesn't even begin to describe them, but they're the camouflage I need for my image at school. Besides, it doesn't matter if they get too close. They'll never be able to read me.

"Hey, girls." We air-kiss before they start talking about the latest stupid reality TV show that I don't watch but pretend I do. It's easy to do that. All I have to do is pick up on what they say and build on it.

Papa is the next prime minister, thank you very much. If I don't have a way with words, who will?

"So, are we going to Ronan's party, or what?" Veronica asks with a dramatic tone.

"Oh, I have, like, the perfect dress." Summer jumps up and down like a giddy kid. "The one we bought from Chanel the other day. Remember that, Silver?"

I nod. "You'll look so hot in it."

"I know!"

"Hey, maybe we should all wear Chanel?" Veronica says. She has chubby cheeks, even after the plastic surgery she made her father pay for as her eighteenth birthday present over the summer.

She went to South Korea for it. No kidding.

"Sure..." I trail off when the clouds above us part, revealing a hint of the sun. That's when I notice it.

A shadow.

It's a larger shadow—a shadow that's too close. It's like they've been copying my steps.

Veronica and Summer are talking about Chanel's latest collection while my heart is about to jump out of my throat.

Still, I don't turn around. I don't alert the person that I've seen their shadow because nature decided to give me a warning.

"Let's go to the restroom, girls," I say.

"Oh, right. I have to check my makeup too," Veronica agrees.

I make them walk at a slightly faster pace. It's not fast enough to alert the shadow, but it's fast enough to get away.

As we round the corner, I pretend to look for something in my bag and I catch a glimpse of him.

He stands at the entrance of the tower.

The shadow is Adam Herran. The captain of the rugby team. His father is one of Papa's party friends.

And he was at the wedding.

SIXTEEN

Cole

Observation is the source of all evil.

If you fail at it, you're screwed. If you're the subject of it, you're also screwed.

Only a few people take the time to observe their surroundings and be aware of their environments.

Most are headed forward, not caring about the opportunities or the chances they miss. If they would just throw a look sideways, if they'd stop to watch, their lives could dramatically change.

Observing my surroundings—especially people—is what has given me a gift very few have…recognising weaknesses.

If you observe someone long enough, you'll pick up their habits and, soon, their telltale signs and their sensitive buttons. It's all in there, laid out for the taking.

There's an art in observing. You can't be too obvious, or you'll be labelled a stalker, a creep, and a whole lot of unflattering terms.

My books have always served as a camouflage for my observation sessions. That way, I can concentrate on the words while figuring out my surroundings. Observing doesn't interrupt my flow—if anything, it enforces it. While observing, I take the necessary time to process the words I've learnt.

For instance, now, during practice. Xander has thrown the ball three times off the pitch. It's not because he's bad—out of all of us, he probably has the best aim. He missed on purpose because he gets to run there and have a better view of Kimberly, who's started to show up for our practices.

He's been hung up on her since we were six or something, but then one day, he decided he should hate her. I figured out his reason some time ago, and I still think it's dumb.

If you want something, go for it. Society and expectations be damned.

Xander doesn't share my philosophy, so instead of acting on his feelings, he keeps getting in her vicinity, begging for a look from her or some proof that she hasn't forgotten about him. But when she does give him validation, he pretends she's the rock in his shoe.

He's pathetic.

Then there's Aiden. His poker face has been cracking whenever a certain Frozen is in sight. She's in the track team and they're practising across from us. He hasn't listened to a word the assistant manager has told us. Instead, he's been watching her with that calculative streak.

He's more discreet than Xander about it, but it's there, and I know, I just know that Elsa is my one-way ticket to break him the fuck off from Silver.

And they will break it off.

The curtains have fallen. They can't fool me anymore—not that they should've since the start.

I run back to defence and cut off the beginning of a counter-attack. I'm good at ruining things before they start. The assistant manager shouts, "Fantastic tackle, Captain!" But his words don't register.

Nothing does.

Since yesterday, I've been on a high I haven't been able to control.

I did it.

I finally took Chaos by the throat and fucked her like I secretly fantasised for years.

It was her birthday, but I got the best gift—being her first.

It wasn't the fucker Aiden or any other loser; it was me. She never broke her promise to me.

My head has been filled with images of her porcelain skin, of her bold flowery scent, of the way she moaned my name.

Fuck, how she moaned my name.

That's the only way I want her to say my name from now on.

I know it won't be easy. Silver didn't just pull away from me as soon as I was out of her, she ran. Not to mention, she's been acting cold and aloof since the morning.

Aiden is my fiancé.

Fuck that.

If she thinks I'll let her hang on to his arm after I claimed her, then she must not know me at all.

I only allowed the fun because I knew there would be a day where she'd be officially mine. After Mum and Sebastian's marriage, that option is off the table, but that doesn't mean I can't work around it.

The first step is done, but there's more to come.

As soon as the assistant manager calls a break to go through the formation, I stalk towards the bench Aiden is occupying, snatch a bottle of water and settle by his side.

He's wiping his face with a towel, his gaze focused on Elsa as she runs. I see it then—pride. He's not just infatuated with her, he's also proud of her. Interesting.

"She's good," I say nonchalantly.

His attention slowly slides to me. He must've noticed me sitting beside him, because even though he acts like he doesn't care, he's also hyperaware of his surroundings. However, he didn't realise I was observing his observation session.

"Eyes. Off," he orders.

There. The reaction I needed. "Relax. I was only saying she's good."

"Don't say she's good, don't even watch her being good, speak to her, or about her. Deal? Deal."

"I would've probably done that if I hadn't realised you're a fucking liar."

"Me? What have I lied to you about?"

"Hey, how do I remove virginal blood from my dick? Should I just wash it?" I recite his text from back then and the words that fucking broke me. "I already washed the blood off my dick. I wouldn't have if I'd known you have a virginal blood kink."

He raises a brow. "Are you trying to prove you have a good memory? Am I supposed to clap or some shit?"

"I'm repeating your lies, King. You really thought I wouldn't find out?"

"It took you three years." He grins. "Three years of thinking I was her first. Three years of dying on the inside imagining I was fucking her whenever we were alone. Three years of constant doubts. Let's not mention how you punched me that night or your petty moves whenever you could dig me a hole. Do you know what I call that? A win."

It takes all my self-restraint not to raise my fist and punch him again, and this time, I'd ruin those features so no one would look in his direction. I'd make him an ugly monster. However, I know that will only give him the reaction he wants, so I drink a sip of water to soothe my throat.

"The fun is over. End it," I say with a calm I don't feel.

That's the thing about plotting chaos. You feel it, but you don't show it—it's the most lethal type to ever exist.

"Why would I?" Aiden flings the towel over his shoulder.

"Because she's mine now." My throat closes around the word. *Mine*. How long have I waited to say that out loud?

Years. Fucking years.

And now, I can't even say it to the world—just to the bastard Aiden, but it's a start.

"I'm surprised she stayed a virgin for you with you being a dick and all that. And you'd think being with me for three years would have upped her standards."

"More like lowered them."

"I don't know what perverted game you're playing, Nash, but does she agree?"

"That's none of your business. Your only role is to end it."

"No can do. You see, Queens and I are *it*. So what if you're fucking her? I'm the one whose ring she'll be wearing and who she'll marry." His face is blank, but it couldn't look any more gruesome if he were smirking.

They made a deal. I can smell it in the air, even without knowing it for sure.

Silver felt threatened and, therefore, pulled on her armour, in which Aiden plays a part.

The fucker must've been offered something that serves him in some way.

I slam the lid of the bottle shut. "Are you sure you want to play this game with me? This time I will crush you."

"Is that a promise?"

"This is your only warning, King. I will not play fair."

"Are you telling me you were all this time?"

"Your choice."

"Show me your worst, Nash."

The break finishes and Aiden saunters back to the field.

After Levi King graduated, I became the captain. He recommended me to the coach because he thinks I'm more level-headed than his dick of a cousin. He chose right. I can pretend to care, Aiden doesn't even try.

I follow close behind him. If it were any other person, they would've backed away, especially if it was someone who'd witnessed how I play unfair.

However, Aiden is made for the challenge. The harder it gets, the more insistent he becomes about finishing it with flying colours.

It's his loathsome competitive nature that resembles Silver's, and probably the only reason why they get along on some level.

What Aiden doesn't realise is that I know his weakness. He didn't have it when he took off with her and played me by sending those texts. Now, he does.

I promised him and I promised her.

It took me years, but I'll make them both fall as far as I did.

I'll make them feel every thread of chaos I felt while riding my bike all night under that pouring rain.

When I go back to Sebastian's house that late afternoon, it's buzzing with energy.

Assistant, PR team, spokesman team, publicist, secretary, and even the driver. They're all there, running about and making calls and turning the house into an elections' hall.

Farewell, my quiet home. Mum kept the house, but it's not like I'll go live there on my own.

I wouldn't anyway. Even with the number of people who are here on a daily basis, being here is worth it.

We're under the same roof. My chaos and I.

"Oh, Cole." Mum fusses with some plates at the kitchen counter. "Be a darling and give me that plate."

"I'll carry them for you."

"Nonsense." She motions at an empty place on her arm. "Just put it there and go have fun."

"I can help, Mum."

"I'll get one thing straight with you, just like I did with

Silver. I don't need your help," she says in a half-stern, half-jokey tone. "When I do, I'll ask for it."

I put the plate where she motioned. Each of Sebastian's team members grab one and thank her with big smiles on their faces. It's like they forgot they should eat.

Sebastian comes down the hall and helps her, then places a kiss on her temple. They smile at each other, like any reserved old couple would do, I suppose—polite and glad they don't have to spend the rest of their lives alone.

Oh, well, if an elections' campaign is their idea of a honeymoon, so be it. Mum knew what she was signing up for, she better not regret it.

On my way up, I greet all of Sebastian's team members by name, ask them about their day, their kids, and the stats. All of them strike up conversations and appear happy someone is considering them humans instead of an extension of Sebastian. He gets all the limelight and will be remembered in history books. They'll vanish as if they were never there.

I do it to appear polite. If you're kind and caring, people lay off you. They don't observe, watch, or dig deeper into you.

I sure as hell don't do it because I'm actually kind. That's Silver. She pretends she doesn't care, yet she goes out of her way to buy gifts for their kids and to make them their favourite tea.

We're opposite that way. I don't care, but I appear as if I do. She cares, but she pretends she doesn't.

I stand in front of my door, and yes, I did choose a room that's right next to hers. She wanted to protest but didn't have a valid argument, so she huffed, puffed, and glared.

I love it when she glares. It means I'm getting under her skin, and I love being there—under her skin, I mean.

Instead of going into my room, I do a discreet sweep of the hallway, and once I make sure no one is around, I step into hers.

Her bed is made, but she's not here. The sound of running

water comes from the bathroom. My cock hardens at the thought of her naked and wet.

There has never been a girl who's pumped so much blood into my dick like she does. And that happens without even touching or seeing her.

A mere thought is enough to reduce me into one of those hormonal teenagers I always thought were fools.

There's nothing I want more than to get in there and own her all over again. But before that, I need to do my ritual.

I don't bother readjusting my trousers as I stride to her bedside table and put in the code to her lock. It's the date her parents announced they'd divorce. She hasn't changed it at all since I figured it out.

At first, I put in her birthday and smiled when it didn't work. It meant she's not predictable. I tried a combination of her favourite number, seven, but that didn't work either.

Then I recalled the reason why she even started writing in her journal, why she needed a piece of paper to cry to a 'silent friend' as she called it in her first entry.

Her parents' divorce.

I tried the actual date her parents finalised their divorce, which is easy to find on the internet, but that didn't work either.

The right one is the day she learnt about her parents' divorce, which, ironically, happens to also be William's death anniversary.

In the drawer, she has ten journals. One for each year. Some days, she talks a lot, on others, she only writes two words.

I pull out this year's journal. Since yesterday, I haven't stopped thinking about what she could've written about last night.

When she drove her Mum home, I did sneak a peek, but she hadn't written an entry yet. Then she returned and didn't leave her room.

I flip to the last entry. Yesterday.

Today was Papa's wedding and my eighteenth birthday.

Mum cried and I felt so guilty for liking Helen when Mum clearly doesn't.

Cole took my virginity today. He just took it and it was so dirty.

Remember when I said I hate Cole? Well, I don't only hate him.

I despise him.

I wish he would disappear from my life.

I narrow my eyes on her words. She hates me, despises me, wishes I'd disappear from her life.

Fuck that.

It's the same as every entry she writes about me. Why does she refuse to admit the truth, even to her bloody journal? She does that with everything else.

When she talks about her parents, her life at school, or even how much she misses Kim, she says it truthfully, but every time it's about me, it's all fucking lies.

We'll see about that.

I place her journal exactly the way I found it, close the drawer, and put the combination back to zeroes.

The sound of the shower is still going. I turn the door's knob and remove my clothes on my way inside her bathroom.

As soon as I'm at the entrance, soft moans stop me with my fingers on my trousers' buttons.

I stand there and watch the most exquisite view I've seen in my entire life.

Silver stands under the stream in all her naked glory. I might have seen the occasional nip slip over the years, or her underwear when she forgot to tuck her legs together when wearing a skirt, but I've never seen her entirely naked.

And fuck me, why haven't I done this before?

Her tits sit high and perky, droplets of water clinging to

the hard pink tips, begging to be licked off. Water soaks her golden hair as it glues to the entirety of her back.

Her smooth waist and long legs are like a porn fantasy. But that's not the best part about the scene, it's her hand disappearing in and out of her cunt as she reaches her other hand to tug on a nipple.

Eyes closed, her head is thrown back, letting the steam soak her. White straight teeth trap her bottom lip to rein in the moans.

It's not working.

The slight noise she's making turns my dick rock fucking hard, if that's even possible, considering it was already ready when I walked in the room.

Yesterday, I signed a no-going-back oath and today, I'm keeping it.

SEVENTEEN

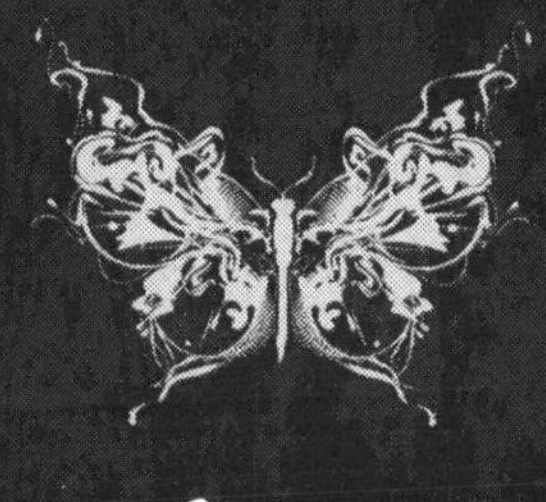

Silver

I'm supposed to take a quick shower and join Papa and his team. They're going to discuss strategy and I want to be there.

The moment I'm under the stream, I start thinking. That's what I do when I'm in the shower—I think. A lot.

Some people sing, but I become a damn bundle of thoughts. Maybe it's the stream of water or the peace of the moment, but it always pushes me to think again about my decisions and choices.

It's my second favourite place after the park. Peace, cleanliness, and a clear head.

Only, it's not clear.

One thing keeps barging to mind…those dark green eyes, his voice and the authority in it.

End. It.

Screw him. I didn't end it. Aiden and I are on the same side. As long as I keep benefitting him, he'll do the same.

I even paid a visit to a certain girl who's been writing him love letters. Cole, not Aiden. Who the hell even writes love letters anymore? Is she from a century ago or something?

Anyway, I told her he has a condition, you know, like a dick condition. She thinks he can't get it up. I only meant that he's a dickhead, but hey, as long as it worked, I'm not complaining.

Then I caught myself smirking when she walked away, thinking no one will get to see his dick anyway. That's when I realised I'm going off track again. I'm sabotaging any sliver of a relationship he has with the other sex.

He's making me lose my sanity along with my better judgement.

The wanker.

And yet, the only images that keep playing in my head are of yesterday. Me against the table while he yanked my dress up.

My hand sneaks down my stomach and to between my thighs. I'm wet, and it's not just because of the water.

A shallow breath leaves me as I thrust a finger inside. I'm still tender and a bit sore.

I recall the way he spanked me while he held me down by the nape. He took my will, my choice, and I got even wetter for him.

My nipples pucker, painfully so, and I close my eyes and roll my head back. I twirl one tight bud between my fingers and tug on it. A moan tries to escape, but I trap it in like I did when he was touching me. His hands and body and chest covered me whole until he was all I felt.

I remember the first time he thrust into me, the force of it, and add another finger, tumbling over with the power of the thrust. I imagine it's him, pounding into me, whispering dirty words into my ears, telling me I'm his, and my pace picks up.

My pounds turn harsher and I'm hurting my nipple, pinching it with my fingernails until it screams in pain.

I've touched myself before, and he's always been the image I've pictured. Him half-naked by the pool. Him sweaty and rugged and freaking delectable after practice. Him running and scoring and being a god on the field.

But I've never wanted to inflict pain with it.

After yesterday, that's all I want. The slight sting of pain that comes with pleasure. The power that comes with being completely at his mercy.

I plunge my fingers quicker, my moans filling the silence of the bathroom.

Oh, God.

The force of whatever is building inside me frightens even me. My legs tremble and my poor nipple begs to be put out of its misery.

My eyes roll back, causing my lids to open a little.

That's when I see someone.

No. Not someone.

Him.

In the middle of my bathroom.

For a moment, I think he's a manifestation of my imagination. That I somehow thought about him hard enough I managed to bring him to life in 3D format.

But then the rest of the scene registers. He's naked.

There's not one piece of clothing covering his body.

I've always wondered about how he'd look naked and it escaped me every time.

And now, there he is, in all his glory. Cole isn't as muscular as Xander. He's leaner and has a quiet beauty about him. Even his wide chest and six-pack appears demure in an irresistible type of way.

Due to playing football, his thighs and long legs are powerful and taut. His chest muscles contract with the way his hand is gripping his cock.

I felt it yesterday—and keep feeling it today—but it's the first time I've seen his dick. It's so big, I'm both appalled and amazed that it fit inside me. I couldn't look away from it or him even if I wanted to.

And I do want to. I just can't avert my gaze.

He's touching himself.

Cole is naked and he's touching himself.

His hand tugs up and down his dick, and for some stupid, irrational reason, I hate his hand right now.

That was me yesterday. It should be me now, not his hand.

My fingers move inside me at a slower pace, my eyes drooping as if they're about to close.

That's when the entire situation filters into my dazed brain. The fact that I'm masturbating in front of Cole. The fact he's doing the same while watching me.

He's in my bathroom.

I gasp, letting my hands fall to either side of me despite my body's protests, and swiftly turn around. "W-what are you doing here? G-get out."

There's no power behind my voice, no matter how much I wish for it. My heart beats loud and fast. The tender skin between my legs is aching, demanding the release I just interrupted. My nipples throb, close to cutting something with how hard they are.

No movement comes from Cole. The sound of water is the only thing in the bathroom. I swallow through my broken breaths.

Did he leave?

Why the hell is my chest falling at that idea?

I need some therapy because I shouldn't be feeling this out of sorts whenever he's in sight. Is it because he became my stepbrother? Am I acting this way because my will was taken by our parents' marriage and I missed the timing?

Do I only crave him this much because I can't have him?

That must be why, because the fact that my heart is nearly bursting out of my chest doesn't make any damn sense.

I slowly take a peek over my shoulder.

Goosebumps erupt all over my wet skin, the hot water doing nothing to alleviate it.

Cole stands right behind me. He's close enough that I smell his scent, spice and his lime gum. Close enough that I get trapped in his warmth. Close enough that he's drenched, his silky hair becoming soaked and sticking to his forehead. Close enough that streams of water drip down his pectoral muscles and down, down —

I snap my attention back to his eyes, refusing to be caught spying on his dick.

"What did I tell you about giving me your back, Butterfly?" he murmurs near the shell of my ear.

My eyes fight to shut at the shiver he's erupting on my skin.

He grabs my arse cheek, and this time, I whimper, my thighs clamping together. "Or are you perhaps tempting me with this? Do you want me to fuck it?"

"N-no." My voice is weak, even to my own ears.

I, myself, don't know what I want him to do. As long as he touches me, has his hands on me, it's like everything suddenly becomes possible.

"No, huh? I'll change your mind one day." He licks the lobe of my ear, murmuring in hot words, "Now, how about I finish the show you started?"

"I didn't start any show." I'm surprised I can speak with the stimuli shooting rampant all over my body.

"Oh, but you did. You kept thrusting in and out of your cunt even after you saw me. Were you fantasising about my dick inside you, Butterfly?"

"No!" My voice is defensive, full of shame.

"You know, the more you say that, the surer I am about how much of a liar you are."

"I'm not lying…ohhh…" My words end in a moan when he releases my arse and plunges two fingers inside me in one go.

The itch from earlier returns with a vengeance and I arch my back, needing more friction. Just more of him.

"Your pussy doesn't lie, she's telling me she wants my dick." He curls his fingers and I moan again, my head collapsing against the tile. "Do you want me inside you, Butterfly?"

"No," I whisper, my voice desperate.

"Are you sure?"

Of course I do, but I'm not saying it out loud. I'm not going to let him break me into speaking it.

He pushes his hard cock into the crack of my arse and I clench, biting my lower lip.

"It seemed like you wanted it earlier when you were watching my dick and fucking yourself."

I shut my eyes, unable to take the assault of his words and his touch at the same time. I'm so close to combusting, to begging, but I'll never do that.

Cole isn't someone I should let do this to me.

I only want him because I can't have him, because if anyone found out about what we're doing behind closed doors, they would shun us.

And that's sick. Just utterly sick.

If my only form of defence is defying him, then so be it. That's what he'll get.

"Open your eyes."

I don't.

He grabs a fistful of my hair and spins me around. His fingers slip out of me and I mourn the loss, my walls contracting as if trying to keep him inside.

My back flattens against the cold tiles, causing me to gasp, but I don't open my eyes.

"Look at me."

"No."

He tugs on my hair. "Are you or are you not going to look at me?"

"No."

"I'm going to fuck that word out of you, Silver."

My insides liquefy at that promise, but I hang on to my façade with blood-coated fingers. "Just get it over with and leave me alone."

"You don't get to treat it as a burden when you've been fucking fantasising about it. You don't get to tell yourself lies just so you can sleep at night."

Watch me.

He wraps a hand around my throat and squeezes. Hard.

My eyes pop open as I struggle for breath. He eases his hold, allowing me tiny gulps of air.

"There you are." He stares down at me with those eyes that I sometimes think have no soul behind them.

They're green, but they feel black.

They're looking at me, but sometimes, it's like they're seeing through me.

He's gripping me by the hair and the throat, and for some foreign reason, it feels like the most right position to be in.

"I'm going to fuck you and you're going to scream." He licks my trembling lower lip. "If you don't, we can do this all night."

I don't speak. I can't.

It's like I've lost my abilities of speech and thought. I've lost everything.

All I can do is watch him. The water forms rivulets down his face giving him an exotic look, the steam of the bathroom swirling around him like a halo.

I'm fucked. So bloody fucked.

He releases my hair and grabs my thigh, lifting it up and, as a result, making my other foot stand on a tiptoe.

"Wrap your legs around my waist," he orders, but I don't.

I want him to do it all.

If I don't participate, I can pretend I didn't want this. It's all his doing, not mine.

He must see it in my face because he grabs my other leg and lifts it, slipping inside me, inch by each agonising inch. I close my eyes, but it's to soak in the sensation.

I tighten my legs around his firm waist to not lose my

balance. The force of his thrusts hits my back against the wall over and over again.

I relish in every one of them.

Cole is harsh and out of control, exactly how I imagined he would be when I was fantasising about him earlier.

He squeezes my throat hard enough to make me open my eyes.

"You don't get to hide, Butterfly." He peers at me. "Not anymore."

Yesterday, when he fucked me from behind, I was slightly grateful he couldn't see the chaotic emotions swirling in my eyes.

Now, he does—in full HD. I've always thought I showed emotions in a way no one understands, but Cole might be able to.

I don't want him to understand.

This position, face-to-face, heart to heart, is too intimate. It's like he's peeling me piece by each bloody piece.

I hate that a part of me wants him to reach the core.

I hate that a part of me is grateful he's doing this, that he's freeing me in ways I would've never used to free myself.

And because I hate him, I hurt him.

I glide my hands around his back and drag my long nails down the wet skin with the intention to cause him pain.

He hisses, but instead of stopping, he picks up his pace and pounds into me with renewed ferocity as he pins me to the wall by my throat.

Then he leans down to the sensitive flesh of my breast and sucks on it before biting—hard.

My back arches off the wall and a terrifying wave spreads over me like wildfire.

"I'll leave my mark as you leave yours, Butterfly," he speaks through loud, erotic sucks that echo in the bathroom. "No one will see you like I do, touch you like I do, fuck you like I do."

I come then.

The force of his pounding and the meaning behind his words bring me over the edge.

Because I know, I just know they're real.

I can deny it all I want, but that doesn't mean they disappear. The same as the monster under my bed.

I shouldn't have looked. Now, I can't unsee him or pretend he's not there.

"Scream," he rasps against my mouth as he slaps my arse.

I do scream. The lust-filled sound reverberates around us like a rondo in the final round of a piano concerto.

That's when Cole empties his load inside me with a deep-throated groan.

My head drops against his chest, my fingers clinging limply to his sides and tiny tremors pulse through my legs.

For what seems like a full minute, we stand there, the water beating down on us as we're tangled around each other.

Who knew showers could get this intense?

"See? It's not hard to listen to orders," he speaks against my ear, licking and nibbling on the shell.

Reality kicks back in.

Damn me and damn him. I shove him away, causing him to chuckle as he pulls out of me and releases my throat.

Unlike yesterday, the feel of his cum only lingers a little before it's washed away by the water.

"I hate you," I murmur.

He pulls on my hair and kisses my nose. "Sure thing, Butterfly. As long as it lets you sleep at night."

Then he leaves. Water drips over his hair and hard body as his feet pad on the floor.

The moment the door clicks behind him, I release a muffled, frustrated scream in the silence of the bathroom.

EIGHTEEN

Cole

We spend the entire early evening with Sebastian and his campaign members.

We eat a meal fit for an army that Mum prepared. Sebastian considers his team a family, too. Since they're working hard for his campaign, they get to eat as family members.

A part of Sebastian's campaign focuses on bringing the classes together, even if there's a clear separation. It's a smart way to look at it. He recognises that there's no way to eradicate classes—at least, not right away—so he thinks the first step should be bringing them together.

Once they think they have enough in common, maybe then, the classes can be abolished. Not that his party will ever agree on that front, but he's only planting the seed for now.

He's a smart politician, and I do believe he'll go far. I have no doubt in my mind he'll become the next prime minister.

That means I'll be the prime minister's son while Silver is the daughter. There's no way in fuck we'll ever be able to have a public relationship.

It's part of the reason why I lost it and took her at the wedding. There was so much angry energy boiling inside me and I had to smile and take pictures and accept congratulations for something I never wanted to happen.

But like Silver, I care about Mum too much to kill her chance at happiness. She was brought up in a closed-off environment by her strict father before she was shipped off to an abusive husband that she spent years recovering from the remnants of his degradation.

Since Sebastian came into her life, she doesn't need the pills to sleep or to eat. She doesn't walk around the house like a ghost, or kiss me like a robot who feels nothing because of antidepressants.

Mum deserves this.

But that doesn't mean I'll do as Silver demands and walk away from her. It doesn't mean I'll let her slip away from between my fingers and go to some other fucker while I watch like a pussy.

She's currently sitting across from me around the conference table in Sebastian's office as the head of his PR, Frederic, goes through the family part of the campaign.

She chose the farthest seat from me, snuggling to her father's side and glaring at me every chance she gets.

I smile back, riling her up even more. After the shower, she changed into denim shorts and a black tank top that moulds to her curves. Her hair is pulled into a tight ponytail, reminding me of how I grabbed her by it while I pounded into her over and over again.

I force myself to focus on Frederic, the leader of the campaign, to prevent getting fucking hard in front of Mum and Sebastian.

Frederic is a short man with a beer belly and piercing brown eyes. He has a look that sees through things and a quick wit that fits a politician's right-hand.

When he asks for suggestions, Silver suggests posting pictures on social media, like the one she made us all take over dinner earlier.

The caption was: *Family dinner #SebastianQueensForTheWin #GoTories*

The selfie looks spontaneous. Frederic and his people are wearing their half-dishevelled clothes—mostly no jackets or ties. Mum, Silver, Sebastian, and I are in house clothes. The casual quality of it has gained a lot of attention on social media. Instantly, many online magazines picked it up with headlines like:

'Sebastian Queens' Daughter Calls Her Father's Team a Family.'

Silver might seem spontaneous, but she's taking a lot after her parents. Her upbringing has made her plot even the most casual moments.

That's why she gets irritated when things don't go as planned—such as Aiden's recent obsession with Elsa.

Or me.

The fact she can't plan me pisses her the fuck off. As it happens, I live to see that expression on her face.

"Posting too much on social media can be interpreted as attention-seeking," I say.

The light blue of her eyes snaps my way. "People want to know about the lives of those they're entrusting with their vote. If we show that Papa lives normally like them, it'll give him a good push."

"But he's not like them." I raise a brow. "He will rule over them, and if that's not in their conscious mind, it's buried in their subconscious."

"So what do you suggest?" She fists her hand by her side. "That he stays away?"

"He should be close, but not close enough that they know about every detail of his life."

"But..."

"Cole is right," Frederic interrupts. "The sense of mystery is what keeps people coming back for more—even subconsciously. You can post as usual, Silver. Your Instagram statistics are doing very well."

She purses her lips, cutting me a glare as Mum tells her she loves her Instagram account.

That may be the case, but the fact she didn't win against me, even in opinions, is turning her cheeks a faint hue of red.

That's exactly the reason why I keep doing it. I'm the only one who gets to wrench that reaction out of her.

She retrieves her phone, seeming to check a message. Her lips part. The reaction is so small, it can be interpreted in different ways.

Silver's lips part when she's surprised, aroused, or scared. The first two are out of the way because her fist is still clenched.

Is she scared? Of what? Or whom?

I need to get my hands on her phone. I did once, but it's fingerprint-protected and takes a photo, then sends it straight to her cloud when someone tries to unlock it. There's no PIN option, so I couldn't get around that.

I'll check it when she's asleep.

Frederic talks about fighting crime. There's a lunatic who's been attacking women as they jog in secluded park areas. He doesn't kill them, but he usually molests them with pens or cuts their skin. None of the victims who filed a report saw him. They were drugged by a needle and the next thing they remembered was either waking up alone or someone else finding them.

It's rare to have a serial attacker around here, so Frederic tells Sebastian about how he should offer his support to the women. Cynthia is already very active in the women associations committee, so he should make friends with her, something that Sebastian refuses and Silver's face slightly falls at hearing it.

Then Frederic moves on to talk about using Mum and Sebastian's marriage to promote to another faction of society. While everyone is busy focusing on him, I retrieve my phone and hide it low under the conference table so Derek, the driver who is currently sitting beside me, doesn't see.

And yes, even the driver plays a part in the campaign. This is almost like a battlefield where even the horses need to be placed strategically. No mistakes are allowed.

Cole: Did you hear what Frederic said? I'm always right.

I observe her facial features as soon as I hit Send. They morph from concentrated to the fired-up expression where she's ready to climb on the table and jump down my throat. Or punch it. Honestly, I wouldn't be surprised if she did both.

She decides to ignore me, thinking of herself as the better person or whatever else might be going on in her righteous, prude brain.

Not under my watch.

I'm persistently out to destroy her innocence, and it's for a reason.

Cole: That includes the fact that you fantasise about me. Admit it and I might not use it against you.

She purses her lips, her fingers flying over the keyboard.

Silver: I do not. Keep dreaming, wanker.

Cole: Do you mean to tell me you haven't been rubbing your thighs together since we got here in remembrance of me?

Her cheeks tint in a rosy colour and she grips the phone tighter.

Silver: I have not.

Cole: I saw you, though. In fact, I bet you're clenching your thighs right now. I bet you're wet, Butterfly.

Her lips part, with arousal this time, but she focuses back on Frederic, refusing to reply.

It takes everything in me not to go there, grab her by the hand, and kidnap her the fuck out of here. Since that option is out of the question, I type.

Cole: Maybe I should check. I bet if I thrust my fingers in you right now, you'd soak me like you did my dick.

Her lips tremble as she reads the text.

Silver: Stop it.

Cole: Why? Are you scared they'll find out you like being fucked by your stepbrother? That you were fucked against this same table when anyone could've walked in and witnessed you losing your virginity?

She swallows and squirms in her seat. If anyone were to pay her the slightest attention, and if she had on a light-coloured tank top, everyone would see her nipples, hard and turned on.

The fact that I can push her buttons makes me smile. Then I pretend I'm agreeing with Mum about some sort of a weekend meal.

That's the difference between me and Silver. She can't multi-task, especially when she's aroused, but I never erase my surroundings, not even when she's the only thing who matters in them.

Silver: Just shut up.

Cole: I will on one condition.

Silver: What?

Cole: End it with Aiden.

It's her turn to smirk from across the table.

Silver: I won't. What will you do about it? Fuck me? *yawn emoji*

I narrow my eyes the slightest bit, then decide to push the button she loathes the most.

Cole: Remember that pic you saw on my phone?

Her brow furrows as she reads the text, and when realisation sets in, her fist clenches harder and her manicured nails nearly crack from the way she holds her phone.

Cole: If you don't do as you're told, you'll regret it.

Silver: Screw. You.

As soon as Frederic finishes the section, I stand up. "I'm going to meet the guys."

Mum smiles. "Ronan's again?"

"Yeah."

"Have fun," Sebastian tells me.

Silver's eyes widen, but she quickly masks her reaction. She already knows that she messed up real bad.

On my way outside, I type her one last text.

Cole: I will be screwing someone. It just won't be you.

NINETEEN

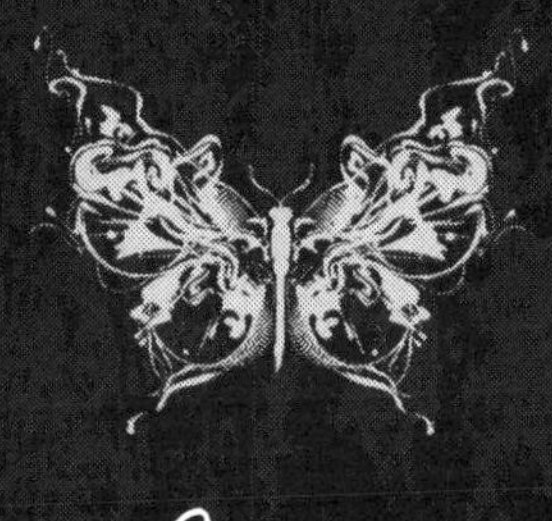

Silver

I lied.

I told Papa and Helen I was going out with Veronica and Summer. Instead, I'm at Ronan's house.

Okay, Veronica and Summer are here too, so it's not like it's a complete lie.

Papa doesn't like it when I party. He doesn't say it out loud, but he thinks it's beneath me.

It's not like I love it myself. Unlike what everyone believes, I don't like attention. Or at least, I like it on my terms, and not twenty-four-seven.

The three of us stroll through the entrance. Lars, Ronan's favourite butler, greets us by name. And yes, when Ronan's earl father isn't around, he has his butlers organise the parties for him, and he practically throws them at every chance possible.

He makes any event a reason for celebration.

Summer and Veronica each flip their hair back. I do too, not to announce my arrival, but to boost myself with some confidence—I need every drop that exists.

For that very reason, I wore my short peach-coloured Louis Vuitton dress. It stops above my knees, the slits at the front and the back giving it a provocative view while still saying 'You can't afford what's underneath this shit.'

I pulled my hair up in a ponytail and put on red lipstick, thinking of Mum's words.

Red kills them, Babydoll.

I finished the look with red nails and heels so high, they make my legs taller and my arse perfect.

Silver Queens is here to conquer.

Aiden and Cole have always been unbeatable at chess, but what they seem to have forgotten is that I also play. I plot, too.

Just because I let Cole invade my body in that brutal, unapologetic way doesn't mean he gets to step on me.

The thumping of some trendy pop music echoes in the air. RES's students dance to the beat, chugging alcohol and grinding against each other.

Some make out openly, clinging to one another as if tomorrow will be the apocalypse.

"Ew, gross," Veronica chirps loudly as we pass them by.

"Get a room, losers," Summer continues.

I stare back at the couple even after we pass them. My chest aches at the view and I shake my head refusing to think about the reason.

"Mission?" I ask them.

"Find Cole before he does something stupid." Veronica readjusts her generous cleavage.

"On it, Sil." Summer gives me an 'I'll call you' sign as we split up.

I told them I can't let Cole do anything that will hurt Papa's image. It's true—but only partially.

One, Cole would never do that. He's too careful.

Two, that's nowhere near the reason why I'm here.

I begin my hunt through the house. The problem is, Ronan's mansion is so damn huge. I get lost in it on normal days, let alone when it's full of people.

Pulling my phone out, I type.

Silver: Have you seen Cole?

The reply comes immediately.

Aiden: Since when are you so obvious about looking for him?

Silver: Answer the question.

Aiden: That would be a no. I don't like being ordered around. Try again in ten years.

Aiden: Best of luck finding him when he chooses to disappear.

I swear I'll punch Aiden one day, but that won't be today or as long as he's agreeing to be engaged to me. I'm not an idiot. I know he'll leave me in a heartbeat if he chooses to, and if that happens, I'll be completely at Cole's mercy—or the lack thereof.

At least now, he feels threatened. Now, when he thinks no one is watching, he looks at Aiden like he wants to murder him.

Cole has always gravitated towards Aiden more than Ronan or Xander. It's like an understanding of sorts. What if he's only hung up on me because Aiden has me, and once Aiden disappears from my side, he'll consider himself the winner and move along?

My chest squeezes at the thought.

Since when did I start to have Mum's mindset?

My phone vibrates with a text.

Summer: Spotted at the eastern wing fifteen minutes ago.

That doesn't help. There are, like, fifteen rooms there.

I type the fastest I ever have.

Silver: Alone?

Summer: With Jennifer from the track team.

My fingers hover over the keyboard and moisture fills my eyes.

No.

I won't allow myself to cry about this.

The moment I lift my head, my gaze collides with Adam's. He's sitting in a small lounge area with the rest of the rugby team. Those guys are popular, too. Not as much as the football team, but they have their share of girls and glory. While his team members are joking, laughing, and drinking, he's not.

A bottle of beer nestles between his fingers as he stares at me. Unblinking. Unmoving. Almost like he's been watching me that way since I came in.

My shoulder blades snap together and I swallow as I quickly cut off eye contact. It's better to pretend I didn't see him

I need out of his vicinity. Now.

I spot Xander pouring juice in his vodka bottle. Before any of the girls start ganging on him, I storm in his direction, out of Adam's view, and grab him by the arm.

He grins down at me, showing me his dimples. "Queen B, I thought this scene is beneath you with all the stupidity around? You know, alcohol and sex. Wait, is that still a taboo word? Sex, I mean."

"Shut up."

Xander laughs and it's charming. *He*'s charming. Why the hell isn't he the one I'm hung up on? Why did it have to be that wanker?

"You still won't show me your tits?"

"No."

"Tell you what, I'll give you a hundred so you make Ronan believe you showed them to me."

"Ronan tried that tactic before you and the answer is still no."

"That fucker." He appears genuinely offended.

"You need to step up your game, Xan."

"I know..." he trails off as Kim appears at the entrance plastering a shy smile on her face.

She stares between me and Xander, her chin trembles the slightest bit, which used to be her habit before crying when we were kids, then she turns around and leaves.

I bite my lower lip, my feet itching to go to her and alleviate that awkwardness of being in a party alone. But I can't. She can't get close or she'd read me. No one is allowed to read me.

"Why don't you go after her?" I ask Xander who's still watching the place she stood in, his fingers strangling the bottle.

"Why don't *you?*"

"I…can't."

"Maybe I can't either."

"You were her best friend, Xan. She needs you more than she ever needed me."

"So now you care? You didn't when you were acting like a bitch towards her."

"You aren't a saint either. She used to always brag about how you promised to never leave her and that you're her knight."

He swallows, his Adam's apple moving with the motion. "Yeah, whatever."

"What happened back then, Xan?"

"Nothing. Or maybe everything." He throws a dismissive hand and chugs down the entire vodka-juice down his throat. "What are you doing here anyway?"

The reason why I came slams to the front of my mind. "Searching for Cole. Helen needs him and can't reach him."

Lies and lies and more fucking lies.

"Oh." He blinks slowly. "Are you sure you want to interrupt him?"

"*Yes.*"

"It won't be pretty."

"Let me worry about that."

"Whatever. He's in the west wing, second room to last."

I kiss his cheek. "You're the best."

"You bet." He winks.

The only reason I don't run is because I'm not supposed to.

You never know where reporters are hiding, Silver. Always be on your best behaviour in public, Babydoll.

Mum's words are engraved in my head like a mantra.

As soon as I ascend the stairs and I'm out of everyone's view, I run all the way down the hall, ignoring both the pain from my heels and the one in my chest.

Images of that bound girl I saw on Cole's phone flash in my head like a horror film.

Stopping in front of the door, I realise that my heart hurts. So much that I feel like I'll throw it all up if I'm touched in any wrong way.

Do I really want to see what's inside? Do I want to witness it with my own eyes?

Maybe I should go back, bring out my journal and curse him in it.

And then what? Cry myself to sleep like a pathetic fool?

I won't do that. I'm not a coward. Cole Nash will never break me.

Taking a deep breath, I grab the handle and push. It's locked.

Shit. Of course it's locked. Why had I thought Cole would not think of that?

I don't leave, though. I knock.

That's what you do when you've decided to attack—you can't pull back. You have to get on with it. Finish it. *Conquer* it.

If you lose, so be it. At least you tried.

I raise my hand to knock a second time, but the door opens and my fist nearly hits Cole's chest. I'm tempted to do just that, but the shadow peeking from inside stops me.

He's still wearing the T-shirt and jeans from earlier. His face is neutral except for the small twitch at the corner of his lips. "Why, Silver, what are you doing here?"

I push him aside and barge inside. The girl, Jennifer, sits on the bed in only her lace bra and underwear. She doesn't even try to hide her nakedness.

My blood boils at seeing her. She's like me, or rather, a fake me with fake blonde hair that's filled with extensions and fake blue eyes and fake everything.

"Silver?" She stares between me and Cole, who's still standing at the door. "I thought we were going to play. What is your sister doing here?"

Sister.

Freaking sister?

"Kicking your butt out." I gather her stupid skirt and T-shirt off the floor and hand them to her. "*Out.*"

"Oh, I'm sorry." She has an annoying voice that I want to hit the mute button for. "What makes you the boss of me?"

I grab her by the arm, my nails digging into her flesh.

She whines. "Stop her, Cole."

He doesn't.

He just stands at the entrance with that blank expression that I'm sure harbours the devil and his minions.

Ignoring him, I drag Jennifer outside and throw her clothes behind her.

She picks them up, shaking her head. "No one mentioned anything about a crazy sister."

"I'm not his fucking sister!" I slam the door shut to mute her voice.

My breathing is shallow and harsh as I stand facing the door.

There. Another one out of the way.

Mum is right. Women can conquer.

"Not my fucking sister, huh?" A sinister voice whispers from behind me.

It's then I realise what I've done and that I'm all alone with Cole.

Now that I stopped whatever he was planning, I can go. I place my hand on the handle when he speaks, "Leave and I'll call Jennifer to finish what we started."

I whirl around and fold my arms over my chest. "What the hell do you think you're doing?"

"Proving that you want me, even if you don't like to admit it."

"We both know that's *not* true."

He strokes a strand of hair behind my ear, murmuring, "We both know you're a liar."

My breathing loses its regular rhythm as his hand stays beside my face.

"You dressed up for me, put on red lipstick, your fuck-me heels, and your favourite Chanel perfume." He sniffles me, and I fight the need to lean in and smell him too. "But I prefer your hair loose."

He tugs on the pin holding my blonde strands, letting them fall in cascades down my back. "You shouldn't be jealous of Jennifer."

"Stop saying that. I'm not."

"Is that why you kicked her out?"

"I kicked her out because she's fake. She's not me, okay?"

"I'm good with that."

"W-what?"

"I don't care as long as there's a resemblance." He runs his fingers through my hair. "What's it going to be, Butterfly? Take her place or should I call her back?"

"If you do that, I'll go fuck Aiden."

He laughs, but there's no humour behind it as he tugs on my hair. "We both know you won't do that."

"Do you want a video this time?"

He pulls me from the door and throws me on the bed. My gasp invades the air when my back hits the soft mattress. I swallow as I get caught in his darkened eyes.

This is the side of Cole he allows no one to see. The side where he's ready to finish lives while he's smiling.

He reaches into a drawer by the bed and retrieves several ropes. My eyes widen. Does Ronan allow him to keep things like that in his house?

"Her or you?"

I lift my chin. "She must be already gone."

"She'll come back with a simple text. What's it going to be, Silver?"

"Do you fuck them after you tie them up?" My voice trembles at the end, and I hate myself for it. I hate myself for asking the question I've been wondering about since the day I saw that picture on his phone.

He raises a brow. "You can find out after I tie you up."

"No."

"No?"

"You can't fuck me. You can just look at me and wish you had me, but you can't fuck me." I won't be one of his others. I'll be *me*. The one he can't have no matter how much he wishes to.

"I don't agree to that." Cole approaches me.

"It's my deal or no deal."

"You're going to regret that, Butterfly."

"We'll see about that."

"Remove the dress," he orders.

"You're not going to fuck me, so no."

He narrows his eyes, but he quickly masks it. "Very well, Silver. Let's do it your way."

Yes, my way.

Power buzzes through me like a high. I lie on the bed, and even though I feel a sense of control, I can't help thinking it's a fake one.

No. I *am* in control. We're doing it my way.

Cole parts my legs and secures them to the poles of the bed. The feel of his fingers against my skin is like lava. The ropes dig into my skin so I test them by wiggling my toes; they tighten around my flesh. He moves to my hands, and when I'm spread-eagled, I realise the mistake I've made.

I've left myself under his control, where he can revoke the stakes on me. Where he can decide to never untie me.

Trying not to freak out, I speak in my most composed tone, "Now what?"

"I'm not done."

He rummages through the drawer and brings out a ball gag and a blindfold. I swallow, then pretend the notion of losing all my senses doesn't scare the shit out of me.

"Do you want me to stop here, pat you on the back, and let you go?" He asks in the same mocking tone he usually uses to ask if I'm a coward. He's saying it without the words.

"I'm not a quitter," I say.

A smile curves his lips as he wraps the gag around my mouth and straps it behind my head, which he lets fall to the pillow. Almost instantly, drool forms over the rubber no matter how much I try to swallow.

Cole's sadistic smile is the last thing I see before he secures the blindfold over my eyes, plunging my world into darkness.

Losing my sight makes me super aware of everything else. Like the feel of the soft sheets beneath me, Cole's cinnamon and lime scent, the goosebumps he leaves behind as he glides his finger down my cheek.

"You fucked up, Silver." His sinister voice fills the silence of the air like doom. "You shouldn't have given me this power over you."

"Mmmm," I mumble, but the gag stops me from forming any words.

He traces my upper lip. "Do you know how much I've fantasised about having you completely at my mercy?"

Cole fantasised about me?

Oh, God. Why does that sound more wrong than the current situation?

And why do I want to look at his face as he says it?

His fingers wrap around my throat and he squeezes. It's not suffocating and nowhere near as hard as when he fucked me against the shower wall, but a full-body shudder grips me and zaps straight between my legs. It could be the helplessness, or the fact that I can't stop him if he does squeeze too tight.

"I can't fuck you, but I can play with you." His hand leaves my neck and his entire presence vanishes.

The loss registers in my chest before I can control my reaction.

Where is he? Did he leave?

What seems like hours—but could be only minutes—pass as I try to control my drooling and count the pulses in my ears.

God, why do I feel so hyperaware of everything?

"Cole..." I mumble his name around the ball gag. It comes out unintelligible.

Where is he? He put me in this situation, the least he can do is alleviate the intensity.

I feel like I'm going to explode. I've never been so helpless in my life, and the fact that Cole is the one who's witnessing it causes small bursts of adrenaline to rush through me.

Then, suddenly, his fingers grip my thighs and I try to clench them closed, but my position and the ropes keep me from making much of a difference.

Cole lifts my dress to my waist, baring my thighs to the cool air. "Stay still, Butterfly. You'll only bruise that beautiful, porcelain skin."

Beautiful.

He thinks my skin is beautiful.

Ugh, brain, seriously? His hand is sneaking up my thigh and all I can think about is that?

He cups me through my underwear and I groan. It's like I've been on fire and he's finally dousing it.

"Fuck, you're soaked." He slides my underwear as far as they'll go down my legs, and before I can focus on the brush of his fingers against the inside of my thighs, his hands are gone.

"You like it, don't you?" He circles my clit with his lean digits, making my back arch off the bed. "The fact that you're under my control, the fact that I get to do whatever I want with you without your brain meddling?"

I want to shake my head, but the sensation he's eliciting in my body turns me motionless. I just want more of it.

More.

"I'm going to taste you. For real this time." And then his mouth takes the place of his fingers, sucking on my clit. I buck off the bed as I immediately fall apart, the orgasm washing over me like a waterfall.

Oh, God.

I'm so turned on that I come by only his lips against me.

"Fuck, baby," he speaks against my clit. "I'm going to feast on you."

And he does.

I'm not even down from the first orgasm when he starts lapping at my folds.

One of his hands grips my thighs while the other slides under my dress and pinches my nipple beneath the built-in bra.

I can't stay still on the bed, my bound limbs jerking at the ropes. The fact that I'm tied up and can't see or scream adds a pleasure I never thought was possible. It's like he's stealing all my senses, all my thoughts, then thrusting them back in so they'll focus on this moment.

His tongue plunges in and out of me with a maddening ferocity, as if he's fucking me with his cock.

I scream, but it comes out muffled as I come again, my head falling sideways and my cheeks flaming.

"You're addictive, Butterfly." The rumble of his voice and his light stubble create a different type of friction against my most intimate parts. "I won't stop until you admit you belong to me. Only me."

Oh, God.

"If you want me to stop, I will. Under one condition." He

crawls atop me. "I'm going to remove the gag and you're going to moan my name."

The moment he unstraps the gag, I pretend that I'll do as he asks. I'll give him what he wants so he'll end this, but instead, I swallow my drool and say, "I hate you."

"Your choice, Silver." His voice is calm, but I can sense the darkness beneath it.

I've pissed him off, and he'll take revenge.

And maybe, just maybe, that's exactly what I want.

After he puts the gag back in place, he goes back to eating me out like an animal, a madman who can't stop.

I come again and again.

By the fourth orgasm, I think I'm dehydrating and will faint.

Cole's knees are on either side of me as he crawls atop me again and removes the gag. "Now say it."

"N-no."

"Fuck your stubbornness, Silver. Do you think I'll let you go?"

It takes all my energy, but I manage to get out, "Show me your worst, Cole."

He chuckles without humour. "You asked for it."

As he straps the gag back in place, I brace myself for more. So what if I faint? I'll never let him break me.

Then the door opens and I freeze, my heart nearly leaping out of my throat.

Oh, no. No, no, no...

If someone sees us and —

"Looks like fun. I should've been invited, considering I'm the fiancé and all."

I release a long breath at Aiden's voice. My body sags and I fight to keep my eyes open behind the blindfold. My breathing starts buzzing in my ears and I can barely register my blurry surroundings.

"Fuck off," Cole says calmly as he smooths my dress and I feel him pulling my underwear up my legs.

The fact he's hiding my nakedness from Aiden should make me grateful, but I hate him too much to feel any sort of thanks right now.

"What was that, brother-in-law?"

"Say that again and I'll murder you." It's the first time I've heard Cole issue such a direct threat.

It's like he's ready to act on his threat right here, right now.

"Can't you see what you're doing?" Aiden's voice. "She's fainting."

"That's none of your business," Cole says.

Hands pull the blindfold away and I squint at the light before I make out Aiden's expression. He's smiling down at me with contempt. "You owe me one."

"Yo," Ronan's stoned voice comes from the door. "The fuck? You have a threesome and I'm not invited?"

Cole shoos him out, and by the time he returns, Aiden is already unbinding me.

My lids flutter closed despite my attempts to keep them wide open.

I don't feel so good.

"Silver." Cole slaps my cheek. "Fuck, Silver?"

"Told you she was fainting," Aiden says. "I know you're giddy, but did you lose the Stop button?"

"You shut the fuck up." Cole focuses on me. "Silver, can you hear me?"

"I hate you," I murmur and then surrender to the darkness.

TWENTY

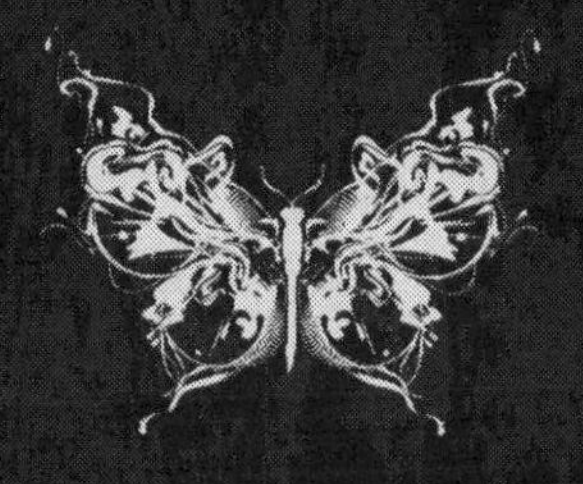

Silver

I don't know how I got home. There were voices, Aiden's and Cole's, and they were arguing about who got to drive and who got to hold me in the back of the car. I recall wanting to open my eyes so I could see them fight.

"I'm the fiancé. It goes without saying that I should hold her. You'll only be the doting brother after all, no?"

"If you don't shut the fuck up and drive, I'll call Elsa to see you acting as a *doting fiancé*."

"Fuck you, Nash."

One of them must've won, because strong arms carried me and then I was submerged in that cinnamon scent and warmth.

I'm half-dazed, floating, and I still smell him, feel him, secretly crave him.

What is wrong with me?

His fingers stroke my hair back, then his lips are on my nose, my temple. He's soothing me, whispering words I can't for the life of me make out.

And that's probably how I surrender to the darkness all over again. I'm coming in and out of it as if I can't stay in one place for too long.

When I come to again, there are different voices—Papa

and Helen. I'm on my bed; I recognise it from the flowery scent and the texture.

Cole says something about me fainting because I didn't eat much.

Dick.

He manages to slip out of everything whichever way he pleases. Not that I want anyone to know what happened. It's bad enough that we were discovered by Aiden and Ronan.

"This is all because of Cynthia's influence and all the diets." Papa sounds enraged as if he's about to barge into her flat and start a fight out of nowhere.

"Take it easy, Sebastian." Helen's quiet tone sooths him—and me—a little. She says she'll get me something to drink and it'll all be fine. That they should all calm down.

I don't open my eyes, even when some of my energy pushes back in. Facing Papa and what I've done is the last thing I want to do.

Besides, I don't want to see Cole's face. Hearing that low tenor of his voice as he tells Papa I didn't mean to starve myself and that I could be stressed is already too much to handle.

This time, I pray for unconsciousness. I want to disappear from this world and somehow wake up in one where I don't feel as if I killed a few puppies.

Helen wipes my hands with a wet cloth that smells like jasmine. The lulling sensation makes me feel serene, at peace almost. She somehow ushers Papa and Cole out, and that's when I surrender to the black behind my lids.

I dream of voices. At first it's my mum's voice telling me I'm a disappointment and that this isn't how she raised me to become.

Deep inside, I know it's the guilt talking, but I can't help the tears that stream down my cheeks. I'm that eight-year-old again wearing the princess dress with butterfly ribbons and running down the street and crying.

"Papa! Mummy! I'm so sorry. Come back please."

They don't. They continue to walk in different directions. I stand in the middle of the street, not knowing which one to follow. My feet are frozen. My heart palpitates faster with every passing second.

"Mummy! Papa!"

They don't turn around or acknowledge me. They just keep going, getting farther with each breath.

"You want help, my beautiful?"

My head snaps up at the suave voice. Adam. He's big, like in real life, and he's wearing his rugby jersey. He smiles as a trail of blood oozes from his teeth and then down his chin.

"S-stay away from me." I step back. He steps in.

The blood is now dripping down his blue jersey and his white shorts. His smile has turned red and his eyes are camouflaged in shadows.

"You're beautiful, a masterpiece." His voice turns monotone like those demons from horror films. "Come with me."

"No!" I keep walking backwards as I stare at the road my father took. "Papa!"

He stops and hope flares in my chest, but when he turns around, a scowl covers his face. "You disappointed me, Silver. You're no longer my daughter."

Then he evaporates into smoke.

"No! Papa!"

Adam and his shadow are getting closer. I'm taking larger steps back, my heart nearly skipping over itself.

I stare at the other road. "Mum! Come back, please."

She does, but she's crying. Her tears are red and her hand is wrapped around her wrist. Blood splashes from it and pools at her feet.

"Why did you do this, Babydoll?" she whispers and then drops into the pool, drowning in it.

"Muuum!"

"You only have me now." Adam reaches a black-coated hand in my direction.

I scream.

The sound is muffled when another hand wraps around me from behind and snaps my neck.

I startle awake to be greeted by the darkness in my room.

My harsh breathing echoes in the silence and my clothes stick to my back with sweat.

He's coming for me.

He'll catch me.

He will —

"Silver?"

The sound of Cole's voice instantly calms me down. I don't know how, but it does.

He hits the light switch to reveal he's been sitting on my bed. Grabbing my hand, he slowly uncurls my stiff fingers from around my necklace. I've been holding it and my chest in a death grip as if that could've saved me from the nightmare I was seeing.

No. I didn't only see that nightmare. I lived and felt it to my bones.

Papa and Mum left me.

Adam was coming for me, and then he or something else killed me.

No one was there for me.

A sob tears from my throat and it's like I've been holding on for eternity to express whatever is lurking inside me.

"Come here, Butterfly." Cole opens his arms.

I don't hesitate as I dive into them, my hands wrapping around his waist and my face disappearing into the hard muscles of his chest.

Whenever I inhale, I take in his clean scent mixed with cinnamon, and it's like my own therapy.

For long seconds, we stay there as he strokes my hair away from my forehead and rubs small circles on my back.

My breathing evens out, and just when I think I'm going back to sleep, his quiet voice surrounds me, "What happened?"

It's like a spell has been broken. Whatever halo I've been trying to pretend exists shatters all around me.

He's the reason why I had that nightmare. How the hell could I take refuge in him?

I start to push away, but Cole keeps me pinned in place by the hand on my back. Literally on my back. He has reached under my oversized T-shirt and has his palm on my bare skin.

Holy shit.

I'm suddenly fully aware that I'm completely naked under the T-shirt.

"D-did you change my clothes?" I stare up at him with horror.

"Mum did." His lips tug in a smirk. "Not that it would be something new if I saw you naked. I can even picture you right now."

I scowl at him, then fist my hand and hit him across the chest. He chuckles, the sound quiet and easy in the room.

"There you are." He strokes my hair from my forehead. "I thought I lost you for a second there."

"It was just a nightmare." A very real one at that.

I feel like it's the nightmare of my life. Since my parents' divorce, I've had similar nightmares of them leaving. After Mum's suicide attempt, I dreamt about blood for months.

However, this is the first time everything's poured out at the same time.

"Nightmares are usually a manifestation of your subconscious." Cole's fingers are still lost in my hair, and I'd purr like a kitten if I didn't want to stab him right now.

"Yeah, and my subconscious, just like my consciousness, hates you."

That nightmare was a symptom of my guilt over what I let happen with Cole. The perverted pleasure I got from it. The heart-pounding sensation I keep on getting whenever he pushes my buttons or challenges me.

It's all because of him and his damn existence that I'm spiralling out of control.

"I didn't know you were fainting," he says calmly.

"As if you would care?" This time I do pull away from him, inserting much-needed distance between us. "Your only goal is to get what you want. What if I faint or die or get hit by a freaking bus? It'll all just be a part of your sick games."

"That's *not* true."

"Not true? Give me a break, Cole. You're only doing this to me to prove you can, to be the winner as usual, to see me shatter and lose."

He interlaces our fingers and lays them across his stomach as he watches me with an unreadable expression. "Is that what you think?"

"That's what it is."

"It isn't."

"Are you telling me you would've done all this rubbish if you didn't feel threatened by Aiden?" My voice loses strength by the end, and I curse myself for being this affected with that thought.

"Stop bringing him up when you and I are talking." His tone lowers. "If it's only us, then it's going to be only about the two of us."

"You want it about the two of us? Fine. Here's a two-of-us talk… I want you to leave me the hell alone."

"See, you have a problem, Silver."

"A problem?"

"You're a liar and you're in denial. You can lie to yourself all you want, but you can't lie to me. You don't get to spy on me when I'm playing football or when I'm swimming and then pretend you don't care about me. You don't get to act territorial about me by chasing all the girls away, then decide you just did that for the family image. You don't get to come all over my fingers, my tongue, and my dick, then pretend you don't fucking want me."

Oh, God.

I swallow the lump in my throat, staring at him as if he's grown two heads.

"But those aren't the only lies you tell yourself," he continues in that infuriatingly calm tone. "You pretend you're happy for your father when you secretly hate his new marriage because you always had a fairy tale dream about your parents getting back together. You love my mum, but you feel guilty towards your mum because of it. You sometimes wish you were never born as your parents' kid, because maybe that would make you feel wholesome like other children with non-separated parents. You feel guilty for dropping your friendship with Kimberly, but you act like a bitch to her because it's your only defence mechanism to keep her away. You don't want her to see the ugly parts of you or how empty you actually feel inside. You're flawed and you hate those flaws, so you use the attitude and the looks to make everyone believe you're a perfect human they wish they could turn into.

"You keep Summer and Veronica as friends, because they're disposable and so you won't feel the pain you still do whenever you look in Kimberly's direction and realise she also left you behind and chose Elsa over you. Truth is, you're jealous of Elsa and it's not because of Aiden. You're jealous not only that she took Kim, but also that Ronan and Xander are gravitating towards her and leaving your snobbishness behind. But you can't tell them to spend time with you, because that will make you seem weak, and you loathe that more than losing all your friends who actually matter. You let guys get close, but never close enough to see who you are, *what* you are. You don't allow anyone to see your makeup-free face, because you're self-conscious about the freckles on your nose. You're also self-conscious about listening to rock music, and you do it in secret because you're worried that if Cynthia or anyone finds out you do listen to it, they'll think you don't deserve to play the piano. You —"

"Shut up!" My voice shakes, then breaks, coming out as haunted as I feel.

It's like I've listened to a distorted retelling of my life. As if someone dipped their fingers inside me and wrenched out a part of me I've always kept under lock and key.

No. Not someone.

Cole.

He once again took my choice and learnt things he has no business learning.

Considering how observant he is, I figured he knew a few things about me, but never in my wildest dreams would I have thought he delved too deep.

"Why?" he speaks casually, as if he didn't just flip my world upside down. "You don't like listening to the truth being thrown in your face? I can tell you about —"

"Stop it." I meant it as an order, but it comes out as a plea. "Just stop, Cole."

He drapes a hand around my nape and pulls me over so our foreheads connect. I gulp in harsh intakes of air, breathing him in with every inhale.

"Here's the thing, Butterfly, I *can't* stop."

"Why not?"

"Because you're my chaos, and I can't survive without chaos."

"I'm chaos?"

"The worst of all. The most beautiful of all. And you know what? You might as well be the deadliest."

My breathing chops off. "Are you ever going to let me go?"

"Are you?"

No.

The word stabs in my head as real and as gut-wrenching as that nightmare. There's no need to think about it. I know for a fact that if I saw any girl near him again, I'd plot her fall and break her to unrecognisable pieces.

But I don't say that, because truth is, I knew Cole lived for chaos. Under his calm exterior, it's the only thing he plans for. The only thing he lives day-to-day for.

He always, without doubt, loses interest once the chaos turns boring.

That's the same case for me. If I stop bringing chaos into his life and disrupting its flow in some way, he'll drop me as if I never existed.

That thought pierces my heart more than the manifestation of my subconscious in that nightmare.

If I even remotely want to have him, then I need to be his chaos.

His only chaos.

And for that, I'm letting Papa, Mum, and even Helen down. I'm free-falling to sin and I have no way to stop it.

"That's what I thought." He grins, drops a kiss on my nose, and pulls me to him again.

He lies on his back and hugs me to the crook of his body so that I'm half-laying over him.

"Cole? What are you doing?"

His eyes are already closed. "What does it look like I'm doing? I'm sleeping."

"You can't sleep here," I whisper-hiss, but when I try to get up, he pins me to his side.

"Sure I can, Butterfly. In fact, I don't like my bed. I'm going to use yours every night."

"You can't do that."

"Watch and see."

"Papa or Helen could come in."

"It's locked; they won't."

"Still —"

"Just shut your busy brain for a second," he cuts me off, sighing. "Close your eyes and sleep."

"You think it's that easy?"

"It is. I'll give you pointers to sleep better."

"Pointers?"

"Actually it's one. Dream of me."

I groan as I place my hand on his chest. Now that he's put the idea in my head, I'm so sure I will.

"I hate you," I tell him.

He smiles as his lips brush against my temple and stay there. "Not as much as you want me, Butterfly."

TWENTY-ONE

Cole

As much as Silver acts like a bitch or directs all her maliciousness towards me, she sleeps like an angel.

Literally like one.

She snuggles to my side, her nails digging into my T-shirt. I inwardly groan at the memory of her dragging them down my back. She thinks she was hurting me, when in fact, she was proving how territorial she actually is about me.

Did she really think I wouldn't notice she was leaving those marks so all the female population would see them? She was basically marking her territory.

Silver might be more low-key about her possessiveness, but it's lurking in the background, waiting to be unleashed on the world.

Her long lashes flutter on her cheeks and her lips part the slightest bit, wishing for my fingers inside them.

The loose T-shirt slides down her cleavage, outlining the pale flesh of her tit and there's a hint of her rosy nipple that's begging for my fucking mouth on it.

I slowly pull the shirt up to hide it. My dick protests, but he needs to wait. Silver might sleep like an angel, but she's a light sleeper. If I touch her, she'll wake up, and I know I won't stop if I start touching her. I have to take care of something else first.

Of course, I haven't slept. One, she's too distracting, moulding to my side like this. Two, this is one of the rarest chances I'll get to take care of unfinished business.

I could've done it in the car earlier after I made Aiden drive us while I held her in the back seat, but I was too focused on her well-being to think of anything else.

Aiden was right—I took it too far. But that's the thing about Silver, it's clear that I have no brakes when it comes to her.

That's not good.

Control is everything I have. I command situations and people before the action even plays out. I'm a director, but my sets are real and my actors are actual people.

However, when Silver showed up dressed like a fucking fantasy at my room in Ronan's house, and not only kicked out Jennifer but also took her place, I lost all common sense.

After the last text I sent her, I suspected she'd follow; I never thought she'd be that direct about it. I never thought she'd actually let me tie her down and gag her and blindfold her. Or that she'd enjoy it the way she did.

Then she pissed me off by refusing to admit she wanted it and I lost track.

I can't do that.

I need a remote control when I'm with her. Or that's what I told myself. Then I found myself sneaking into her room again.

It was a bit easier when I didn't have her. Now that she's mine, I can't stay away. Not touching her has become equivalent to physical torture.

And now, I need to know what's bothering her. No one fucks with her.

Or at least, no one but me.

Moving slowly, I retrieve her phone from the nightstand and use her forefinger's print to unlock it.

She mumbles something, but then her breathing evens out again.

Her wallpaper is a picture of the four of us from the wedding. She's hugging Sebastian's waist and I'm standing beside Mum.

I grind my teeth.

I know what she's doing. She's reminding herself every second of the day that the world sees us as siblings—even if she doesn't.

We'll see about that, my Butterfly.

I open her gallery and scroll through her recent photos. They're mostly a few selfies she took with Summer and Veronica on their way to Ronan's party.

Then I find a picture that makes me stop and click it.

It's a shot of her out of the shower, wearing a towel, her wet blonde hair falling on either side of her. It's a selfie, but her entire face isn't visible—only from the nose down.

She's trapping her lower lip under her teeth. Her towel is slightly loose around her tits to show the hickey—the same one I left above her right tit when I fucked her in the shower.

Silver took this picture right after I left. She wanted to memorise it, to store it for safekeeping.

I smile down at her. If hickeys are what she wants, I'll bathe her body with them until the entire fucking world knows she's taken. They might never know it's me, but they'll know she belongs to someone.

After sending the photo to my phone, I delete the text to myself and go to her messages, ignoring her group chat with her shallow friends. I don't have to search long to find what I'm looking for. *Unknown Number*.

My muscles tense the more I read the texts. They started years ago—three, to be exact. It was around the time she became glued to her phone, sometimes smiling, other times frowning.

The number sends texts almost daily. In most of them, he tells her she's beautiful, and in others, he'll mention details about her daily life he wouldn't know unless he watches her closely.

The Queens' mansion has high security. No one but the family members and Sebastian's team is allowed inside without supervision. And Cynthia. Somehow, Sebastian allows her free access to his house.

He hasn't sent texts about her home clothes. They're mostly about what she wears to go out. So this means he's close, but not too close.

The last text he sent was on the day of the wedding.

Unknown Number: You look beautiful today, like a rose finally deflowered. Happy eighteenth birthday. You're a woman now.

My grip tightens around the phone as my senses skyrocket to high alert.

I stare at Silver's sleeping form, at the way her fingers are gripping me close, almost as if she's afraid the same nightmare from earlier will repeat.

Her other hand clutches her butterfly necklace, the one I gave to her which she's never removed.

Silver has someone who's obsessed with her, watches her, probably masturbates to her pictures in the darkness of his room.

Someone who's slowly but surely becoming threatening.

And she's hiding it from the world.

Silver has someone who wants her chaos.

Just like me.

TWENTY-TWO

Doll Master

Do you ever get the feeling that you're so close? That one step is all it'll take for you to get it? That you've taken several steps, but the last one is the hardest?

I do. All the time.

However, it hasn't been working out so well lately. Too many eyes. Too many people. Too much security.

I need to get my doll out before it's too late.

I'll protect her. I'll bathe and wash her. I'll feed her.

And eventually, she'll realise her fate has always been with me.

She's wasted her life enough on people who don't deserve her. I do.

In fact, I always have.

I deserve her more than she deserves life.

I have to act fast because the other one is picking up on what I'm trying to do.

The plan is already in motion. I just need to get all the annoying things, called people, out of the way.

No one gets between me and my doll.

My art.

My masterpiece.

TWENTY-THREE

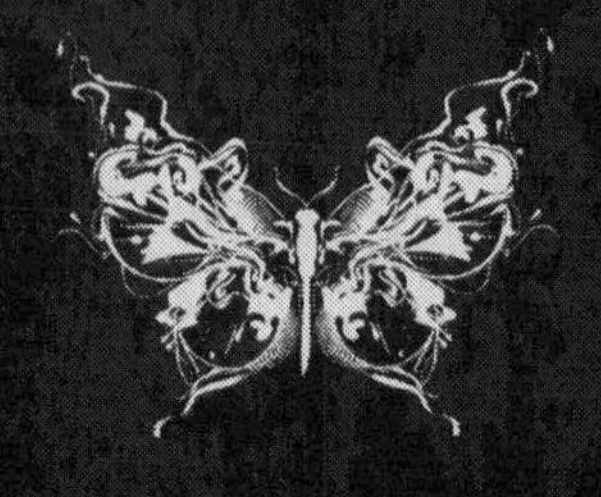

Silver

A week passes and Cole leaves me alone.

Partially, at least. He still uses every chance to get on my nerves and make me lose at everything, even if it's a debate I started.

He never backs down. I swear he lives to see me suffer.

However, he hasn't tried to have sex with me since that time in the shower. He hasn't even tried to tie me up like in Ronan's house.

Well, I *have* locked my room's door every night, but I haven't heard it being turned, which means he hasn't tried. I mean, he's the one who said he doesn't like his bed and would prefer to use mine.

Not that I'm disappointed or anything.

I wasn't even disappointed when I woke up that morning after I fell asleep in his arms and found myself alone in my bed.

I *wasn't*.

The thing is, I never felt my bed was empty until he slept in it, dwarfing me in his hold, just to disappear as if it never happened.

Why hug me to sleep if he planned to leave? Besides, how come I didn't feel him leave? I was tangled all around him. I should've sensed it when he untangled himself from me.

What would I have done if I had? It's not like I would've told him something stupid like 'stay'.

So anyway, I've been at peace. Complete peace. I've visited Mum and we've had lunches. She still seems out of sorts, but she's working and campaigning for the party. Mum does better when her head is occupied with work. Besides, she's seeing a successful French businessman, Lucien, whom she introduced me to. He appears to be fun and has an older man charisma that might actually rival my father's.

Not in my eyes, obviously, but in hers. If she introduced him to me, he's not going to be one of those guys she goes out with once and then ghosts.

This means my parents will never get back together. Not that they had any chance when they were both single.

Papa's campaign has been doing fantastic. I love reading the comments on our social pictures and how most of the people respect him even if they don't agree with him.

There are often comments about how good-looking Cole is, and asking whether he'll follow in his father's or his stepfather's footsteps. Business or politics. I want to reach out and poke their eyes out. I have comments that compliment me on my social media, but I have no idea why I become enraged when it's about Cole.

Fine, so I get worked up about everything to do with Cole. Believe me, I want to control it, to somehow get over it, but every time I lie in bed, my fingers find my pussy and I imagine him there lying beside me as I bring myself to orgasm. They never feel as intense as the ones he brings me and I always feel dirty afterwards, and yet, I repeat it every night.

I need help.

But I refuse to admit that out loud, so I focus my efforts on breaking Elsa and Aiden off.

He's starting to stray away from me and I don't like it. I need a constant backup plan and Aiden is that plan for me.

And okay, maybe I've been keeping an eye on Cole. Since his 'I know it all' speech from the other night, I've been discreet about how I act. I doubt he knows about the girls I told lies to about his dick or about how cold he is—they seem to dig the latter, so they keep coming back for more, and that's when I have to threaten them.

Sometimes, I feel guilty about it, and other times, I feel like I'm doing the world a favour and protecting those girls from the craziness that is Cole.

And no, I'm not jealous.

Then there's Aiden. When I mentioned him seeing Elsa and told him we had a deal, he brushed me off.

"And I can end the deal whenever I wish," he said. "I've had my fun, and I'm free to end it. Besides, you're a cheater, Queens."

He laughed as he passed me by. Wanker.

I'm a cheater? What about his damn sexcapades with Elsa?

Not that it matters. I know I'm holding on to a wobbly thread, but I can't simply let go.

As I head towards the school car park, there's no one in sight. I quicken my pace to my car because Cole just left, and he told Helen he'd be home late today. He doesn't have practice and Ronan isn't throwing a party tonight, so I need to figure out where he's going.

A small *tap-tap* sound comes from behind me and I freeze. My shoulder blades snap together and it's as if someone is grabbing me by the gut.

I pick up my pace and the *tap-taps* do too.

Shit.

A hand grips my shoulder. "Hey, Silver."

I gasp as I whirl around so fast, I nearly fall. That's when I come face-to-face with Adam. He stands with a hand in the pocket of his uniform trousers as he holds out something for me.

The nightmare hits me across the face again. Blood. A black hand. A —

"You dropped this." He gives me my pen that I don't remember dropping. I actually remember losing it a few days ago. I'm too detail-oriented, so I notice when I lose things.

"Thank you, Adam." I smile, taking the pen instead of calling him out on it.

If I want to escape him and his clutches, I need to pretend I don't suspect him at all.

"You know my name." He grins in a welcoming way.

Adam's grandfather from his mother's side holds a baron title and his father is an influential figure in Papa's party. He's not bad looks-wise. He has a buff physique, fit for playing rugby. His face is handsome too. His eyes, though, are usually bloodshot and he always appears as if he wants to ruin someone's life.

Last year, he made a fake confession to Kim, and when she showed up, he poured a bucket of paint on her head, then mocked her, saying, "Do you really think someone would love a fat pig like you?"

Although I make it my mission to stay away from Kim, I went to the principal about it. Adam crossed an unforgiveable line.

I should've suspected him after that.

"Of course I do." I offer him the impersonal smile I save for reporters. "We've studied together since Royal Elite Junior."

"Yeah, but I didn't know you noticed me."

"I notice everyone, Adam. Listen, I have to go. Best of luck with your game."

I'm about to leave when he places a hand on my arm. I freeze, my heartbeat escalating in my chest. "Is something wrong?"

His face turns blank, and with his bloodshot eyes, he appears like a demon rising from the earth. "He doesn't deserve you."

He smiles, and I automatically smile back, even though red alarms are blaring loud in my head.

I need to get out of here.

Now.

Trying to maintain my cool expression, I start to pull my arm away.

He squeezes it once before letting me go. "See you around, Silver."

As he turns and leaves, I jog the fastest I can to my car without actually sprinting.

Something tells me I just opened Pandora's box and I'll never be able to close it again.

The feeling doesn't go away, not even after I throw the pen out the window as soon as I'm out of the car park.

Thankfully, I do catch up to Cole. He got on the motorway.

I feel like a stalker as I make sure to keep two cars between his Jeep and my Audi.

He's hiding something. I just know it.

What if he's out to ruin the family image? What if he's going out to meet some girl and then he'll bind her and do what he did to me the other time?

I shake my head and continue my super silent, super professional stalking.

It only becomes a problem when he leaves the motorway and starts taking secondary routes. I can't keep up without being noticed and there aren't as many cars that I can hide behind.

So I wait until he takes a turn before I follow. I'm starting to feel like Sherlock—or rather, a loser policeman at a stake-out.

I slow the car as much as possible while I make the turn.

I hit the brakes and reverse back. Cole stopped in what seems like a back street. There are several German and expensive cars lined up along what appears like the rear entrance to a club—or a morgue.

There isn't even a name or an indication of what goes on in here.

Could it be some underground gambling ring? I know Xander fights in underground places with gangs and stuff. I heard him talk about it to Ronan the other time, but neither of them mentioned Cole.

Besides, violence and gambling always felt beneath him.

I park my car at the adjoining street and stay in there for a few seconds, contemplating my next move. What if the people inside are dangerous? Should I have a backup plan?

Yes, of course I should.

I pull out my phone and text Derek.

Silver: If I don't text you in half an hour, trail me to my phone's GPS.

His reply is immediate.

Derek: Yes, Miss.

Silver: And please don't tell Papa or Frederic.

Derek: Yes, Miss.

That's what I love the most about Derek. He doesn't ask questions. He just makes things happen.

Like a miracle.

Taking a deep breath, I exit my Audi and beep it locked. I turn around to pull on the handle. Mum taught me to always make sure the car is actually locked and not trust the beeping sound.

A hand wraps around my mouth from behind and I scream, but the sound is muffled as a strong body slams me against my car.

TWENTY-FOUR

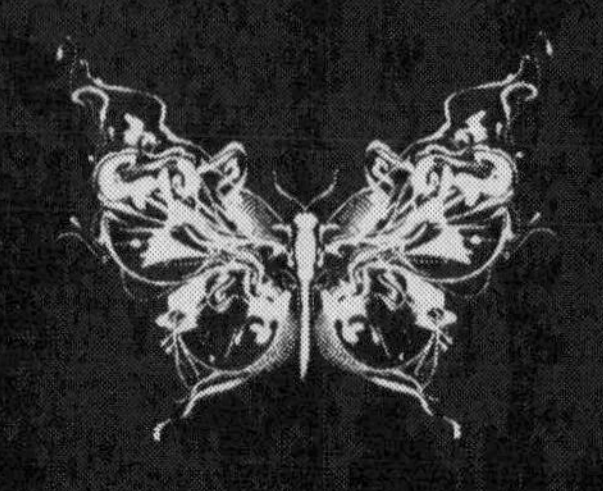

Silver

My fight mood rushes forward and I'm about to kick him, bite him, stomp on his foot, and punch him in the crotch.

But then, something happens.

His warmth.

His damn warmth mixed with cinnamon and lime.

"What did I say about giving me your back?" Cole whispers against the shell of my ear.

I release a long breath and then realise I did it against his hand. I push him away, turning around to face him.

It's worse in this position. Now his chest is close to mine and my breasts are an inch away from his shirt.

He lost the jacket and has the sleeves of his shirt rolled up to his elbows, revealing his strong, veiny forearms.

Focus, Silver.

"You scared the shit out of me." I fold my arms over my chest.

He raises a brow. "You shouldn't roam around in places that scare the shit out of you."

"And neither should you."

"This place doesn't scare me, Butterfly." He pauses, staring me up and down as if I'm a case study. "So?"

"So what?"

"Why have you been following me since I left school? Do you perhaps miss me?"

"No."

"If you say that word one more time, I'm going to fuck you right here, right now." He leans over and lowers his voice. "They have cameras on these streets."

My eyes widen, but it's not only at the prospect of being caught. It's also because of the fact that he mentioned fucking me.

Why did he have to paint that picture in my head after a whole week of depriving me of it? Is this a game?

"Or you can come with me," he offers with nonchalance. "You followed me here so you might as well see what I'm up to."

"N..." I trail off at the dark look in his green gaze.

"What was that, Butterfly?"

"Nothing." I clear my throat. "What is this place anyway?"

"Come with me and you'll find out." His voice is smooth, suave, like I imagine the devil sounded when he tempted Eve.

But he's right—not that I'll ever admit it. I'm already here, so I might as well meet the other side of Cole.

I walk ahead of him, and when he doesn't follow, I toss a glance over my shoulder. "Aren't you coming, coward?"

He throws his head back in laughter and I freeze in place. My heart thrums hard in my chest at the view of his happy face. That sound of laughter is as rare as a passing unicorn in Cole's case.

I wish I could somehow steal it and store it away for safekeeping.

The moment ends when he soon joins me and we're going through the entrance he parked his car near.

Someone who looks like a bouncer tips his chin at him, and it's then that I'm positive we're at some type of a club.

"She's with me." Cole motions at me and the bouncer just nods again. I nod back, not sure about the protocol here.

If Cole is known enough to be recognised and even given a free pass, this should mean he's somewhat of a regular.

A petite woman wearing a satin gown and a black kitty mask smiles at us. "Welcome to *La Débauche*."

Is this some sort of a costume party? If so, I'm not dressed for the occasion. I actually have the perfect Chanel dress for it. Also…

"Debauchery?" I whisper-hiss at Cole.

He ignores me and motions with his head at the girl, leading us into a room with black wallpaper and no furnishing except for a sofa and a rack with hangers full of black clothes. "Should I arrange a separate room for the Miss?"

"No, we're fine, thank you." Cole flashes her his kind smile that can melt ice.

"The show starts in ten minutes, sir."

"Arrange a private viewing session."

"Yes, sir." The girl bows and closes the door behind her.

Yes, sir? What the hell was that all about?

I take a quick sweep of the black gowns and trousers in their plastic bags. There are also masks like the one the girl was wearing.

The reality of things slowly filters in. The secrecy, the club's name, the girl's clothes and her words. I swing back towards Cole. "Did you bring me to a sex club?"

"You came on your own. You can leave at any time." He unbuttons his shirt. "But you're not a coward, are you?"

Damn it. He always gets me with that argument.

"What are you doing?" I murmur as he shrugs off his shirt, revealing his taut muscles, before he moves on to his belt.

"There's a dress code for this place." A smirk tugs his lips. "Why are you shy when you've already seen me naked, Butterfly?"

"I-I'm not."

"Are you perhaps eager because it's been some time since you've seen me naked?"

"You wish."

He yanks his trousers and boxers down in one go, standing fully unclothed before me. I force myself to stare at his face to stop myself from ogling his dick and the way it's pointing at me.

Cole takes his time to retrieve black trousers and pulls them up his legs. I stand there, crossing my arms and pretending I'm irritated, when in fact, I'm boiling from the inside out.

I shouldn't be in a place like this, and most of all, I shouldn't steal peeks at his nakedness.

"If you're not going to leave, you should change."

"I'm not a coward, but I'm not going to have sex in front of a bunch of strangers—even with the masks on."

"It'll be the other way around."

"What?"

"I don't come here to have sex. I come here to watch it."

Oh.

I bite my lower lip. "And…um…did you bring someone else in the past?"

He approaches me in slow, predatory steps. When he's in front of me, he places two fingers under my chin and lifts it up. "You're my first."

"And last," I speak before I even realise it. It's out now; I'm not taking it back.

"Last?"

"I'll stay if you promise I'm the only one you'll bring here."

"Deal, but you have to come with me all the time."

I gulp, nodding. This is a drastic step, but the thought of him bringing another girl here makes me delirious. I'll never allow that.

"And you'll let me dress you."

"Cole!"

"That's my condition."

"Fine, but there'll be no sex while you're dressing me." I stop, then quickly blurt, "Oral included."

He smirks as he removes my jacket. "You're learning."

Not that I have a choice. I need to keep up with his devious mind. Cole is like the tiny clauses you don't see in a contract. It's as if he searches for opportunities to turn people's decisions against them.

I pretend to be unaffected as he loosens the ribbon from around my neck and unbuttons my uniform's shirt. He takes his sweet time with it. He's watching my face the entire time, probably hoping for me to squirm or something.

In his dreams.

"How do you know about this place anyway?" I try to focus on something else other than his fingers as they brush over my skin.

When my shirt falls open, I let it drop from my arms and join the jacket on the hanger.

"It was my father's."

Oh. "Helen knows about it?"

"She just knows it's one of the gazillion businesses William Nash owned. She doesn't get too involved."

"And…you do?" My voice turns breathy as he opens the zipper on my skirt and it falls down my shaking legs.

I step out of it and let him pick it up and hang it.

"I do. That's why you were allowed in. There's a brutal screening process of applicants here. You have to be eighteen and older, but not just any legally aged person can walk through those doors. They have to be investigated and proven to have both the financial support and power to be accepted. It was my father's way of gaining dirt on the dark and depraved minds of most of his board of directors. So he didn't want many other outsiders around, unless he could collect some dirt on them, too. I get a free pass for being the heir. Aren't you glad you know me?"

I can't concentrate on his words, because his fingers are

running over my stomach. He stands up again so that his front is nearly glued to mine and he reaches behind my back to unhook my bra.

As it drops to the floor, he groans. "I love your tits. I've loved them since you refused to show them to me when we were fourteen. But do you know what I love more?"

I couldn't speak even if I tried, so I keep my mouth shut. He takes my breasts in his hands and runs his thumbs against the hard tips over and over until my breathing is chopped to bloody pieces.

"Marking them." His lips latch on to the flesh of my left breast where he left a hickey the other day. It's like he wants to mark the same place.

He sucks and nibbles, and it's almost as if he's fingering or fucking me. My thighs clench and my heartbeat picks up.

At this rate, I'll beg him to take me right here and now. But I'll never do that.

I put my hands on his shoulders. "I said, n-no sex."

"Sex is when I'm pounding into you until you scream, Butterfly." His eyes glint as he pulls away from my tortured breast. "I'm only touching you ever so gently."

Wanker.

His fingers hook on either side of my underwear and he slides them down my legs, leaving goosebumps in their wake. I step out of them mindlessly.

"I don't have to touch you to know you're turned on. I can smell you." He bunches the underwear in his hand and sniffs them.

My lips part and I feel as if someone's doused me in fire.

That's not supposed to be so hot, right?

"S-stop it," I murmur.

"You didn't make a rule about this. You don't get to now." He watches me and my toes curl as I resist the urge to cross my arms.

It doesn't matter how many times he sees me naked. I always feel this sense of intimidation.

I shouldn't, and if it were anyone else, I probably wouldn't, but it's Cole.

Anything sex-related has happened with him. My first kiss, and second and third and all, actually. My first fantasy, my first sex dream, my first masturbation, my first oral, and losing my virginity.

All of it.

He's like the definition of sex in my mind and it's nearly impossible to shed away that image.

He yanks the black dress off the hanger and throws it over my head. I help him, letting the sleeveless outfit fall to my knees, confused about his reaction. It's almost as if he doesn't want to see me naked. But why? He's the one who wanted to undress me.

Instead of placing the underwear with the rest of my clothes, he shoves it in his trousers' pocket.

"Hey!" I protest. "That's mine."

"Not anymore."

"Are you a pervert?"

He places a kiss on my nose, his voice teasing. "I've always been a pervert for you, Butterfly. It's not my fault you're only just figuring it out."

I shove him away and he chuckles as he puts on the mask before strapping the other around my eyes.

Cole stops to watch me, then he nods with approval before interlacing my hand with his.

I start to pull away, but he keeps me in place. "No one will know who we are. This is a private room only I use. Besides, the masks."

He's right. Now that I study him closely, he's a bit unrecognisable and I must be too with the help of the mask.

After we make our way out of the room, Cole leads me

down a long hall with dim red lighting and black flowery wallpaper. A few black chandeliers hang from the ceiling.

I'd never tell Cole this, but I'm glad he's holding my hand. I feel like demons will jump from the walls and devour us.

Or me, to be more specific. Cole would probably make friends with them.

We stop in front of a door. "This is a viewing room."

"What does that mean?" I whisper, not sure why it feels like I should.

"It means we get to watch a couple have sex through a one-way window. They know they're being watched, but they don't know who's watching and they can't see us."

"People *like* that?"

"You'd be surprised, Butterfly."

He clutches the handle.

"Wait." I swallow. "I don't want to watch with other people."

"Why? Are you shy?"

"I just don't want to. That's like watching porn."

"Porn is fake. This isn't. Besides, I usually watch alone anyway. Perks of being the heir."

I release a breath and let him guide me inside.

"Ah, they've already started."

I don't focus on what Cole is saying because I'm trying to adjust to the darkness in this room. It's almost like a film theatre, but the seats are sofas—bigger in size and fewer in number.

Instead of a screen, there's a large window that gives a view of another room. It has the same black wallpaper. There's a table in the middle on which a petite brunette is tied, spread-eagled, and a bigger black man is fucking her.

The sound of their groans and moans echo around us like a symphony.

Oh. God.

My thighs clench at the power of his thrusts. He looks as if he's hurting her with his size, and yet, she's screaming, "More... faster...harder!"

I watched porn once. Just that one time after being intrigued by all the praise Ronan and Xander have for it. I wasn't impressed. It seemed staged and fake and all the sounds they made turned me off.

This isn't porn. This is...humans at their truest, rawest, most real form.

I don't realise I've stopped walking until Cole tugs me by the hand to sit me beside him on one of the plush chairs.

"Isn't it beautiful?" His hot breaths cause my skin tingle as he whispers into my ear.

I want to call him sick for having such voyeuristic tendencies, but I'm too enthralled by the scene to build my defences.

The ecstasy on both their faces grips me by the gut and I couldn't look away even if I tried.

My nipples tighten against the dress, and although the cloth isn't a harsh material, it feels like they'll cut through it.

A strong hand clutches my thigh and I jolt as a zap of arousal flashes through me. I slowly focus on Cole, on his shadowed face and cut lethal, yet handsome, features. My eyes are so droopy, I'm not sure he can see them.

"You want me to relieve that ache, Butterfly?" His hand sneaks under my dress, up my thigh, electrifying my skin along the way.

I part my legs. I don't know why, but I just do. It could be the different setting or the couple's groans, how he's pounding into her and owning her.

I want that.

But not with just anyone. Only Cole.

"You know, it's not obligatory to remove your underwear around here," he muses.

"Then why did you?" I'm so turned on, my voice turns breathy.

"Because it gives me straight access to this." He dips two fingers against my folds and I moan, my heart lurching in my chest. "You want me to finger you?"

I open my legs farther in answer.

"You'll have to do something better than that."

I stare at the couple, then at Cole's arm disappearing under my dress, and I don't think as I slip my hand into his trousers and grip his thick, hard cock.

A groan slips free from Cole's throat as I work him up and down. I've never done this before. I'm being driven by pure instinct and the need for more. I do it fast and strong because I suspect Cole wants everything intense.

"Ah, fuck." His voice is filled with lust as he circles my clit. "I love your hand on me, but you have to say the word for me so I'll finger you, Butterfly."

The woman's moans echo louder as she screams, "Harder... harder...harder!"

"C-Cole, please..." I pick up my pace and he finally thrusts his fingers inside me.

Three in one go.

I nearly collapse from the sensation alone. I don't stop working him up and down as he pounds into me in a rhythm that matches the man's.

I can't see their faces because of the masks, but I can feel the passion, the raw claiming, and I moan with her. I arch my back like her.

My whimpers fill the space as I focus not only on my pleasure, but also on Cole's. I'm going to bring him to orgasm, I'm going to be the reason...

He hooks his fingers inside me and teases my clit. I fall apart around him, my thighs shaking and my moan mixing with his groan.

At first, I think he has come too, but he didn't. He stands up with my hand still around his cock. "Put me in your mouth."

My thighs shake at the image as I part my lips and guide him inside. I can't stop staring at him, at the rippling of his chest muscles and his God-like presence. I only glide my tongue over him a few times before he comes all over my tongue. His cum drips down my lips and chin.

He gathers it with his thumb, his eyes shining with raw possessiveness as he smears it over my lips.

"Hmm. You look marked and mine."

Cole thrusts his fingers inside my mouth and makes me swallow every drop. He licks his fingers that were inside me at the same time.

As I stare up at him, I realise two things.

One, he's ruined me for anyone else.

Two, I'm screwed.

TWENTY-FIVE

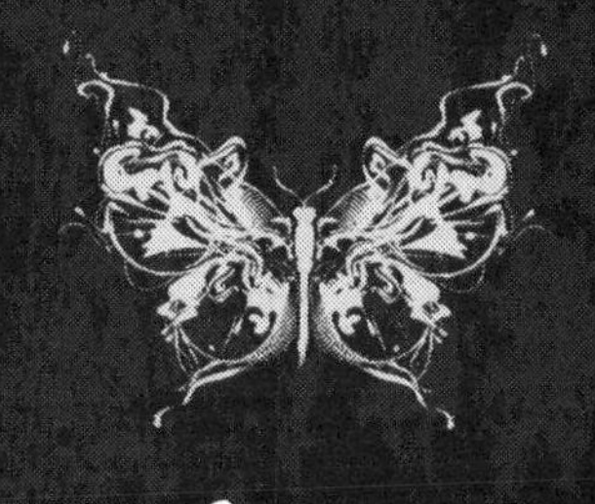

Silver

We don't go home right away.

Instead, Cole says we have to eat. When Derek showed because I might have forgotten to text him, Cole told him to find a way to drive my car back as I was going with him.

All the way, he's been trying to finger me under my skirt because I stole my underwear from his trousers when we changed back. I've been slapping his hand away, to no avail.

But that's the thing about Cole. He never gives up. If he wants something, he doesn't stop.

Not even close.

We end up at a secluded restaurant that's not on the main street. It's like he knows all the hidden areas, which shouldn't be a surprise, considering the secret life he's leading through that club.

My core still tingles in remembrance of that couple, of their ecstasy—and mine.

It's an experience I'll never be able to forget. I never knew I liked voyeurism until I came undone around Cole's fingers. He's slowly but surely ruining me.

The restaurant is Italian and has wooden decor with tables and chairs in the shape of trees. We settle across from each other and order wood-fired pizza. I placed an extra order of French fries with mayonnaise.

If I'm getting in the calories, might as well go all in. I'm too hungry after that experience in the club and I can't trick my stomach into accepting salad.

"We could've eaten at home." I study my French-manicured nails to not look at Cole.

Even though he's reading from a book, he's also been watching me in this intense way that turns me into a self-conscious fool. I'm not the type to get self-conscious. Ever.

Except when this wanker is involved.

"I'm hungry." His voice drops with clear seduction.

"Well, you could've eaten at home."

"I can't wait until home."

"Stop it," I hiss, watching our surroundings. Thankfully, the place isn't full at this time.

"Stop what? I'm only saying I'm hungry."

"I know what you're thinking, okay?"

"I doubt it."

"You're recalling what just happened in the club." I lower my voice. "Don't you dare bring it up to anyone."

"Yes, Miss Prim and Proper," he mocks. "But that's not what I was thinking about."

"No?"

"I was actually picturing eating you instead of the food we ordered."

My lips part and I gulp, the image stabbing through my mind without permission. Just like Cole. He's toying with my brain in more ways than one.

I clear my throat, opting to change the subject. "Is that book as depressing as the other book from that author?"

He's reading *Kafka on the Shore* by Haruki Murakami. When I was fourteen, I read *Norwegian Wood* by the same author after that quote. I spent the night crying with how the story turned out. I loved the hero so much, and I hated how fate dealt with his emotions.

"Haruki Murakami's books aren't depressing. They're unique."

Cole doesn't read much fiction, if at all. He usually has his head buried in philosophy and psychological books. I know he loves Helen's books, but they're mostly psychological crime thrillers. I take a pause when he says he loves a certain fiction author who doesn't write in the psychological vein.

"What's so unique about them?" I ask.

"It's his imagery. He wrenches you out of the world and he offers riddles without solutions, letting the readers solve them themselves. Everyone's interpretation is different from the other. It's art."

I see it then. The gleam in his eyes whenever he reads said books. Cole likes the challenge and being immersed in something so deep, he forgets his surroundings. It's his own form of chaos.

"Most find it frustrating, of course, and bombard the publisher with endless questions."

"I think it's beautiful."

He lifts his head, raising a brow. "You do?"

"Yes, I think many people need surrealism and to be able to find their own solutions." *Like Cole.*

I like Haruki for producing books that keep Cole invested and excited. I even forgive him for breaking my heart in *Norwegian Wood*.

The waitress brings us our pizzas and bats her lashes at him. Bitch.

"Uh, excuse me?" I force a fake smile. "I ordered mayonnaise with my French fries."

"Coming right up." She smiles one final time. I glare at her back as she leaves and even when she brings it to me.

"The service here sucks," I grumble.

Cole smiles.

"What are you smiling at?"

"Your jealousy can be adorable, Butterfly."

"I'm *not* jealous." I take my first bite of pizza and burn my tongue. *Ow!*

Cole slides the cup of cola to me, still smiling in that blood-boiling way.

"I'm not jealous," I insist, taking a slurp of the drink. "I just wanted my mayonnaise."

"Who even eats mayonnaise with French fries when they have pizza?"

"I do." I stuff one in my mouth.

He leans over the table so his face is mere inches away and he reaches a hand to me. I freeze. What is he doing? Is he going to kiss me in public or something?

Oh, God.

Cole wipes my nose and then sits back down. "You had something there."

I release a long breath, not knowing if I should feel relieved or disappointed. What the hell is wrong with me?

We spend the rest of the meal in easy conversation about other fiction authors Cole reads, which aren't a lot. Aside from Haruki Murakami, there's Helen, John Le Carré, Honoré de Balzac, Kahlil Gibran, and Lee Child.

Speaking of, Cole says there's a new release by Lee Child that he needs to buy, so we swing by the bookstore after we leave the restaurant. He teases me all the way about my mayonnaise eating habit. He really does enjoy getting on my nerves.

So in the bookstore, I load the dice against him. "Hey, nerd. You're supposed to live your life, not spend it stuck in books."

"I have both." He retrieves a few copies from the new release shelf. "I have fun *and* read books."

"No, you don't."

"Didn't I just prove it in the club, Butterfly?"

Touché.

"You're still a nerd, Cole."

"You still find it hot. I know you watch me when I read." He winks. "I watch you when I read, too. Especially in the pool."

"Pervert."

"I think we've already established that. But so are you."

"I'm not."

"You are for me."

"I said I'm *not*."

Fine, so maybe I watch him a little. Okay, whenever I get the chance. Now that we live under the same roof, I can't actually take my eyes off him, even if I try.

He runs his fingers over the books as he moves from one row to another and I swallow, recalling those same lean fingers inside me not so long ago.

I follow him like a lost puppy, unable to cut eye contact with his hand.

"Remembering something?" He smirks at me.

"No." I stare at the opposite shelf.

"What did I say about that word?"

"What are you going to do about it?" I place a hand on my hip. "Fuck me in the middle of the bookstore?"

He stalks towards me, and before I know it, he cages my nape with his hand. He pushes me until my back hits the shelf, then he slams his free hand by my head. His lips inch forward until they're a breath away from mine, as if he's about to kiss me.

"You think I wouldn't do it?"

"C-Cole, stop." I search our surroundings, my heart beating fast.

"Don't test me, Silver. I'm barely able to keep my fucking hands off you in public."

"Silver and Cole sitting in a tree, K-I-S-S-I-N-G!" Ronan appears in front of us with a huge grin, grabbing Xan by the shoulder.

I push away from Cole, my cheeks flaming.

"By all means." Xander motions between us. "Continue. We don't even need popcorn."

"There's nothing to continue," I say in a cool tone. Mum says even if you're caught, act as if you did nothing wrong.

"Yeah, right, Queen B," Xander huffs.

"*Merde*!" Ronan's face falls. "Does this mean we can't see your tits anymore?"

"Don't mention them again or life as you know it will be over, Astor." Cole's face and voice remain calm, but the menace is clear in his eyes. "You too, Knight."

"I knew you were the jealous type," Xan grins, showing his dimples.

"You knew?" Ronan hits his shoulder.

"I suspected they were making babies at your house the other night."

My face heats. "We weren't!"

"Yes, you were." Xander waggles his brows. "Aiden had to help drive you home after one of Cole's sessions."

"Under my damn roof and yet I'm the last to know? *Again*?" Ronan speaks in a dramatic voice. "I feel left out again. Now I have to see my therapist. Are you going to pay for his bill or take responsibility for the emotional damage? Are you? That's what I thought. Why am I always left out of the cool stuff, *merde*?"

"It's not what it seems." I try to keep my calm façade, but I'm trapped with no way out.

Cole holds his paperbacks nonchalantly to his side. "It is."

"Cole!" I glare at him.

"I knew it." Xan extends his hand to Ronan. "Hand me my hundred."

"Wait." Ronan stares between us. "Are you fucking? Because that's the only thing I bet on."

"No!" I shriek.

"Yes. Every night," Cole says in a cool tone.

"Fuck *me*." Xan shows his dimples. "Make that two hundred, Ron."

"You get five, *mon ami*. This shit is interesting." Ronan grins. "So you, like, do it under your parents' roof at night? Or in the shower? Are you open to threesomes?"

A scream fights to be set free, but I bottle it inside and storm past them. Ronan calls behind me that he's only here to get his mother a new book and won't bother us, but I'm not hearing him.

It isn't until I'm in front of Cole's Jeep that I realise I don't have my freaking car because the arsehole sent it away.

He comes right after me and as soon as he opens the door, I climb inside, arms folded and nostrils flaring.

"What's gotten your knickers in a twist?" he asks casually after getting behind the steering wheel.

"Are you acting as if you don't know? Why the hell would you tell Xander and Ronan about...about... You know!"

"Us. It's called *us*." His voice turns edgy. "And they at least need to know you belong to me. It's not like they'll tell anyone."

"There is no us, Cole. Stop fooling yourself."

He angles his body in my direction and I push back against the seat, expecting him to do something—not sure what, but he can't kiss me here where everyone can see us.

Instead of touching me, he pulls the seatbelt and straps me in. "There *is* an us. In fact, that's the only thing that exists. The sooner you stop fighting that, the better for you."

He tugs on my hair—hard—before he settles back in place. I pretend he's not there on the ride home. Or I try to anyway. I've never managed to succeed at that.

As soon as we're inside, Papa and Helen greet us for dinner.

"I'm glad you're getting along," Helen says.

"Your meal was well received," Papa adds.

"Meal?" I ask, staring between them.

Helen shows me an article.

'Sebastian's Family: The Future'

There's a sneaky picture taken of me and Cole while we were eating and smiling. It was when I got the mayonnaise on my nose.

I return Papa's welcoming expression, even though I die a little inside.

I make sure to stay away from Cole for the rest of the evening. No sitting near him or across from him. No looking at him during Frederic's briefing. When it's time for bed, I lock my door and hide under my sheets, barely holding in the tears.

I dial Mum and she picks up after the second ring.

"Mum..."

"What is it, honey?" Her voice is weak but concerned.

"I just miss you."

"Oh, Babydoll. I miss you, too." She sniffles.

"Mum, are you crying?"

"I miss you. I miss home. I even miss Sebastian. What is wrong with me?"

I sit up, my heart racing. "Mum, are you drinking?"

"No. I'm watching *The Notebook* and hating my life."

"How many times have you watched that one? I thought you hated romantic films."

"I do." She pauses. "Is he happy with her?"

I swallow, but I choose to lessen the blow. "I'm not sure."

"He is. You just don't want to hurt me." She releases a breath. "I'll be better, Babydoll. I promise."

"Mum, if you still care about Papa, why did you guys get a divorce?"

"I do *not* care about him. Your father will realise his mistake with Helen and beg me to be with him, and do you know what I will tell him? No. Besides, I have Lucien."

"You're the most beautiful woman I know, Mum. Any man is lucky to have you."

"What's the point if I can't have the only one for me?" She releases a sigh. "Anyway, tell me about your day."

We talk for a few more minutes about school and piano. After she hangs up, I keep thinking about what she said.

What's the point if I can't have the only one for me?

Really, what's the point?

I'm about to switch off the bedside lamp when a shadow appears at the balcony. There's a rustle of the curtains before someone barges inside.

My mouth opens to scream, but then I make out Cole.

He's in simple grey cotton trousers and a white T-shirt, but he appears like a model in those home shoots.

"What the hell is wrong with you?" I pant. "What are you doing here?"

"Sleeping."

"Get out. I locked the door for a reason."

"The locked door can't keep me away. Besides, why do you think I chose the room next to yours? I always come through the balcony. I have to keep my door locked, too, in case Mum comes to check on me."

"Is there anything you don't think through?"

"You." He dives beside me under the covers and holds me close to him. His chestnut strands fall haphazardly across his head.

"M-me?"

"You're the only thing I've never been able to think through."

My breath shortens, but I whisper, "Because I'm your chaos?"

"Because you're the reason I look forward to new days." His hand slips under my oversized shirt. "Mmm. Nothing. You're on the naughty list this year."

"I'm not."

"Yes, you are. My naughty girl." He yanks his trousers down and I bite my lip as he aligns the tip of his cock with my entrance. "I'm going to fuck you like that man did that woman today. It's going to be hard and ruthless, and you're going to moan my name."

My limbs liquefy and I'm about to moan from the assault of his words alone.

I don't get to reply as Cole slams inside me in one merciless go.

And then he keeps his promise.

TWENTY-SIX

Cole

There are right days and wrong days.

Today is the latter.

I know the right days—or rather, I discovered them over the past couple of weeks.

Right days start with Silver's face opposite mine before I wake her up with my tongue inside her cunt, and her muffling her screams into the pillow so no one hears.

Right days include leaving hickeys all over her tits and stomach and even her neck, then spying on her as she secretly stares at them in the mirror with a smile.

Those days include sneaking behind everyone's backs whenever we have dinner, and fucking her against the bathroom's counter until her orgasm face is the only thing visible in the mirror.

Those days can also be spent in the club, where we watch people have sex until she becomes so hot and bothered and starts to touch me. Where I'm fucking her then and there until my name comes out of her mouth in a stifled moan.

Right days end with me slipping into her room and fucking her before hugging her to sleep, only to wake her up in the middle of the night to fuck her again.

That's the problem with Silver... It's impossible to get

enough of her. I have no pause or stop button when it comes to her. The moment I think I'm done, she'll moan in her sleep or absentmindedly stroke my chest, and all I want to do is own her again.

The resistance never really withers away from her. It doesn't matter that she comes undone around me, or that she still goes behind my back to threaten any girl who comes close to me. After every time I take her, every single orgasm, and every single kiss, she doesn't fail to murmur that she hates me.

Her body might open to me willingly and without any resistance, but she still has her heart and mind under lock and key.

On right days, I couldn't give a fuck about that. The only thing that matters is that she's mine. So what if no one knows? I'm still the only one she comes for, begs for, and whose name she moans.

I'm the only one who sees the hickeys and the only one who puts them there. I'm the only one who witnesses the rolling of her eyes and the 'O' on her lips when she orgasms. The only one who feels the shaking of her legs around me and hears that small satisfied noise she makes when she's spent.

But on wrong days, like today, I want to grab her by the throat and kidnap her the fuck out of here.

Out of this city. This country. This world.

Since we're at school and have many witnesses, I can't actually do that. So I watch her like I always have.

When we're here, Silver pretends I don't exist as she goes on about her day. I've told her a thousand times over that the more she acts like a bitch towards me or anyone else—the more she fakes her life—the harder I'll fuck her that night.

I think she's doing it on purpose. Her eyes will shine with both excitement and fear whenever I corner her, then she'll flip her hair and tell me she's not scared of me.

She is sometimes. Or she's probably scared of the depth of her desire for me.

Whenever I sneak into her room at night and find her in one of those oversized T-shirts, she jumps in bed, realising just how much she's fucked.

I tie her down most of the time, and she comes harder than any other type of sex.

As soon as we finish practice, Silver decides to have a one-on-one with Aiden near the pitch.

Recently, after Elsa nearly drowned in the pool, she broke it off with Aiden. Silver is using that chance to stake her claim again, and Aiden is doing it to make Elsa jealous and go back to him.

Silver's smile is fake at best. I know her genuine smiles, and they're usually reserved for her parents and home. She offers them whenever she compliments Mum's food, or when she kisses her dad good morning and tells him she loves him.

They also come out when she sleeps wrapped around me. But she'll never admit that.

At every reminder that we're siblings, she physically pushes away from me. If she's sitting across from me, she'll squirm. If she's somehow beside me—which is rare as hell—she'll inch away.

The fact that I can't be with her in public used to be fine at the beginning. I used to like knowing that she's a bitch on the outside but turns into a willing submissive whenever I touch her. That I'm the only one who sees that side of her.

On wrong days, like fucking today, it isn't fine.

Aiden can be with her, can touch her, can even fucking marry her and get everyone's blessings. The fact that I can't has been worsening the chaos that's been in my head since they got engaged when we were fifteen.

It's not like I can say to Mum, 'Hey, you got your fun with Sebastian, now leave him.'

Not only is that selfish, but I also care too much about Mum's well-being to ever do that to her.

Doesn't mean I don't think about it.

"Whoa. Look at them go." Ronan clutches my shoulder as I stand by the bench and pretend to drink from a water bottle.

Resisting the urge to glare at him, I feign nonchalance. "Look at who?"

"What?" Xander runs towards us, panting. "Who? Drama?"

"Captain is pretending he doesn't care about King and Silver."

Why should I? They're both playing a game. But I don't say that in front of these two fuckers or they'll use it as a chance to think I care.

"I don't think Silver likes King." Xander shrugs. Finally, someone seeing the truth. "I don't think she likes or cares about anyone, actually. Everyone calls Elsa Frozen, but Silver is pure metal."

She's not. She does care. Silver calls her mum five times a day and makes sure her dad stays hydrated and Mum stays focused whenever she has a deadline. She watches Kim's disintegration from afar with a sad expression that she wipes away before anyone can see it.

The reason Silver seems like an uncaring, self-centred bitch is because she doesn't show her concern. She considers it a weakness and does everything to smother it.

"Nonsense." Ronan points at himself. "She likes me."

"She likes no one," Xander says.

"Except for *moi*." Ronan grins. "Everyone likes me."

"Not me," I taunt.

"Me neither most of the time," Xan agrees.

"Fuck you both, *connards*. I'm really filing a report for neglect." Ronan switches to a dramatic tone. "My abandonment issues are coming back to me. I need therapy."

Xan raises a brow. "Party tonight?"

"Fuck yes." Then Ronan goes on about the ladies who

will be available to him and how he'll forget our betrayal with them.

I tune him out, even though I still get the gist of his words.

All I can focus on is the look in Silver's bright blue eyes. The way they lighten under the hint of the sun. The way they sparkle with excitement whenever her father wins a poll, or Derek hands her the bag of mini Snickers bars she still uses as comfort food.

Or when I step into her room every night.

Look at me, I speak to her in my head. *Not him. Fucking look at me.*

I stand there for a few seconds, counting, waiting for the moment she realises she's not supposed to be talking to Aiden.

That I'll find her in Ronan's party, drag her to that room where I first tied her, and do it again.

I know that's exactly why she's putting on this show. She loves the thrill, the slight fear, and even the forbidden aspect of it. She gets wet when I ask her if she's scared someone will walk in.

But the fact she's not looking at me, not even a glance, is fucking with my head.

It doesn't help that this is the most wrong day of all.

She, of all people, should know that.

I leave Ronan and Xander in the middle of their usual bickering, take a quick shower, and head to my Jeep.

Instead of going to Sebastian's house, I drive back home.

My original home that Mum still keeps.

I go straight to where my mind has been living for the past ten years. I drop my messenger bag on the chaise lounge and stand at the edge of the pool, placing both hands in my trousers' pockets.

The water is blue; I know that. But all I see is red. Deep, dark red and blank eyes and a hand.

Ever since that night, I haven't been able to swim in this

pool. I swim in other pools, and I never imagine their colours changing.

This one is different.

Even now, the water is turning a murky red. A hand will come out from there. He'll gurgle words.

I still don't remember the last words he said. Which is ironic for someone with an excellent memory.

Were they even words?

I do remember the first part, though. I'll never forget it. Maybe that's why I can't recall the rest.

You're a monster.

My monster of a father called *me* a monster. How ironic is that?

Not ironic enough apparently, because I can't get it out of my mind. It's like an old, distorted disc that plays in my head on repeat.

I can't forget the blood or the hand or the gurgled words he said before he stopped speaking altogether.

Today is the anniversary of William Nash's death. Ten years later, I'm still standing at the edge of the pool as if I'm that small kid.

I still wonder why I extended a hand to get him out.

Why I didn't want him to drown, even though he deserved it.

I still wonder why I didn't scream and yell and cry when I couldn't reach him. When he floated in the bloody water. Why did I turn around and leave? That's not how kids my age should respond to seeing their father drowning in his own blood.

I should've gone to Mum. I should've at least had a reaction.

I didn't.

It was…nothingness. It's there, but you don't feel it, see it, or smell it.

Slender arms wrap around my waist from behind. Her flowery perfume envelops me as her pale, manicured hands grab each other at my stomach.

For a second, I close my eyes and cut my connection with the bloody water.

Silver is my chaos. She's the first person I saw after all that blood, and for that reason alone, she's associated with it.

She's not supposed to be my calm. And yet, when her head falls on my back and her warmth mingles with mine, I realise she's the only calm I've ever had in my life. Even books don't compare—and that says something.

Silver is the beauty and the ugliness.

The calm and the chaos.

"How did you get in?" I don't attempt to face her.

"I asked Helen for the code. I figured you'd come back home for the anniversary." Her voice catches. "I wanted to tell you this at the funeral, but you were being mean, so I didn't."

"Tell me what?"

"I'm so sorry for your loss, Cole. You were too young to lose a parent."

"Or maybe I was old enough to realise it's better I lost that parent."

She lifts her head from my back but doesn't release me. "What do you mean?"

"My father was abusive. He hit me and Mum, especially Mum, whenever he was drunk."

"Oh. I didn't know that."

"No one did. Mum and I are great actors." I don't know why I'm telling her this—her, of all people. It must be because it's a wrong fucking day. I get weird on wrong days.

"I don't think you wanted him dead, though." Her voice softens.

"Maybe I did."

"If you did, you wouldn't come to stand here on every anniversary."

"How do you know that?"

Silence. Her hands tighten around me, but she doesn't answer.

I untangle them and spin around to face her. "You've been watching me?"

She's staring at the ground, kicking imaginary pebbles. "Maybe."

I lift her chin with two fingers until her huge blue eyes are trapped with mine. "What makes you think I come here to pay tribute? Maybe it's because I feel guilty."

"It doesn't look like guilt." Her voice is gentle, emotional. "It looks like you want to grieve but can't. It was the same at the funeral, right?"

I have no words to say, so I remain quiet, letting her interpretation soak in. How could she know me so well?

"It's a black day to me, too, Cole. My parents decided to split up on this day ten years ago. People say it gets better, but it never has. I still feel that loss and it hurts, but I grieved. Why don't you try it?"

How can you try something you've never felt? I don't even know what grief means.

A crazy idea hits me and I voice it before thinking about it. "Jump with me, Butterfly."

"Jump with you where?"

"In the pool."

"Now?" She stares between me and the water. "But it's freezing."

"Are you a coward?"

"No."

"Then do it."

"Fine —"

Before she can finish her reply, I grab her by the arm and we both jump. The splash of the water mixes with Silver's gasp before we go under.

Down...

In blood.

The water is blood.

Red engulfs me in his clutches. A black hand pulls at my ankle, yanking me to the bottom. I don't fight it. I can't. If I do, he won't let me go. If I do, he'll just grab me tighter. He'll tell me I'm a monster and that I should —

Two hands touch my cheeks—soft, tender hands—and guide me to the surface.

Silver.

Her golden hair is wet, sticking to her temples, and her frantic, bright eyes search mine. Her palms are still around my cheeks as her body moulds to mine under the water. Only our heads are on the surface level.

The water's still bloody, but it's slowly returning to that blue colour. There's no hand pulling me under into nowhere.

"What is wrong with you? You scared the shit out of me, Cole." She pants. "Are you okay?"

I wrap my hand around her nape and take claim of her lips. I kiss her in gratefulness. I consume her as my form of thanks.

Silver wrenched me from the water, not only now, but also ten years ago.

My chaos.

My damnation.

TWENTY-SEVEN

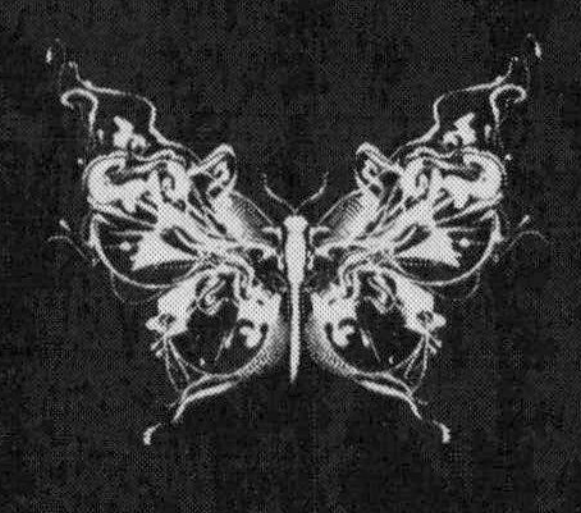

Silver

"I'm off!" I run down the steps, juggling my bag and the containers.

"Darling," Helen calls after me, carrying my thermos. "You forgot the tea you made."

"Oh, right. Thanks, Helen. You're the best." I hug her and slap a loud kiss on her cheek.

I feel like a cheater whenever I'm with Helen or with Mum. Why can't I have both mothers?

She waves at me as I step out of the house. "Be careful, darling."

"And you go write." I usher her inside. "Deadlines, Helen. Deadlines."

She smiles, joy sparkling in her eyes. "I'm going, I'm going. You're worse than my agent."

I wave at her again, grinning as I place my overnight bag, the thermos, and the food I spent the entire morning making—or rather, helping Helen make—in the passenger seat of my car.

When I'm about to head to the driver side, Papa's car comes to a slow halt near mine. Derek gets out to open the back door, but Papa beats him to it.

Running to him, I wrap my arms around his waist. "Papa, have you had a successful party meeting?"

"Aside from Cynthia challenging every point I suggested?" He strokes my hair. "Sure."

"I'm sorry."

"That's just her and she'll never change. I'm starting to think she's double-crossing us using the Labour Party."

"You know she'd never do that. Your principles run in her veins."

"Only when I don't voice them." He watches me. "Are you going over to hers?"

I nod slowly. "I'm spending the weekend."

"Do you have to? You can always stay. There are no custody laws that we need to obey now that you're an adult."

"She'll just end up coming here."

"Let her," he says in a dispassionate tone. "We can continue the debate."

"Papa." I stroke his jacket. "I want to spend time with her. She's my mum."

There might have been times in the past when I disliked her choices and her decisions and what she turned me into, but as I grew up, and after I saw her in that tub, I realised just how fragile Mum actually is. Deep down, she's being this strict with me because she doesn't want me to end up as a shell like her, no matter how proud she is that I look like her.

"I understand." Papa kisses my temple. "Do you know why she's been grumpier than usual lately?"

"I don't know." Mum would kill me if I said something to him about her personal life.

That day she slit her wrist, she made me swear not to humiliate her and said that she'd do it again if I disrupted our oath. I cried as I begged her to go to the hospital. She didn't, because that would have humiliated her and put her name in the headlines.

I watched her suture herself by following online tutorials. I'm pretty sure she had an infection, but she self-medicated with antibiotics and tranquilisers. She did everything herself and refused to have any medical staff take a look at her.

Since then, she wears thick watches to hide the scar.

"Is it because of that French businessman she's seeing?" Papa raises an eyebrow. "Poor bastard. Maybe I should warn him that she'll challenge him every step of the way and eventually suck the life out of him."

"Papa, no. Lucien is great. They actually get along."

"They do, huh?"

"Yeah." I stop myself before saying, 'They don't fight like you two', and instead I tell him, "You just take care of Helen, okay? She's on a deadline."

"Fine." He kisses my temple again. "Have fun. Though I doubt Cynthia will let you in the midst of nagging about everything."

Shaking my head, I kiss him on the cheek and wave at Derek before I get in my car.

On my way out, I watch the entrance to the house, searching for that familiar black car. Not that Cole comes home this soon.

He has late practice before the game tonight.

Ever since the day of his dad's anniversary a few weeks ago, something has changed between us.

I can't put my finger on it, but I feel it in the way he watches me, the way he seizes every chance to kidnap me somewhere out of view, yank my skirt up, and fuck me.

It's as if he can't get enough of me. And the more he does that, I can't seem to get enough of him either. It's like I'm caught in a maze with no way out.

He still sneaks into my room every night, no exceptions. He still takes me to that club. My favourite part about it isn't the watching—though I love that—it's the fact that we wear masks where no one can tell who we are.

At first, I looked over my shoulder, expecting someone to recognise us, but that anxiety withered away with time.

In *La Débauche*, I get to touch Cole and even let him kiss

me in front of other people without worrying that we'll be on the headlines the following day.

If anything, Cole recognises most of the people we watch. Even though they wear masks, he sometimes plays a quiz with me to guess that politician's/influential figure's/CEO's name.

The game is simple—with every wrong guess, he gets something from me. Since I always lose, I usually end up against one of the sofas as he eats me out or fucks me until my voice turns hoarse.

Needless to say, all of Cole's games lead back to sex. Seriously. He comes up with all sorts of schemes that result in me naked and splayed out or tied up.

If he's sick and I secretly love the devious ways he takes me, what does that make me?

I guess we'll never know, because I would never tell him I enjoy what he's doing to me. It's not about him and me; it's about Papa, Mum, Helen, Frederic—who would kill me if Papa doesn't—and the world, basically.

Cole and I are in a particular category and we simply can't jump to another one.

As much as I'm careful so no one picks up on our relationship in public, I always feel like maybe someone will. Maybe someone will notice the way I absentmindedly watch him when he's practising, or when he's reading alone in the school's garden.

Maybe someone will know I don't shoo all those girls away because of the family image, but because the idea of him touching anyone else makes me a red bull.

It's hard for me to show a facet of myself when, on the inside, I'm scratching at it, wanting to rip it away and be set free. That part of me wants to let Cole kiss me in public, to call him mine in front of the world while giving them the middle finger.

But that part is an idiot.

That's not how the world works—especially not the one we live in.

This won't only ruin our future, but also our parents,' and for that reason alone, I know whatever Cole and I have will never last.

It's a fling.

An adventure.

And like any adventure, there will come a day when it'll eventually end.

Something in my chest constricts at that thought, but I shake my head, pushing it away.

He'll get passive-aggressive today. He always is whenever I spend nights with Mum.

She hasn't been doing that well lately, so I'm visiting, even if it's not the weekend.

Truth is, I'm not really that selfless. While I do it to make sure she's fine, I also do it to take time out from Cole.

Sometimes, it gets too raw and too…much. Sometimes, when I wake up and don't find him beside me, tears come out of nowhere.

And that's not okay. That's not how flings are supposed to work.

So I detox at Mum's.

It's useless, though. The moment I go back and he takes out all the lost nights on my body, it's like I've never been away.

My phone dings. I smile at Mum's impatience. She must be asking if I'm there yet. For the third time in the past half an hour.

My smile falls when I read the text.

Unknown Number: You look so enticing in that short pink dress.

I swallow, my heartbeat picking up speed as the silence—and the emptiness—of the underground car park registers.

Does this mean he's here? Or did he follow me from home?

Since I became almost sure it's Adam, I blocked the

number. A few days later, I had a text from another unknown number saying I can't escape him.

So I asked Frederic to change my number a week ago, pretending some reporters have it and are bothering me.

I could've done it myself, but that would mean I'd have to register the new number with my personal details. Papa's campaign team have special security measures to keep all our personal information classified.

Frederic immediately got it for me, and I thought I'd be done with Adam's stalking habits.

The text in front of me is proof that it's not over.

How the hell did he get my number? Sure, his father is a member of the party, but he wouldn't possibly ask Papa for it, right?

Deep breaths. You can do this, Silver.

I can keep it to myself until after Papa wins the elections. Then I'll tell Frederic all about Adam.

It's not only the creepy, stalkerish texts but also the way he keeps watching me at school. I pretend I don't notice how he follows me around, or how he glares at anyone who gets in my way.

When he greets me good morning, I greet him back because his type can't and shouldn't be provoked.

Grabbing my bag, I open the car door, only for it to hit something—or rather, *someone*. I gasp as Adam appears right in front of me. He's wearing jeans and a simple black T-shirt, a smile grazing his lips.

My first thought is that I need to run.

Right now.

I pull on the door's handle, but my rapidity and strength fail against his.

He grabs the door and leans in so he's blocking my exit and caging me within the confines of my own car.

"Hey, Silver." He smiles, showing me his teeth.

I plaster on my own fake smile. "Hey, Adam. What are you doing here?"

"My uncle lives here. Such a small world, huh?"

"Yeah." I pretend to gather my things.

"Who are you visiting?"

I can't tell him I'm here for my mum. I don't want this psycho to know where my mother lives, but at the same time, I need to get myself out of this situation without being suspicious. "I'm meeting with friends."

"Anyone I know?"

"Just Aiden and the guys."

"I see."

Still smiling, I motion at the way he's blocking me. "Uh, excuse me?"

He doesn't move. Not even an inch.

My heart is about to stop beating. What if he has other plans instead of letting me go?

Maybe I should call for help or Cole?

"Sure." Adam moves away, still holding the door open.

I release a breath as I step out, carrying my bag and the food containers. "Thank you."

He closes the door for me, his smile sinister at best. "No, thank *you*, Silver."

I offer him a nod and walk as fast as I can down the car park without actually running. I keep peeking over my shoulder, expecting Adam to be following me.

My only relief is when one of Mum's neighbours exits his car and uses the lift with me.

On the way up, I can't erase the disturbing look on Adam's face from my brain. Or the fact that the first person I thought about when it came to getting help was Cole.

I would've hit my head if my hands weren't full.

Then I recall Adam's reason for being here. He said he was visiting his uncle, but he didn't come up.

In Mum's building, you can't go up unless you have the floor's code.

Besides, I know all the residents in this building from when Frederic was screening them prior to Papa's campaign. There's no one with the last name Herran in the tenants' list.

Of course, Adam could've meant an uncle from his mother's side, but there's only a slim chance of that.

I throw him and that thought at the back of my mind as I step out of the lift and go into Mum's flat.

She squeezes me in a hug as soon as I'm inside, and I close my eyes, breathing her scent in.

Safe.

It feels safe to be here.

She pushes away, staring at what I've brought. "What are those?"

"Food and my special tea."

Mum scowls, folding her arms. She's wearing a blue satin gown and a robe. Her hair is wet, which means she recently came out of the shower. "Helen made them?"

"She just gave me pointers."

"Yeah, right. You're as hopeless as me when it comes to cooking." She scoffs. "Sebastian must be *delighted* to have a wife who can cook. Good for him."

"Come on, Mum. It's just food."

"Helen must think I'm a charity case that she can make food for."

"That's not true. She only helped when she saw me struggling."

"Saint Helen." She rolls her eyes. "I'm telling you, she's a snake underneath it all."

"Mum!"

"Whatever." She hugs me again. "Don't let her take you away from me, too, Babydoll."

"You're my mum. No one will take me away from you."

"That's my girl."

"Does that mean you'll eat it?" I ask hopefully.

"I'm only drinking the tea you made." She strolls to the living area. "I'm on a diet, anyway."

I place the containers in the refrigerator for when she gets hungry. Mum has so much pride, it's insane.

Papa, too, I guess. That's why they're always at each other's throats.

I pour us each a cup of tea and join her on the sofa. She's watching *The Notebook*. Again.

"Mum, seriously?"

"What?" She takes the mug from me. "Romance in films and fiction is much better than real life."

"You're the one who told me it's all lies." I settle beside her.

"That's why it's better than real life."

I run my finger over the hem of the cup. "How's it going with Lucien?"

"Fine," she says in a dispassionate tone.

"Mum, are you even trying?"

"Of course I am. Lucien isn't a loser like the others. We talk a lot and he's not intimidated by my brain."

"That's great, right?"

"Uh-huh. He wants to take me to France."

"Why don't you go? It'll be so romantic."

"What was I just saying? Romance doesn't exist in real life, Babydoll. Anyway, I'll think about it." She faces me. "Now, tell me about you."

"M-me?"

She smiles in a sly way. "Don't think I haven't noticed the way your features have brightened up lately."

"T-they haven't!" My cheeks are so heated, they're about to explode.

"Oh yes, they have." She narrows her eyes. "It's not even Jonathan's son, is it? My daughter is a man slayer."

"Mum!"

"What? You're with two men at the same time and you get to choose which one is best. As long as you end up marrying Aiden, all is good."

I swallow at that. Not only is Aiden so caught up in Elsa that he's physically unable to see anyone but her, but there's also no way I'd marry him.

The sole reason I'm still keeping up with the engagement is because of the camouflage and Papa's campaign.

"Don't let it consume you." Mum strokes my hair off my forehead. "You're the only one who'll suffer."

I abandon the cup on the table, wrap my arms around her waist, and hide my face against her chest. "What if it's too late, Mum?"

"Oh, Babydoll." She places the mug on the table and hugs me. "Why did you have to repeat my mistakes?"

I'm not repeating her mistakes.

I'm going one step further.

I'm making it so much worse.

Mum falls asleep on the sofa after drinking two glasses of wine. I cover her with a blanket and take away Papa's campaign plan from between her fingers.

It's the same one he presented to the party today—the one she criticised harshly. She said it can be better.

I kiss her on the temple and then clean the dishes before retreating to my room in Mum's flat.

She decorated everything to make it like the one I have back home. Only, this one doesn't have a balcony from which 'someone' can sneak in.

Pulling out one of my oversized T-shirts, I put it on and

go commando. In the past, I used to wear knickers, but since Cole has become a constant part of my nights, I've developed the habit of wearing nothing underneath.

It's…liberating.

I retrieve my phone and scroll through Instagram. Elites lost today because Xander and Aiden were too distracted.

Ronan posted a selfie with the other three horsemen a few hours ago—right before the game started. Cole stands in the back as Xander clutches him and Aiden by the shoulders.

He's not smiling or scowling. It's his default face. I zoom in on him and my heart does that same little flutter that happens whenever I look at him.

My fingers trail to my necklace and I close my eyes for a brief second, imagining him coming through the non-existent balcony and jumping me on the bed.

Is it healthy that I miss him when I just saw him this morning?

My phone pings and I startle, my eyes flying open.

If my heart could spill to the ground, it would right about now.

A text from Cole. It's almost as if he's telepathic and knows exactly when I'm thinking about him.

Cole: I'm in your room. You aren't.

My breathing hitches as I type.

Silver: What are you doing in my room?

Cole: What I do every night, Butterfly. Getting my dose of you.

An involuntary smile grazes my lips.

Silver: But I'm not there.

Cole: Your sheets are. Your smell is. Even your underwear drawer.

Silver: Don't you dare look in there!

Cole: Already did. Do you honestly think there's something of yours that I haven't already looked through?

Silver: You're such a pervert.

Cole: Admit it, you're turned on thinking about me lying naked in your bed as I jerk one off to you.

I wasn't, but now I am.

I can't get the image of Cole touching himself on my bed out of my head. My nipples strain against my T-shirt and I readjust it, only for them to ache more.

Still, I type the lie.

Silver: I'm not.

Cole: How come I don't believe you?

Silver: I don't care what you believe.

I type with shaky fingers as my other hand disappears between my legs and I let my head fall back against the pillow.

My fingers circle my clit and I muffle my moan with my teeth as I slip two digits inside me, pretending it's him sneaking into my room again.

Cole: You know what I think, Butterfly? I think you're wet and you're aching to touch yourself. That is, if you aren't already. You'll imagine it's me like you did in the shower. You'll think of your fingers as my cock and you'll thrust hard and deep, wishing it was me.

My moans echo in the air as I let the phone fall to the side and pinch my nipples under my T-shirt. The moment I run my fingers over the hickeys he left there, I come.

"C-Cole..." I moan his name in the silence of the room as a sigh falls from me.

I'm still panting as I grip my phone again.

Cole: Touch yourself all you like, but we both know it won't be as satisfying as when I'm there.

The arrogant bastard. He's right, though. It's nothing, intensity-wise.

I hate it when he's right.

Cole: Come back early tomorrow. I miss you, Butterfly.

I miss you, too.

I allow my brain that thought as I fall asleep, hugging the phone to my chest.

TWENTY-EIGHT

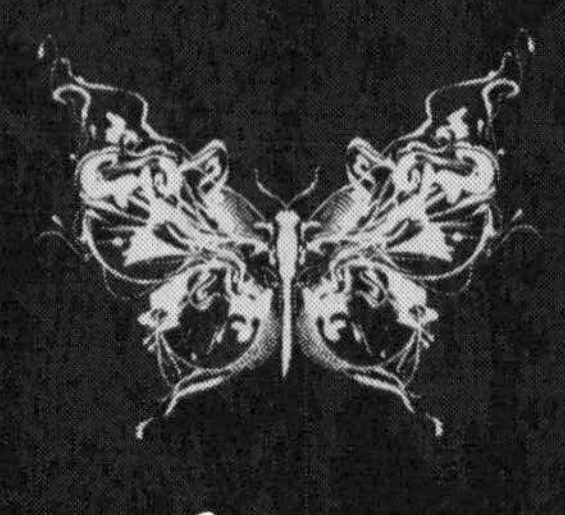

Silver

Nausea.

It's the second day I wake up feeling it in the span of a week.

I felt it a few days ago when I was preparing the food with Helen before I went to Mum's. Then yesterday, when Summer made me smell the new perfume her mum got her.

Today, too.

That's when I had a look at my calendar. My period is two days late.

It shouldn't be a big deal since I've always had a non-regular period.

Besides, I've been stressed about Papa's campaign, Mum's mental state, and keeping the whole thing I have with Cole a secret. I lose a few months of my life every day because of stressing out and even take tranquilisers.

That's what I tell myself.

That's what I keep chanting in my head during piano practice or even when I notice Adam too close to the girls' restroom soon after I come out of it.

I tell myself I'm on the pill. I first started taking them to regulate my cycle. After I became sexually active, and with Cole not using a freaking condom, I took them religiously.

Not once have I missed a pill.

"Now, remember, the pill is ninety-nine per cent effective, and only if you don't miss taking any." My GP's words have been playing in my head on a loop for days now.

Yesterday was the day I started freaking out.

Yesterday was the day I read horror stories from women who also trusted birth control pills and got pregnant.

So last night, I pretended to be asleep when Cole snuck into my room. It didn't stop him from hugging me from behind, wrapping himself around me.

I couldn't sleep.

All I could focus on was his hand on my stomach as he slept.

My stomach.

I'm not stupid. I know that I can't pretend to be asleep every night. Not only will Cole see straight through me, but he'll also confront me. He'll pick up on my mood changes.

And then what?

What if this nausea and the need to throw up isn't normal? What if the pill has failed me and I fail myself and my parents and everyone else?

That's off the table.

I stay in my car across from the pharmacy, wearing my huge sunglasses and watching my surroundings as if expecting a reporter to jump me.

I can almost imagine the headlines:

'Spotted: Sebastian Queens and Cynthia Davis's Daughter at a Pharmacy, Buying a Pregnancy Test.'

'Scandal: Sebastian Queens and Cynthia Davis's Daughter is Pregnant Before Marriage. The Father is her Stepbrother.'

I nearly throw up at that thought.

No.

I drive out from in front of the pharmacy and head to school, listening to my playlist with the volume turned all the way up.

My nerves are on the verge of spilling to the ground by the time I finish my first class. Cole keeps watching me, and I know, I just know he'll pick up on it.

I have to do something.

For the rest of the day, I bide my time practising the piano in the most distracted way possible while forming my plan.

I wait until the end of the football practice to make my first move. For the first time in ever, Elsa isn't with Aiden. Ronan mentioned something about how she was going to meet them in Aiden's house so they could watch the game together.

Perfect.

I'm at the car park, standing by Aiden's Ferrari. As expected, he comes out first, his hair still damp and his messenger bag slung carelessly over his shoulder. He hasn't even bothered with wearing the jacket.

He's like that when it comes to Elsa. Since she's meeting him at his house, he's skipping unimportant steps so he can get to her faster.

He dismisses me with an impatient hand. "Get out of my way, Queens."

"I think I'm pregnant."

He pauses his dismissal game and narrows his eyes on me before he returns back to his poker face. "Congratulations. I'll send gifts. I won't offer babysitting services, though."

"I'm not kidding."

"And I honestly can't give two fucks. You made this mess. Clean it up."

"What mess?" Cole's voice rips me out of the moment like doom.

"Make a sound when you approach, damn it." I glare at him.

"Why?" He tilts his head to the side. God, I hate how good he looks fresh out of a shower, his wet chestnut strands falling over his forehead and his lips a bit redder. "You have a secret with King?"

I lift my chin. "Maybe I do."

Aiden grabs me by the shoulders and pushes me into Cole's embrace. "Here, your mess. You're welcome."

He gets into his car before starting the engine. I try to go after him, but a strong hand at my waist pins me in place.

Cole stands behind me, his front glued to my back and his hand wrapped around my middle. He whispers in low, frightening words against my ear, "What the fuck do you think you're doing?"

I gulp, but my mouth is dry, so it doesn't soothe the thing lodged in my throat. "We're at school. Let me go."

"Not until you tell me what the fuck is going on with you? First, you pretend you're asleep. Then, you don't have breakfast with us. And now, you're running after Aiden?"

He picked up on all of that.

Of course he did. Cole is perceptive to a fault. That's why I need to get the hell out of this before he figures out the rest.

I have no idea how he'll react, but I know whatever it is, I won't like it.

So I need to take things into my own hands.

I force my voice into its most neutral tone. "I decided to announce my engagement with Aiden for publicity. Uncle Jonathan thinks it's a great idea."

He does. It's always been one of the things he's insisted on since the engagement started.

I wait for Cole's reaction, brace myself for his wrath, but his calm response takes me by complete surprise. "Why?"

"What do you mean, *why?*"

He's still speaking against my ear and every word out of his mouth injects a shiver straight up my spine. "You're not doing it for the publicity alone, so why don't you cut the bollocks and tell me the real reason behind it."

"You." I whirl around to face him. "It's so I can get rid of you."

Hot scorching emotions whirl inside me and I feel like crying, like screaming.

Cole laughs. The sound is strong and hollow, making me stiffen.

"You're so cute to think you can get rid of me." He grips me harshly by the chin. "You should know already that the harder you push, the meaner I turn. The louder you say you hate me, the more ruthless I become about owning that hate. It doesn't matter which game you play. You can even invent a new game, but I'll learn it and still bring you to your knees in front of me. So tell me, Silver, do you honestly think you can ever win against me?"

No.

The answer is loud and clear in my head, but I also know I have to win this one.

I have to push Cole away.

"This time, I will." I jut my chin in his hold. "Now, if you'll excuse me, I need to catch up to my fiancé."

His grip tightens until I wince, but I don't push away or cut off eye contact.

For a second, we're suspended in time, almost as if we're the only people on the face of the earth. My skin prickles and goosebumps erupt on my arms. Something tells me it's not because of the cold.

The moment ends abruptly when Cole releases me.

Wait. He's letting me go?

"If you follow Aiden and play this game, you won't like how I'll react."

Despite my tries not to be affected, tremors erupt on my skin at his softly-spoken words.

I know, without doubt, he'll make good on his promise, and while my shoulder blades are pulling together with ominous feelings, I won't give in.

I turn around and go to my car.

It doesn't take me long to arrive at Aiden's house.

It's raining heavily by the time I park beside his Ferrari right after he comes out of it. I don't bother with an umbrella as I block his way to the entrance.

The King mansion has always felt a bit gothic. It could be because of the sad angel statues pouring water in the fountain. They gave me weird sensations when I was a child.

Ronan, Xander, and Cole pass us on their way inside.

The latter doesn't even spare me a glance. He already issued his threat. Now he'll wait to see how I act before he reacts.

He's so calculating, it drives me freaking insane.

Aiden tries to push me towards him again, but Cole tells him to clean up his own mess, then follows Ronan and Xander into the house.

"In case you didn't realise, this is called stalking." Aiden places a hand in his wet trousers' pocket.

"As if you'd know anything about stalking."

"What is that supposed to mean?"

I curse myself for letting that slip in front of Aiden. Here's to hoping he says nothing to Cole, because I really have no state of mind to deal with all of this nonsense right now.

Folding my arms over my chest, I pin him with a stare. "I wasn't done talking in the car park."

"Well, I was." He turns to leave.

"I'll tell Elsa the baby is yours."

Aiden stops and whirls around, his left eye twitching.

I've got him.

That's the only reaction Aiden hasn't been able to school over the years. It means he's pissed off and will be out to destroy lives.

A risk I'm willing to take.

"It's not," he says.

"She doesn't know that."

"The DNA test will prove it isn't."

"Seriously?"

"*Seriously.*"

"You really believe someone like Elsa will wait until the DNA test comes out? She doesn't trust you as it is and will leave you in a heartbeat the moment I plant the idea that you're my baby's father in her head."

Silence.

I've got him again. Someone like Aiden, who's never allowed himself a weakness, now has one.

It's not like I'll hurt him in any way. He has the complete ability to help me, but because he's a psycho, he won't do it unless I have something that benefits him. Or, in this case, doesn't ruin him.

"What the fuck do you want?" he asks.

"Don't break it off with me, and if any of this gets out, you'll announce you're the father."

"That would be a no. I'm not taking responsibility for Nash's bastard."

"Hey! Say that again and I'll kill you."

"Sorry, Mama Bear," he mocks. "But that negates the whole point of this deal. Remember Elsa?"

"I'm saying, *just in case*. I'll find a solution."

He tilts his head. "I can search for underground clinics and *poof*. Gone. No one will know the future prime minister's daughter aborted."

I place a protective hand over my stomach, my lips trembling. But...but I don't want that.

"We'll go with my plan." I stand my ground.

"I'll only agree to not breaking the engagement off. *For now*. Everything else is a no."

"Aiden!"

"Silver." He smiles.

"I'll tell Elsa."

"And leave yourself with no options?"

"If I'm going down, I'm taking you with me."

"If you speak to Elsa, I'll speak to Nash. Believe me, you can't win against me on this. Ruin me and I'll ruin you back."

"Remember our deal back then?"

"What deal?"

"You said you'd fix it." I stomp. "You promised, King."

"I promised you fuck all."

"But you said —"

"I said nothing. You assumed everything yourself. The game was fun while it lasted, but I'm not playing anymore."

"You're not playing?" I huff. "So when it's to your benefit, you're all in, but when it's not, you just drop out?"

"Exactly. Smarten up, Queens. All of what you're doing is a temporary solution."

"That's none of your fucking business." I grind my teeth. "I knew you'd change your mind because of that little bitch."

He pushes into me and I step back so I'm glued against my car. "Watch it. If you call her that one more time, I won't let you be, Queens."

"You can't do fuck to me, King. You know why? Because Uncle Jonathan is on my side."

His left eye twitches again.

Aiden will help me. I don't care what I have to do so that he'll cover this up for me, but he will.

I can't ruin my parents' careers. But the thought of killing my own flesh and blood makes me want to vomit my guts out.

"How about Nash, then?" Aiden asks in a neutral voice. "Whose side do you think he's on? If he finds out about your little games, who do you think he'll lash out at? Spoiler alert. It won't be me."

My heartbeat skyrockets at the thought that Cole will find out and make me give up the baby. "Don't you dare, King."

"Then fucking disappear, Queens. This is your final warning. If you threaten what's mine, I'll destroy you until there's nothing left for Nash to pick up."

Tears barge into my eyes despite my tries to keep them at bay. I've never felt more alone in my entire life than I do right now.

There was that day my parents announced their divorce, but I had Cole back then—or I like to think I did.

Now, not only do I not have him, but he'll also throw me away the first chance he gets.

I'm about to threaten Aiden some more when a hand pushes him away.

Elsa.

I didn't sense her presence when she crept up on us. She did it the other time, too, when she grabbed me by the hair.

I'm about to shoo her away when she slams her fist into my face. Hard.

A burning sensation explodes in my cheek and I raise a trembling hand to clutch it, not sure what just happened. I know Elsa hates me because she's possessive of Aiden, but to hit me?

No one hits me. I'm Silver Queens.

Right when I'm about to hit her back, she punches me in the abdomen. Something inside me moves. Or maybe it's my imagination, but I feel it.

I shriek, wrapping both my arms around my midsection.

My baby.

No.

My baby.

I can't focus on anything but that thought. Did something happen to my baby?

Elsa grips me by the collar of my shirt. "I told you to stay the fuck away from what's mine!"

And then she punches me again. I push her away, keeping a hand around my midsection. But Elsa is like a bull who's not only out to hit me but also out to kill me.

Oh, God.

My baby.

He's going to die.

I bend over, trying to shield my stomach while pushing blindly at Elsa.

No, no, no…

Aiden grabs Elsa by the arm and pulls her back against his chest.

She fights him off, trying to get to me again. I've fallen to the ground, trembling and still holding my stomach.

If something happens to my baby, it's all because I couldn't protect him.

Aiden squeezes Elsa's neck and she finally stops trying to reach out for me. She blinks a few times and looks at Aiden who whispers, "Don't go there again."

She nods and he hugs her as she buries her head in his chest.

"Make her go," Elsa murmurs. "Make her go away."

He glares down at me. "Leave."

I stand on unsteady feet, ready to bring hell on her head. My face burns and I'm sure that bitch left bruises, but all I focus on is the damage she might have done.

The fact that she may have hurt my —

My gaze strays to behind them and all the words I meant to say disappear.

Cole stands at the entrance of the King mansion, camouflaged by a creepy angel statue. Both hands are in his trousers' pockets and a smirk tugs his lips.

If you follow Aiden and play this game, you won't like how I'll react.

He'll come for me. He'll find me. And I'll pay.

Blindly reaching behind me, I open my car door with trembling fingers, barge inside, and speed out of the premises.

I know it's a matter of time before he finds me, so all I can do is run.

TWENTY-NINE

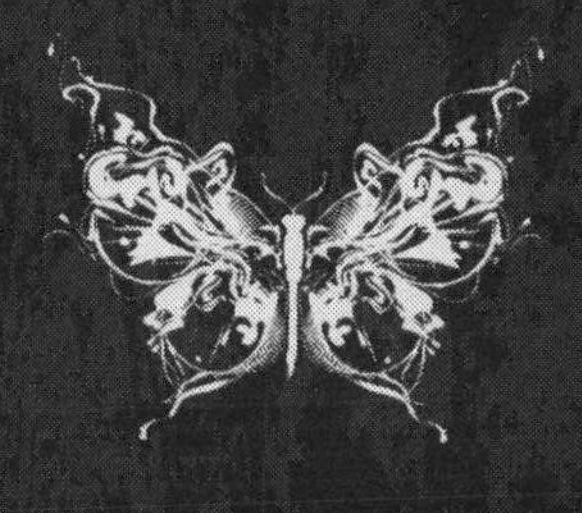

Silver

I plan to drive as far as my gas can take me.

Maybe I can leave and never come back.

I can go to an Eastern European country and live there alone forever. I can go to Finland. They have the most beautiful landscape I've ever seen.

Instead, I find myself in the park.

The same park I ran to when I was eight. The same park I run to whenever I feel like the world is closing in on me.

I ignore the rain and park my car, step out of it and head inside. The rain soaks me in an instant.

My hair glues to my face and my clothes stick to my back all over again.

I stand in the middle of the empty park, my breathing harsh. My face burns, but it's nothing compared to the thing clawing and beating inside me.

It needs to be out.

Throwing my head back, I stare at the dark grey sky and scream.

I scream so loud, I think someone will call 999.

I scream for all of the accumulating emotions and the pain, none of it having to do with the burning bruises Elsa left on my face.

I scream because the option of going to another country is impossible. No matter how much I theorise about it.

Mum, Papa, Helen, and all my life are here. Even the bastard, Cole.

I place a hand on my stomach and let the tears loose. The thought of getting rid of the baby rips a harsh sob out of me.

It's weird how I haven't even taken a test, and yet, I somehow feel it. It could be my imagination, right? I could be making up a pregnancy because I'm going out of my mind.

Or it could be real and I'll have to deal with it.

On one hand, I have my family, my future—*our* future. Cole and I are eighteen. We still haven't gotten a proper start into life. We still have our entire futures ahead of us. I'll never be able to go into politics if I become a teen mum—or worse, go through childbirth before marriage.

Aiden is out. I know his limit is to stay engaged to me. He'll never—and I mean, *ever*—hurt Elsa by taking responsibility for the baby.

Worse, Cole and I are stepsiblings. He can't take responsibility, even if he wants to. Our world doesn't work that way.

On the other hand, there's a life growing inside me. Little hands and feet. A human being. How will I ever live with myself if I murder it? How will I have a future? How will I wake up every day and pretend I'm not a killer?

I scream again, the intensity popping my ears. There's so much pent-up frustration inside me, broken pieces and wishes for an alternative reality.

A shadow appears in my peripheral vision and I jump back, my heart stammering in my chest. If it's Adam, I swear to God —

"You're kind of predictable, Butterfly. The park, really?"

Cole comes into view and pauses when he notices the tears in my eyes, the way my hands are balled into fists, my trembling lips, and the general mess I'm in the midst of.

His brow furrows. "Why are you crying?"

"Why am I crying?" I hit his chest. "Why am I fucking crying? Fuck you, Cole, okay? It's all because of you."

He lets me hit him, curse him, and doesn't attempt to stop me. "Correction, Silver. It's because of *you*. You shouldn't have provoked Elsa. You knew she'd snap one day."

He thinks it's because of Elsa? I hit him over and over again. *Hit. Hit. Hit.* "Idiot. Wanker. Bastard. I hate you. If it weren't for you, none of this would've happened. You barged into my life and invaded my space and now...now look at this mess!"

"*I* barged in?" He grabs both my hands, forcing me to stop, but he doesn't yank them away from his chest. "*I* did it? How about you? Why the fuck did you have to be here that day? Why did you jump me, push me to the bench, and cry your glitter tears on me? Why did you refuse to let me go and promise me your firsts? If you want to blame anyone, blame yourself. You made me obsessed with you to the point I can't fucking breathe until I see you."

Oh, God.

Oh. My. Freaking. God.

That's the first time he's ever said anything like that to me.

I hiccough, my fingers splaying on his wet shirt, feeling over the muscles of his hard chest. "Cole..."

My voice trails off when I can't find words to say. Should I be mad or touched right now? Should I kiss him or bite his lip off?

Cole has always been an enigma I couldn't figure out, even if I tried.

"What?" His voice softens.

"Why did it have to be you?"

"What kind of question is that?"

"Stop answering my questions with questions, wanker."

He strokes my wet hair away from my face and I shiver,

then wince when he touches my bruised cheek. "Come take shelter from the rain."

Cole leads me to his car that is parked nearby. After we slide inside, he brings out a towel from a grocery bag.

"Did you make a stop to get this?" It looks new.

"Shut up." He throws the towel over my head and dries my hair and face. He brings out a tube of ointment and applies it on the area where Elsa hit me.

His ministrations are gentle and I find myself caught up in his tender touch. Cole doesn't show this side. Ever. At least not in a genuine way, so I know not to take it for granted.

"Take off your clothes."

I cross a hand over my chest. "No. We're in public."

"The windows are tinted. Take them off before you catch a cold."

"No."

His jaw tightens, but he continues speaking in that infuriatingly calm tone. "What did I say about that fucking word?"

"I won't take them off."

"I'm mad at you right now, so don't make me rip them off you."

"You…won't." *Right?*

Just as I'm contemplating the option, Cole reaches out for me. I wiggle away from his merciless clutch at the last second.

"Fine, I'll do it!" I remove my jacket and unbutton my shirt, murmuring under my breath, "Brute."

"I heard that."

I make a face, then grimace when my bruises burn.

By the time I'm down to my underwear, Cole yanks the bra away and I shiver, even though he already turned on the heater.

I grab the big towel and wrap my body in it, peeking at him through my lashes. His shirt is also wet and it's completely transparent, showing his muscular chest and hard nipples. "You'll catch a cold, too."

"I don't catch colds." He reaches into the grocery bag and retrieves a thermos.

"What is it?"

"Hot chocolate I got from Aiden's kitchen."

I try not to be touched that he not only came after me, but he also thought it all through.

Sipping from the thermos, I let the warmth seep through me. "What else do you have in that bag?"

He retrieves a Snickers bar and my eyes double in size. I snatch it away and eat almost half of it in one go.

I don't even think about the calories in the big bar. I usually eat small ones, and only occasionally or when I'm feeling really down.

"No one will take it away, Silver. Eat slowly."

I face away from him to finish it. What if he changes his mind?

"Damn. You're really not you when you're hungry."

I throw him a dirty look over my shoulder, still chewing on my bar.

He chuckles, the sound like music in the quietness of the car. I pause chewing to listen to it and memorise it as if it's a piano sonata. Will there be a day where I won't stop and stare when he laughs?

"What are we going to do now?" I ask to distract my brain.

"We'll wait until you're warm, then we'll go back home."

"Right."

He raises a brow. "Unless you want to stay the night here?"

I don't want Papa and Helen to see me like this, and I don't want to feel the guilt I do whenever I stare at them and realise I'm letting them down. Besides, I'm in no mood to explain the wet clothes and the bruises.

"I want to stay the night here," I whisper.

His eyes widen a little. "I was only throwing it out there, but wow, it worked."

"Remove your clothes, though. You'll catch a cold."

"Just admit you want to see me naked." He unbuttons his shirt, and then his trousers, throwing them amongst the wet clothes in the back seat.

Water forms a sheen on the smooth ridges of his abs and thighs. His dark blue boxer briefs tighten around his semi-hard cock.

"That's not true." I clear my throat, pretending I'm not ogling his half-nakedness. "So what are we going to do?"

"What do you want to do?"

I think about it, and an idea hits me. "Read to me."

"Read to you?"

"You've always read quietly, even when you were a child. I've wondered how it would be like if you read aloud."

Or rather, I've fantasised about him reading aloud to me.

"What do you want me to read?" He reaches into his glovebox. "I have a few books here."

"No. Not one of your boring philosophy books."

He raises a brow. "Boring, huh?"

"Yeah, well, you can read me those when I want to sleep." I reach into my bag, retrieve my phone, and open my Kindle app. "Read me this novel."

"I don't read from e-books." He stares at my phone with distaste as if he wouldn't touch it with a long stick.

"Stop being a paperback snob. Besides, the Kindle app has all your books in one place. You don't have to carry a few tons with you whenever you want to go somewhere."

"I don't carry tons with me. I only take the ones I want to read."

"Come on, try it."

"I did and the answer is no."

"Just this time."

"Still a no."

Smirking, I use his own tactics against him. "Are you a coward, Cole?"

He narrows his eyes on me but snatches the phone from between my fingers. As soon as he sees the text, his snobbish expression withers away, making way for a smirk.

"What do we have here? Erotica?"

"Nope, erotic romance. There's a difference." Okay, fine, so maybe I went overboard with that, but I wanted to see his expression.

"This is a sex scene, Butterfly."

"So?"

He raises a brow. "You want me to read sex to you?"

I nod, wrapping the towel tighter around me.

"Why read it when I can perform it? I can even do a lot better than what's written here."

"Stop being an arrogant bastard and read."

He taps his thigh. "Lay your head here."

"Why?"

"Do it or I won't read."

I pretend to grumble as I rest my head on his hard thigh. The view from below is ethereal. The way his face turns serene whenever he reads has always been one of my favourite sceneries. I thought it'd appear somewhat disturbed when he reads a sex scene, but it remains the same.

"Their clothes lay in a heap on the floor beneath them. He pulled her by the waist, slammed her back against the door, then lifted her up so her legs wrapped around his hips. He started to thrust into her heat and she moaned in pleasure as he hit her womb." He pauses. "Can he do that? Hit her womb, I mean."

"Cole."

"I'm asking an innocent question. I'm genuinely curious."

"Well, you don't get to be. Read without commentating."

He goes back to his cool narration voice. "She writhed against him and all she could think about was his cock ramming into her over and over again until she couldn't breathe.

He was taking her to lengths she didn't know were possible. At that moment, everything turned clearer and she knew she would take the next step. Her decision was made."

He pauses again.

"Why did you stop?" I frown at him.

"Do all women think too much about things during sex?"

"Which part of no commentating do you not understand?"

"Fine." He focuses back on the phone. "His hands grabbed her waist and he picked up his pace until the whole building could hear his grunts and moans. That's when she knew she'd orgasm."

Once again, he stops.

"Now what?"

He stares down at me with a gleam shining in his dark greens. "Does this turn you on?"

"Why are you asking?" I pretend my core hasn't been tingling since he started reading. Only, it has less to do with the scene and more to do with his voice.

"This is your form of porn, isn't it?"

"Shut up and read."

"The sex could use more intensity, like, let's say, ropes?"

"Not everyone is into kink like you."

"They should be. They're missing out. After all, I converted *you*, Miss Prim and Proper, to the dark side. Admit it, you've been thinking about it since you saw that picture on my phone."

"I have not!" My voice is too defensive.

He chuckles but goes back to reading. I fall asleep listening to his soothing voice, hoping that tomorrow I'll find a solution to this whole mess.

THIRTY

Cole

A perk of being observant is having the element of surprise. If you can predict everyone's moves before they make them, it gives you the chance to take them out at their own side of the battlefield.

The disadvantage is if someone knows you're observant and hides from you.

Like what Silver has been doing the past couple of days.

She doesn't avoid me, but she's been cautious around me, immediately pulling away any chance she gets. She's been spending nights at her mother's so I don't sneak into her room.

Then I heard her whispering to Frederic yesterday to ask if there's a possibility someone outside her father's team might have her phone number.

I knew she changed it because of the stalker. The fact she's doing it now after years of receiving them means he's upped his methods.

He couldn't have possibly come into contact, right?

My theory is that her change has to do with him, and in order to get her back, I need to take care of it.

But first…

After everyone leaves the locker room, I thrust a hand against the wall, blocking Aiden's exit.

He didn't come to practice and only showed to make sure that we were going to visit Elsa in the Meet Up because she needs company after a health problem. Or, rather, that Xander, Ronan, and Kim are. He specifically told me not to go. I know why. He doesn't trust me around Elsa anymore, not with the damage I can inflict on his relationship with her.

"Now what?" He raises a brow. "You want to start a polyamorous fling? I don't think Queens could take it, though."

I suck in a breath and smile as I grab him by the collar. "Speak of her that way again and I'll rearrange your features."

"Have you forgotten the part where she's my fiancée?" He smooths something on my jacket. "You're my brother-in-law. Isn't that full of unicorns, or what?"

I maintain my smile, even though I want his head in the middle of the blood pool in my old house. "This is my final warning, King. End it with her. Officially."

"Let me think about it…hmmm. I'm going to go with no."

"It's your choice. Don't blame me later." I leave him and stride outside.

Silver told Sebastian she'll be staying at her mum's for a few days. I only get to see her in school where she makes sure her friends are always with her.

After that night we spent in my car as I read to her, I thought she was coming around. That she was finally giving up her damn stubbornness and resistance, but Silver isn't the type who gives in. Not even if you put a knife to her throat.

She's the type you have to challenge, then make her lose.

Run while you can, Silver.

I head to my car and when I open the door, I notice someone standing near the entrance.

Adam Herran.

Captain of the rugby team and son of one of the Conservative Party members. Usually, I wouldn't give two fucks about him, but the position he's standing in is in direct view of where Silver usually parks her car.

She already left; I saw her not so long ago.

The fact that he's standing so close to where she was could be a coincidence, but here's the thing, I don't believe in coincidences.

Everything happens for a reason. Coincidence is merely a term to interpret things that seem to not have an explanation.

They do. You just have to look deeper.

I tilt my head to the side as Adam brings out his phone and smirks while staring at it. There's a slight twitch in his fore-finger, which I assume is excitement, thrill...gratification.

I tuck all those reactions at the back of my mind. Adam Herran is under my radar right now and nothing—absolutely nothing—will save him from me if he indeed did what I think he did.

But first, I need to make true of my promise to Aiden and drive all the way to the Meet Up.

When I arrive, I ignore Ronan's and Xander's protests about how I shouldn't be here. Elsa appears dishevelled, in a mess, almost as if she hasn't been able to sleep. There's some-thing about her relationship with Aiden that isn't what it seems. Everyone calls her Frozen, but I believe there's always a reason behind the ice.

Aiden's ice exists because of the kidnapping.

Silver's ice exists because of her parents' divorce that she still hasn't gotten over, no matter how much she loves Mum.

Mine is because of that blood pool and the need for chaos.

And in order to get back at Aiden, I need to melt Elsa's ice. The only way to do that is to tell her a truth Aiden would never reveal.

While Xander and Ronan bicker, and Kimberly watches them with dreamy eyes—or rather, she watches Xan—I take Elsa outside and tell her about the kidnapping.

I tell her everything that happened from my POV. Of course, I don't tell her about meeting chaos or that I didn't want to be found. That would make me seem like a psycho and I don't need that baggage thrown onto Elsa.

She needs to trust me, not be wary of me.

I'm about to tell her about Aiden's engagement with Silver when Xander cuts us off like a little bitch.

Fine. I might have lost my chance this time, but not next time.

Elsa will know about the engagement and Aiden will have no choice but to break it off with Silver.

And then she'll be mine.

All fucking mine.

When I get home, the house is eerily quiet. Sebastian has some sort of a media debate going on, so his entire team is with him.

Mum has a deadline, so she must be writing. The mood has been calm and peaceful around here lately.

And empty.

Silver's absence makes this place feel like a fucking cemetery.

What's wrong with me? I'm supposed to see her as my chaos, but now she's the reason behind the calm?

She'll come back, though. I'll get rid of Aiden and anything that keeps her away from me until she has no choice but to run back into my arms.

When I was reading on the history of Europe, I had a small fascination with Hispania—modern-day Spain and Portugal. One story has remained with me. During the Muslim caliphate conquest of Hispania during the eighth century, there was this Berber leader who sailed a small army from the North of

Africa to Gibraltar, which is now named after him. His men were scared because they were greatly outnumbered.

What did he do?

He burnt all their ships and told them the famous line, 'The enemy is in front of you. The sea is behind you.'

He gave them no choice but to fight. Not only did they fight, they also won and ruled Hispania for over seven centuries.

That's what I'll do to Silver. I'll burn her ships so she has no choice but to fall back into me.

To be mine for seven fucking centuries—or whatever is close to that in human years.

I prepare Mum's favourite jasmine tea and take it to her office that she had made up as soon as we moved in here. Mum has always needed her space to write. If anyone interrupts her, she loses her train of thoughts and might never go back to that 'zone'.

Instead of knocking, I slowly open the door, planning to put the drink on the table and leave.

Mum stands in front of her board, scribbling what seems like ideas. They always look like another chaos to me. Words scattered all around with no apparent purpose or meaning. How she manages to put them into something coherent afterwards still escapes me.

However, Mum is an artist and no one is meant to understand them. She says even artists find trouble understanding themselves sometimes.

I place the cup on the table and plan to leave without disturbing her, but she turns around and smiles. "Darling, you're home."

"I brought you some tea." I motion at the board. "When can I read it, Mum?"

"Not yet."

"I thought I had the perks of being the son and getting to read early." There's a lot of buzz going on about Mum's upcoming book, and like any of her other fans, I can't wait to get my hands on the masterpiece. Mum has a way of titillating the human mind without romanticising it. I fell for her writing since the time I stole her first book and read it in Aiden's house.

She laughs. "Fine. I'll give you a copy the same time I send it to my agent. Happy?"

"Yes. Now, have you eaten?" Mum forgets her pills and her meals when she's on a tight deadline, and I have to constantly remind her of them. Silver has been taking on that role, too.

Mum's had insomnia lately, but that's only because she's been writing. She always seems to backpedal a little when she's on a deadline. Her therapist told me it's nothing to worry about, because she's stressed and will eventually go back to normal once she makes sure she's met her deadline.

"I have." She comes close and pats my cheek. "Look at my little boy grown into a man. Have I told you I'm proud of you today?"

"You just did."

"Where's Silver?" She stares behind me. "I was planning to make some lasagne for dinner."

"She told Sebastian she's staying with her mum." I grin. "Let's make it a date for two?"

Her expression falls since she's all about family gatherings, but then she smiles again. "Absolutely."

I'm about to leave her be, but I stop at the door and turn around. "Mum?"

"Yeah?" She glances at me over her shoulder.

"Are you happy? With Sebastian, I mean." I would say yes. He's attentive and gives her the space she needs, but the devil in me wants her answer to be 'no' so bad, it's disgusting.

"Why, of course." Her face breaks into another warm, gutting smile. "I finally have the family I've dreamt of."

"I'm happy for you, Mum." *I'm not.*

Yes, I want Mum to smile more, and she has since we moved in here, but now I'm starting to have regrets.

I'm starting to think, what if I hadn't agreed when she first told me about Sebastian? What if I'd told her no instead of hoping they'd eventually get tired of each other and break up?

And the funny part is, I don't do what-ifs. I'm the type who doesn't look back on past events but chooses to face forward instead.

However, there has always been an exception to my rules.

Her.

My Butterfly.

My chaos.

I stand outside of her room for a second, but choose to go into mine.

While her Chanel scent helps me sleep at night, it's also a form of torture to imagine her there when she's not.

I change into a pair of home trousers and a T-shirt, then sit on my bed, lean on one hand, and open my book of choice again.

Nausea.

Could be because I'm feeling a sense of nausea myself, or that I'm about to go into a different type of nausea.

I should probably read history instead of focusing on someone else's existential crisis. Just when I'm about to go with that idea, my door barges open. I expect it to be Mum, but she doesn't barge doors open.

Slowly, I lift my head to find those blue eyes—furious, dark blue, like a storm.

Silver stands at the threshold of my room. Her denim dress's straps are falling off her pale shoulders. Her golden hair is all over her back and in her face.

She slams the door shut and strides towards me as if hell is resting on her head.

She came back and she's in my room. Silver never comes

into my room unless Mum or Sebastian ask her to call for me. And she usually disappears all too soon.

"Miss me?" I smile, still gripping my book.

"Miss you?" Her voice raises. "More like, I'm here to choke the life out of you."

"Huh. I thought I was the only one into choking."

She thrusts her phone into my face. It's a conversation between her and Aiden from not so long ago.

Aiden: Nash fucked Johansson from the track team.

Silver: What the fuck?

Aiden: I thought you should know.

That fucker.

He must know what I told Elsa, which I expected, considering Xander was there and Elsa looked like she was on the verge of a breakdown.

What I didn't expect was his childish ways of retaliating.

The joke's on him, though. His text brought Silver straight to my room.

I'm the one who burned the ships. The enemy is in front of her and the sea is behind her.

"When was this?" she blurts. "How dare you fuck her?"

"I don't see why I shouldn't." I pretend to be bored. "You have a fiancé. Why can't I have a fuck buddy?"

Her lips part. They tremble before she seals them into a line, and I know, I just know that I won't like what she'll say next.

"I'm going to get a fuck buddy, too."

"Funny." I force a smile. "We both know you're too conservative for that."

"Well, you made me less conservative on Papa's fucking wedding day, so I guess I have no principles anymore." She flips her hair. "I'll send pictures."

I jump forwards and drag her by the arm so hard, she squeals as she falls back on the bed.

I hover over her, pinning both her wrists to the mattress while my knees are on either side of her waist.

She stares up at me with wild, huge eyes that are puffy. She's been crying, all alone, in dark corners, so no one—not even her mother—would see her pain.

Silver and her fucking phobia about image are starting to grate on my nerves.

"Let me go," she speaks in a clear, firm tone. "I'm done playing your games, Cole."

"Games." I push into her, causing her lips to part as my hard dick digs into her stomach. I didn't bother with underwear so she can feel every detail. "Does this look like a fucking game to you?"

"Well, apparently it is," she says in the same tone, even though she clenches her thighs. "I won't be your side dish or your toy."

"Sounds like jealousy to me."

"Fuck you, Cole. Okay? Let's see who's jealous when I go find myself another dick."

"Another dick?" My jaw tightens. "You think that will ever happen in this life?"

"You can't watch me twenty-four-seven."

"No. But I can fuck you so hard, there'll be nothing left for anyone else." I grab both her hands with one of mine and yank her dress up. She tries to kick me in the crotch.

I slap her legs apart and she stops, a gasp falling from her lips. Taking advantage of her stunned reaction, I pull her underwear and my trousers down.

She shakes her head when I'm at her entrance.

"Stop resisting me when your cunt is dripping for me," I speak against her neck before I latch onto the skin, leaving a hickey for the world to see. "Tell me to fuck you."

"N-no."

"If you don't, we'll be here all night." I glide the crown of my dick over her folds, slow and unhurried until she moans, her eyes rolling back.

"Cole, stop..."

"Tell me to fuck you, Silver. This time, you're going to ask for it."

"No!" She grits out even as her body shudders beneath me. "I'm not a side dish. You don't get to fuck me after you've dipped your dick in someone else."

"Dipped my dick in someone else, huh?" I bite the sensitive spot on her throat and she whimpers.

Her voice is shaky and tears barge into her eyes, but she keeps her ground. "I don't care how much I want you, Cole. I can be a fool for you, I can let you crush my damn principles, but I won't let you humiliate me. I'm Silver Queens. I don't take other people's sloppy seconds."

"You never did."

She blinks up at me through the frustrated tears forming in her eyes. "W-what?"

"That time at the wedding was my first, too."

Her lips part and she remains silent for so long, I start to suspect she's lost her voice. "But...but...but...that time when you were all discussing your virginities at the Meet Up, and Ronan said —"

"I lied so they'd leave me the fuck alone. So you got Miss Goldman fired for no reason. Though she did seduce me."

She bites her lip, suppressing a smile. Silver might be harsh, but she's the most real thing I've ever seen. "You knew about that?"

"I know everything about you." I nuzzle my nose against her neck, inhaling her flowery Chanel scent. "After I thought you gave up your virginity to Aiden, I was going to try with others and then rub it in your face, but I stopped at the last minute. All I ended up doing was tie them up."

"Why?"

"Why what?"

"Why couldn't you do it with others?" Her voice is low, emotional.

"They weren't you, Butterfly. No one is you."

A full-body shudder takes hold of her and her legs willingly open. But before I can do anything, she lifts her head. "How about Johansson?"

"Aiden lies when it fits him. Besides –" I brush my lips over the hollow of the tender skin of her throat"– do you think I have the energy to focus on anyone but you? You drive me fucking crazy."

"Not more than you do me."

"Is that so?"

"You're a bastard and I hate you most of the time."

"Most of the time? Does that mean there are times you don't hate me?"

"Maybe."

"Maybe is good enough." I study her soft features, the faint freckles visible on her nose because she ran over here without putting on any makeup. She forgot her sacred makeup for me. "Do you have something to tell me, Silver?"

If she lets it out, if she talks about it, or at least trusts me enough with whatever is bothering her, I can deal with her rejections.

"Yes." She gulps. "Fuck me, Cole."

My whole body sharpens at her softly spoken words. It's the first time she's ever asked me to fuck her.

The first time she's admitted she wants me without me having to extract it out of her body.

I claim her lips and place my fingers around her throat as I thrust inside her in one long go. My balls slap against her pale skin and I take a second to relish the feeling of her completely with me.

She whimpers into my mouth as I kiss her with a violence that matches the force of my thrusts.

"Wrap your legs around me," I order, and she complies, caging me against her. I fuck her into the bed, her wrists pinned and her hair splayed out on the sheets her as her body slides back and forth on the mattress.

Silver's not only chaos, she's also a goddess. The type everyone can watch from afar, but I'm the only one who gets to worship at her altar.

The one who gets to own every inch of her.

"C-Cole," she moans, nibbling on my bottom lip. "Go slower."

"Since when do you like it slow?"

"J-just do it."

When I don't listen, narrowing my eyes on her, she places several kisses on my mouth, my chin, and even my nose. "Please."

Fuck me.

I'll do anything if she does that. If she moans my name and kisses me as if I'm the only one she'll ever want.

Rotating my hips slowly, I take her unhurriedly for the first time. I don't like slow fucks, it feels like a caress, and I don't get the entire intense experience.

Silver's back arches off the bed and she clamps all around me, strangling me inside her.

Something shifts in the air. It's like that sense of excitement you get when turning a new page in a book.

Her moans mingle with my groans as they fill the room. I take my time pounding into her slick heat in slow, measured thrusts, moulding her entire body to mine.

"Oh, oh, Cole…I-I think…I'm…oh…" Her mouth remains open as she shatters all around me.

I spill inside her at the same time, and my release is the hardest I've ever experienced.

Silver Queens is officially fucked.

There's no way she'll ever escape me now.

THIRTY-ONE

Doll Master

Contrary to popular belief, it's not hard to observe and go unnoticed while doing so.

It's not hard to get close enough to smell my doll's Chanel perfume and touch her soft skin.

It's not hard to do that in my head and then somehow bring it to reality.

All I have to do is move in patterns neither she nor anyone else can detect.

She's started to notice me, she's started to get scared of me. She's stopped responding with those soft smiles when she reads my texts and is now changing her number to escape me.

Doesn't she know that's impossible?

Right. She doesn't. She's just a little girl who's scared. She only fucks like a whore, thinking no one knows about her forbidden romance.

It's okay, though, because the doll will eventually fall at her master's feet.

She already has.

She simply doesn't know it yet.

I guess this is the part where you give the doll some breathing room. Let her believe that she got rid of me.

After all, the hunt is more thrilling this way.

Just when she believes she's safe, I'll come out, wash her, smell her, touch her.

Be with her.

Until then, I have to keep myself busy. Another doll lies in front of me, unconscious, in the darkness of the forest.

This doll secretly craved the high, the element of surprise, or she wouldn't have run in a deserted place this early in the morning.

Her blonde hair is similar to Silver's, but not really. Her white skin is the same shade as Silver's, but not as soft.

For now, I have to settle for the second choice when the first is all I ever wanted.

Soon, my doll.

Very soon.

Do you see the sacrifices I make for you?

THIRTY-TWO

Silver

Today is off.

It started off.

I was supposed to have breakfast with Mum, but she said she has work at the party and can't get together.

Then Helen brought me the packet I ordered. I dislike ordering online, only because I prefer seeing things, trying them on, and touching them before buying them. But desperate times, right?

I couldn't possibly risk going to a pharmacy for a pregnancy test, so I ordered one, along with a bunch of makeup and clothes that I'll probably never wear just to cover the initial purchase.

I have my own bank account, and since I turned eighteen, neither Papa nor Mum have the right to see my statements without my approval, so this is merely a precaution.

"Thanks, Helen," I tell her, helping with the pack.

"What have you gotten in here, darling?" She drops the box on the bed. "It's so heavy."

"Just stuff."

"Don't take long. Breakfast is ready."

"Okay." I kiss her cheek, then lock the door behind her. I also close the balcony's door for good measure.

As soon as I open the box, I rummage through the rubbish I bought until I find the test.

My fingers tremble as I clutch it.

You can do this. You've got this.

I read the instructions carefully before I go to the bathroom and follow them. As I wash my hands, I keep staring at the test.

Two lines means pregnant.

One line means not.

The instructions say I have to wait for five minutes. It's been ten seconds and I'm already freaking out.

It took me some time to buy this test. As in, more than a couple of weeks. I kept thinking that if I didn't know for sure, then nothing would happen. In a typical running from responsibility kind of way. Every day my period doesn't show up, I freak out more.

During all this time, I've been letting Cole fuck me slow and deep until I think I'm going to faint from the amount of softness he actually possesses.

Other than that, weird stuff has been going on all around us.

Like when Uncle Jonathan took me to the Meet Up so he could announce to Elsa that I'm engaged to Aiden. There was a whole shitshow that involved her father and a lot of other things.

I wanted to run from there, and I did as soon as I could. Aiden is still after my head because I didn't warn him about his father's surprise visit, but fuck him. He made me believe Cole fucked Johansson when he never had sex with anyone else but me.

A small smile tugs on my lips at that thought and I gently bite my lower lip.

Cole was a virgin until me. It's hard to believe that he never had sex until our parents' wedding day.

I'm Cole's first and last.

I frown at that. Last?

That can't be possible. Not with the situation we're in. That's why I got the test. I need to figure out what to do about what's growing inside me.

I glimpse at the timer, then at the test. Three minutes to go.

Letting my head fall into my hands, I pretend to play "Moonlight Sonata" in my brain.

I'm not here. I'm in another universe where I get to be with who I want without any restrictions.

Then I can even have this baby. I can be a mother and promise not to throw my emotional baggage on to him.

God. I sound like a bitch about my parents in my head.

The timer goes off and I release a breath as I peek from between my fingers.

Two lines.

Pregnant.

I'm pregnant with Cole's child.

Holy. Shit.

I apologise to Helen, pretending I have a meeting with Summer and Veronica so I can't have breakfast at home.

If I sit at the same table as Cole or Papa, I'll eventually crumble, and I can't do that.

My head is in complete chaos during the entire day. I can't focus. I can't play the piano. I can't even take two steps without being in a daze.

It's like I've been pushed out of my own skin.

I know I'll eventually have to make decisions. I have to go to the doctor and either ask him about the baby's health or tell him to kill him.

Tears prickle into my eyes at that second option.

I don't want to kill my own child. I don't care that I'm eighteen and that the father is my step-freaking-brother. Why does an innocent soul have to pay for that?

Every time Cole is in sight, I act cool, then run away.

He'll know I'm avoiding him. He always does, the wanker.

Besides, I can't possibly fall asleep without him reading me one of his boring books now. He's so snobbish about paperbacks, I gave up trying to make him read to me from my Kindle.

The thought that I'll lose all of that once the truth of what I'm carrying comes to light makes me sick to my stomach.

Maybe I can crash at Mum's for a few days until I figure out what the hell I'm going to do.

Unless she finds out and kind of kills me.

And Papa.

He's so old-fashioned and conservative. He'll be so disappointed in me if he finds out I haven't only been fucking my stepbrother under his roof, but I also fell pregnant.

I call it a day as soon as the last class ends. Usually, I'll linger around the football team's practice and pretend they bore me out of my mind while I secretly ogle Cole.

What? He looks hot as hell in his football jersey and with that captain band around his thick bicep.

All the girls are head over heels for Aiden and Xander because they're the strikers who scores the goals. Or Ronan, because he makes a show out of everything he does. But Cole is the secret weapon.

I think only the coach and the players themselves understand how important his position on the team is. Ninety per cent of the assists that lead to goals are made by him. All the possessiveness of the ball in the midfield is also ensured by him. Most of the attacks are orchestrated by him. The defence is literally his bitch.

He's the only one who gives one hundred per cent in both defence and attack. Ronan might be midfield too, but he goes forwards more. Cole goes forwards and back.

Cole is the strongest player on that team and people are idiots for idolising the other three.

Just because he's silent and doesn't brag, doesn't mean he doesn't work hard.

But then again, it's not like I want everyone to idolise him.

I'll crush every last one of them.

And yes, I learnt all that football rubbish since Cole started to have an interest in the game. I've always pretended I didn't care about it, and I don't, not really, but I care about how *he* plays.

How he owns the field and everyone in it without them noticing. He's the master behind the game because he plots everything to a T.

Today, though, I won't stay and watch. I need to gather a few things from home and flee to Mum's before he returns.

I'm about to get into my car when a shadow creeps up behind me. I startle, turning around.

"Hey, Silver." Adam smiles at me. His eyes are bloodshot and his shoulders seem tense underneath the uniform. A waft of alcohol comes from him.

The hell is he doing here?

I haven't received a text from him in more than a week, and he's been keeping his distance at school, so I thought he finally got himself together.

I don't like the look on his face. Not one bit.

"Hey, Adam." I try to sound distracted, even though I'm on the verge of a panic attack. "I'm in a hurry so —"

He grips my arm so hard, I smother a squeal. "Why the fuck do you always do that?"

I try to wiggle free, but his hold is like steel, fingers digging into my flesh. "Adam, let me go. You're hurting me."

"Hurting you." He barks out a laugh. "You know how to be hurt, Silver? Because you've been stomping on my heart over and over again."

Shit. Shit.

Swallowing, I watch my surroundings, searching for help. There's no one here—of course.

"I don't know what you're talking about, Adam."

"You mean you pretend you don't know." His other hand caresses my chin. "You know, I've been in love with you for such a long time, but you keep playing hard to get. I've done everything for you. When that bitch Kimberly was bothering you, I mock-confessed to her and spilt paint on her head. I've done everything to protect you."

My mouth hangs open.

He's a psycho. I can't believe he did that to Kim because of me. She was hurt so badly, it pushed her into a Nazi-style diet that's been sucking the life out of her.

There's no telling what he'll do to me. God, I should've told Papa about those texts since I first got them. Why did I have to fill my emotional gap with them? Just how stupid could I be?

"Go out with me, Silver." He smiles like a maniac. "You and I are meant to be."

I squirm away from him, pushing back against the car and wrapping a hand around my baby.

"Back off. Don't mistake my silence for weakness."

"Do you know how long I've dreamt about this?"

My insides are about to liquefy with terror, but I keep the harsh tone I learnt from Mum. "Back off or I swear —"

"Shh, shut up. Shut the fuck up." He jams his fist at the roof of the car beside my head.

My eyes widen as I try to keep my calm. I'm Sebastian Queens and Cynthia Davis's daughter. I will *not* break.

Taking a deep inhale, I speak in a slightly cracked voice,

despite my attempts to keep it neutral, "Adam. If you don't stop, I'll tell —"

"Shut the fuck up, Silver." He punches the car again.

"What's going on here?"

I release a breath as someone approaches us. Elsa. I've never been happier to see her in my entire life.

"Fuck off, bitch. This is none of your business," Adam snarls at her.

"Silver?" she asks me carefully.

I slightly shake my head and mouth, "Cole."

For some reason, he's the only one I want to see right now. Besides, I know he can keep Adam's claws off me.

And I need Adam's damn claws off me.

Elsa retrieves her phone, shoulders pushing backwards. "Back off right now or I'll call the principal, Adam. Maybe it's *his* business."

He takes a step towards her.

She jams her hand in her backpack. "Come any closer and I'll blind your fucking eyes with pepper spray."

Adam's gaze roams over me one more second, and I hold my breath, only releasing it when his attention breaks from me as he snarls at Elsa, "Stupid fucking bitch."

Elsa keeps watching him with that rigid posture and determined look until he gets into his vehicle and leaves.

I fall back against my car, hugging my stomach.

It's going to be fine, baby.

It's over.

It's all over.

"Are you…okay?" Elsa stops in front of me.

I can't believe she, of all people, helped me. After all the drama I've brought to her relationship with Aiden, I would have expected her to beat me up again or something.

At least, that's what I thought when she caught me vomiting in the bathroom the other day.

Instead, she asked me if I needed help.

She's the polar opposite of Aiden, and maybe that's why they fit so well.

"You didn't have to do that," I whisper. "I…I need to go. Forget what I said earlier. Don't mention a word about this to Cole."

If he knows, he'll blame me, not Adam. He'll come after me for hiding this from him.

I need to talk to Frederic about it. He's a PR genius, he can tell me how to deal with this in the best way that won't hurt Papa.

He'll also want to murder me, but I'll take that.

I wish I could also tell Frederic about the pregnancy, but he'd tell me to get rid of it. That's what everyone would say.

Cole included.

And that hurts more than I'd like to admit.

"You should tell Aiden," Elsa says.

"What does he have to do with anything? King didn't tell you?"

"Tell me what?"

"Whatever. It's not my place." I open my car's door and slide inside. "I won't say anything until you talk to him."

"About what?"

"What do you think?"

After what she did for me today, I might consider Aiden's order and actually confess it all.

What's the point of holding on to this engagement if he won't take responsibility for the child?

As I drive out, I place a hand over my stomach and a tear slides down my cheek at the thought that I might be forced to lose this life after all.

THIRTY-THREE

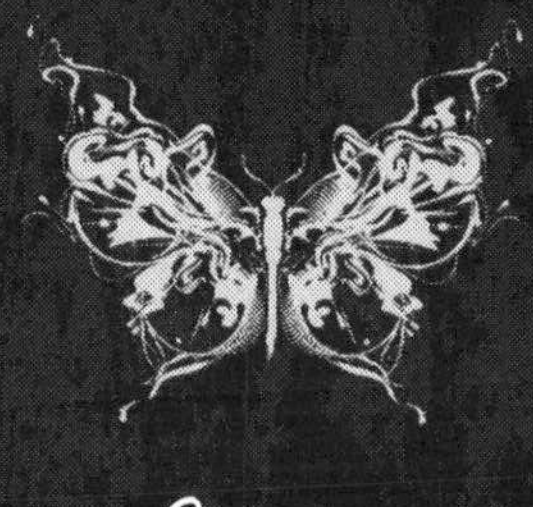

Silver

Every day that passes is like a ticking bomb.

Every time Papa or Mum say they want to speak to me about something, I jump in my own skin.

Every time Helen brings me food, I wince, thinking I'll get morning sickness.

Every time Frederic and Derek tell me 'Good morning, Miss' or 'Good evening, Miss,' I'm screaming inside, *They know!*

I spend the entire week with Mum so I can avoid Cole.

At first, he corners me, demanding I tell him what I'm hiding and threatening that I'll pay if he has to find out himself.

His form of payment isn't toying with my body as I wish. Instead, he completely tunes me out.

For the first time since we started whatever we had, Cole isn't speaking to me.

He says he won't unless I tell him what's going on.

Whenever I pass him by and he pretends I don't exist, I die a little inside. Cole has a perfect blank face, so he can make you feel like you're no different from the dust on his shoe.

It hurts.

It makes me sleep with tears in my eyes every night.

But what hurts the most is the thought of what he'll do when he finds out I'm carrying his baby.

Today, I turned down a dinner date with Mum and Lucien. Usually, I love the Frenchman's company. He's cool and charismatic and reminds me of Uncle Jonathan—without the frightening ruthlessness. As long as he makes Mum smile and forget about her demons, I approve.

Despite Lucien's pleasant company, I decide to return to Papa's house, hoping, *praying* Cole will actually sneak into my room.

He doesn't.

He doesn't pay me much attention at dinner, as if I'm not sitting right there in front of him. Even Helen asks me if Cole and I are going back to the time we couldn't stand each other.

I guess we are.

Why did he give me all those moments just so he'd take them away? We were doing fine being at each other's throats before the wedding.

Who am I kidding? I hated the times from before. He was always far.

Just too far.

I scroll through both Ronan's and Aiden's Instagram accounts, hoping to catch a glimpse of Cole's picture like a bloody fool.

Aiden made fun of how Cole's not speaking to me. That arsehole doesn't deserve the huge favour I did for him.

A few days ago, I told Elsa the engagement and everything in between were fake. Although she won't completely forgive him yet, my freely-provided confession is a start.

I've turned so soft over the days.

My phone vibrates and I sit up, excitement whirling inside me. Is it Cole?

Unknown Number: Meet me.

I gulp. That's the first time he's ever asked that. Is it because of what happened in the car park a few days ago? It's a new number. He keeps changing them as if playing hide-and-seek with Papa's team's security measures.

Unknown Number: I'm behind the fence of your house.

Unknown Number: If you don't come out, I'll post a naked picture of you for the world to see.

I can call his bluff and tell him he has no such picture, but what if he does? I can't risk Papa's campaign or Mum's reputation.

Tears prickle my eyes as my chest closes in on itself.

What the hell is wrong with me? Why do I find myself in screw-up after screw-up? First Cole, then the pregnancy, and now a damn stalker.

Could I be more of a disgrace to my parents?

I was always a good girl. When did I start losing myself? When did I become this damn loser who sees a failure in the mirror every morning?

Swallowing my tears, I type with unsteady fingers.

Silver: Why are you doing this, Adam?

Unknown Number: Because I love you. Remember when that bitch Elsa was bothering you? I'm the one who pushed her into that pool. For you, my love. For your beautiful blue eyes.

Unknown Number: I know you broke it off with Aiden for me. Because you've always loved me too.

Oh. God.

He pushed Elsa for me. She could've drowned and died.

I have to see him and put an end to this.

Stumbling from the bed, I run out of my room, only to be halted by a broad frame.

Cole.

We're standing in front of my door. He's wearing a hoodie and cotton trousers. His chestnut hair falls all over his forehead.

"Where the fuck are you going dressed like that?"

I stare down at myself and realise I'm only in a see-through oversized T-shirt with nothing underneath because I wanted to seduce this bastard.

"N-nowhere."

He narrows his eyes on my face, then on my hand, and I subconsciously hide the phone behind my back. He snatches it away and when I try to fight him, he uses my finger to unlock it.

I didn't even exit the chat.

He keeps it out of reach and his eyes darken with every passing second.

Damn it.

"So it was Adam," he says coolly, with almost no emotion at all. This side of Cole has always scared the shit out of me.

I can never tell what he'll do next—whether he'll rage or leave. Though I've never seen him rage, not really.

"That's what you've been hiding from me, Silver?"

I hate when he calls me by my name.

"I have to meet him," I murmur. "He'll post a picture and there'll be a scandal."

"He won't."

"How would you know that?"

"If he had it, he would've attached it to the text and threatened you with it. He's bluffing."

"What if he isn't?"

He grabs me by the arm and pushes me inside my room, then slams me against the door, keeping me pinned in place. "He won't. Even if he does, you'll only make it worse if you meet him."

"But —"

"Shut up."

"Cole…" I plead.

"Shut the fuck up, Silver. I told you I won't be lenient if I find out on my own." He retrieves his phone and puts it to his ear. "Frederic. How are you? I think there could be an intruder near the back garden. Can you have one of the security guys check?"

I fidget with my back glued to the door, my toes curling against the floor before I release them.

"Won't he get mad if we provoke him?" I whisper.

Cole places a finger against my mouth, shushing me. My brain has other thoughts, though, like kissing that finger and telling him everything bottled inside me.

"I see," he says to Fredric. "Thank you. Have a great night."

"So?" I ask as soon as he hangs up.

"There was no one. He must've left."

"What if he didn't?"

"What are you going to do about it? Go out like that and meet him?"

"No. I was in a hurry. I didn't think."

"You don't seem to be doing a lot of that lately."

It's more like I'm thinking too much.

"I'm confiscating your phone. Go to sleep."

I peek at him through my lashes. "You won't sleep with me?"

"I thought you hated me. Why would you want me to sleep with you?"

Ugh. The arsehole.

I huff as I climb under the covers, pulling them to my chin. He pulls out my chair and a book we're reading for literature and sits opposite me.

"You can go. I don't need a babysitter." I try not to sound frustrated that he prefers the chair over me.

"Considering you were going out to meet your stalker in fuck-me clothes, you obviously do," he says without lifting his head from the book. *Wuthering Heights*. Fitting.

"What do you care? I thought you weren't going to talk to me."

"I'm not."

"Well, you clearly are right now."

"Go to sleep. You're confessing tomorrow."

"Confessing? To whom?"

"To Elsa, who almost drowned because of you. Because

you were self-centred and enjoyed having a stalker say you're beautiful."

Tears prickle my lids and I hide farther beneath the sheets. "You know that's not the case."

"Uh-huh."

"You think I want to hurt other people? What is wrong with you? Are you crazy?"

"Watch that fucking attitude, Silver."

"And if I don't?"

"Go to sleep," he repeats quietly.

I do, with tears in my eyes and emptiness in my chest.

For the first time since he moved here, Cole doesn't hug me to sleep.

For the first time, he's so disgusted with me, he doesn't want to touch me.

I hate myself for hating this.

And I hate him.

I hate him so much, I dream of him hugging me.

In the morning, Cole takes me to the Meet Up.

More like, he drags me.

He's still not speaking to me and I'm starting to feel pitiful.

I loathe being pitiful. It brings back memories from when I was a child and every single one of my parents' friends gave me that look.

Poor Silver.

Since then, I've built walls and a whole new persona so no one would give me that look again.

Cole and I are sitting in the small cottage, and I recall the pain I felt when I thought he'd lost his virginity to Miss Goldman.

So what if it didn't happen? He made me believe it.

Well, I made him believe I lost my virginity to Aiden, so there's that.

Ugh. I hate this tension.

I sit on the chair, waiting for Aiden and Elsa. Cole stands right behind me like the Grim Reaper.

True to his Grim Reaper image, he's not speaking either.

I'm too scared to look behind me, so I murmur, "Are you going to keep up the silent treatment for long?"

"Not a word, Silver. I don't want to hear your voice."

I pretend he didn't slash my heart open with that and mutter, "Screw you, Cole."

The door opens and Aiden and Elsa come inside.

She watches me as if I'm a freak while Aiden appears mostly annoyed. "What are you doing here, Queens?"

"Ask Cole," I speak low.

Elsa steps inside, observing Cole and me carefully, as if we'll jump her. "Hey."

Cole offers her his signature polite smile that he offers to everyone. The good boy image. The good son, good stepson, good freaking citizen.

But I know Cole the best. I know the image he puts out and the one he keeps tucked underneath layers of practice.

He's a gentleman in public. A monster in private.

With me.

He's being a monster to me right now and I hate how much it hurts.

"Elsa," he says. "Sit down. There's something you need to know."

Aiden throws his weight on the sofa and she settles beside him, still watching us closely, as if she's trying to get a read on the situation.

I wonder if she sees the pain in my eyes.

No one should see your pain, Babydoll. Your pain is yours, not for the people. They will only use it against you.

I inhale deeply, remembering Mum's words.

"Tell them," Cole orders in a low, calm tone. "If you don't, I will. Do you want them to hear my version?"

He'll tell them I wanted Elsa hurt. I wanted Kim hurt.

That I'm scum.

That I disgust him.

"Get it over with, Queens," Aiden says impatiently. "I don't have all day."

I lift my head and focus on Elsa. "I don't know why we keep getting involved, you and I."

She gives me a look that says, *Same.*

"This is my final warning." Cole's merciless voice cuts through my head like a knife. "Talk or I will."

Taking in another deep breath, I speak in the most composed tone I have, "Remember Adam?"

"Did he hurt you again?" she blurts.

Shit. Why did she have to mention that?

"*Again.*" Cole's voice lowers. "So it's happened before, yes?"

He won't let me live this down, will he?

Aiden grips Elsa by the shoulder, hard. I can almost imagine the tightness I'd see in Cole's jaw if I were brave enough to look at him. "How do you know about that, sweetheart? Hmm?"

"He was bothering her in the car park; I stopped him," she says.

"You stopped him," Aiden repeats. "How did you stop him exactly?"

"I just threatened him with calling the principal and using pepper spray."

"You don't have pepper spray."

"He believed I did. What are you so agitated about?"

"What am I so agitated about?" His words are clipped. "Why do you fucking think? He could've taken both of you to God knows where in his state. Do you have no sense of self-preservation?"

"I only did what I thought was right. Okay?"

"Not okay. It's not fucking okay to throw yourself in danger like that." He glares at her and she glares back, unyielding.

I respect that about Elsa. Aiden is a psycho, but he's met his match in her.

During their entire exchange, I try to ignore the gloomy energy at my back but fail.

"Very well, Silver. Very well." Cole's voice is the equivalent of being stabbed with a thousand knives. "Tell them why we're here."

"I only found out yesterday." I stare at my nails. "Adam came over and...well, he said a lot of shit."

"Say it," Cole whips out his order.

"Adam said that..." I lick my lips. Damn. Why do I feel so guilty about this? "He was the one who pushed Elsa in the pool."

Elsa's blue eyes double in size, but she stays silent.

"He did, huh?" Aiden drawls.

"Go on," Cole urges. "Tell them why he did it."

"He said he did it to get in my good graces, okay?" I slide my gaze to Elsa's. "I swear I had nothing to do with it. I only just found out myself. If I'd known, I would've told you."

"But you knew Adam's intentions." Cole digs the knife deeper. "And apparently, you've known about them for a long time."

I swallow. "Cole —"

"Not a word."

"Cole —"

"Go wait in the car."

Ugh. Seriously. Why does he keep doing this?

You know what? Enough is enough.

I jerk up, throwing my hands in the air. "Come here, Silver. Go there, Silver. What do you think I am? Your fucking toy?"

He remains motionless as he repeats, "Go wait in the car."

Then I do something I've never done in public before. I flip him off.

I flip Cole Nash the bird.

And because I'm somewhat of a coward, I storm to the entrance.

Before I reach it, I stop, recalling something important. I face Elsa and whisper, "I'm sorry."

I slam the door shut behind me, but I don't leave. The thing is, this door isn't soundproof—most likely because it's old. I discovered it once when I came here and listened in on Levi, Aiden's cousin, having sex with his girlfriend, Astrid. But I ran away before they could discover my perverted tendencies.

That was my first voyeurism experience. Well, it was just audible, but it counts. That was when I started to think that maybe I enjoy things on the edge.

Maybe that's why I became entangled too fast with Cole. Not only does he not judge me, but he also shares those tendencies with me and he's not at all apologetic about it.

"Let's meet later," Cole says—to Aiden, I assume.

"I'll get in touch," the other dick replies.

"And, Elsa?" Cole calls.

"Yeah?" She sounds distracted.

"She only learnt this information yesterday. Don't beat her up again."

My heart nearly bursts at Cole's words. I can't believe he just said that when he's mad at me.

"Says the guy who watched while she was beaten to a pulp." Aiden scoffs.

"She brought it on herself that time."

And he had to ruin it.

Doesn't matter, though. He stood up for me.

Before he comes out, I run to the main street and walk for some time before I catch a taxi.

Yes, I'm a coward and I really don't want to deal with his wrath right now.

I know I'm only delaying the inevitable, but he'll eventually cool off.

Right?

THIRTY-FOUR

Cole

Silver ran away to her mother's house.

Again.

She's starting to make a habit out of it and I'm going to fuck it—amongst other things—out of her.

But first, I have to take care of business.

Like the sorry fuck who's now going home after a drinking session in a pub.

Aiden, Xander, and I wait for him in the dark car park. Adam chooses this poor neighbourhood because it gives him some much-needed camouflage. He gets to drink as much as he wants without anyone bothering him or threatening to tell his father about it.

Xander is the one who gave us this piece of information since he does the same whenever he wants to escape his father's wrath. Though he still doesn't want to admit that he's developing a drinking problem.

However, that's not important right now. The fucker who's going to come out is.

"Where's Ronan?" Xander asks.

"He's stoned," Aiden says. "I'm going to fuck up his face if he complains that we're keeping him out."

"He wants to be kept out." I place a hand in my pocket to

prevent it from curling into a fist. I've been planning for this moment since last night. Since I saw the fear in Silver's eyes as she dashed out in see-through clothes. She's not the type who goes out unprepared, which means she was scared about her parents' careers more than she showed. The fact that that bastard Adam has gotten under her skin this way makes me want to eradicate him from this world.

No one gets to toy with her under my watch.

That game is mine and Silver's alone. No outsiders are allowed.

"Astor wants to be left out?" Aiden raises a brow. "Are we talking about the same person?"

"He puts on a façade." I throw Aiden a condescending glance. "If you weren't so self-centred, you would've noticed it."

"Hashtag burn." Xander grins. Aiden and I never go at each other's throats—at least, not in front of the others. So whenever that happens, Xander and Ronan act like monkeys who've found a banana.

"I told you it's over with Queens. I ended it officially in front of Jonathan." Aiden levels me with his own condescension. "Stop being a petty little bitch."

Before we met here, Aiden told me over the phone that it was all over.

He's no longer engaged to Silver.

She'll also speak to her father about it soon.

Despite the relief I feel, it's not enough. It's as if I can't get the thought of her engaged to someone else out of my head. Despite knowing it was fake all along, she was still someone else's fiancée.

Not mine. *His*.

The part I'm most pissed off about is the fact she'll never be my fiancée. She'll never be fully mine no matter how much I own her.

Then she had to be secretive about that fucker Adam. She's

slowly but surely pushing me out of her life, and soon enough, I'll only be a fling in her past.

Silver will eventually choose her parents' image and hers. I've never belonged in that picture-perfect frame.

Maybe that's what makes me feel even more pissed off than I should be about this whole fucking mess.

"Whoa, Captain." Xander clutches me by the shoulder. "Now you get Silver all to yourself, huh?"

"Which can't be said about your case." Aiden smirks at him.

Xander's grin falls and he flips him off. They both think they can keep secrets from me, but I've already figured it out. I'm curious to see how Xander will handle it.

"Here he comes," I whisper as Adam stumbles from the pub. It takes him a lot of swaying to reach his car.

He doesn't see us since we're hidden in the blind spot near the wall. Adam curses under his breath when he's unable to find his keys.

Aiden's shoulders tense and his expression blackens. Ever since he confirmed that Adam was the one who pushed Elsa in the pool, he's been out for blood. Almost like me.

Xander just joined because he likes to punch things lately.

No one here wants to fuck up that arsehole more than me. He didn't only terrorise Silver, but he also thought he could have her.

He thought he could own what's fucking mine.

Aiden goes first, but he doesn't bother with the ski mask. He punches Adam straight in the face.

Adam wails like a schoolgirl, clutching his nose.

"Payback time, fucker." Aiden raises his fist again.

Adam's eyes widen when Xander and I join in. The moment he realises the clusterfuck he's got himself into, his face contorts like a whore faking an orgasm.

He has no idea what's coming for him. I'll have fun

dissecting him to bloody pieces, but I won't need violence like Xander and Aiden.

Mental pain is more destructive than the physical one.

After Aiden punches him for the second time, Adam shrieks, blubbering nonsense.

"Hey…hey…" He puts both hands up, his eyes red and bloodshot. "L-let's talk it out. Our parents are friends. We can find a solution."

"Yes, let's talk." I place a hand on Aiden's arm, bringing it down. My voice is surprisingly composed, considering the chaos stabbing inside me. But I've always been the type who gets eerily quiet and calm in a time of crisis.

At first, I thought it was because of the calm night of the kidnapping, but maybe it's more because of the blood pool William drowned in. It was so fucking calm after he floated.

So silent.

So dead.

Like this lowlife will be once I'm done with him.

"Right, Cole." Adam smiles as he straightens. "I knew you'd be more reasonable."

"I am. See, I don't think violence fixes anything. You eventually heal from the cuts and bruises. They don't live inside you and remind you of what you did every day, do they? Unless we can get you in a state of stage four cancer for at least ten years—without medication—I don't see how we can make you pay physically."

Aiden and Xander smirk as all hope vanishes from Adam's eyes. It always feels euphoric when they realise I'm the worst choice they could've ever gotten. People are afraid of Aiden and think they can take refuge in my apparent kindness and welcoming smiles, but they don't know me.

None of them do.

Except for my Butterfly.

And it's for her that Adam will regret the day he got into

her immediate vicinity. He'll regret every time she read those texts with a frown or looked over her shoulder in fear.

"Here's how it will go, Adam," I continue. "We already know you use performance-enhancing drugs. But that won't do you much damage, even with the school, so we planted a few stashes of cocaine in your locker this afternoon. The cleaning staff should have found them by now and reported back to the principal. He should be on a phone call with your father, but that's not the only phone call he'll receive, is it, Xan?"

"Nope." Xander feigns sympathy as he speaks, "My dad, you know, Lewis Knight? Anyway, he's kind of a big shot in your father's party and he'll tell him that if he doesn't send you away, his position might be in jeopardy. If he does, however, it might end up being beneficial for him. He can move up in rank, you know." Xander winks. "Politics."

"My mother also has your mother's chain of restaurants." I take a step forward. "Considering Dad's company is one of their biggest shareholders, I'd say I can crush your mother's business with a simple BOD meeting, don't you think?"

I had to tell Mum about Adam. It was either that or get Sebastian involved. And as much as I'm fucking pissed off at Silver, I know she did everything she did to keep this out of her parents' political lives.

So I respected her wishes and didn't tell them. Mum loves Silver, so she agreed immediately and said she'll do anything to keep our family protected.

Our family.

I hate those fucking words.

"And that, my friend —" Aiden clutches Adam by the shoulder, and the bastard is too stunned to even flinch "— is only the beginning. We still haven't gotten Jonathan King and Sebastian Queens involved. Do you want a preview?"

"W-what do you want me to do?" Adam stares between the three of us as if we're his Grim Reapers.

I stalk towards him and smooth his shirt. "You'll accept your fate and leave for the military academy without a fucking protest. If you don't, I'll crush you."

And I will. Adam won't get away with only being transferred. As soon as I grow up enough to take hold of my father's businesses, I'll hunt him down and destroy him all over again.

I'll make his life a hell so deep, he will never find a way out.

He'll pay back in instalments.

He'll look over his shoulder in fear, just like she did.

That's my best form of revenge.

Once Adam thinks I'll release him, he sighs. I lift my fist and punch him in the face until my knuckles sting.

True, violence never solves anything, but it's liberating in a way.

It's ironic that I've only ever punched two people due to anger—Aiden and Adam.

Both times were because of Silver.

Everything in my life has turned around and revolves around her.

One way or another.

I go home late.

Partly because of Adam. Partly because I considered going to Cynthia's building and barging inside.

The only reason I stopped is because of Cynthia. She doesn't like me—because of my mother, I suppose—and would start a riot before allowing me to see Silver this late.

By the time I arrive home, it's around one in the morning. It's dark and quiet, so Sebastian and his team must be pulling an all-nighter in the party's building. They seem to be doing that a lot lately.

Perhaps he knows how much Mum needs her quiet when

she writes. Besides, it's more convenient than moving back and forth between the house and his workplace.

As I open the door to my room, my mind fills with ways to drag Silver back here tomorrow.

I need to catch her at school before she runs to Cynthia's. While I hate missing practice, because of the control I feel during games, I probably have to so I can —

I stop on the threshold of my room, my thoughts coming to a halt, too.

Silver sits on the chair by my desk—or, rather, sleeps. Her head lies on a book she must've been reading, her blonde strands half-camouflaging her face.

Her oversized T-shirt for the day is pink and barely reaches the middle of her naked thighs.

For a moment, I stand there and watch her.

For a moment, I soak in the image.

She came back.

Not only did she not stay at her mother's, but she also came to my room.

She was waiting for me.

Fuck. I shouldn't be feeling like a giddy teenager with a crush on the school's queen B, but it's there. The…joy.

Silver has never come to me before, not willingly. Not even as a pretence. She has walls so high, I thought I would never be able to climb over them no matter how much I tried.

And I did try.

I tried every fucking trick under the sun.

A part of me is still pissed off about the whole Adam thing, but now that I know he'll disappear for good, some of that anger vanishes.

Besides, I can't actually be mad at her when she's sleeping. She looks so pure and peaceful.

I gently pull her hand away to catch the title of the book she's been reading.

Nausea.

A small smile grazes my lips as I carefully wrap one hand around her back and the other under her legs and carry her in my arms. Her head falls against my chest with a satisfied moan.

She's so beautiful, it's fucking me up.

And it's not only her external beauty, it's everything about her, from her insecurities to her affectionate and responsible side.

It's just her.

I sit on the bed and manoeuvre her so she's half-lying atop me, her back leaning against my chest and her legs tucked between mine.

My fingers stroke the sensitive spot in her neck. She moans, and this time, her eyes flutter open.

Fine, so I was being a dick and woke her up. But I needed to see those baby blues.

For a second, she seems disoriented, then her lips break into a smile as she stares up at me, her head lying on my bicep.

"What are you doing here, Silver?"

The smile slowly vanishes. "Mum has a late-night meeting at the party and I don't like staying there alone. Besides…"

"Yes?"

"I don't want to run away anymore."

"And you decided to come to my room?"

She nods.

"If I remember correctly, you ran away when I told you to wait in the car earlier. Do you think you can come and go as you wish, Silver?"

"Cole…"

"Answer the fucking question."

"I was scared, okay? You can be scary sometimes." She half-turns so she's tucked in my lap and glides her fingers across my chest. "But when I got to Mum's and knew she wouldn't be home, I was restless. I met Adam there the other time, you know. He said his uncle lives there, but he doesn't. So I was scared he'd come find me."

That fucker. I should've punched him a few more times.

"I couldn't stay there," she murmurs. "You're the only person I wanted to see."

I try not to let those words consume me, but I fail. All I can do is watch her—the rosy hue on her cheeks, the relaxation in her shoulders as she snuggles into me.

"Are you still mad at me?" she whispers.

"Depends."

"On what?"

"On whether or not you hide things from me again."

She gulps. "I won't."

"You won't, huh?"

"No."

"Adam is gone," I tell her. "He'll be forced to transfer tomorrow. You won't have to worry about him again."

Her eyes light up and widen like when we were kids. And just like then, I would do anything to bring that expression again. "Really?"

"Yes."

"Thank you." She plants sloppy kisses on my lips, my cheek, my jaw. "Thank you, thank you."

It's like she's back to being a little girl, but I'm the only one who gets to see this side of her.

Just me. And it'll remain this way for as long as we both breathe.

I reach my fingers under her T-shirt.

"Cole, what are you doing?" She swallows, her expression morphing from excitement to arousal.

"Punishment."

"P-punishment?"

"You think you can hide things from me, flip me off and run away without paying the price?"

My fingers find her bare pussy and I grunt as her arousal coats my skin. "Looks like you've come ready for your punishment, Butterfly."

Her breathing hitches as I thrust two fingers inside her.

"You'll never lie to me again?"

"N-no." Her thighs clench around me.

"Run away from me?"

"No…" It comes out as a moan as I pound into her and play with her clit.

"Take someone else's side over mine?"

"Oh, God. Cole…" She tightens against my fingers, her lips forming an 'O'.

Using my other hand, I slap her arse and she gasps even as her walls grip me like a vice. "That's not the word."

"No, no…" She falls apart around me.

"You're mine, Silver. Only fucking mine," I whisper against her ear.

She doesn't nod. She doesn't agree, but for the first time after an orgasm, she doesn't tell me she hates me.

THIRTY-FIVE

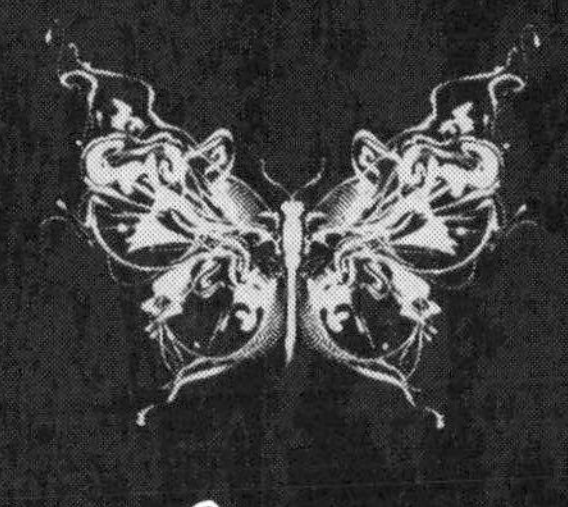

Silver

Unlike what I feared, Papa doesn't say anything when I tell him about breaking off the engagement with Aiden.

He simply pats my back and tells me my happiness matters more than anything else. Besides, it's not like Jonathan will stop backing him just because there's no in-law relationship. Apparently, Papa can help him with a partnership with a duke's family in return.

Jonathan hasn't been as tolerant with Aiden, though. I think he's taken him somewhere in China.

Mum is the same. She hasn't been talking to me since she learnt the news.

She showed up here and started her usual fighting shows with Papa.

"You're such a horrible influence, Sebastian. It's because of you that Silver has no sense of responsibility."

"Me?" He laughed with menace. "Do we really want to go down that lane, Cynthia? Because you're the one who's trying to make her a carbon copy of you, and not in the best way. If she doesn't want to marry for money and status, she will *not* marry for money and status. I will not sell my own daughter like a whore the way you're selling yourself to that Frenchman."

Their fight just got more intense after that, it was like those divorce days all over again.

I squeezed Helen's hand as we listened to them from outside Papa's office. Helen was pale and I could tell she was uncomfortable, but she didn't interfere or face Mum. If it were any other person, she would've kicked her out, and honestly, Mum would deserve it.

I apologised on her behalf to Helen and she stroked my cheek and told me it's not my fault.

That was yesterday.

I haven't heard a word from Mum since then. It's the weekend, so I have no idea where she could be. Usually, she'd invent work, because unlike what she won't admit, Mum is also a workaholic, just like Papa.

We're supposed to spend time together, but she hasn't returned my calls or texts. She's not in her flat either and it's freaking me out.

I plan to gather my thoughts and keep my promise to Cole—the part about not hiding anything from him again. I've been thinking of ways to tell him about the pregnancy because, like he did with Adam, I know he'll take care of this. Or at least help me make the decision, since obviously I can't do it.

A part of me is scared he'll tell me to get rid of it.

What else should I expect? That he'll suggest we leave the country or something?

Damn it, Silver. Stop being a naïve fool.

Cole has an early practice today because of a game in the evening, so I don't have to look at his face and feel guilty that I'm hiding something from him.

Besides, Mum's disappearance feels like a weight perching on my chest, looming over me like a demon.

I feel like that girl who walked in on her while she drowned in her own blood.

She hasn't answered my calls in fifteen hours. She promised to never do that to me again.

I tap on Papa's office door, balancing a tray of tea on my hand, and go inside. A forced smile grazes my lips as I serve Papa, Frederic, Derek, and the rest of their team.

"Thank you, Miss." Derek smiles but quickly hides it.

I return it, then ask Papa, "Can I talk to you for a second?"

"Absolutely." He nods at them before following me outside. We're standing in front of his closed office door. "What is it, Princess?"

"Mum is missing."

His jaw tightens. "She's a grown woman, Silver. Stop worrying about her as if she's a child."

"Papa..."

"Why would you even want to talk to her after the show she put on yesterday?"

"You don't understand. She can't be left alone for too long." I clink my nails against each other.

His expression morphs from anger to contemplation. "What do you mean?"

Mum will kill me if she finds out I told him, but she pushed me to this. I can't take this pain anymore. I can't keep it from Papa.

"Remember that time I went to spend the weekend with her and didn't want to leave her side for a whole month?"

He nods. "I thought you felt guilty about leaving her alone."

"I did. She cut her wrist, Papa."

"She *what?*"

"She doesn't want to show it, but she suffers in silence. The image you see, the debates and smiles and social media goddess titles are just her way to appear strong."

"Princess." He wraps an arm around my shoulder, appearing as shocked as I did back then. "You dealt with all of that on your own? Why haven't you told me?"

"She wouldn't let me. You know her; she'd rather die than show any type of weakness. During your divorce, she spoke high and mighty in front of the cameras, but she cried when she thought no one was there. She fought you every time she saw you, but she always worked on improving your plans for the party's future when she was alone. It's not that she doesn't care, Papa, it's that she doesn't like to show it." And I think I inherited that trait without even realising it.

"That loathsome habit of hers." He sighs, stroking my back. "She'll be okay. She loves you too much and would never leave you."

"But she was so mad yesterday." I sniffle. "What if she... what if..."

Papa's brow furrows in concern. "She won't." Even as he speaks the words, he doesn't seem to believe them. "She'll stay, Princess. If not for anyone, then for you."

"What do you mean?"

"You know, Cynthia was always the type who didn't want children, because she thought they'd get in the way of her ambitions and her plans. I tricked her into it, sort of, and the moment she knew she was pregnant with you, she said she loved you without even seeing you. When we first met you, she cried and thanked me for changing her mind." He smiles with nostalgia and shakes his head. "Then she said she'd kill me if I told anyone she cried. Point is, Princess, you gave her life and mine a deeper meaning. For that, we would never leave you, even though we left each other."

My arms drape around his waist and I fight my own tears. "I love you, Papa."

People say you can't choose your own parents, and many wish they never had their parents. Not me. I hated the fights and the divorce and everything that came with it, but I wouldn't change my parents for the world. Flaws and fights be damned.

My phone vibrates and I pull it out faster than I've ever done in all my life. It's not Mum. It's Lucien.

I called him earlier but only got his voicemail.

"Hey, Lucien."

"Hello, Silver." He has a charming French accent that I can listen to for days.

"Is Mum with you?" My heart beats loud as I wait for his answer.

"Yes, she is."

Oh, thank God. "Can I talk to her?"

"I'm afraid not. She's asleep."

Oh. "Can I come over?"

After Mum introduced us, we usually had meals either in his place or at her flat. He's a very private man and doesn't like eating in restaurants. Since I met him, I've always thought he'd be the one who would get Mum out of her funk.

She enjoys his company and hasn't been quick to break things off with him. I never actually felt more than friendship between them, and I thought that was enough for Mum's state of mind.

"Yes, of course," Lucien says. "But we're not in London."

"Not in London?"

"Yes, we're taking some time off in my mansion in Nice."

"You're in France?"

"*Exactement.*"

Oh, Mum. Couldn't she let me know about that little detail? Though she'll probably call me back when she wakes up.

Or maybe she won't.

I need to see her and make sure she's fine.

"Can you send me the address?"

"I'll do better than that." There's a smile in his voice. "I'll send a driver and my private jet."

"Thanks so much, Lucien."

"Any time. How about you spend the weekend with us, yes?"

"Okay."

After I hang up, I release a breath and realise Papa has

been standing there the whole time. From the tightening of his features, he seems to have heard the entire conversation.

"See? She's been with her lover while you were worrying about her. Cynthia will always be Cynthia. She's only using your guilt against you."

"Papa, how can you say that?"

"Do you mean to tell me she doesn't?"

"Well, sometimes, but she really does suffer in silence."

"Clearly. In France. During a romantic getaway." He briefly shakes his head. "You don't have to go."

"I want to. I need to make sure she's fine."

He kisses my temple. "Call me when you get there."

After Papa returns to his office, I quickly pack a bag. Lucien's driver pulls in at our house's entrance half an hour later.

Just when I'm about to climb in, Cole's Jeep comes to a slow halt in front of the mansion. My heart flutters and I have to remind myself to breathe as he walks up to me, wearing black jeans that hang low on his hips and a grey T-shirt that stretches over his shoulders.

I was planning to text him once I was in the car, but I guess this is better.

"Where are you going?" He watches the Mercedes and the driver with a critical eye.

"To see Mum in France."

He raises a brow. "Now you're running away to France? You think I can't follow?"

"She went with Lucien and I want to make sure she's fine." *And not mad at me.*

He watches me for a few unnerving seconds. The way he observes with that blank look on his face makes me feel as if he's dug inside me and figured everything out.

Like he can see the baby and will now confront me about it.

"I'll go with you," he finally says.

"You're coming with me?"

"If you're not running away, you wouldn't mind, right?"

"But..."

He pushes past me to the car and slides into the back seat. "Are you getting in?"

I join him, closing the door. "Shouldn't you tell Helen?"

"She's writing and won't come out until tomorrow. I'll call her then."

"Don't you have a game tonight?"

He shrugs.

Cole never skips practice, let alone games. The fact he's willing to do that to be with me sends tiny butterflies to slash the bottom of my stomach.

As the car leaves the mansion, I allow my thoughts to creep in. Deep down, I'm happy he's coming with me. I've been on trips before, but this is my first time with Cole.

The driver takes us straight to a special landing place where a plane is waiting for us.

"Wow. Lucien went all out. Maybe he wants to marry my mum."

"I don't think so," Cole says as a beautiful flight attendant leads us to our seats.

"Why not? What's wrong with my mum?" I snap.

He smiles. "Easy, Tiger. I don't think they're in that type of a relationship."

"Why would you think that?"

"They only seem to be close friends."

I clamp my lips shut, refusing to admit I also had that same thought.

The captain welcomes us, tells us the flight will last about two hours, and wishes us a comfortable trip.

Soon, we're flying in the air and I take pictures of the clouds, then a selfie.

As Cole sleeps, probably exhausted due to practice, I lean closer to him and, like a total creep, take another selfie.

When the flight attendant offers me food, I accept the fancy pasta. Soon after I finish, I regret eating it. Nausea hits me out of nowhere and I run to the bathroom and empty my stomach.

I haven't vomited in so long. It feels sticky and my stomach feels as if tiny needles are poking it.

Strong hands pull my hair to the side and Cole pats my back with a gentle touch. "Hey, are you okay?"

"I'm not." Tears barge into my eyes as I face him.

"What's wrong? Have you eaten something bad?"

"No."

"Then what is it, Silver? And don't even think about lying to me."

I'm tired of lying, of hiding, of watching days pass by like a ticking bomb. I want someone to share this with me. And not just anyone, him.

Cole.

Standing on wobbly feet, I wash my mouth out and head back to the seat. Cole follows me with that furrow in his brow. I let my head drop between my hands, breathing harshly. The seat creaks when Cole settles beside me and inches closer.

"Silver, what is it?"

All right, this is it. The moment of truth.

Meeting his dark greens, I murmur, "I'm pregnant."

THIRTY-SIX

Silver

Cole stares at me with that unnerving silence that nearly splits me open.

Nothing changes on his face.

Absolutely nothing. Almost like he's in numb state of mind.

Out of all the times he could've been blank, this is the worst. Why does he have to be so unreadable?

I've known him forever, so I'm usually able to reach behind that mask and get a glimpse of what he's hiding.

Not now though.

Peeking at him through my lashes, I watch with bated breath, waiting for his reaction.

He says nothing.

Not even a word.

Maybe he hates me. Maybe he's disgusted with how I'm ruining his future with this news.

The flight attendant comes to our side again, her presence interrupting our non-existent conversation. "Are you okay, Miss? Can I get you anything?"

"No, I'm fine," I murmur.

"Water with honey," he says. "Lime, too, if you have it."

She nods before disappearing to where she came from.

So he does have a voice. He just doesn't use it to speak to me. He continues observing me as if I'm an alien who's come to occupy the planet.

"Are you going to say something?" I meant to snap, but my voice comes out quiet, almost scared. "Anything?"

"Did you go to the doctor?" he asks.

"No."

"Then how do you know you're pregnant?"

"I took a test."

"You should go to the doctor."

"I can't just go to the doctor, Cole, okay? What if someone recognises me? Sebastian Queens and Cynthia Davis's daughter at the OB-GYN. Do you realise how scandalous that would be? I couldn't even go buy the freaking test and had to order it online."

"Would you stop thinking about the scandals and your parents and start thinking about yourself?" Cole snaps. Whoa. He never snaps. "This is your health, your life. You're carrying a baby inside you. Do you think that's a game? Or that they won't eventually find out?"

Tears sting my eyes and it takes everything in me not to break down right then and there. I feel like a kid being yelled at for idiotic behaviour.

"You think I haven't thought of that? I have. For weeks. I suspected this for damn weeks before I finally took the damn test, Cole. I'm the one living with this reality day in and day out, picturing all the possible scenarios and hating the fact that I might have to kill this life. So don't sit there telling me I'm not taking it seriously, because I am. More than you'll ever know."

He narrows his eyes. "You've suspected it for weeks and didn't tell me?"

I lift a shoulder, staring out of the window.

"Why?"

Because he could say the words that scare me the most. That I should abort.

Instead, I say, without facing him. "Because I hate you."

"Silver..." he warns, seeming to rein in whatever emotions he could ever show.

"Just forget it, okay? I'll figure it out."

He grabs me by the chin and spins my head around. My eyes are filled with tears and it's taking superhuman power for me to keep them at bay.

"*We* will figure it out. Both of us are responsible for that life."

"Cole..." A tear slides down my cheek and he wipes it away with the pad of his thumb.

"You thought I would abandon you?"

"No, but I thought you would be against it."

"It's already happened. I can't exactly be against it."

I pull away from him. "So if it hadn't happened, you would be?"

"No, but *you* would be."

"What?"

"If it were up to me, you'd be fucking mine in front of the entire world, and yes, I would be planning to put a football team worth of babies inside you so you'd always be glued to my side. But you constantly think about your parents and your image and everyone else's fucking opinion, so it's you who won't let anything happen. *Not* me."

My lips tremble as I face away from him again.

Damn him.

He lifts me up just so he can bring me down soon after.

The attendant delivers the cup of water he requested. He takes it from her hand and thanks her.

I don't miss the way she speaks in sultry words when she says to call her if he needs 'anything'. I'm going to tell Lucien to fire her.

What? Flirting must be against her code of work ethics.

When Cole offers the glass to me, I refuse to drink.

"Drink it."

"No."

"Stop acting like a baby," he says.

"Oh, wait. Is that because I have a freaking one inside me?" I mock. "No thanks to you."

"Drop that attitude and drink the fucking water, Silver."

"Or what? You'll make me?"

He wraps a hand around my nape and pulls me closer. I gasp and he uses the chance to make me drink. When I close my mouth, he holds my nose, forcing me to breathe through the only other opening.

Cole doesn't let me go until I finish the entire glass.

I wipe my mouth with the back of my hand, glaring at him. "You're a brute."

"And you hate me and you wish you'd never met me. I know the mantra." He slides his gaze up and down my body, and I feel self-conscious at the intense way he's watching me. "I'm also the one who put a baby in you."

"That's not something to be proud of."

"Maybe it is." He smirks.

"Can't you see what it'll do to us? It can destroy everything."

"Well, here's the thing, Butterfly." He leans over and brushes his lips against my nose. "I don't mind self-destructing if it's with you."

As soon as we land, Cole tells the driver to take us to an address he gives him.

It's an OB-GYN he looked up on the internet when we were flying.

I begged him not to take me to the doctor, because the driver will tell Lucien who could tell Mum, but all my protests fall on deaf ears.

Cole speaks in French to the receptionist. I speak it, too, but his accent is the best with foreign languages. It's barely there. I sound like an English snob when I speak French.

The doctor, Dr Qasim Laurent, is an older man with olive skin and light green eyes. After he does the test and asks me a few questions, he says we should wait.

Cole tells him we want to make sure the baby is fine. After the doctor leaves us alone, me on the table and Cole standing beside me, I swallow. "Why do you want to know if the baby is fine? Are you…thinking about keeping it?"

"Are you?"

"I asked first, Cole."

"You never come first, Miss Number Two."

"Dick," I mutter.

"What was that, Butterfly?"

"Come on, answer me."

"You had better chances of getting an answer before reducing me to my dick. I know you love it, but, well, it doesn't work in such situations," he teases.

"Cole!"

His expression returns to the serene blankness. "I do want to keep it."

If my heart could burst into pieces, it would've been all over the white room by now. "Really?"

He nods.

"But we're…you know…I'm your sister in front of everyone."

He gives me a dirty look. "You're not my fucking sister. I hate that word."

I hate it too.

I thread my fingers into his. If he and I want to keep it, then we can figure something out, right?

He watches me peculiarly for a second, his intense gaze sliding from my face to my abdomen and then back again. His eyes aren't only seeing me, but they're tearing through my flesh and peering into my soul.

"What?" I whisper.

"Did you… I mean, were you pregnant when Elsa beat you that time?"

The memory of that fear of being alone and not being able to protect my baby assaults me. I nod.

"I'm so sorry, Silver. I wouldn't have stood still if I knew. I would've protected you." He lifts our interlaced fingers and brushes his lips on the back of my hand, eliciting sharp tingles.

"I know." My throat closes around the words.

"You do?"

"Yeah, you were a dick, but you made up for it when you showed up at the park. I heard when you told her not to beat me again in the Meet Up."

His lips tug in a smirk. "Eavesdropping, Miss Prim and Proper?"

"Shut up. You're lucky I forgive you."

He kisses my fingers again.

We remain silent after that, just interlacing our fingers together and Cole caressing the back of my hand with his thumb. It's like we can't figure out what we want to say.

So I imagine Cole and me living in a faraway country. Well, not that far away—somewhere like France. Actually, no, it's still too close to home and can reflect back on our parents. We can go to Asia or Africa or even Australia.

By the time the doctor returns, all sorts of scenarios have formed in my head.

"*Alors*." Dr Laurant clears his throat and speaks in a thick French accent. "You have an ulcer that can be treated with *des IPP*. That's the reason behind the vomiting and nausea. You've had stressful times, yes?"

I nod. "But what about the pregnancy?"

"Is the child okay?" Cole asks.

"There's no child." The doctor smiles in an impassive kind of way. "You're not pregnant, *mademoiselle*."

Not pregnant? What does he mean I'm not pregnant?

"I took a test." I stare between him and Cole. "I took a test and it said positive."

"It's rare, but it can be... How do you say *faux positive*? Ah. A false positive."

No, no, no...

"How many tests have you taken, *mademoiselle*?"

"One."

"A false positive then. If you had taken another one right after, it would've come out negative. If you take tranquilisers a lot, that can alter the test. That's why we recommend you take multiple tests."

"What about my period? It's weeks late."

He flips through his pad. "Yes, from the form I can see that you used to take the birth control pills to regulate it. Since you haven't been doing so lately, it affected your cycle. Again, stress and tranquilisers play a part."

"So, I'm really not pregnant?" My voice breaks at the end.

"You're not. Your blood test shows normal HCG levels—that's the pregnancy hormone."

"Can't it be wrong?"

"No. Blood tests are the final verdict." He scribbles something on his pad. "I'll give you something for the stomach aches."

I stare at Cole.

He appears as dazed as me. As speechless as me.

I'm not pregnant.

It should make me happy, but all I want to do is cry.

THIRTY-SEVEN

Cole

Silver hasn't said a word the entire way.

She's slumped in her seat, staring out the window and trying her hardest not to break down.

It's like she's there but isn't.

Not really.

She left a part of herself at that doctor's office. I know, because I left a part of me too.

For a moment, I allowed myself to consider the prospect of becoming a father. Despite what I told her on the plane, my vision of fatherhood appeared a lot like blood in a pool.

Being a father meant becoming my own version of William and I would never be that fucking man.

However, the idea of being the father of Silver's children… Well, that's an entirely different thing altogether.

I started plotting where we'd go. How we'd live. All of it.

I started picturing a future where I wouldn't have to sneak into her room or pull her into a dark corner to be able to touch her.

A future where she's all mine in front of the world.

The doctor killed it. He aborted a dream that hadn't fully formed yet.

Not knowing what to say or how to say it, I remain silent.

I've always loved silence—it allows me to read in peace and let my thoughts be loud. Silence is my sanctuary.

Not now.

Now, I want to slice through it with a knife and end it once and for fucking all.

By the time we arrive to Lucien's house, it's almost evening.

Silver steps out of the car like a robot, hugging her bag, as I follow after. A butler greets us in front of the property. It's built near the cliff of a beach. The nearby town is visible from here, but it's far enough that no one would wander around the house.

Lucien must be a private man.

"*Bonsoir,*" a butler greets us at the entrance with a welcoming smile and motions at Silver's bag. "*S'ill vous plait.*"

She hands him the bag and asks in a tired voice, "Where's Mum?"

"*Madame* Davis?" I ask when he seems to be lost. I doubt he didn't understand; he must be one of those French people who refuses to acknowledge any language other than their own. The level of his snobbishness is similar to Ronan's favourite butler, Lars.

"*Ah, oui. Madame Davis a retourné à l'Angleterre avec Monsieur Lucien.*"

Really? Cynthia went back to England with Lucien without telling her daughter about it?

"*What?*" Silver retrieves her phone and winces. "Ugh. I forgot it's on airplane mode." She dials a number, then places the device to her ear. "Mum? Where are you?"

Silver paces the entrance while the butler just stands there, completely oblivious to the scene.

"I'm already in freaking France. Lucien must've told you I was coming. How could you leave?" She listens for a second. "It's always emergencies this, work that. What about me, Mum? *Me?* Have you ever thought about me in all the decisions you make?"

Realising she snapped at her mother, she quickly backpedals. "I'm sorry. I didn't mean to…okay… Talk to you later."

She hangs up with a sigh and keeps concentrating on her shoes as she speaks. "Mum had a work emergency. Lucien will be able to send the jet back to us tomorrow evening. I'm going to stay the night. You can catch a flight at the airport if you want."

And with that, she steps inside and the butler follows her with a nod at me.

I release a long sigh, then go after her. My shoulders are tense and the back of my neck is about to snap with how rigid it feels.

I find Silver upstairs, standing in the middle of a room.

It's similar to that time when I first touched her, first tasted her, when Mum and Sebastian announced they were getting married.

I've never been a believer of the butterfly effect, the fact that one simple alteration of initial conditions in a non-linear system can cause a catastrophic outcome later on.

However, I believe that small incidents, like Silver hearing that I lost my virginity that time, have led to a whole lot of clusterfuck. It's because of what she heard that she retaliated. She fought back. And since then, we've kept on fighting and challenging each other in a vicious cycle.

Now, we're here and nothing can be undone.

"Why are you still here?" She fiddles with her bag on the bed. "Go home. The driver can take you."

"I know what you're doing and it's not going to work. You'll never be able to push me away, so you might as well stop trying."

She pretends to not hear me as she yanks all the clothes out of the bag, her back bowing and rigid under the denim jacket.

I stride to her and grip her arm, forcing her to face me, to look at me. She can't be alone right now.

Tears glisten in her eyes as she pushes at my chest. "What do you want from me? Just leave me alone."

"I can't."

"Why not?"

"Because you're in pain. I hate it when you're in pain, Butterfly."

She breaks down then. A sob tears from her as she wraps her arms around my waist in a vice grip and hides her face in my chest.

I pull her close, a hand on her back and the other protectively around her head. I let her pain soak mine because if I had the option to take the hurt in her cries or the rawness of her grief, I would.

I've been emotionally fucked up since I was a child anyway, what's one more pain to add?

Only, this one has an entirely different meaning.

Silver is the type who doesn't cry often, and when she does, it's like she's breaking your heart. It's in those small sounds and the sniffles. It's in the way her whole body shakes with the force of her pain.

"It hurts. Why does it hurt so much, Cole? It's not supposed to. I should be happy I won't be forced to have an abortion, but why do I feel like I killed a baby that was never there in the first place? Why do I feel so horrible?"

"You're not horrible. You're just human, and you feel pain. It'll eventually go away."

"W-what if it doesn't?" she speaks through her hiccoughs. "What if I always feel this…this *loss*."

"Then we'll feel it together."

She peeks up at me with her tear-streaked face and bloodshot eyes. "What do you mean?"

"I told you, you're not the only one responsible for this. Your pain is my pain, Butterfly."

THIRTY-EIGHT

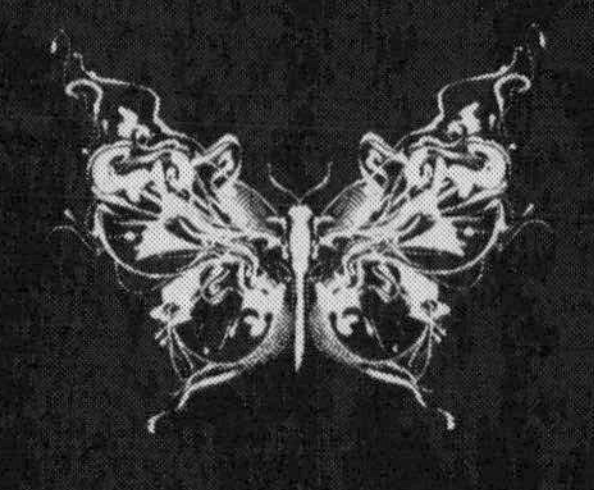

Silver

That night, Cole holds me as I cry myself to sleep.

I cry for something that was never there. But just because the test was negative doesn't mean I don't feel the loss.

It doesn't mean I don't feel like I'm missing a part of me. A chance of an alternative future, of a different life, another… possibility.

Because I know, I just know that if it were real, Cole and I would've fought for it. He would've taken me somewhere none of the reporters or the people from back home could find us.

Now, I have to return to the reality that I'm fucking my stepbrother and that while there isn't a baby this time, life as we know it will be over if anyone catches us.

My head's been in the clouds and now I have to drop back to the ground.

The next morning, Cole tries to drag me into town. He ambushes me after I'm out of my shower, standing in front of the bathroom in his stylish jeans and T-shirt with his hair combed.

No matter how much I love his appearance, I'm in no mood to leave my bed today. "I want to stay in my room until it's time to go home."

"Huh." He stares down at me with his signature blank expression.

"What?"

"I didn't know you were a bore aside from being a coward."

"Hey!" I punch him in the shoulder.

The faintest smile grazes his lips. "Forget it. I'll go without you. I don't need cowards on my tours."

I hear him greet the butler good morning and tell him he'll have breakfast outside.

That wanker.

I throw on a cute peach-coloured mini-dress with a strappy back and gather my hair into a ponytail. After I shove my feet into the first pair of shoes I find, I storm out behind him.

It's when I'm by the entrance that I realise I haven't put on any makeup. Whatever. I'm in no mood for that.

I catch up to Cole by the hill of the house, walking slowly.

"I'm not a coward." I pant as I keep up with his pace.

He smiles but says nothing. Instead, he threads his fingers with mine. The softness of his touch nearly breaks my heart all over again.

Your pain is my pain, Butterfly.

That was the first time I'd been able to breathe since the doctor said it was a false positive. Knowing that Cole, of all people, understood that pain made it less sharp. It's still there, but I feel a certain type of peace knowing I have him with me.

Wait. He's holding my hand. He shouldn't.

I stare over my shoulder and try to wiggle away, but he doesn't let me go. "Cole! We're in public."

"We're not in England. No one knows us here." He drags me closer into his side. "Stay still."

No one knows us here.

The only one who does is probably Lucien's butler, and he's out of the picture now.

A surreal sense of levitation takes hold of me as I let Cole lead me in the direction of the nearest town.

Renewed energy engulfs me. I soak in my surroundings,

the bright blue sky and the warm sun. In the confines of the tight streets and vintage feel of the roads, it's like a scene from a novel.

"There was a destructive battle here during the world war," Cole says as we pass old buildings. "Our troops fought for the French on these same streets."

I grin, watching him study the old pavement with that curious glint in his eyes. It's so rare to see him unleash his inner nerd. "Well, it wasn't our battle, and yet, we lost so many soldiers for it."

"Do you honestly believe that?" He gives me a curious look.

"Yes, the French got themselves into that mess. We didn't have to act like knights in shining armour."

"We were anything but. That's called a precedent fight, Butterfly. We were going to get involved anyway, so we made the first move and fought the enemy on foreign soil. Those types of battles happened many times over the course of history, like in the Ottoman Empire's colonisation wars, or the Persians against the Romans."

"You're such a nerd."

He releases my hand and tugs me to the crook of his body by the waist. It's the first time he's touched me so possessively in public. It's almost as if he's announcing his ownership. "Who are you calling a nerd, Butterfly?"

"You." I hide my smile. "I bet you can give accurate retellings and even recite what those generals said before every battle."

"Of course I can. The pre-battle part is the most important. That's the moment before death. Before chaos."

Cole called me his chaos before, and I still don't know whether that's a good or a bad thing. Since he associates it with death, it's clear on which side it falls. My heart shrinks as I try to fight off the feeling.

"It's beautiful," he says.

"Beautiful?"

"Yes. It's the unknown, and the unknown can be the most beautiful thing."

"Or the most horrible one."

"You never know at that moment. When troops stand there listening to their generals, they don't know whether they'll die, be injured, or stay alive. They don't know if they'll see their families again or if it's all over. It's human nature at its truest form."

"It's called survival."

"It's called life." He brushes his lips against my nose. "It's chaos."

My heart thumps so hard, I'm scared it'll stop beating or something.

Oh, shit.

I'm not supposed to be so caught up in him like this. I'm not supposed to wish I'm still his chaos and that he'll never ever find a replacement.

"Do you want to do something chaotic?" I bite my lower lip.

"Like what?"

I motion at a tattoo parlour across the street from which a couple are exiting, appearing half happy, half in pain.

He raises a brow. "You want to get a tattoo?"

"Together. You and I." It's a crazy idea, but I want to commemorate this moment. I want to remember the pain, but also the way Cole held me through it.

We'll eventually go home, and I want to keep the moment where we got to hold hands in public as a permanent reminder of today.

I expect him to refuse since Cole isn't the type who likes to mark skin—at least not permanently, but then he says, "I get to choose what you put on your skin."

I jut my chin. "And I get to choose what you put on yours."

His lips tilt in a charming smile. "Deal."

In the parlour, we decide to get tattoos on our sides since they can be easily hidden by clothes. Cole demands that the woman take care of me, not the man. Which is fine by me since that means she won't be touching him.

Two hours later, and after so much pain that almost brought me to tears, we stand in front of each other in the middle of a room with dark walls.

"Show me." I motion at his T-shirt.

"You first."

"At the same time?"

He nods and we lift our clothes, baring our skin at the same time. Cole got the tattoo I chose for him and it's even more beautiful than I imagined. The skin around it is red due to how fresh it is, but the design is clear. It's an open book with tendrils of smoke coming out and on top of it, written in a neat font is the word 'CHAOS.'

"It's so beautiful," I breathe out, approaching him to get a better view.

Cole holds me at arm's length. "Stay there, I still haven't gotten my fill."

I remain in place, swallowing at the intense way he's examining my tattoo. It's a butterfly. And not just any butterfly. Cole sketched something that's identical to the butterfly pin I wore that day ten years ago in the park.

The tattoo came out perfect with all the small details in the wing. It's an exact match to the pin and similar to the necklace around my throat.

"So?" I ask. "You like it?"

"I love it." He plants a kiss on my nose.

My toes curl like they do every time he does that. It's softness where Cole is usually hard. It's something he only does with me.

After we leave the tattoo parlour, we roam the streets, hand in hand, as Cole tells me more history.

The smell of baked goods lures me in like a cartoon character when we pass by a small pastry shop.

"Let's try croissants," I tell him.

Cole buys us croissants *au chocolat* and we sit at a small table in front of the shop. There are a few old patrons at the surrounding tables, and they seem relaxed, enjoying the bright weather.

I take a bite of the hot croissant and moan in pleasure. "Now I'm craving a Snickers bar. Let's find some afterwards..."

I lift my head and stop chewing when I find Cole's darkened eyes zeroed in on me.

He's sitting opposite me with the small table separating us. He's close enough that I smell his cinnamon scent and inhale it into my lungs.

The way he's looking at me is so sinister, it's like he'll grab me and fuck me on the table right here, right now.

I clear my throat, but my voice comes out breathy anyway. "Why are you looking at me like that?"

"Why did you just moan?"

"I-I didn't."

"Yes, you did. Don't lie to me."

"It was because of the croissant."

"And here I thought you were seducing me."

"I-I wasn't."

"Well, it worked."

"C-Cole —"

My words die in my throat when he grips my chin with two fingers and pulls me close before his lips claim mine. It's an open-mouthed kiss, all tongues and teeth and...*freedom*.

Neither of us worries that we're in public or that we shouldn't be doing this or that someone will see.

Fuck them.

Fuck everyone.

Because this thing that beats between us is way stronger than their words and their judgement.

The loss we felt is way deeper than societal standards and forbidden relationships.

It's us.

As twisted as it is.

We don't stop kissing that day. We make out in the streets. In the grocery store. Everywhere. We give the people in town a PDA they never signed up for.

I take pictures with a barely-willing Cole who hardly looks at the camera and refuses to pose unless it involves a kiss or me touching him.

I commemorate every moment and every second. I document the time where I get to kiss him anywhere I want.

Because real life will strike again.

Real life will rip us apart.

And the only place I can have him is behind closed doors.

THIRTY-NINE

Doll Master

Once upon a time, there was a doll.

You thought you could get rid of me because I'm not sending you texts anymore.

I'm close even when I'm far.

I'll follow like a star.

And that star will eventually become your fate and your only reprieve.

It'll follow you as you grow. As you fall. As you stand up just so you'll fall again.

You can't run. You can't hide.

Little doll, what have you done?

The fun has only begun.

And soon, you'll come undone.

FORTY

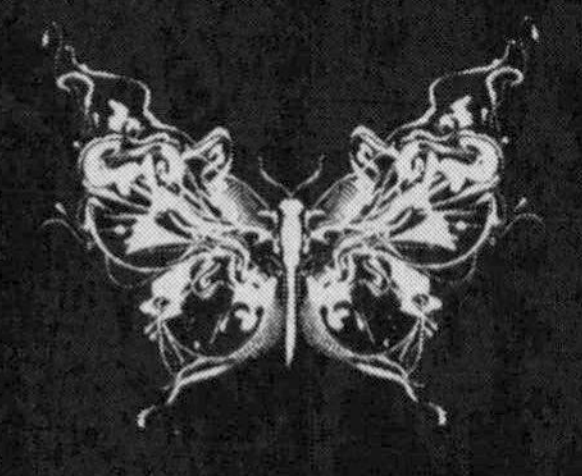

Silver

In the end, life goes on.

Mum was fine, and in her words, she only needed to clear her head in a place where Papa doesn't exist. Usually, she makes him appear as the villain every chance she gets, but not this time. Maybe she's finally moving on? I hope so, at least. I feel so sorry for Lucien.

After that weekend we spent in Nice, Cole and I evolved. I can't find the words to describe it properly, but we just took it to the next level.

Could be because we shared a loss, or because we became more careful.

Or I did.

The anxiety and stress I felt when I thought I was pregnant was torture. It's Papa's election year—the dream he's worked his entire life for. The one he divorced Mum for because he wanted to focus on his political career.

I can't be self-immersed and ruin that for him.

Or Mum's social popularity. Or Helen's success.

So the only time Cole gets to touch or even be near me is when he sneaks into my room at night. When both our doors are closed and the outside world ceases to exist.

I still pretend I don't want him there and he fucks me

harder each time I do. It's like he's punishing me for our screwed-up situation.

Cole likes punishments. The control and the fact that I fall completely at his mercy is his driving force.

Whenever I act like a brat at school, or when he tells me to do something and I don't, he sends me texts like:

Cole: I'm going to spank your arse so hard, you will remember me every time you sit tomorrow.

Cole: You better be naked and splayed out on the bed when I come in or there will be no orgasms for you tonight.

Cole: What did I say about talking to Aiden? Do you want to be punished, Butterfly? Is that it?

Let's just say, I did most of those things on purpose so he'd unleash his intensity on me. There's something so mesmerising about Cole shedding the cool mask and going all out when he's with me.

I'm the only one who gets to provoke that side of him. The only one who gets him on more than one level.

And he gets me.

He knows when the doubts creep in, when my heart shrinks whenever I see a kid on the streets and recall the loss of what we couldn't have.

Every time I run to the park, he follows with a Snickers bar and kisses me on the nose.

Last week, I won a piano competition. Well, Cole let me win. I know he could've beaten me, but that day, he barely played. When I shoved him, demanding he not take pity on me, he said, "That wasn't pity. I've always wanted to see that spark you get in your eyes when you win."

"But you've made it your job to crush me in everything."

"That's because you were with Aiden. Now, you're not."

To say Cole gets jealous would be an understatement. He doesn't like any male in my vicinity, but he's so subtle about it. Like kicking Aiden down every chance he gets, or plotting Ronan's demise just because he put an arm around my shoulder.

Aiden calls him petty and he is in some ways. Cole doesn't stop when he's on a mission—everything in his environment becomes a means to reach a goal. He doesn't sleep a wink until he achieves it.

Not that I'm any better in the jealousy department. I make it my job to make sure no other girl hangs around him or in his immediate surroundings.

The other week, Teal, Elsa's foster sister, was sitting with Cole in the school's garden and reading from a book he specifically ordered from overseas.

My relationship with Teal—if you could call it a relationship—is better than the one I have with Elsa. Partly because we crossed paths in *La Débauche* and we're both into voyeurism. And okay, I might have pushed Cole away when I recognised her because I didn't want to be associated with him anywhere in public.

That fantasy of us being together for the world to see started and ended in that small town in France.

Seeing her with him, and knowing that they got along on some level when Cole never actually showed any interest in the opposite sex in the past, made me rage like a volcano.

I'm the only one he's supposed to read to. The only one who falls asleep listening to his voice, dreaming about a parallel world where he can read to me in the park while my head lies on his lap.

So I flirted with Ronan as double payback. Teal is Ronan's fiancée; he wasn't amused to see her with Cole either.

That evening, Cole tied me to the bedpost and fucked me the entire night. No kidding. He only let me sleep around dawn.

Well, he didn't let me. I fell asleep on him when he went to run a bath for me.

I'm still not talking to him because of the whole Teal thing. She almost kissed him back there. He didn't stop her, Ronan did. If he hadn't, Cole would've let her fucking kiss him.

Now I'm the one who's being petty, but whatever. It's enough torture that I don't get to kiss him in public, that I don't even get to hold his hand or flirt with him, that I don't get to shout it to the world that he's mine. I don't need to see other girls' claws on him on top of everything else.

"Have fun, kids." Helen waves at us from the front door.

Her face looks worn out, which is understandable considering she's about ready to submit the final manuscript for her next release to her agent. He read the first half and was thrilled, calling it her best work yet.

She kind of died a little in the process of meeting her deadline. I feel sorry for her since Papa isn't around much anymore.

Most of his nights and days are spent at the party. Although he barely shows up at home, Helen's been nothing but supportive. Now that I think about it, most of my parents' fights were because they didn't find time for each other in the midst of chasing their careers.

Helen is kinder and less outspoken than Mum. It's been several months, but she's never called Papa out or blamed him. She's simply left him to his devices and taken care of the house and us as if she's lived here her entire life.

I love Helen, but sometimes, I miss having Mum around. It's crazy given that she moved out ages ago, but before the marriage, she always dropped in unannounced just to fight with Papa.

Now, it doesn't happen anymore. And to an extent, I'm grateful to Helen for that.

I snap the seatbelt over my simple soft pink dress that falls to above my knees as Cole drives his Jeep away from the house. Ronan is throwing a party in the Meet Up. Since his parents returned from their overseas trip, he doesn't have full access to his mansion, so the Meet Up is his next best option.

Parties have never been my thing, so I considered skipping and lounging around to watch the latest political debate. However, the brute, Cole, barged into my room and told me we're going.

I know for a fact he doesn't like parties and that the only reason he attends them is to observe everyone, to tuck in their habits and weaknesses for later use—especially his friends.

He feels like they could be the most threatening to him considering they've known him the longest, so he needs to be prepared for them.

When I told him he's too distrustful, he said he's only prepared because they're fuckers. His words, not mine.

He's wearing jeans, a T-shirt, and his Elites royal blue jacket. They won tonight, so this is some sort of a celebration.

I try not to focus on how the colour blue suits him so well, or how strands of his chestnut hair fall across his forehead, or how good he smells straight out of a shower.

Considering the tingles between my thighs, I'd say I'm failing.

"Why did you drag me out again?" I fold my arms over my chest.

He keeps his attention on the road, driving with one strong hand on the bottom of the steering wheel. God. I've always loved how he drives—it's so effortless and masculine. And he does it with so much confidence, like he could do it with his eyes closed.

They say a person's driving style speaks of their character. I often get worked up with idiot drivers who don't respect road signs or etiquette, but Cole tunes them all out as if they don't exist, as if they're the dust on his shoe.

His dispassionate disregard of others is so weird given how much he observes people, but I guess he doesn't observe them because he likes them. It's more because he needs to see how they'll fit in his plots.

"You didn't come to the game, Silver."

"That's because I said I wouldn't." *I'm mad at him.*

"And what did I say?"

I don't reply. He grips my half-bare thigh with his free hand. It takes everything in me not to clench my legs together at the way he's touching me.

"What. Did. I. Say?" he emphasises each word.

"That I should come." I keep my voice level. "Did you really expect me to show up after the whole picturesque scene with Teal?"

"Jealous much, Butterfly?"

"Screw you, Cole, okay? I ha —"

He tightens his hold around my thigh so hard, I wince. "Don't finish that sentence."

"Or what?"

Cole shakes his head. "You don't want to know."

My insides nearly liquefy at the promise. So I whisper, "I hate you."

The car comes to a screeching halt. I would've hit the dash if it weren't for the seatbelt.

I swallow, expecting Cole to jump me here and now, but his next words surprise me. "Get out."

"W-what?"

"You heard me."

"You're abandoning me here?" I throw a glance out the window. The way to the Meet Up is a bit deserted. The street lights are few and far between and there's no human soul around. "This is the middle of nowhere. What the hell is wrong with you?"

"Get. Out." His words are firm and final.

My chin trembles as I release my seatbelt and open the door's handle with unsteady fingers.

I can't believe he's doing this to me.

Once I'm outside, I stand near the door as I slam it shut, then I flip him off through the window.

If he expects me to beg him to take me along, he'll be waiting for a long time.

I turn away from the car, fiddling with my bag so I can call an Uber. The sound of a door opening catches my attention.

Wait. He didn't leave?

Slowly spinning around, I spot him lifting the Jeep's boot. His dark green eyes cut a path to my soul as he aims them at me.

"Get in here."

"Get in where?"

He motions at the boot.

"Have you lost your mind?"

"Apparently *you* did when you said what I told you not to say." He's so calm, it's disturbing. "Are you going to get inside or not?"

I'm about to say no, but he interrupts me. "A crime happened around here a few days ago. A blonde girl who was running alone in this deserted area got attacked and molested. She's currently in the intensive care unit."

I gulp. Even I had heard about that.

"It's not the first incident. Remember what Frederic said about this serial attacker?" The chilling tone he speaks with covers my skin in goosebumps. "Many women who wander alone early mornings or late evenings in places like these get ambushed. But here's the plot twist, perhaps the serial attacker will turn into a serial killer, considering he already has a pattern and a victim profile. All the girls are blondes and with fair skin."

"S-stop it."

"Blue eyes, too, Butterfly. Just like yours."

"Fine, arsehole." I go to his side. "You didn't plan on leaving me here, did you?"

"Of course not, but you don't get to ride with me after saying you hate me."

I scowl at him, then climb into the boot. Thankfully, it's vast enough to fit me, but I have to bend my legs.

"You're sick," I tell him.

"You love it."

I do. I really, *really* do.

He reaches behind me, and I shiver as his hand brushes against my bare shoulder.

Damn him and his touch.

Cole retrieves some ropes.

"Here?" I whisper-yell as he ties my ankles together. The tightness of the ropes feels so familiar now. So *exciting*.

When he's finished with my wrists, he steps back and watches me with a sadistic gleam in his eyes. "There. Much better."

"You'll really leave me like this?" Usually, the tying up part is followed by sex and mind shattering orgasms. That's why I like them. What's the point of appetisers if there's no main course?

"One more thing." He rummages by my head, then retrieves a ball gag and straps it around my mouth.

My protests turn into muffled sounds. Oh, come on! The car boot shouldn't be the setting for this.

Ropes and a gag. Maybe *he* is the psycho attacking women. He even knows about the victims' profiles and everything.

Where the hell did that idea come from?

His fingers caress my cheek before gripping my chin. His thumb strokes my lower lip. I want to taste him.

"You really thought you could tell me you hate me and get away with it, Silver? I'll eventually fuck that word out of you."

I shudder at the promise. Right now? Here?

"Be a good girl." He closes the boot, killing my hope, and turning my world black.

I swallow back my frustration as the car moves down the road. He's an excellent driver, so I don't bump into anything, not even once.

When we come to a halt and the sound of people filters in, I realise we must've arrived at the Meet Up.

"You want to come out?" he whispers without opening the boot.

I hit the roof with my foot.

Laughter comes from him as he opens the boot a slit. I squint at the light from the party. People from school buzz all around the car park, laughing and ready to have a good time.

My eyes widen. They can't see me like this.

"What do you say?" Cole's eyes gleam as if he knows exactly what I'm thinking about.

I shake my head, mumbling around the ball gag.

"I thought so." He strokes my cheek again. "Be good."

And the darkness returns.

The bastard.

I can't believe he's leaving me like this to go a party.

It feels like I stay there for hours, if not days. Okay, I'm exaggerating. It's probably been fifteen minutes, but I'm restless. I move around and I accidently hit the boot a few times before I realise someone might hear.

Shit.

A commotion comes from outside. I can hear Cole's and Ronan's voices, but I can't make out what they're saying.

Soon after, all the voices disappear and the car starts moving.

Thank God.

By the time it stops again, I'm so ready to give Cole a piece of my mind.

He opens the boot and I blink a few times to readjust my vision.

We're at the park.

The bastard knows where to take me to lessen my anger. He removes the gag and I swallow all the drool that's gathered in my mouth.

Cole undoes my wrists. I push him away as I try to free my ankles, but I end up making the knots tighter.

A chuckle rips from him as he takes over the task. "Stay still."

Once I'm no longer tied, I jump out of the boot and punch him in the chest. "What if I was claustrophobic, you arsehole?"

"You aren't. You hide in your closet every time you write in your journals."

My lips part. "Y-you know about them?"

"Maybe."

Oh. My. God.

He's not supposed to. Why the hell does he even know about them?

"How far did you read?"

"All."

"You…you…you're such a pervert!"

"Not as much as your entries about me lately."

My cheeks heat to a deep shade of red. "Shut up."

"Why? Are you shy you admitted that night-time is your favourite time of the day?"

"Whatever." I fold my arms. "If you do that to me again, you'll read about the black magic and the voodoo doll I'm preparing for you."

He grabs me by the arm and tugs me close so I end up flush against his front. "If you say you hate me again, this will only keep escalating."

"Escalating?"

"Uh-huh," he whispers against the shell of my ear. "And that includes the fucking journal."

I push away from him, about to get into the passenger seat, but he doesn't release me.

Cole throws me into the back seat, closes the door, and pulls my dress up.

"S-someone will see," I breathe out even as my legs wrap around his waist the moment he yanks his trousers down.

"They won't."

"What if they do?"

"What if they do, Silver? What if they fucking do?" He thrusts inside me in one long go that tears a moan out of my throat. "That won't change the fact that I fuck you and sleep with you every night. It doesn't change the fact that you're mine."

A shudder grips me in its clutches as he owns me in every sense of the word. Lately, it feels as if he's not only fucking my body, but he's also screwing my heart and soul.

He's owning every part of me whether I like it or not.

At first, I thought this would be a fling and would soon end. I thought I'd get bored, tired, or maybe everything would fizzle out.

But it's been months, whole damn months, and it's only been fizzling up—not out.

What was I thinking? This is Cole. He's owned a part of my soul ever since that day in this very park.

He's always had me. One twisted way or another.

As we fall apart together, the realisation hits me like a thunderstorm. The feelings I have for him were never temporary and they never will be.

None of this will be temporary.

It's all wishful thinking.

"Fuck," he murmurs against my neck. "You're messing me up, Silver. Why can't I stop thinking about you for even a second?"

"They're not real."

"What isn't real?"

"The feelings. Everything. They only exist because we can't be together."

"What the fuck are you talking about?" He lifts his head from my neck, watching me with disapproval. With anger.

I shove him away, and thankfully, he doesn't protest as he pulls out of me, his cum dripping between my thighs.

Retrieving a tissue, I clean up, not wanting to meet his imploring gaze. "Take me to Mum."

If I spend the night with her, surely I'll clear my head and come up with a better plan for the future.

One that doesn't destroy both our families.

Because at this pace, we're heading straight to a cliff where both of us will fall.

Cole's jaw ticks. He doesn't say a word as he tucks himself in, gets out, and takes the driver's seat.

I remain at the back, pretending to stare out the window, when I'm actually stealing looks at him.

Once we're in the car park, he throws me a Snickers bar through the window, his face blank. "I bought it earlier. It's melting."

My heart warms. Cole doesn't eat Snickers, or chocolate in general, but he always buys them for me. "Thanks."

"I'm done playing your games, Silver. This is the last time you run from me."

"What do you expect me to do?"

"I expect you to be with me because you want to, not run away because you can't admit it to yourself."

"What about everyone else?"

"Fuck everyone else. They don't matter more than you and I."

And with that, he leaves. I hit the button to Mum's flat, my shoulders drooping as I absentmindedly eat the Snickers bar.

Maybe I should save it for when Mum and I watch a film—not *The Notebook*.

I enter the code to her flat and go inside, still nibbling on the chocolate.

It's dark inside, the only light coming from her room. I'm just outside of it when the sounds filter in.

Moans. Groans. Slaps of flesh against flesh.

My cheeks heat. I probably should've called first. But then again, Lucien barely comes to Mum's flat, and I kind of thought they were in a non-sexual relationship.

I turn around to leave when I hear the unmistakable name.

My fingers slowly push the door open. What remains of my Snickers drops to the ground. I'm scarred for life.

Mum is on her back as a man fucks her hard.

And that man isn't Lucien.

It's Papa.

FORTY-ONE

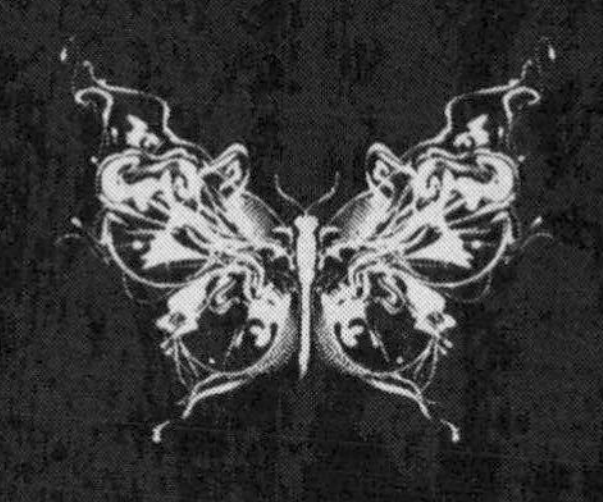

Silver

The three of us sit in Mum's living area.

To say the air is awkward and full of tension would be the understatement of the century. This isn't how I've imagined our family reunion.

Mum ties the satin robe around her nightgown and keeps touching her hair, trying to submit the dishevelled blonde strands to order.

Papa appears completely normal, all tucked in his suit as if he were born in one.

God. I can't believe I walked in on my parents having sex. It's even more disturbing now considering they're no longer married.

They sit beside each other while I'm across from them, arms folded like a judge out to prosecute her defendants.

Mum flashes me an awkward smile. "It's not what it seems."

I scrunch my nose. "I think I saw exactly what it seems."

"Princess." Papa clears his throat. "We're sorry you had to witness that."

"Shouldn't you be sorrier about other people? I don't know, like Helen and Lucien?"

"Lucien and I are just friends, Babydoll. We only go out together to avoid the hassle of finding dates to the countless of events we attend."

"How about Helen then?" I jut my chin at Papa. "How could you do this to her?"

Mum studies her red nails. "They're not sexually active."

"Cynthia," Papa reprimands

"What?" She feigns nonchalance. "Silver is old enough to understand that. She's sexually active herself."

"I did not need that image." Papa looks at me weird, almost horrified, as if he's just realising that I'm not his little girl anymore.

"Mum!" My voice lowers. "How do you know that?"

"I know everything about you, Babydoll. You think I wouldn't notice that you're in love?"

"I-I'm n-not in love." I clear my throat. "Anyway, this isn't about me. Papa?"

"Helen and I only got married for convenience. She had no idea how to handle the fortune William left behind, so I offered to help. One thing led to another and we sort of formed a partnership."

"And a marriage." Mum huffs. "She thought if she had you long enough, you'd probably fall for her graces. That woman is a snake."

"Cynthia." Papa releases another breath.

"Still, this isn't right, Papa." I'm such a hypocrite. I'm fucking his stepson under his roof every night, after all.

"Didn't you always want us to be together?" Mum asks. "You planned it for years."

"Not at the expense of someone else's happiness. This isn't right by Helen, and you know that, Papa. These are your core principles and you betrayed them."

"Silver!" Mum scoffs. "I can't believe you're taking that snake's side over your mother's."

"She's right." Papa's lips thin in a tight smile. "I'm sorry I disappointed you, Princess."

"Give me a fucking break." Mum throws her hands in the air. "So now I'm the bad guy in all of this?"

"Language, Cynthia." Papa's voice lowers.

"You didn't mind the language when you were fucking me earlier."

"Mum!"

"Cynthia!" Papa says at the same time.

"Fine." Mum jerks up. "I'm always wrong. I always say the wrong things. Apparently, I can't make any personal relationship work and should focus on my job instead. If my own daughter and the man I thought was the love of my life don't understand me, it's useless to keep trying. Go back to your soft, sweet Helen."

She's about to storm out, but Papa and I stand up. He catches her by the wrist before she can go.

Tears glisten in her eyes and she tries to hide them. Feelings have always been Mum's curse. I see it now. The fact she couldn't keep up with her career and her married life at the same time was her doom. She never forgave herself for giving up on her marriage, and that's why she developed depression after the divorce. But she had too much pride to ask Papa to try again. As did he. So they kept fighting every chance they got instead.

Papa's face softens for the first time in…years. For the first time since Mum left the house. "Helen is indeed soft and sweet."

"What are you waiting for then?" she snaps. "The door is right there."

"But she's not the woman who drives me crazy with every word out of her mouth. She's not you, Cynthia."

My heart nearly explodes as Mum's expression becomes gentle, almost as if she's ten years younger.

Papa caresses her hand. "I'll end it properly with her tonight, and we can have a family breakfast tomorrow?"

Both Mum and I nod.

As much as I feel sorry for Helen, I believe in fairy tales. I believe in Mum and Papa. I always have. The only reason I gave up on them is due to thinking they were more at peace apart. Turns out, they were both miserable.

Mum and I walk Papa to the door. I hug him and tell him that I love him, that I'm proud of his decisions, even if this turmoil can damage his campaign.

He kisses me on the temple, then Mum on the lips. "I love you both."

"And I love you, Bastian." Mum closes her eyes, inhaling his scent. "I never stopped."

Papa kisses her again and leaves. After Mum closes the door behind him, she squeals.

No kidding. Cynthia Davis *squeals* and wraps her arms around me. Her happiness is infectious and I hug her back as she whirls me around in place.

"I knew he'd eventually choose me." She pulls away and flips her hair. "Helen, who?"

"Mum, you don't have to be a bitch about it."

"Oh, but I do. She knew about our feelings for each other and pretended to be Mary Sue. I hate her goody two-shoes type." Mum's expression falls. "Okay, I lied. I didn't know he'd eventually choose me. I thought I'd lost him to her for good."

"I'm afraid to ask, but since when did you two start your affair?"

"Since I came back from France." She smiles, her cheeks reddening. "Your father was jealous about Lucien."

After he found out about the cutting. But Mum doesn't need to know I told him that.

In a way, I participated in this reunion.

I'm happy for my parents, but I feel so sorry for Helen. She doesn't have feelings towards Papa, right?

"I love you so much, Babydoll." Mum hugs me again, and this time it feels warmer. "I'm sorry we had to make you live through our fuck-up, but you know, sometimes it takes a loss to realise who you really want to be with."

"A loss?"

"I lost your father, and that's when I realised how much you both mean the world to me. Even more than my career, my principles. Everything."

Mum hugs me to sleep that night—in my bed, not hers. I'll never sleep in hers after the scene I've just witnessed.

Her words keep playing at the back of my mind. The part about needing to experience a loss to realise who you really want to be with.

The only person who keeps barging into my mind is Cole.

Since that day at the doctor's office, something shifted and now I know why. I also know why my feelings for him scared the shit out of me in the car park.

It's because they're the truest I've ever felt. Despite his dickhead nature and how twisted he can be.

I might be his chaos, but he's also mine.

My chaos and my safety.

Now that Papa will end it with Helen, we can finally have a chance. It'll take us some time because of the media attention, but we can do it.

I contemplate texting him, but he was so mad earlier. I'll speak to him in person tomorrow.

The next morning, he texts me first.

I nearly jump out of my skin when I find his text message after freshening up.

Cole: Meet me at my old house.

Silver: Okay! I'll see you there!

I sounded a bit too excited in that text, but whatever.

After I throw on last night's dress and a pair of shoes, I snatch my mother's keys. "I'm borrowing your car, Mum!"

"Hey, where do you think you're going, young lady?" She emerges from her room wearing a stunning red dress. "Your father will be here any second."

"I'll let you guys catch up and join later." I grin. "He'll need to catch up when he sees you like that."

"You think?"

"I'm sure. Bye!"

I'm flying down the hallway and into the lift before she can reply.

Mum isn't the only one who's excited. I feel like I'm going to fly out of my skin. Cole might be possessive to a fault, but he gives an infuriating silent treatment. If he's angry at me, it takes a lot for him to break his silence.

Not that I make it any easier... I've got Mum's stubbornness. And while it's good to not let anyone step on me, it's not so good when I recall how I kept denying what Cole and I both craved.

I arrive at his house in record time. Since I know the code, I put it in and step inside.

The house is empty. I think he mentioned something about moving back in after he's out of RES.

Is that why he called me here? Will this be our place after we leave school?

I bite my lower lip to suppress a smile.

Don't get ahead of yourself, Silver.

Pushing the door open, I step inside the mansion. "Cole, I'm here —"

My words die when something pricks my neck from behind. My tongue feels heavy in my mouth.

Black spots form behind my eyelids as my body hits the ground with a thud.

"Cole..." I murmur

"Shh. Your master is here, Doll."

The world goes out.

FORTY-TWO

Cole

It's strange how you spend your entire life with someone and it turns out you don't know them at all.

You don't know yourself.

You wake up every day and take yourself for granted when that self has dissociated into something else.

Something potent.

Something criminally insane.

I spend the entire night reading the book. *Dolls*.

The alter ego never allowed me to read the book before, or come near it until completion.

Until I went in to search for that alter ego and didn't find it.

I found the book, though. The full manuscript was left in an envelope on the table for the agent.

I found the clever words that hinted something real but still remained in fiction land.

What Gav did to his dolls, though? Yeah, that was described in meticulous detail.

But Gav didn't want any of those dolls. They were plastic. They weren't real.

Gav's father didn't let him play with dolls. After Gav's mother's death, his father brought him to his knees and told him he'd now take his mother's duties.

Gav's father hit him and touched him. Gav's father took his virginity when he was nine because he had the right to before anyone else. He made him, so he got to own every part of him.

Gav's father was depraved.

Gav became insane.

He didn't know it, though. Gav is like Antoine Roquentin from *Nausea*. Antoine didn't know he had an existential crisis, and Gav didn't know he was insane.

Criminally. Psychologically.

Gav hid his favourite doll under his pillow and kept looking at it while his father fucked him, pushing his head against the pillow to muffle the sound so no one in the house could hear.

The doll had long blonde hair and bright blue eyes.

The doll smiled at him every night his father came for him.

The doll kept him sane.

The doll made him feel safe.

He became her Doll Master because that was the only thing in his life he had control over.

Gav's father fucked him until he was eighteen. Every night. No exceptions. He told Gav he loved him and he couldn't live without him, as he bled him. He told Gav he was his one and only as he whipped his back.

Gav just looked at his doll. Even when he grew older. Even when everyone at school called him a nerd, and the most popular girl told him to watch it when he tripped into her.

Gav promised to ruin that girl's life.

Then Gav's father died in an accident. Gav was no longer tormented, but he cried that night. He cut himself to feel the blood his father used to extract out of him.

He cried when no one hit him and fucked him.

Gav masturbated with his doll, but he wasn't satisfied anymore.

So Gav decided to find a replacement for his father. He

married an abusive woman who spoke like his father did and raped him in the same way.

Gav got his father back. He got his balance back.

And every night, when his wife was asleep, Gav stared at that doll. He'd smile and tell her, "Your master is here, so you can sleep, Doll."

She didn't listen to him sometimes, so he placed her between his legs and punished her.

Gav had a daughter, but she wasn't a doll. She was just an extension of him. He didn't love her like he loved his doll.

His daughter was a reminder of his cruel wife, too. She looked so much like her, and every time he saw her, he wanted to push her away so that his wife would only beat him.

Gav knew he had to act normal. He was good at acting normal. No one suspected him—not even in his father's mansion. His wife didn't suspect him either.

Gav was a good boy.

He raised his daughter to be a good girl. He knew when to cry and how. Gav practised smiles and tears every day. He practised people, too.

He watched them and knew how to get to them—how to make them like him. The more people liked him in parties, the harder his wife raped him. So Gav made himself more likeable until his wife nearly killed him with her beatings.

Gav smiled when he fell asleep hugging his doll.

Then Gav's wife found the doll. She made fun of it and of him. She told him he was a psycho and threw the doll into the fireplace. Gav screamed as the smell of burnt plastic filled the air.

His wife killed his doll.

Gav didn't know how it happened. One second, his wife was laughing as she left. And the next, Gav ran behind her and pushed her.

She fell and then she no longer breathed.

Something inside Gav unlocked. His father was dead. His wife was dead. No one understood him or his needs.

The night his wife died, Gav cried because he couldn't smile anymore.

He'd lost his doll.

But then he found *her*. He'd seen her before, but he had his doll at the time, so he didn't care much about any other doll.

But that night was different. That night, she was crying. His doll didn't cry, she only smiled.

Now, she cried for him. She was sad for him, and Gav decided he'd found his doll again.

Gav knew that he'd own that doll.

He didn't want to hurt her, though. He didn't want to unleash how much he missed her.

So he found other dolls, temporary ones. He hit them from the back, masturbated to their helpless bodies, then left them in the forest.

They had golden blonde hair and bright blue eyes. They looked like his doll, but weren't.

Now, Gav has his doll. She comes to him. She smiles at him and compliments him.

He cooks for her, washes her, and brushes her hair. He changes her clothes and takes pictures of her. When no one is looking, he masturbates to them.

To her.

His doll.

The one he'll own forever.

No one believed in his happily ever after, but he did.

He believed that he and his doll would have forever. One way or another.

My hands are unsteady as I find the pictures in the box. Countless pictures of Silver in several indecent positions—while she's asleep, half-naked, through the shower peephole.

The door to the office opens and I glance up.

Sebastian stares at me. "What are you doing here?"

"Do you have a gun?" I ask in a voice I don't recognise.

He nods.

I never saw it coming when I should've.

That's what happens when you watch everyone else except for yourself. When you observe everything except for the thing that's right in front of your eyes.

I never recalled Dad's last words, but now, I do.

When I ran outside that day, I was scared because I'd heard Mum scream.

I thought something had happened to her.

Dad is drowning in the pool, blood oozing from his head.

The sound of gurgling nearly suffocates me. Dad is going to drown.

I don't want him to drown.

He reaches his hand out and I extend my smaller one. The red water is pulling him under. The red water is taking him away.

"Dad..." My whisper is haunted, my small hand trembling along with my entire body.

His face contorts. Chaos. It's coming back.

Just like it took me to the dark, it's now taking him.

"Y-you're a monster," Dad gurgles on the water. "R-run, Cole."

Then he's gone.

Run, Cole.

Those were his last words to me. Not the 'You're a monster' part. He wasn't looking at me when he said those words.

He was looking behind me.

At the shadow I couldn't possibly sense because I was shaking, watching Dad drown and not being able to do anything about it.

He was looking at Gav.

Or what's written in the book as Gav.

Gav is my mother.

Silver is her doll.

FORTY-THREE

Doll Master

"Moonlight Sonata" echoes from the phone and I hum along with it as I wipe my doll's hands.

It's her favourite piano piece. It's grown on me, and it makes me think of her.

She's still out. Maybe I put too much propofol in the syringe this time?

Well, I missed.

I was a bit angry all night.

Everything that I've done to be close to my doll is slowly withering away. That bitch Cynthia has always been a sore thumb since high school. Her only saving grace is giving birth to my doll.

Now, she and Sebastian think she can take her away from me?

He said we should divorce. I should move out. I can't see her anymore. I can't cook for her, wash her, brush her hair, kiss her, watch her fuck my son.

I'm not jealous of Cole. He's always been an uninteresting doll, but he's the only one who can make her eyes roll back and her lips part with so much pleasure. So I let them have it their way.

Even if they lock me out sometimes.

Now, because of Cynthia, Sebastian says I can't live with my doll anymore. I offered him everything William left me with the sole condition that I stay with him—with my doll.

I was only going to keep watching from afar. I was going to brush her hair and kiss her goodnight and good morning and have her kiss me back.

That's all I asked for.

I was even hurting other dolls to not lose my cool and touch her.

None of those sacrifices worked. She was going to leave me anyway. No matter what I did, she'd choose the bitch Cynthia over me.

I'll kill Cynthia as soon as my doll wakes up and gives me a kiss. Then we can stay here.

She used to always come and cook with me here. She'll love it.

Silver moans as she slowly opens her eyes. Those blue, *blue* eyes. Like my previous doll that I used to hide beneath my pillow as Dad loved me.

She's better than that doll, though. Silver is more sophisticated, and her smile is more real.

"H-Helen?" She cradles her temple as she slowly sits up. "What happened?"

"You're okay, darling." I caress her arm, her soft skin, her porcelain doll complexion.

I'm the master of this doll.

So much pride fills me at the thought.

"I came here to meet Cole and..." she trails off, finally taking note of her surroundings.

We're sitting on the edge of the pool.

Where it all started.

William's death freed me. It gave me so much I didn't know I could have.

It made me a genius. The type of person who can toy with people's emotions through writing. I disguised myself in every character I wrote. People hated me, were enraged about my actions, but most of all, they were intrigued by me.

I was William. I was Sebastian and Cynthia. And, last but not least, I'm me and with my doll.

I always liked bringing my doll to the pool and bathing her in it.

We swam in it before, but I couldn't touch her like I wanted to, because she was smart and she would've freaked out.

My son is smart, too, so I had to wear the mask I perfected so well from when I was in my father's house.

I had to play on his guilt and love for me so that he'd forget about his infatuation with my doll, and let me date Sebastian, and eventually marry him.

Cole pitied me. He felt guilty because I got hit on his behalf.

I didn't. I simply didn't want to miss any of William's beatings. I wasn't protecting Cole. I was pushing the brat out of the way so he didn't take what was rightfully mine.

My son is so intelligent; he takes after me, but he's not at my level. Cole is a bit too blinded by my doll, so he misses the small things.

Like the stalker messages. He came to me for help, saying some wannabe stalker at school wanted to hurt my doll. I took care of him, of course, and I stopped the texts so he and my doll believed it all ended with Adam.

It never would.

My doll smiled for me when I first sent her those texts and she'll continue to.

"Why are we here?" Silver appears more confused than suspicious.

"We're going for a swim."

"I…I've got to go." She starts to stand but falls right back down again.

"Easy." I stroke her cheek. "You're still under the influence of drugs. I don't want you drowning."

Tears shine in her mesmerising eyes as the realisation starts to trickle in. "Helen?"

"Yes, darling? Although I'd rather you call me Master." I frown. "My other doll was never really able to do that, but you're better than her, aren't you?"

Her lips part—those beautiful lips like a rosebud—and her hand shakes in mine. "W-what are you doing?"

"Your parents are trying to break us apart. Aren't you sad? Because I am. No one can break us apart."

She tries to push back, her fear rising and suffocating the air like grey smoke. I grab her harshly, and when she falls again, her head bumps against the tiles with a thud.

Silver shrieks as blood oozes bright red from the back of her head and on to the tiles. Just like William's that day.

Blood is beautiful. It's the truest human form.

"Silver," I scold. "Look at what you've done."

"Helen, please." Her voice is wobbly as she grabs my hands while tears stream down her cheeks. "D-don't do this. Think of Cole."

"Why should I think of him? He should get his own doll and not share mine."

"P-please…stop…"

I never thought I would love this expression—the way her lips tremble and how she's pleading with me, how she's calling me her master without saying the words—but I do.

So very much.

What can I do to deepen it?

Oh, I know.

I push her into the pool. She screams before her voice is swallowed by the water. The blood from her head engulfs the blue as she flails around.

I crouch on the edge, waiting for her to surface. Like William.

He begged me to save him. Then Cole came and I had to hide behind the tree.

Now, my doll will come out and beg me.
My doll will tell me *please, Master.*
Love me, Master.
Own me, Master.
And then she'll smile at me.

FORTY-FOUR

Cole

By the time Sebastian and I arrive at my old house, my chest is so heavy I can barely breathe properly.

A hand squeezes my shoulder. Sebastian. I told him the entire story on the way.

After I pulled an all-nighter reading the book, I found the message Silver left me this morning.

Okay! I'll meet you there!

Mum deleted the message she sent her from my phone, but I know where she'll take her.

To where it all started. The fucking pool.

I told Sebastian how I stumbled upon Mum's special edition version of her new book—the one she said she won't release—and I had to read it because I'm a fan of her work.

I told him about the pictures and everything in between. I told him how she wrote her life into Gav's personality, and how she's used her alter ego to be a part of every story she's written.

The Killer and the Father.

Serial CEO.

The Doll Maker. Cynthia. She wrote an entire book about her and made her a serial killer.

I should've seen the signs. I should've found the stash of unused pills she eventually flushed down the toilet. I should've stopped to question the manic way she wrote on her plotting board.

I should've gone with her on those jogs instead of believing it was her 'me' time.

I should've noticed more.

But then again, I couldn't have. Mum lived her double life so perfectly, it's crazy.

Yes, it is. Crazy. My mum is a criminally insane person, and the weight of that realisation hits me like a brick wall.

But that's not the reason for the heaviness in my chest.

It's the fact that she lured Silver here. That she's been watching her for years.

She noticed her the first time I did in that fucking park. She followed me, to make sure I hadn't seen her kill William, and then she found her doll.

Her crying doll who's even more beautiful than her previous plastic doll.

I led her to Silver.

I'm the one who made her stop seeing Silver as Cynthia and Sebastian's daughter, but her long-lost doll.

It was me.

"You have to be careful," Sebastian says. His face is hard, but he keeps a cool head. "From what we've learnt thus far, she's unpredictable."

I nod as we hurry to the pool area. He's carrying his gun in case anything happens. He called Frederic during the drive, and his head of PR said he'll meet us here.

"Doll?" Mum calls in a serene voice. "Come out. Stop hiding."

I stop near the pool. A body floats in the water. Red water.

Blood water.

Her golden strands float around her while she remains unmoving.

Like that day.

Just like that day.

Run, Cole.

My father's scratchy, drowning voice plays in my head like a distorted record.

"Oh, Cole, darling." Mum smiles, her eyes kind. She's always looked so kind and approachable. She's never had a malicious look or action. At least, not on the surface. "Silver is playing hide-and-seek."

"Silver!" Sebastian runs towards the pool, but I beat him to it and jump in.

It takes everything in me to ignore the blood changing the colour of the water as I grab her by the arm and wrench her to the edge.

Her face has paled. Her chest doesn't move up and down.

She's not breathing. Fuck.

"Silver!" My hand shakes as I pull my palm away and see the blood oozing from the back of her head, turning her blonde hair red.

I lay her on the tiles and press down on her chest.

Come on, Silver. Come on, you can't leave me!

Please don't fucking leave me.

"M-my doll?" Helen runs towards us. "Why isn't she smiling?"

Sebastian blocks her way, pointing his gun at her head. "Stay the hell away from my daughter."

"Sebastian, can't you see? She needs me. My doll needs her master."

"Not a move, Helen," he growls.

"Or what?" She tilts her head to the side. "You'll kill me? We both know you can't do that. Let me see my doll."

I continue pressing on Silver's chest. Her lips are turning purple. With every second passing, she's dying.

Every single second, she's slipping through my fingers.

A shriek comes from Mum, but I don't look at her. I don't

pay her attention. Then I hear her wresting with Sebastian for the gun, but all I care about is Silver.

Come on. *Come on.*

"Leave her alone." Mum stands above me, holding the gun. "Let her go. You're killing her, Cole."

"You killed her! *You* did!"

"No." She shakes her head frantically, stepping back. "I didn't. It's not me. It's not —"

Her words are cut off as she trips. Her head bumps against the railing of the pool with a sickening thud, and then she falls down…

Down.

Down.

Her blood turns the water crimson.

She doesn't float.

Neither Sebastian nor I move to help her.

I'm still compressing Silver's chest, my own chest feeling as if it's clearing out of oxygen.

She doesn't open her eyes.

She doesn't respond.

That day, the doll dies.

FORTY-FIVE

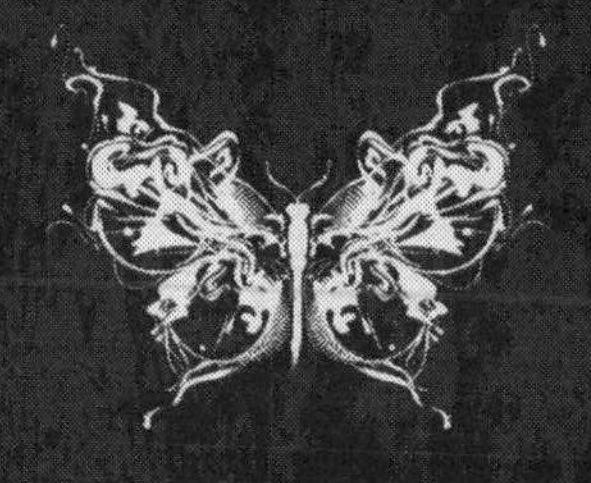

Silver

It's strange how fast things can end.

One moment you're there, in the middle of your happiest moments, and the next, everything ends.

Not really, though.

It's been two weeks since everything went down. Since Helen turned out to be a psychopath who had an obsession with me.

Who hurt other women so she wouldn't hurt me.

Who wrote books so she wouldn't kill the other women as much as she wanted to.

A part of me died that day. The part that believed in Helen. The part who loved her and felt sorry for her.

As that part died, Cole revived me back to life.

I took my first breath of resurrection the moment after she died.

A death for a life.

We didn't go to the hospital, though. Frederic brought the hospital to me—or rather, a team of doctors. He made them all sign NDAs that would cost them three generations of intensive labour if they were to disclose anything.

I ended up with a few stitches and a sore, scratchy throat, but that's not the pain that's stayed with me.

It's everything else.

It's the fact that I didn't see Cole after that day.

The fact that he's not answering my calls or talking to me.

The fact that he told me through Papa that he's moving out until he has to go to university.

The fact that he didn't let me console him or be there for him.

Even during Helen's funeral, he nodded at us, accepted my parents' condolences, and spent the entire day with his arsehole friends. And while I was glad he had someone by his side, I wanted that someone to be me, not Aiden, Xander, and Ronan.

Police procedures didn't take long to be wrapped up. Frederic worked his magic on all the media play and it was labelled as an accident.

Papa wanted Helen exposed, but Frederic and Mum talked him out of it. He'll have no chance to stay in politics if he does that.

If he's known to have been married to a psycho, a serial attacker who threatened his daughter's life under his own roof, he'll be shunned forever and our lives will turn into hell.

However, if he's known to have lost his wife during his campaign due to an accident, he'll gain sympathy.

"And I'll pretend to console you," Mum said. "Then everyone will say I suit you better than that bitch who, by the way, I said was a psycho. I can't believe she hurt my baby."

She hugged me to death then. Mum has been hugging me every night and has practically moved back in with us.

Her and Papa's affection and consolation help, but they don't close the hole in my chest. They don't heal the wound that's been open since that day.

A wound that burns and makes me cry every night.

So today, I decide to close that wound myself.

I go to him.

To the house he moved back into.

The house of ghosts and dolls and blood pools.

Coming back here is the last thing I want to do, but I also didn't sign up to be separated from Cole.

After putting in the code, I walk in slowly, watching my surroundings as if someone will jump me and jam a needle into my neck.

I stop when I make out his tense back. He appears melancholic, his shoulders drooping underneath his jacket. He's standing in front of the pool, only, it's empty now. No blood water or any water.

Several boxes are stacked above each other outside.

Is he moving out? Where to?

I tried asking Aiden how Cole was doing, but that bastard wouldn't give out any information and I'm too exhausted to plot anything to force him.

"Are you going somewhere?" I stop beside him.

Cole's gaze snaps to me. His dark green irises appear bottomless, hollow, almost as if they've already moved someplace else. "What are you doing here? You shouldn't be here."

"Then why are you standing here?"

He stares back at the empty pool. "Go home, Silver."

I barge in front of him, wrap my arms around his waist, and rest my head against his chest, breathing in his scent.

"What are you doing?" he asks without hugging me back.

"You told me to go home. You're my home, Cole."

He shoves me away, shaking my shoulders. "I'm not your home. I'm the son of the woman who almost fucking killed you."

"You're not her."

"Maybe I am. I've lived my entire life thinking I inherited the fucked-up genes from my father, but it turns out, they were from her. Maybe I'll grow up to be her."

"You won't."

"How would you know that?"

"Because you shared my loss. You called it *our* loss, Cole, remember? You told me my pain is yours. You'll never be her, because you care. In your own way, you care."

He breathes harshly as if he's still fighting that notion. That reality.

The fact he's not his parents. He never will be. I know that for a fact.

"And I'm your chaos." I smile through the tears pricking my eyes. "So you can't leave me alone or I'll haunt you."

"You'll haunt me?" he asks with a little smile.

"Yes, I will. You know why?"

"Why?"

"Because I love you, Cole. I've been in love with you since you found me in the park that day and pulled my hair and told me you wanted my firsts. I've loved you more through the years, and I hated every time I had to face the reality that I couldn't be with you."

"I thought you hated me."

"That was my way of saying I love you."

He taps my nose. "You're so weird."

"Not more than you. You've been a dick to me for a long time."

"That's because I wanted you to stay interested in me. To never get tired of me. I beat you in everything just to see that fire in your eyes as you challenged me for a rematch. I beat you to keep you coming back to me."

My lips part. I didn't know that. "Really?"

"Really. I might have been in love with you for as long as you've been in love with me."

Tears glisten in my eyes. "Oh, Cole."

"Moan it. My name, I mean," he says with mischievousness.

"I love you, Cole." I sigh.

"Does that mean you're mine now?"

"I always have been."

He wraps a hand around my throat and his lips claim mine.

EPILOGUE 1

Silver

Three years later

"What the hell are you doing here?" I whisper-yell as Cole leans against the bathroom's door and clicks it closed behind him. "This is the ladies' room."

"I know." He stalks towards me, and every step he takes is like he's walking straight to my heart.

I was right. There's no way my feelings for him would ever fizzle out.

With every passing day, I fall harder and faster into him.

With every day, he becomes my everything.

We moved to Oxford for university, and soon after, we told Mum and Papa about our relationship.

I can't be with him officially. At least, not yet. Papa won the election and became the prime minister, then remarried Mum a year after Helen's death.

That caused quite a ruckus in the media, despite their strategic approach. Frederic made it look like Mum consoled Papa and they rediscovered their initial attraction.

It's true that Cole and I don't live under the same roof anymore, and he eclipsed himself from the family circle to not be associated as my brother. But it'll take years for the world to come to terms with us.

We're bigger than the world, he and I. They're not ready for us.

Papa and Mum are the Conservative Party—despite their non-conservative actions with that affair. I can't exactly bring their votes down by announcing I'm in love with my ex-stepbrother.

I can only do that once Papa is out of 10 Downing Street.

Because of that, our relationship is just known on a familial and close friends level. As in only Aiden, Xander, and Ronan from our friends.

But even with that, Cole shouldn't be here.

"Everyone else is outside," I scold. "We're supposed to be celebrating Xander and Kim's engagement."

"I know." His eyes gleam as he cages me against the counter, his hands on either side of me.

I wrap both arms around his neck. "We can't do this."

"I know."

And then his lips devour mine. I climb up his body as he fiddles with his belt, and soon enough he's plunging inside me.

I kiss him like a madwoman as he fucks me hard, fast and dirty against the counter of the bathroom.

I'd be lying if I said this was our first time violating public indecency codes. Cole doesn't show it, but he's the adventurous type. He doesn't stop when he wants something done—that something being me.

Nothing deters him, whether we're at the university dorms or during a night out while everyone is getting drunk. And even during family dinners.

Mum calls him out on it every time, and he merely shrugs.

"C-Cole..." I grip his shoulders hard.

"Close, Butterfly?" he grunts against my mouth.

"Yes, oh, yes."

"Who do you belong to?"

"You."

"Say it."

I bite my lower lip as I murmur the words that drive him crazy, "I've only loved you. Just you. You're my first and last."

He wraps his hand around my throat, squeezing as he pounds into me faster, making me fall.

Fall into him.

Fall into us.

He comes inside me at the same time as I shatter around him, biting his shoulder over his shirt to muffle my scream.

Once the wave subsides, I sigh, resting my head against the crook of his neck, breathing him in. "I love you."

Instead of all the times I told him I hate him after sex, now I make it a habit to say my true feelings.

"And I love you." He kisses my nose as I stand to my unsteady feet, stupid gravity pulling me down.

After I clean him and myself up, I face the sink to check my makeup. Cole remains at my back, wrapping both arms around my middle.

Not a day goes by where we don't keep our hands off each other. We might not touch in public, but in private? We're everything no one should know.

We're kinky, we're dorks, we're nerds. Or, rather, Cole is. We're in love. We're happy.

As long as I have him, I know I won't need anything else.

He rests his chin on the top of my head. "You'll marry me, right?"

I freeze, the lipstick suspended in front of my parted mouth as I meet his gaze in the mirror. "W-What?"

"You'll marry me?"

"Is this because everyone else is getting married?"

"Fuck everyone else. I'm asking *you*." He kisses the top of my head. "I know it'll be a long time until I actually marry you, but I want confirmation."

"Oh, Cole." I spin around and face him. "Of course, I'll marry you. You're the only one for me."

"The only one, huh?"

"The *only* one."

"And you're the only one for me, Butterfly." He kisses me so passionately on the lips, I nearly climb his body all over again.

"Repeat that in front of that fucker Aiden when we go outside."

I laugh. Cole is still low-key mad at Aiden for the three years I was engaged to him, and he seizes every chance to take revenge.

Cole will always be Cole.

I'm just glad he finally put Helen behind him. We both did. Now, we only focus on us.

When he demanded my firsts, I saved them for him. In return, he saved me his. We're each other's everything.

Hugging him, I whisper, "One day, I'll shout at the top of the world that you're mine."

"And you're mine, Silver, always."

"Always."

EPILOGUE 2

Cole

Seven years later

Ten years.

It took me ten fucking years to finally shout to the world that Silver is mine.

Well, not exactly shout, but show it by marrying her.

We had to wait until Sebastian got out of office and then give the world time to forget before I could marry her.

We tied the knot in France—literally and figuratively. In that town where I first kissed her in front of everyone. Where we didn't care who saw us and got our tattoos together.

The place where we had our first loss. Where she cried, but also laughed.

Now she's not only mine; she's my home, my only family.

After Mum's death, I never felt like I lost a family member. I think I stopped considering Mum family the moment I read that book. The moment I knew she was out to harm my Butterfly. My infinite chaos.

Silver is my family. Even Sebastian and Cynthia are my family. They're the ones we spend holidays with. We have the most heated conversations during those dinners since our opinions clash a lot.

Let's just say, Silver took after her Mum in the stubbornness department and they're not afraid of showing their fiery side every chance they get.

Now, I have her as both my wife and my partner. Silver decided against politics after all. She said politics suffocated us while we were younger, so she won't put our children through that.

I converted her to the dark side and she graduated in business with me.

Now that we have complete control over Dad's fortune, my wife and I are still competing about who brings in the best investments.

Currently, she's in the hospital, carrying the most beautiful creature I've ever seen.

Our baby girl, Ava, was born a day ago. Silver and I haven't been able to stop staring at her.

She's playing with Silver's butterfly necklace and blinking slowly.

"Oh, my God. Look at her, Cole." Silver nearly bursts into tears.

"I know." I stroke her shoulder and kiss her nose, then Ava's head.

For years, Silver has had worn a sad expression whenever she's seen kids. She dotes on Aiden's, Ronan's, and Xander's children, but it's always with that loss lingering deep within her.

I worship her body afterwards and try to take her mind off it, but it's a reality that we've had to live with.

Now, we've made that non-existent child possible.

Our friends are here: Aiden and Elsa, Xander and Kim, Ronan and Teal. It took them some time, but Silver eventually made peace with Elsa and Kim. She had to apologise for those years at school. Elsa apologised for beating her up, saying she shouldn't have. Kimberly didn't take long to forgive Silver after she learnt from Xander and Teal that Silver had always asked about her and looked out for her. At uni, Kim and Silver built back their friendship from when we were younger.

She's now sitting on the other side of Silver, about to cry with her because she knows how much Silver has dreamt of this child. Kimberly has always been a softie, and unlike Silver, she's not afraid to show it.

Elsa's hostility towards my wife has lessened since Silver told her about Adam pushing her into the pool. With time, they became friends, considering that they share Kim and Teal. The latter, Ronan's wife, has always had some sort of an agreement with Silver. Both of them are the most furious when making crucial decisions. They never—and I mean, *never*—hold back.

Ronan is always grinning like a proud idiot whenever he sees his wife in action.

The eight of us have never broken apart. We share the same world and business ventures. We often meet to watch games and even go back to the Meet Up. Levi and his wife Astrid join us, too. Knox, Teal's twin brother, comes too when...well... when he's not so caught up in his new life.

The nights start and end with Ronan and Xander's antics. Aiden and I pretend that we tolerate them. Truth is, we need the vibrancy they bring to our lives.

Not that we'll ever admit it.

Ronan holds Teal by the waist and leans over to speak. Their height difference is so noticeable, she always appears so tiny compared to him. "Should we marry off our Remi to little Ava, ma belle?"

She chuckles. "Stop trying to marry everyone off to our son."

"Yeah, Ron." Xander hits his shoulder. "I thought you wanted him to marry my daughter."

"You said no." Ronan pokes him back.

"Still, how dare you exchange my Cecily with anyone else?"

Xan scoffs. "Not that I would ever let her get married. She'll stay with us forever."

Kim shakes her head, smiling, but says nothing.

"Daddy." Eli tugs on Aiden's trousers, awe filling his features. "She's so pretty."

"Not bad for Cole's spawn." Aiden lifts his six-year-old son so that he can kiss Ava. He goes straight for the mouth.

Silver and Elsa laugh.

I glare at Aiden. "Keep your son away from my daughter. *Far* away."

"What's wrong with my son?" Aiden glares at me, then ruffles Eli's head. "Don't listen to your Uncle Cole, Eli. If you want his daughter, go for it. I'll support you."

"Not if I break his legs first." I hold Silver close and she jokingly hits my shoulder.

"Stop it."

Fine, so I still hold a grudge against Aiden, but it's not only because of the engagement. He took a first of hers that I was never able to get back—a waltz. And yes, I remember she had her first waltz when we were fourteen. I remember everything about her.

I'm *that* obsessed with this woman. Addicted to her. Fucking in love with her and the beautiful chaos she brings to my life.

I kiss her head again and we both smile as we watch our miracle. Our Ava.

Our story might not have started in the best way possible, but we wouldn't have it any other way.

Silver is mine and I'm hers.

In the past. In the present. In the future.

Always.

THE END

WHAT'S NEXT?

Thank you so much for reading *Ruthless Empire*! If you liked it, please leave a review.
Your support means the world to me.

If you're thirsty for more discussions with other readers of the series, you can join the Facebook group, Rina's Spoilers Room.

Next up, there's Jonathan King's book, *Reign of a King*. This book is the definition of epic. Stay turned for the prequel Novella, *Rule of a Kingdom* that will be available for free.

Royal Elite Series will have a final book, the epilogue.

ALSO BY RINA KENT

For more titles by the author and an explicit reading order, please visit: www.rinakent.com/books

ABOUT THE AUTHOR

Rina Kent is a *USA Today*, international, and #1 Amazon bestselling author of everything enemies to lovers romance.

She's known to write unapologetic anti-heroes and villains because she often fell in love with men no one roots for. Her books are sprinkled with a touch of darkness, a pinch of angst, and an unhealthy dose of intensity.

She spends her private days in London laughing like an evil mastermind about adding mayhem to her expanding universe. When she's not writing, Rina travels, hikes, and spoils cats in a pure Cat Lady fashion.

Find Rina Below:

Website: www.rinakent.com

Newsletter: www.subscribepage.com/rinakent

BookBub: www.bookbub.com/profile/rina-kent

Amazon: www.amazon.com/Rina-Kent/e/B07MM54G22

Goodreads: www.goodreads.com/author/show/18697906.Rina_Kent

Instagram: www.instagram.com/author_rina

Facebook: www.facebook.com/rinaakent

Reader Group: www.facebook.com/groups/rinakent.club

Pinterest: www.pinterest.co.uk/AuthorRina/boards

Tiktok: www.tiktok.com/@rina.kent

Twitter: twitter.com/AuthorRina